EYE OF HEAVEN

MARJORIE M. LIU

LEISURE BOOKS NEW YORK CITY

A LEISURE BOOK®

December 2006

Published by

Dorchester Publishing Co., Inc.
200 Madison Avenue
New York, NY 10016

ISBN 0-8439-5765-4

Visit us on the web at www.dorchesterpub.com.

WATCHED

"You always like to spy on girls while they sleep?" Iris asked the darkness. The shadow moved and walked toward the pen.

"I'm sorry," said the man, quiet. "But I was only trying to help. You shouldn't be here. Not like this."

"And you're my protector?" Iris tilted her head. "I can take care of myself."

She thought he smiled. "I guess that means you're bulletproof, then. Nice talent to have."

"Yeah," she replied, standing. "I'm remarkable that way."

He was lean, with broad shoulders and narrow hips, garbed in clothes with dark clean lines that looked highly tailored and expensive. Good taste, if nothing else. A man who was primed and ready for a night in a high-end yuppie club, a martini—shaken, not stirred—in his large elegant hand.

Other books by Marjorie M. Liu:

THE RED HEART OF JADE
SHADOW TOUCH
A TASTE OF CRIMSON *(Crimson City Series)*
TIGER EYE

"A lover doesn't figure the odds."
—*Rumi (1207–1273)*

EYE OF HEAVEN

CHAPTER ONE

The package sat on the damp concrete of the Jakarta alley for almost thirty minutes before anyone inside the *warung* food stall made an attempt to retrieve it. Smaller than a lunchbox, brown, and completely unassuming, placed just beside a stack of dirty pans that no one inside the plastic tent felt like washing, it was passed over, ignored, and forgotten by everyone except Blue. A fact that made him very uneasy.

It was the rainy season—miserable and humid, the damp only worsening the terrible suffocating heat inside the tumbling slums of Indonesia's capital. No cool showers, just dirty water hurtling from the sky in terrible sheets, pounding the blue tarp roof and tied-down walls of this transient eatery—here today, gone tomorrow, to another alley or parking lot or street corner; the tables at which Blue and others sat would be easy to fold and load into the three-wheeled cart parked behind the portable stove at the back of the tent. The owner, a thickset woman only a shade browner than Blue, worked furiously over a cutting board, wielding her cleaver in hard bursts of frantic chopping. No knife fights with her; Blue knew who would win.

He also knew better than to complain about the food. Easier just to ignore the paper plate of *nasi goreng* sitting in front of him. The fried rice was too greasy, the shreds of chicken un-questionably raw. Blue had an iron gut—which was currently growling and hungry—but no time for stupid risks like making himself sick on a toilet. If he could even find a toilet. His hotel was on the far side of town, a fine and glittering oasis just begging for his return. Cold air, cold showers, cold bottled water ...

Stop it. Get your head in the game. You didn't come here for a vacation.

Right. Because if Blue had wanted a break he would be in Colorado on some mountain, sitting his ass down on a cliff to watch the sun dip low on an empty, silent world, instead of here now in Jakarta, surrounded by thirteen million people scratching out an existence in an impoverished city that teetered constantly on the edge of racial and religious unrest. And he would *not* be sitting in a dirty transient café, sweating, filthy and tired, risking his life, his sanity, for just one glimpse of a quite possibly fruitless clue, some connection that would finally set him upon the path of a man who needed to die.

Yeah. All in a day's work. Too bad he had a conscience. Even worse that he was in a position to follow his conscience. Being a good person was a hell of a hard way to live, though he could not truly complain. He had chosen this life for himself, after all. And as an agent of Dirk & Steele, he had the resources and skills to go where others could not—to be an asshole of mighty proportions when the bad guys got out of hand. No trading that privilege for the entire world.

Like now, when he was so close. It had taken money and patience for Blue to cultivate his current network of informants; the latest had given him the time and date of a drop-off—promised that it would be a special delivery, straight to the hand of the big bad man himself.

Plastic rattled; Blue tilted his chin, and from the corner of his eye watched as a woman ducked into the tent, rain dripping from her face. His breath caught when he saw her—she was just that unexpected: a tall drink of water, leggy, wearing a sweat-soaked tank that showed off her sinewy arms, smooth skin tanned to a deep gold that was almost as rich a color as her short blond hair. Large sunglasses obscured most of her face, which was strikingly angular and sharp. A little too sharp for his taste—far too hard—but oh, what a body. She stood out in this crowd—and that was a problem.

It was damned hard not to stare as the woman passed his table, but self-preservation limited Blue to nothing but a quick glimpse. That was more than enough to revise his first impression. From a distance he had guessed she was in her thirties; up close, he saw the wrinkles around the blonde's mouth, the leather of her taut skin, the streak of silver hiding in her hair. Fifties, maybe. A really great fifty.

She took a seat near the food cart, easing gracefully onto a collapsible plastic stool that wobbled on the uneven alley concrete. Her pants were loose, her feet clad in sandals. She acted too confident to be a mere tourist, but her clothing was inappropriate for the locale; Indonesia was predominantly Muslim, and though Jakarta claimed to be cosmopolitan, women—foreign and local—were encouraged to be … modest.

But the woman seated in front of Blue did not appear concerned, and not one of the men in the *warung* paid her the slightest attention. Again, odd. Besides himself, the woman was the first foreigner Blue had seen on this side of town all morning, and in this area, with her looking the way she did, people would have almost no choice but to stare. No way around it. Hell, even he got looks, and he was trying to blend in.

So she lives here. The people are used to seeing her.

Or perhaps Blue was paranoid for a good reason.

The woman did not look at the menu written in permanent marker on the tarp behind her; she simply sat drumming her fingers on the table. She did not speak; nor did she appear to make eye contact with anyone inside the *warung*. Yet, less than a minute after her arrival, the elderly owner of the food stall delivered a glass of *teh talua*, yellow with egg yolk and batter and sugar. The blonde woman did not thank her. She did not smile. She did not pay. She picked up the glass and tossed back the drink in one long swallow.

A painfully skinny boy dressed in shorts and nothing else ducked around the back end of the tent. He was soaked, dripping—but the owner, who had gone back to her cutting board, did not spare him a glance. Instead, her gaze flicked to the blonde, whose fingers still drummed, unpainted nails *click-click-click*ing on the plastic, like a drumbeat to a song.

Same as the blonde, the boy did not speak or place an order. He stepped near the dirty pans—careful, hesitant, his bare foot nudging the brown paper package. Testing the waters. Blue did not react. No reason—not yet, not until he was sure. The hunt had already been difficult enough without mistakes; he could not afford impatience, haste.

But Blue's hand was forced all the same. The boy kicked out his foot, the package popped into the air, and quickly, almost a blur, he caught it in his small palm and turned on his toes, whirling like a dancer on the run, and Blue thought, *Good, that's good, kid. You run. Run, run, run. All the way to your boss.*

And the boy did. For all of two seconds. The elderly owner of the *warung*, who up until that moment had completely ignored him, stepped out from behind her workstation and slapped the flat of her cleaver against the boy's chest, spraying garlic and onion as she stopped him cold. The child cried out, staggering backward . . .

. . . right into the blonde, who'd shot up from her stool, moving with incredible speed across the small confines of the *warung* to catch the boy as he fell away from the cleaver. He tried to escape her touch—moved like it burned—but she held on tight. The boy cowered, staring up into her sharp, tan face with his eyes rolling white, mouth all twisted like he was ready to scream or cry.

The woman's lips moved. Blue could not hear her voice, but the child dropped the package into her outstretched palm and shuddered. Game up, game over.

Blue got ready to move, but the woman did not hurt the

boy. She pushed him away—a shove toward the fluttering plastic exit—and the spindly child ran as if death were on his heels, a big, bad death, and Blue thought he just might be right.

He did not allow his gaze to track the child. He watched the woman instead, studying with new eyes the lines of her body, checking for any bulges beneath her clothing that might be something other than muscle or bone. The woman saw him watching and tilted her head. A smile played along her lips and it was sharp like her face, with just a hint of teeth. Blue did not allow his gaze to falter, but all around him he felt movement: men sliding quietly from their seats, sidling away from tables and unfinished food, slipping like ghosts from the damp shadows of the *warung*.

Time for the reckoning. Blue did not blame them for not wanting to stick around. He wanted to run like hell. Run far and hard, away from the nightmare of this place that had already sunk too deep into his skin—like a tattoo, like the worst kind of mark on his soul. The things he had seen in this city, the things he had seen that had brought him here . . .

The woman did not approach Blue, but she held up the small brown package, perching it on the tips of her fingers. Her nails were extraordinarily long.

"So," she said, in a voice that was softer than her face, with a gentle lilting accent that Blue could not quite place. "You thought this was cleverness, yes? You, here, tracking this small bit of nothing?"

"I suppose," Blue said. He was alone now. Even the *warung*'s old owner had disappeared, though her cleaver now rested on the work surface directly to the woman's right. Blue thought of his pistol, holstered at the small of his back. He was not comforted.

You should be. Forget the gun. You could stop her heart if you wanted to. Just one thought, and dead, gone.

Not that he would ever really let himself consider that possibility.

The woman tossed the package to Blue. He caught it with

one hand, but it was heavier than he expected, and he had to fumble to keep from dropping it. The woman laughed—again, soft, oh, so gentle—and said, "Did you really think we would not notice that someone was making inquiries? Did you truly believe we would lead you to our employer or send anything of importance to this place, knowing that you were tracking us?"

"I'm losing my touch," Blue said, staring into her sunglasses, fighting for his poker face. He set the package on the table. "I wasn't always this obvious."

"Perhaps," said the woman. "But I am very good at my job."

"Protecting an animal. You know what Santoso does, how his entire family makes their fortune."

"Flesh." The woman's smile did not fade, but it turned brittle. "Flesh and blood and the sale of such things. Yes, I know."

She unzipped the bag hanging at her side. As she lowered her head, Blue glimpsed a hint of the eyes beneath the rim of her sunglasses. Large, full of shadows. Maybe beautiful, maybe not. It did not matter either way.

"I believe this is what you think you are looking for." The blonde removed a small steel canister from her bag. It was just a little larger than her hand, and almost the same size around. A digital display blinked at one end. Like she had with the little brown package, she perched it on the tips of her fingers like a jewel or bauble. Blue wondered just how strong her hands were.

Strong enough to hurt you, he told himself, and let down his mental shields. Just a crack, a fracture, a tear inside his head—

—and the city roared through his mind, dripping with power, razing his skull with hard currents as every surge of electricity within a half-mile radius touched him for one brief, blazing moment. An old pain which was part of his gift: Blue's ability to control electronic devices simply by focusing his thoughts.

He bit the inside of his cheek, tasting blood, and that was

enough to keep him from being overwhelmed by the initial rush of power. He rode the fire of Jakarta's electronic soul, feeling the burn in his buzzing bones, and though the pain dulled to a simmer, a stream of cold sweat broke out between his shoulders, and he wondered—*don't look back, do your job, live for now or nothing*—how long he could keep doing this and stay sane, whole, healthy—because the heart ran on electricity, too, and one day his was going to give the hell out.

Blue focused on the canister. He sent his mind through its metal surface, sinking into that place where his eyes could not follow, searching electronics, tasting voltage, the thrum of heat in current and wires, and there—familiar—he found the pump, the heartbeat, and he imagined fluids sloshing, hypothermic perfusion sending that chemical solution into the central chamber like blood, and by God, it was small—the smallest such device on the private market, easy to mistake for a bomb.

Blue had seen something similar only once before: in an illegal backwater operating room in Cairo, where a small boy lay near death on a kitchen table while some butcher with a medical degree removed both his kidneys. And there, a transport container like this one, or its larger cousin, had been the first and only clue that had brought Blue on a hunt around the world. Something so distinctively ingenious could be designed by only a handful of people. Parts, too, had to be bought. Manufacturers hired. Paid.

So. Three months searching, requiring long trips overseas, tapping wires, conducting surveillance, bribing people to talk face-to-face. Blue's own private mission—and only because he could not stand to see such terrible arrogance, such blatant cruelty—could not bear to stand by when it reminded him so much of his own flesh and blood.

His diligence had paid off, though, leading him straight to Santoso Rahardjo, the richest man in Indonesia. So rich, in fact, that his family owned the national bank. And, by extension, the government.

Which was exactly why, against the better wishes of his boss, Blue had come here without a partner. Too dangerous. More than one foreign man asking questions would certainly draw attention.

Although, apparently, Blue had managed to do *that* just fine on his own.

So why am I still walking free? It would be easy enough to bribe the police to arrest me, to haul my ass down to some prison where an inmate could stick a knife into my gut the moment I step into a cell. Problem solved. No more questions asked. At least, not by me.

Though the other agents at Dirk & Steele would certainly take matters into their own hands. They would swarm like a sign of the Apocalypse, because hell had no fury like gun-wielding psychics pissed off and hungry for revenge. Not where his friends were concerned.

God. He loved his life.

"What you *think* you are looking for," Blue repeated, the memory of the woman's soft voice distracting him from his mental search of the canister. "Carefully chosen words."

The blonde smiled and, in an astonishing show of agility, twirled the canister on the tips of her fingers like a basketball. She walked toward him as she played with the transport device, and Blue fought the distraction of spinning steel, keeping his focus on her face, on her free hand, which hung close to the open mouth of her bag. He stood slowly from his stool and stepped back, placing the table between himself and the woman. Her smile widened.

"You act as though I am dangerous," she said, the canister still dancing over her fingers. It looked as if it were floating, but Blue could feel the faint charge between her skin and the steel. No magic, no telekinesis. Nothing more than impossible reflexes.

Blue did not return her smile. The woman stopped at the edge of the table and placed the canister back into her bag. She pulled the zipper tight and let her hands hang loose and empty at her sides. Sweat glistened over her skin, softening the hard lines of muscle. A burst of wind cut through the *warung,* shaking the plastic tarp, making her tank top cling even tighter to her perfect body. Blue watched a strand of silver hair touch the corner of her mouth.

"You want me," said the woman. "I can see it in your eyes."

"I'm a man," replied Blue. "But don't mistake attraction for action. Or trust."

"Oh, never." Her smile faded, her gaze flickering to the brown package sitting between them on the table. Blue spread his focus, widening the crack in his shield, and was not entirely surprised to find an electric current hidden beneath the simple paper wrapping. He had anticipated another kind of transport device. Only, after a moment, he realized this felt slightly different. Less complex than that canister again resting snugly inside the woman's bag. Less complex but more dangerous. Blue's breath caught.

"You *see,*" said the woman, narrowing her eyes as she backed away. "I knew you would. Consider it my gift to you. My warning."

Blue watched her turn slowly, as if the air around them were thick as tar, as if she were begging for capture, and though he wanted to follow, to run and run and never mind the questions and answers or that enigmatic smile, he did not. He watched the woman disappear around the wrinkled tarp and closed his eyes, closed them tight, and threw his mind into the device in front of him.

The bomb was easy to disarm. No remote. All it required was a simple disruption of electricity into the timer. Nothing that Blue had not done a thousand times before during his stint in the navy. Nothing that should have been a real threat, given his skill with electronics.

Only this time, something still felt wrong.

He opened his mind wider, casting out his senses, searching hard for another trace, a whisper of dangerous currents, but there was too much around him—cell phones, televisions, cars, radios, power lines, even human bodies—and his mind drowned in the sensations. His bones rattled with them. Blue turned—

He felt the explosion inside his head before the blast wave hit him. His feet left the ground. He learned how to fly.

Later, Blue remembered screaming. He remembered the scent of smoke and blood and, somewhere near, a child wailing as if its heart were breaking, broken, gone. He remembered sirens, shouts, the sensation of needles in his arms. Another voice, a woman's voice, soft and gentle.

He also remembered guilt.

But that was later. Blue slipped away and lost track of his life.

The world changed. Blue felt the difference while still unconscious, trapped inside his dreams—dreams that were unending, a plague upon his soul, which tossed and turned inside his body, fighting to crawl from his flesh. He did not want to stay in darkness. He did not want to see what his memories showed him again and again. But he was slow to wake. A sluggish process, a struggle into awareness.

He noticed his skin first, because he felt movement on it— gentle, a warm breeze maybe—and he heard the rustle of leaves, smelled flowers and ocean salt and vanilla bean. At first he thought those scents and sensations were part of another dream, but only because they were quiet, removed, deliciously low-tech. Nothing electric touched his mind. And that, in this day and age, was quite unnatural.

Blue opened his eyes. A white canvas ceiling stretched above him, shadows flickering on its pale surface. He stared, orienting himself, trying to remember—*Why this? Where am I?*—and he heard paper rustle.

His gaze slid left, and images passed through his brain— *flapping blue tarps, rickety tables, sweaty men*—as he looked at a long wooden table covered in thick white candles, backpacks overflowing with bottles of water and food. Again he heard a rustle, this time of cloth, and he looked past the table and flickering points of flame at . . . *a woman in sun-glasses, sharp, with*—No. Not her. But blond hair, yes. Blond hair that framed a lovely round face, a face he recognized. Blue felt a laugh rise up his throat, though the only sound he made was a dry croak.

"Dela," he said. Delilah Reese. Artist, weaponsmith, best friend, and one hell of a woman. What a sight for sore eyes. Her hair had grown out, and her clothing hung dark and loose. Bands of leather covered her forearms; steel glittered. Throwing knives.

She grabbed a bottle of water before approaching his bed and held it to his mouth. Blue was not quite certain he was not thirsty, but at that first touch of water to his lips he felt the cracks, tasted the blood, the dry thickness of his tongue and throat, and latched on like a baby, gulping down great painful swallows. Dela reached under his head, cradling him close and steady as he drank the entire bottle.

"You want more?" She shook the last drop into his mouth. Blue glanced past her and saw mosquito netting instead of walls; beyond, darkness.

"No." He tried to wipe his face. His arm worked, barely. His muscles felt weak. He also had a short beard, which was a shock. "What happened to me? And why are *you* here?" Why, when Dela and her family were supposed to be in California on their mountain ranch, *not* in Indonesia . . . ?

Unless *he* was not in Indonesia anymore.

Again, Blue pushed outward with his mind and caught the edge of nothing. No electrical devices, no wires, no batteries or engines. The silence made him uneasy. Made him feel as though he was caught in a void, like there was a muffler wrapped tight around his head. Under any other circumstances, great, relaxing—but this was not a good time for unexplained surprises.

Dela smiled sadly. "Do you remember anything, Blue?"

"I . . ." He stopped, heart sinking. "Yes. Yes, I remember."

Remembered in a flood, a rush, one fat gag of sound and pain that made him close his eyes and fight down vomit. He held on, on and on, and after a moment felt the warmth of Dela's body as she leaned close. She touched his hand.

"How many died in the blast?" he asked.

Her fingers tightened. "Three. All men."

"There was a child. . . ." Blue swallowed hard. "I remember a child screaming."

"There were some injuries. Nothing fatal. This was not your fault."

"Of course it was. What happened afterward?"

Dela hesitated. Blue peered at her knives. Danger, danger, and more dangerous, still—Dela did not go armed unless she thought there was a need for it.

She tossed the empty water bottle on the ground. "We're not certain what happened after the explosion. Roland received a message saying you had been hurt, but no location, no contact information, nothing. He had Dean do a remote viewing. Found you in a run-down medical clinic by the quay. Only patient, no doctors to speak of."

"You shouldn't have come. Santoso might have had his people watching me."

"And leave you dead or dying? Right, Blue." Dela shook her head. "Hari and I were in India, so we got tagged. Roland filled us in on what and who you were hunting, so we came prepared for anything."

"And your son?"

"Mahari is safe. He's back home in California with my grandparents."

Blue slowly released his breath. Yes, Dela and Hari's small child would most definitely be safe with Nancy Dirk and William Steele. The elderly founders of the agency still had sharp teeth—and vast resources to match.

Dela reached for another bottle of water and lifted it up to Blue's mouth. "I think we got there just in time. Whatever hit you was from a high-order explosive. The shock wave alone caused abdominal hemorrhaging, and that doesn't include the crush injuries or the burns. You've been in a coma for almost two weeks."

Blue choked on his water. "Coma?"

Dela grinned. "Sorry. I shouldn't have sprung that on you."

Blue pushed her hands away. A *coma*. Abdominal hemor-rhaging. Crush injuries. Blue knew exactly what a high-order explosive could do. But here he was, still able to move. He could feel his entire body. Wiggle his toes. He ached, but not horribly. Not enough to believe that he had lingered near death, that he had suffered injuries that might debilitate him for years to come.

"How?" Blue asked. *How am I still functioning?*

Dela sighed. "Elena and Artur arrived not long after we did."

Which was all she needed to say. If Elena Baxter-Loginov was involved, anything was possible. The former Wisconsin farmer might not be an agent of Dirk & Steele—not yet, anyway—but she was married to one of the agency's most valued members, and was, hands down, the most powerful psychic healer Blue had ever encountered.

As in, start up your own revival, Mrs. Miracle Jones.

"Where is she? I need to thank her," Blue said. Maybe get down on his knees and kiss her feet.

A faint flush touched Dela's cheeks. "She and Artur already left."

Blue frowned, but before he could ask where they had gone, and why Dela could no longer look him in the eyes, her hand fluttered over his chest, down his arm. "As soon as she stabilized your body, we got you out of Indonesia. Had to take a boat to do it because of the effect you were having on cer-tain ... electrical devices ... but we managed the trip. We're in Malaysia at the moment. My grandmother owns an estate here, though we've set up camp about a mile from the main house."

"Good accident prevention," he said, though it bothered him that extreme measures had been necessary. Years since his last exodus, a forced retreat into the mountains, far from the modern world. Alone for six months, just to rest his mind, and since then other similar trips—brief sojourns in his remote Colorado cabin. Precautionary measures, enough to keep him from running too close to his breaking point.

You've pushed yourself too hard over the past several months. And now you're paying for it.

Him and anyone else in his vicinity. He was not entirely certain he wanted to know how bad it had been. Blackouts? Communication failures? Car accidents and chaos and the international news?

"Dela," he began, but she shook her head.

"The trouble was localized," she said, though her voice was uneven, rough. "It took city officials only an afternoon to restore power to the affected areas."

One afternoon. Lucky break.

"You weren't followed here?" he asked.

"Not to our knowledge, but we doubled security. Hari and I have also been taking shifts."

"Making sure no one finishes the job, huh? I'm flattered. You'd think, though, that if Santoso or his crew really wanted me dead, they would have killed me when I was alone and helpless." Blue tried to sit up. "I need to get back there, Dela. I have to finish what I started."

"Two weeks out of the game? You must be joking. Santoso won't let you get close, Blue. I don't know why his people didn't finish the job the first time around, but they won't make the same mistake twice. You step foot in Indonesia, and we'll never find your body."

"Dela, there are people dying because of that man. Every day, people die. And those who do are probably luckier than the ones he leaves alive. Santoso is a harvester, a flesh peddler. He strips people of their vital organs to sell on the black market, and then ditches the leftovers, breathing or not, in some gutter to rot. I've seen it with my own two eyes."

His own eyes, his own hands, in Egypt and Brazil, the Philippines and Vietnam—*hands covered in blood, trying to hold together the wounds, shouting for help, shouting his throat raw, and no one for miles willing to step in because it was just business as usual, good money, and why rock the boat, why help when you could be the next target?*—and he could not shake it. He could not stop hearing the stories, the crying, could not stop seeing the dead and dying—young men, young women, too many children—giving up their lives for the promise of cold, hard cash. And even that, a lie.

Blue could still feel the blood beneath his nails. "I can't walk away, Dela. I won't."

She might have responded, but her gaze flicked right, and he followed her line of sight to the loose walls of mosquito netting. Beyond, in the darkness, he sensed movement. Felt on the edge of his mind a flicker of bioelectricity, a heart-charge. Dela's hand crept to her knives. Blue lowered his shields even more, but sensed nothing mechanical.

The netting pushed inward. A giant stepped into the tent, seven feet of hard muscle and bone, wearing loose linen pants and nothing else. Blue almost expected to see the hilt of a sword behind that broad scarred shoulder, or some other arcane weapon close at hand. Not that the man needed them. It was easy to see the tiger in his body, the shape-shifter he had once been still humming beneath his skin. Magic; another marvel to add to the miracles in Blue's life. Which, despite all its gifts and resources, was still not enough to stop one man from committing mass murder.

The giant paused on the threshold of the tent, ignoring everything but Dela, and Blue watched that hard golden gaze drink in her face and body as though she were a lifeline—the perfect embodiment of breath and heartbeat. Blue wished he could be anywhere but there, caught between them. It was too intimate, and he felt like a stranger to those kinds of emotions. Nothing so deep, not ever. No passion for just one.

Blue suffered, for one instant, a pang of jealousy that this man should have found that kind of connection with another human being, that at any time he could simply reach out and . . . there, love.

"Hari," Blue said, forcing himself to speak. "Hari, it's good to see you."

Hari tore his gaze from Dela. His eyes were grave, and when he spoke, his voice rumbled low like thunder. "The same to you, my friend. It is good you are awake. Had you still been unconscious . . . " He hesitated.

Dela stood. "What is it? Have we been compromised?"

Hari shook his head. "I was just up at the house. Roland called. He had . . . news from Blue's mother."

"My mother?" The rush of fear that swept through Blue was as crippling as any bomb blast. *Goddamn*. If Santoso had kept him alive only to go after his mom . . .

He tried to sit up, but Dela pushed him down, made soothing noises. Hari crossed the small distance and knelt beside the cot, placing one massive hand on Blue's shoulder.

"No," he said quickly. "No, Blue. She is fine. Unharmed. She simply had news, that is all. Bad news."

"Bad news," Blue echoed dully, barely able to hear himself over the hammering in his chest. What kind of bad news could possibly compel his mother to call the office? *Dear God.* The woman had practically refused to pick up the phone during her last heart attack. She hated asking for help.

"Hari," Dela said sternly, and Blue thought, *Just spit it out, tell me now, don't make it linger, don't make it hurt worse than—*

"Your father has died," Hari said.

It took a moment to sink in. And when it did . . .

Blue broke out laughing.

CHAPTER TWO

Death was an inconvenience that Blue could have done without, and if it hadn't been for the two highly moral individuals breathing down his neck, he probably would have pretended amnesia and simply ignored the news. After all, he was practically an invalid, newly awakened from a coma. Barely out of the bomb-blasted woods. He had an excuse. And for Christ's sake, if his father was dead, there really wasn't much that Blue could do about it now.

No such luck, though. Three days later Blue found himself bundled onto a commercial airliner, flying solo to San Francisco. He was the only person seated in the first-class cabin—not a surprise, knowing Dela and her credit card—but Blue did find it rather disconcerting to discover that the flight crew had been given instructions on how to handle him.

As in, with kid gloves. Which meant that for fourteen hours straight, Blue found himself under the carefully pressed and brightly smiling care of three women, who—though he objected strenuously—showered him with books, magazines, hot towels, a private DVD player, and one very large box of chocolate-chip cookies that resembled, in the vaguest way possible, large and bloated zoo animals. Blue felt like a stinking-rich twelve-year-old being sent on his first airplane ride. The only thing missing was a tour of the cockpit and a pair of those little plastic wings. If kids even got those anymore. Airlines were turning into cheap bastards.

More unfortunate than all of the unwanted attention, however, was the fact that the flight gave Blue a lot of time to think. As in, about all the different ways he was fucked till Sunday. Going home to his father's funeral was just the icing on the cake. And so very convenient.

Convenient enough that he briefly considered the possibility of a conspiracy between his mother and Roland. Something— anything—to keep Blue from running away to continue his now fruitless hunt for Santoso and the core leaders of that organization. His mother, God bless her, was capable of such deception, and Roland . . . well, he was a master at games of manipulation, especially for good causes. Like keeping his people alive.

Because Dirk & Steele is a family, Blue thought, hearing the echo of Dela's voice inside his head. *All we have is each other.*

Misfits, outcasts—even some pillars of the community— hiding in plain sight, brought together by an uncommon bond formed by nothing more than the odd genetic quirk and an unbending devotion to helping others. Living lives less ordinary—off the beaten path inside another world where telepaths and telekinetics and honest-to-God shape-shifters rubbed elbows with the mundane. Secret lives standing in line at the grocery store, at the gas station, sitting on the toilet in the stall next door, flying in an airplane—*this* freaking airplane—concentrating the entire time to prevent an accident, a short in the system, one tiny glitch that might send everyone down in a massive ball of flames.

Breathe, Blue told himself, gripping the arms of his seat. *Breathe in, breathe out. Relax. Just . . . relax. Your mind knows what to do. This is nothing. Nothing.*

Yeah, and there was nothing like thinking about *nothing* to make a person fixate utterly and completely on *something*.

He was so screwed.

And yet, halfway into the flight, with the lights turned down low, he finally began to relax. His shields felt strong, solid and tight, and though he could feel the hum of power surrounding him like a cocoon, it did not rattle his bones or buzz his tongue. Everything was quiet inside his head. Safe and very still.

And feeling very safe, and very still, he began to think again of Santoso Rahardjo. And of the woman who worked for him.

Blue's gut ached, as did his ribs and right leg. His knee popped when he straightened it. His left hand was weak. The backs of his eyes felt odd, which coincided with the occasional bout of stars bursting in his vision. No complaints, though. He was still walking, talking, and if he had his way, he would be doing more than that in no time. Because even though Dela and Roland had assured him that someone was going to take over his investigation—that all his work ferreting out the hierarchy of body parts and money would not go to waste—Blue was not going to be satisfied until he was back in the game, danger or no.

You're a control freak. A micromanager. Trust your friends. They know how to do their jobs.

And if they got hurt? Better him than them. Besides, it seemed to Blue that despite his miraculous survival, there was still a big, fat target painted on his head. And sooner or later, someone—probably that blonde—would come and finish the job.

Stop it, he told himself, digging into the box beside him for a cookie. *Focus on now. On what you have to do when you get home.*

Which was very simple. Heal up, take care of his mother— if she would let him—and attend a funeral where no one would know his name. Easy as pie.

Or not. Because soon after landing in San Francisco and hobbling through customs, Blue encountered a long row of mounted television monitors, all of them tuned to CNN, and it was like watching—in awful visual stereo—one long eulogy. He did not notice at first—he was too busy trying to act as if he weren't in pain—but through the chatter and crush of the airport crowd, the background noise crept in. A woman with a deep, pleasant voice. Blue heard her say the words *tragic loss* and *a great man,* and then, quite suddenly, there was a name to go with those adjectives, a memorable name, a name Blue knew as well as his own, because it *was* his own.

Felix Perrineau. Dead at the age of seventy. Heart attack in his sleep.

A long time since Blue had heard that name spoken out loud, and though the announcement was no surprise, it triggered something inside of him: not laughter, but something worse . . .

The lights in the terminal flickered. Blue clamped down hard on his emotions, fighting himself, but it was too late: Sparks shot from the ceiling fixtures, the electrical sockets, raining down as people ducked and shouted. Static leaped like baby lightning bolts from the carpet.

Blue said nothing. His hands curled into fists. He closed his eyes.

The lights did not go out.

But a moment later his cell phone began to ring.

The call was from a stranger, a man who knew his real name. Blue did not like that, but he agreed to meet the fellow because he also knew Blue's mother's name—and he had a message from her. In her native language.

The stranger's Farsi was bad—or maybe it was the cell phone connection—but Blue caught enough, and all the worry he felt for his friends transferred in one gut-wrenching second to his mother.

"Sleep," said the man, his voice cracking, his accent poor. "Sleep, my son. I wish that sleep come to your eyes and you will sleep like a stone in the water."

Words from an ancient lullaby, one that Blue had not heard for years on end. His mother did not sing anymore. She did not speak her language. She did not do anything that reminded her of Kandahar, of Afghanistan. Too much pain. Her sisters had died there.

But if his mother had shared that lullaby with a stranger—a song Blue knew meant a great deal to her . . .

Something's wrong, Blue thought, dialing her home number. *And it sure as hell isn't grief.*

She was not at the house. She was not at the law office, either, and her secretary was no help, confessing only that Mahasti had been gone for the past several days, away on a family emergency.

Some emergency. Blue tried her cell phone. No luck there, either.

Limited options. No time to call in the agency. *Damn.* What a time for an ambush.

And if it is Santoso involved? If this really is a ruse?

Time for a fight, then. No holds barred. No misguided ethics or hesitation. No tricks or subterfuge, either. Blue gathered up his strength and walked through the airport terminal. He did not try to slip away without being seen—or better yet, wait out the stranger and follow him. Instead, he marched straight into baggage claim, searching for an older gentleman wearing a blue suit and purple tie, as he'd been instructed.

Blue found him easily, the man standing out like a diamond in the slag of straggling airport humanity. Tall, elegant, and lean, he was waiting quietly beside carousel one, all easy strength, easy class, good breeding oozing from his pores. The man's silver hair was thick and full, his jaw set, his keen eyes a very bright shade of silver. He looked remarkably like Blue's father.

"You're family," Blue said to him, when he was close enough to say anything at all. Introductions on his part, he thought, were completely unnecessary—and somewhat of a relief. Because maybe Santoso wasn't involved, after all, and this was just what it seemed to be: a family matter, overdue and difficult. Nothing Blue needed to fight over. Not yet, anyway.

The man did not smile. "My name is Brandon. I'm here to take you home, Mr. Perrineau."

Mr. Perrineau. Blue could not remember the last time he had been addressed by his given name. He thought perhaps never.

"You can call me Blue," he said cautiously. "That's good enough."

"Good enough," Brandon echoed, mouth crooking upward. "If you like. Though I can assure you there's no need to hide from the other. It *is* your legal name."

"Really." Blue tried not to laugh. "If you spent any time around my father, *Brandon*, I think you would understand why it would be totally … inappropriate for me to take his name."

"Bygones," murmured the man, and pointed toward the double doors leading out of the airport. "If you don't have any bags … "

Blue did not. What he did have was a burning desire to go home to his apartment and get his gun.

"Where are we going?" he asked, unmoving. "And why would my mother pass on a message to you instead of calling me herself? Where is she?"

"At your father's house." Brandon walked slowly backward, toward the exit behind him. "She is safe, she is healthy, and the only reason she did not call you herself is that she wanted to make a point. Something that would make you … sit up and listen."

"My mother doesn't need messengers to make me sit up and listen," Blue replied sharply. "Something else is going on here."

"Of course," Brandon said. He turned and walked through the exit. This time Blue followed.

It took them two hours to drive to his father's estate, a rambling drive over winding roads that curled and curled into the mountains. Blue occasionally caught wild glimpses of the sea, heard the cries of gulls mixing with the rasp of ravens.

The air was sweet. Beyond the confines of the Audi, his mind encountered only silence.

Brandon did not talk; nor did Blue encourage him. No energy to waste. Blue's body hurt. He could not stop thinking about his mother. Santoso was there, too, but more distant. For the first time since waking up in Malaysia, Blue was ready to hand the case off to his friends.

"We're close." Brandon's posture was relaxed, his voice easy and deep. The road ahead cut through deep forest, shrouded from the sun.

"Are you his brother?" Blue asked, because sitting beside Brandon was like being next to his father, and that was more disconcerting than he wanted to admit. Even more so than the sudden spike of electricity buzzing in his brain. Close, yes. Damn close.

"Does it matter?" Brandon replied. "I thought you wanted nothing to do with the family."

"I don't believe I ever had a choice. I know my mother didn't."

Brandon said nothing. He merely tapped on the brakes, slowing the car to a crawl until he pulled onto a narrow turnoff that appeared, quite suddenly, on the far side of a massive cedar. Blue glimpsed a blinking red light—some laser sensor set in the ground—and knew that ahead of them, someone had been alerted to their presence.

"This is your first time here," Brandon said.

"Yes," Blue lied.

Brandon glanced at him, and for a moment Blue wondered if he knew the truth. But all he said was, "Your mother arrived several days ago. I promise you she's safe."

"Safe's not enough," Blue said, clenching his hands. "She'd better be healthy, happy, ready to dance the tango—because if she's not any of those things, if my *father* has hurt her, all of you are fucked, and good."

"So little trust?"

"No trust. At all."

Brandon's only response was a grim smile—which Blue did not find comforting in the slightest.

The house looked the same as he remembered: a mansion made of logs, some California dream of rustic wonder that had always caused Blue to speculate how a man like his father—who had a heart as small and hard as a hollow walnut casing—could possibly appreciate—or even *want* to live in—a place of such wild beauty. The mind boggled.

Men in dark clothing moved along the periphery of the house, deep in the woods. Blue saw some of them with his own eyes, but there were others waiting out of sight. They carried radios, earpieces, Tasers; Blue could feel the electrical currents in his head. He thought about shorting them out, but held back. Later, maybe.

Brandon parked the car in front of the house. Blue glimpsed movement behind the windows. He began to open his door, but Brandon caught his arm and said, "Careful now."

Blue stared at his hand. "I thought this was supposed to be safe."

Brandon released him, but his eyes were hard. "For your mother," he said, and Blue could not read the terrible emotion that swept his face. "But for you? Be careful."

Blue heard the crunch of gravel; Brandon looked away and quickly got out of the car. Blue stared at his back for one brief moment, gave up the question on his lips, and, gritting his teeth, opened up his own door to follow. His knee popped; the entire right side of his body felt stiff. His confinement to the plane—and the car—had not done him any favors. He tried not to hobble.

A security guard stood nearby, rifle in hand, a pistol strapped to his side. Blue thought about shattering the man's eardrum—one high-voltage shock from the radio device in his ear would do it—but again, control won out. *Caution, be prudent.* Timing was everything.

Brandon gestured to Blue, and together the two of them walked up to the house. The front doors—carved and embedded with stained glass—opened wide as they neared. Inside were shadows, the outline of hardwood furniture. No lights. The curtains were drawn. Blue caught the edge of movement, and a woman stepped into the light.

"Mom," Blue said, and his relief was nothing less than a sucker punch. He forced himself to breathe.

"Felix," she said. Her voice was soft but firm, no sign of fear or weakness. She wore a dark gray gabardine suit, closely tailored to her full figure. Her thick black hair—courtesy of a good dye job—curled in smooth waves to her shoulders, framing a round face that might have been sweet if her eyes had been as soft as her body. Instead, her gaze was black, sharp, narrow—closer to an eagle than a dove—and Blue did not miss the shadows in her gaze, the appearance of a new wrinkle in her forehead.

Mahasti glanced at Brandon. "Did you explain anything to him?"

"Of course not," he replied. "It wasn't my place."

"Not your place," she echoed sarcastically, and shook her head. She held out her hand to Blue. "Come here. Let me look at you. Your employer said there was an accident."

"Mom," he said firmly, ignoring her scrutiny. "What's going on?"

"Your father," she said, and the disgust in her voice was profound. "Your father and his tricks."

"He's dead," Blue said, searching her face. "Tricks are for the living."

Brandon stepped past them and entered the house. The moment he disappeared around the door, Blue moved in close and grabbed his mother's shoulders. She was a short woman; he had to bend over to peer into her eyes.

"We can leave right now," he told her quietly. "Say the word and we're out of here. No one will be able to stop us. I won't let him ruin your life again."

"Ever the optimist," she murmured, looking away. "I am so sorry, Felix. So very sorry. If it were just myself involved, I would never have allowed this to go so far. Would never have agreed to *anything*. But it is not just me, and I cannot . . . I *cannot* find a way out. Not this time."

"Mom."

"No." She pulled away from him. "I am a poor mother. I am a terrible mother for this. A mother who cannot protect her child . . ." Her mouth tightened, and the fear that Blue had pushed away returned again, hard and strong.

They entered the house. It was not the first time Blue had been inside his father's mountain estate, but the previous occasion had been uninvited, of the breaking-and-entering kind. Under the cover of darkness—a teenage exercise—creeping through the woods, disabling security measures with nothing but a thought. Shutting down the grid for a mile around. A reckless act, but one that Blue knew could never be traced back to him. No fingerprints, no tools, no explanation. Just a faulty system. A glitch.

Nothing had changed. Blue felt the security cameras tracking their movements as they walked through the main living area—an open space divided by pieces of expensive furniture and sculpture, vases and statues that were distinctly Asian in origin. They looked very old. Illegal acquisitions, probably. Blue had learned more about that sort of thing over the past three months than he had any interest in knowing, but a man had to be polite, and his best friend was newly married to an archaeologist who had strong opinions on the theft and sale of ancient artifacts on the black market.

Better rocks and glass than flesh and blood, Blue thought. *Better those things any day.*

Their footsteps echoed; the house appeared empty, but Blue felt security lingering just out of sight. An odd feeling began rumbling through his gut; a terrible suspicion. He said nothing, though, simply watched his mother walk with a straight spine, watched as she turned her head to stare at Brandon, watched as Brandon slowed to look back at her with an expression that could only be called unhappy. It was a look of familiarity, as though Brandon had known his mother much longer than a simple handful of days.

And it made Blue nauseated all over again, a sensation that worsened as he pushed his mind ahead and found a fat wad of electricity—a collection of circuits and power so concentrated, so tangled and twisted, his teeth buzzed with the energy. Close, so close—they rounded a corner in the hall, a hall with only one door, and Blue thought, *You're there. Goddamn it, but you're there.*

Brandon did not hesitate when he reached the door. He opened it, and there on the other side was an electronic fortress, a web of wires and monitors and flashing screens, which provided the only light in the room: a blue, shimmering glow. The monitors surrounded, covered, and were suspended over a giant bed dressed in creamy satin sheets and overstuffed pillows. And on that bed, snug within the cocoon, lay a familiar man who was, unfortunately, very much alive.

"Huh," Blue grunted, staring at his father. He looked the same as his pictures, and almost the same as the last time Blue had seen him. Only thinner, with more hollows in his face. A fine resemblance to Brandon's aged elegance.

The old man did not look at him. His fingers skimmed the keyboard in his lap, his gaze flickering over the screens in front of and above him. His mouth moved; he spoke silently to himself. Off to the side, a flat-paneled television broadcasted a muted CNN. Blue saw his father's picture flash briefly, followed by overhead shots of a funeral in progress. Men in dark suits were carrying a casket. Blue recognized the faces of several heads of state.

"I'm being buried in France," his father suddenly said, voice low and sardonic, still with that elegant edge he remembered so well. His fingers never stopped moving and his eyes remained trained on his computer screen, which cast a blue glow on his face. "Nice little show, isn't it?"

"Only if you're psychotic," Blue replied. "But oh, wait. You *are.*"

Perrineau smiled. "I prefer being referred to as *complex.* Besides, a diagnosis of actual psychosis is dependent on the perceived normalcy of the rest of society. And to everyone outside this house? I am—or rather, *was*—as sane as apple pie."

And richer than God. Which, in Blue's opinion, mattered more to most people than morals or loose marbles.

"Felix," Mahasti said, stepping toward the bed. "Don't play word games with your son. I want this over and done with."

"My son," murmured the old man, finally looking at Blue. His eyes were small and hard; the dim lights of the room only accentuated the shadows on his pale skin. His fingers stopped moving. "I don't believe he ever wanted to be my son."

"I had a good reason," Blue replied, refusing to look at his mother. "And even if I didn't, I don't believe you ever wanted to be my father. I wasn't ... white enough for you."

Perrineau narrowed his eyes. "God doesn't love whiners, boy. *I* love them even less."

"Felix," Brandon murmured.

"*Felix*," Perrineau mimicked. He tossed aside his keyboard, but it did not land far. Not for any lack of effort, either. Blue was surprised at the show of weakness, but before he could comment, the old man said, "Wipe that look off your face, boy. I didn't bring you here to gawk."

"Could have fooled me. But since we're on the subject, why *did* you go to all the trouble? Because pretending to be dead? That's rather ... extreme."

"Maybe I want to reconcile," Perrineau said, but there was a sly glint in his eye, and Blue shook his head, folding his arms over his chest. His ribs ached. His heart ached, too, and that was unexpected.

You should have been cold to this. Should have expected it. You can't let it bother you anymore. Not after all these years.

Years spent telling himself he did not need a father, that his mother was enough, that his friends were family and that nothing else mattered. But here, now, a mouthful of words and the old storm was back, with all the same disappointment. It made Blue sick with anger.

"Forget this." He reached for his mother's hand. "We're out of here."

"You leave, you pay," Perrineau said immediately, voice hard. "Trust me when I say the price will be steep."

"You better not be threatening my life."

Perrineau smiled. "And your mother?"

Brandon made a small sound. Mahasti pulled her hand away. Her eyes were hooded, dark.

"Do *not* use me against him," she said to Perrineau. "Felix, I thought we had an understanding."

"You're a lawyer, my dear. *And* I fucked you. Surely you know me better than that."

Blue's hands spasmed into fists. "Don't talk to her like that."

"Or what? You'll kill me?" Perrineau bared his teeth. "Good boy. You be good and do that. See what it gets you."

A one-way ticket to hell and back, Blue thought, forcing himself to breathe. He uncurled his fists, but that was all; the knot in his chest simply got tighter and harder, like some bitter plug pushing up against his heart. Blue tested his shields; they were still strong, but much more of this and that could change. And if it did, with his temper running so high …

He felt his mother watching, her careful mask fracturing, the cool woman beginning to fear. She knew. He could see it in her eyes. Blue wondered if she still remembered the feeling of the shovel in her hands, digging those graves.

"Boy," Perrineau said, drawing out the word, saying it like a slow hammer fall. One word, one statement, one question— all of which demanded a response.

"Yes," Blue said, swallowing his pride.

His father relaxed against his pillows. "Better. No room for indulgence here. No room for anything of the sort. You come here, you listen, you do as you are told. If you don't, I have a remedy. I have an answer. Might be I'm dead to the world, but that doesn't mean no one will hear me. I'm a Perrineau, boy. I'm the goddamn Good Samaritan. People think angels kiss my ass."

Blue said nothing. His mother did not move. Brandon stood near, a shadow at her shoulder.

Perrineau looked him dead in the eye. "I have another son. Did you know that? He is twenty-seven years old. His mother was a waitress in one of my New York restaurants. She was beautiful and stupid, and I married her because she looked like she would be a good mother. And she was. Very good. My son? His name is Daniel. Thanks to you, Felix was already taken. So, there. Thanks to *your* mother, you have another piece of me. Blood and a name. Felix Junior." He shook his head, smiling. "Your brother, though, is legitimate, legal, and my heir. The only problem is that he doesn't want anything to do with me."

"Smart," Blue said, fighting his emotions, schooling his face—trying not to reveal how shaken he was that he had a brother. He glanced at his mother, but her mask was back in place: cool, quiet. And, he thought, unapologetic. She did not look at him, which was a clue—but Blue was in no position to pin her down. He could feel his father watching, resting still as a corpse, and it almost seemed as though his pale skin glittered beneath the light of his electronics, sharp as diamond. Cold and perfect.

"Daniel is smart enough," Perrineau finally replied quietly, his gaze unflinching. "Smart enough to evade me for the past six months. I kept his existence a secret, you know. Until now. I worried about enemies, kidnappers, bounties. A rich man's son is never safe. Never really himself until it is time to take his father's place."

So what does that say about me, you son of a bitch? What does that say about how you feel toward me?

A whole damn lot.

"So you lost him," Blue said. "Another son went bye-bye. So fucking what?"

"I need to find him. Right *fucking* now. I've certainly poured in enough money. Hired all manner of discreet pro-

fessionals. A wasted effort. If his mother were still alive, I
might have some control over him. She was not the running
type. As it is, though, Daniel is ... slippery."

Slippery enough to make his father desperate. Very truly
desperate. Reckless, even. For a moment all Blue could do
was stare, wondering if the sudden chill on his skin was a
sign of hell freezing over.

"You staged your own death to draw him home," he murmured. "All of this ... just to lure him out into the open. Goddamn. You *are* crazy."

"Maybe," Perrineau said, just as softly. "But it hasn't worked.
Which implies that my son either hates me more than I
thought, or he isn't in any position to return."

"If he's dead, you mean."

The old man narrowed his eyes. "*I'll* be dead soon
enough, and that's no lie. So if Daniel *is* gone from this world,
and I join him ... "

"Brandon will be a very rich man."

His father laughed. "Clever. You don't even act tempted."

"Because I'm not." Not tempted in the slightest. Blue did
not want his father's money. He did not want the power or
the name. All his life, struggling to be his own man—*I don't
want your place, never, not ever*—and he was not about to
turn and tuck tail now.

Blue glanced at his mother. Mahasti was not a timid
woman. She was not shy or easily cowed, and even now
when she returned his gaze, he saw that her fire, her sharp-
ness, had not dulled in the slightest. Yet still, silence—and he
could not imagine it, even if Felix had threatened her.

We could leave here, he thought again, ready to tear down
his shields. To disable the network, the grid, and if anyone
tried to hurt them—

No. Blue clenched his jaw. *No, not that.*

But still, escape. The problem was what to do afterward.
His mother had a life. She had a career, friends, a home she
had paid for after years of hard work. Her freedom meant
everything to her, was a testament to everything that had

been denied the family left behind in Afghanistan more than thirty-five years before. Live life on the run? Never.

Blue looked at Perrineau. "What do you want?"

His father briefly shut his eyes. "Isn't it obvious? I want you to find him. I want you to ferret out your brother and bring him home."

"And you think I can do it?"

Perrineau laughed. It was a weak laugh—a choke, a gasp—and the slight undertone of a wheeze sounded sick, tired, as if there were not enough breath left in his lungs for anything so strenuous.

"What is wrong with you?" Blue asked softly.

"Age," Perrineau replied flatly.

"No," Blue said. "No, it's more than that."

"More is not your concern," the old man snapped, spittle flecking the sides of his mouth. "As I said, I want you to find your brother."

Blue said nothing.

Perrineau sneered. "Your silence is no denial."

"I know you can. I know you can and I know you will, no questions asked." Perrineau shoved his hand beneath his pillow and pulled out a thick brown file. He tossed the paperwork to Blue, who caught it against his chest and flinched. More cold swept over his skin.

He opened the file. Read the first line, *Regarding the operation of Dirk & Steele,* and stopped cold.

His father began to laugh. Mahasti stepped in front of Blue and pulled the file from his numb fingers. She flipped through the pages and returned it to his hands, pointing. Blue saw his name and a candid shot of his face. Below the picture was his military history, age, and address—as well as some speculation, but no conclusions, about his "paranormal ability."

"He knows almost everything," his mother murmured. "There are dossiers on your friends. Pictures, too. The proof is all there. I examined it myself."

"Impossible," Blue hissed. "Most of what we do isn't visible to the naked eye."

His mother stared. "There is photographic evidence of a man turning into a crow. And another, a cheetah."

Blue tasted blood—the inside of his cheek. He looked over his mother's shoulder at Perrineau. "No one will believe this. *No one.* They'll accuse you of falsifying the pictures."

"Certainly," said his father. "*If* I intended to disseminate them to the general public. Fortunately, I have better contacts than that."

Blue's vision blurred; he could barely see past the stars, the spinning. He bit down on his tongue, hard, and tasted more blood. The pain helped. "And if I find your son—my brother? What then? You won't share the pictures? Forgive me if I don't trust you."

His father's smile widened. "I must admit, the temptation is considerable. I have never in my life considered the possibility of such ... wondrous things. The military applications alone ... " He stopped, sly. "Well, it makes me wonder what *you* can do."

"Stop this," Mahasti said. "*Stop.*"

"I can make it stop," Blue said, and he meant it. He would do it, if he had to. For his friends, for his mother. For himself.

Perrineau's smile turned brittle. "I have copies. And if I do not call my agent within the next thirty minutes, I can promise you that everything in that file will be released to the proper authorities. And by authorities, I mean my contacts at the Pentagon. Which, I confess, has its own ailing program of psychic warriors. Pitiful creatures. Barely able to bend spoons. Nothing at all like my own flesh and blood. Or his friends."

Breathe, Blue told himself. *Calm down. You have options. You're not alone. You are not alone.*

"Time frame?" he asked. He could do this. He could say yes, which would give him time to stall, to call Roland, to get a fix on this thing. He could eat his pride and anger a little longer. Anything for the people he loved. Anything.

"Quick. No more than a week."

"Be realistic. It's taken you at least six months."

"And I don't have that long. Not anymore."

Good. "A month, then."

"Two weeks, and that is generous on my part."

Blue hesitated. "Why do you want him?"

"A father can't say good-bye to his son before dying?" Perrineau smiled and closed his eyes. "No, you don't think well enough of me for that."

"You're going to hurt him." Blue felt sick. "I'll bring him here and you'll hurt the hell out of him."

"Just bring me my son," said the old man, voice dropping to a whisper. "Let me worry about the rest."

Brandon was instructed to give Blue a large padded envelope, and then they were dismissed, turned away with a wave of his father's hand like they were servants, beggars, clods. The business meeting was over. Time for other affairs, weightier schemes that could be conducted from beyond the grave.

Blue did not appreciate the illusion of freedom. He knew it for what it was—knew, too, that it was not so easy, that his father's reach, even dead to the world as he was, was impossibly long. But Blue asked no more questions, just shut his mouth and walked out. Kept walking until he was out of the house, standing in the sunlight that trickled sweetly through the trees. He sucked in his breath, thought about putting his head between his knees. He was afraid he would not be able to straighten up again.

A familiar hand touched his back, a light touch. "I'm sorry."

"Don't be," Blue said to his mother, reaching back to hug her. "But you have to tell me what he has on you. What he did to bring you here. Back in his room I was afraid to ask."

"I am his backup plan," she said in a tired voice. "Or maybe I was his original plan. He will send me back to Afghanistan if you fail him, Felix. Or maybe he will have me deported just for spite, regardless of what you do for him."

Oh, he really needed to lie down now. "You're an American, Mom."

"And that means nothing to men with money. It means nothing if you are of Arab descent in this day and age. All he needs to do is have one of his men call me a terrorist, perhaps plant some incendiary documents in my home. And there, my life is ruined." She laughed weakly. "Forget deportment; I will probably be put in jail for the rest of my life."

If it was an American jail, that would still be better than going back to Kandahar. Blue knew his mother would not last a day. The Taliban might be gone—sort of—but plenty of the old remnants remained. He tried to imagine her in a burka, alone with no friends or family, and the idea made him sick.

"It won't come to that," he told her. "I promise you. My friends—"

"You and your friends have enough problems," she said firmly. "Take care of that, and then we will see what can be done for me. Besides, I am not without my own resources." She touched his arm. "Felix, I meant what I said. I would not have come here, or allowed myself to be used, if it had not been for the file on your agency."

Blue grimaced, unable to hide how much it pained him to think of her ready and willing to ruin her life just to protect him. *Goddamn.* He was going to find a way out of this or die trying.

Gravel spit. Blue looked up and found Brandon behind the wheel of another black Audi, just like the one they'd come in which was still parked nearby. He leaned out the window and tossed over a set of keys. "I'll take Mahasti home. Drive the other car."

"Like hell," Blue said, but his mother touched his arm and drew him down for a tight hug. Then, before he could stop her, she slid into the passenger seat beside Brandon. Blue stared, numb. He was going crazy. Yes, finally, this was it.

"Wait," he managed to say. "Stop. What's going on? You can't trust him."

"She can trust me," Brandon said. Blue wanted to reach through the open window and punch his lights out.

His mother looked him straight in the eyes with that cool dark gaze that had always been maddening in its utter lack of expression, its seamless stubborn strength. "I have to do this. There are things I can do to protect myself. I won't be used against you. I *refuse*."

"Mom."

"I'll be safe. If nothing else, Felix, trust *me*."

As if he had a choice. That glint in his mother's eye was the conclusion, the set of her jaw nothing more than a solid end to the conversation. Blue gave Brandon one long, hard look and then pushed out with his mind, scanning their vehicle.

"No bugs, no trackers," he said, telling his mother, giving up the ghost and risking the truth in front of the older man. Brandon, however, did not show the slightest surprise at Blue's announcement; there was no question in his gaze.

"I already checked it," the man agreed, revving the engine.

Blue frowned. "Who are you, really? Why are you involved in this? Why do you care what happens?" *And what kind of relationship do you have with my mother, you son of a bitch? Why in God's name does she trust you?*

Brandon smiled, but it was cold, ugly. "There are no stronger ties than blood, Mr. Perrineau. Nothing more beautiful or more hateful. But I suspect you'll learn that lesson again when you find your brother."

His mother did not wave or say good-bye. She gave Blue a long, grave look, and then Brandon drove them away. Blue thought about racing after, following in the car given to him, but he had a very strong feeling that was the last thing his mother would want. She, apparently, had a plan. Something *he* needed to get, and fast.

He glanced one last time at the house. No one stood in the windows watching him, but he felt the security cameras tracking his movements. Men, too, but they were also out of sight. Giving him the illusion of solitude.

Blue slid into the Audi and shook out the contents of the

envelope. A thick wall of cash fell onto the passenger seat—
several thousand dollars at least—as well as a credit card
with his name on it. Blue ignored the money. He kept shaking, and a moment later a photograph dropped free, along
with a folded piece of paper that, at first glance, seemed to be
a letter to Daniel's mother.

Blue did not read the letter. Instead, he held the picture in
his hands, staring. The face that looked back at him was
handsome, tanned, with short brown hair and blue eyes, a
smile that was slightly twisted, as though his brother disliked
the person taking the photograph. He wore glasses. He
looked smart.

Smart enough.

Blue flipped over the photograph. Height, weight, a list of
impressive academic credentials that consisted of a brief stint
at Juilliard, followed by undergraduate and master's degrees
in arts education from Harvard. He had worked briefly as a
teacher in Chicago, and then given up his profession to participate in various aid groups, most recently the International
Committee of the Red Cross. His father had tracked Daniel's
movements everywhere, from Pakistan to Thailand, right up
to New Orleans.

And then, nothing.

Blue shook his head and put away the photograph. He
tossed the money and credit card out the door—he was not
quite that stupid, thank you very much, nor did he want the
taint of being paid to do his father's dirty work—and cracked
open his mental shields to scan the car. He immediately discovered a tracking device in the engine, as well as a bug in the
air vent: two pinpricks tickling his head, floating on the surface of the electronic currents running through the car. Separate and unequal.

Blue shut off the devices, pushing farther with his mind. He
found two cars idling on the other side of the house. Waiting
to follow him, no doubt. Blue shorted out the circuits running
to each battery, and for good measure wreaked havoc on the
three other cars in the garage. He thought about disrupting

the entire electrical grid, but held himself back at the last moment. There was no telling just how much his father knew about him or what he would do to retaliate.

Play it safe, Blue told himself. *For now.*

So he did, remaining on high alert for the first hour of his drive off the mountain, scanning the road ahead and behind with his mind. He even checked the skies for low-flying aircraft: helicopters, a Cessna. He could not discount the possibility that his father was also using satellite technology to track him—the old man had supplied enough technology to the private sector and various world governments to qualify for his own personal feed.

His cell phone rang. It was Roland.

"We have a problem," Blue said.

"Yes," Roland replied. "You have a beard."

Blue rolled his eyes. "Not funny. My father knows about us. He has pictures of Koni and Amiri shifting shape, and he's using the information to blackmail me. If I don't do what he says, not only will he turn the agency over to his friends at the Pentagon, but he's going to tell the authorities that my mother is a terrorist."

"Actually, that is pretty funny, you little fuck. Tell me another one."

"I wish I could."

Blue heard the beginnings of a laugh, followed by a choking sound. "Christ, you're serious. But I thought your old man was dead. It's been all over the news."

"He's not dead enough," Blue said. "It's a setup, Roland. Pure lies."

"Fuck."

"Yes." Blue clenched his jaw as the car went around a steep curve in the road. He pulled the wheel too hard and his ribs throbbed, pain curling up the back of his neck into his skull. Too much he did not need.

Roland muttered something under his breath; Blue heard pencils snapping. "Did he give any indication how he found out, how he even knew to look?"

"No, but according to my mother, he has a dossier on every one of us. I only had enough time to see mine. No direct proof, but there was some inconclusive speculation about what I'm capable of."

"So it's not a complete breach."

"That's not what the shape-shifters would say."

"And there's no reasoning with him?"

"There's no fixing crazy, Roland. You run or take a shotgun to it. That's all."

"Jesus." Roland blew out his breath. "I know there's no love lost between you and your old man, Blue, but this is ridiculous."

Right. What was really ridiculous was that Blue had never been able to count on his father for anything, had never had a father, had never in his life been able to say the word *father* and have it mean anything except deceit, danger, anger.

"Roland," Blue said slowly. "When you first hired me on, I told you my real name. I told you who my father is. And I made you promise to never share that information, not with anyone. Didn't you ever wonder why?"

"Hell, Blue. Your father was—is—one of the richest men in the world. He's a legendary philanthropist and inventor. In some circles, his word is God. That's a shitload of baggage, especially if you don't want people to treat you differently."

"Yeah," Blue agreed. "But that's not the reason I don't use his name."

Roland sighed. "What's he blackmailing you for?"

"I have a brother who ran away. I'm supposed to find him. No reason given, but it can't be good."

"And you're going to do it? Turn your brother over to the old man?"

"It's my brother or the agency and my mother, Roland. How do the scales weigh in your head?"

"Like shit. But even if you play along, Perrineau might still burn us to the ground—or try to use us. And that won't stand, Blue. Not at all."

"So we have a plan B. I go find Daniel, and you guys ... "

What? What was he asking of his friends? This was his fight, his father, his responsibility. If anyone should fix this it was him, and him alone. No one else needed to get hurt.

"Oh," Roland said, ugly laughter running low beneath his voice. "Oh, Blue. I know that look on your face. You can't fool the eyes inside this old head of mine."

"Your clairvoyance is real bitch sometimes, Roland. You know that, right?"

"Sticks and stones. But you're not going solo on this one, Blue. Never you mind what we'll do to your father. You just worry about finding your brother. *Get to him first*. And when you do, you find out why the hell he's so important to Perrineau. Because, kid, after hearing what you just said, it ain't love. Your brother *has* something. And if it's so important that your father is willing to fake his own death for it, then goddamn, you need to keep it out of his hands."

Which did not answer the question of what to do if push came to shove. If Blue was forced to choose one life over another.

Easy. You choose the agency. You choose your mother. You don't know Daniel. You don't owe him anything.

Maybe not. But he did know what it was like to be his father's son, and the idea of returning anyone to that …

"Are you coming by the office?" Roland asked.

"Yes. Is Dean in? I want to see if he can do a locate on Daniel. At least give me a start." Because if the elder Perrineau, with all his resources, could not find his son, then extraordinary measures would have to be taken. And no one got much more extraordinary than the agents of Dirk & Steele.

Even if it was a secret. Even if most of the world simply thought the detectives at the agency were nothing more mundane than human, and just very good at their jobs. And if it was up to Blue, the truth about their gifts would stay a secret, a mystery. It had to be that way, for all their sakes.

It took him several more hours to reach San Francisco, and after that, yet more time to check in at the downtown office and report on the situation. He made inquiries into Santoso—tried to call Artur and Elena, but only reached his friend's voice mail—and when Roland was done with him and he was tired and hungry and hurting, he passed off Daniel's letter to Dean, who—in a highly unusual show of solemnity—made no wisecracks as he held the paper in his hands, eyes closed, searching for a trail.

He discovered one.

Two hours later, Blue left the office. He ditched the men following him and drove to the airport, paid cash for a ticket. Then he boarded a plane and flew to Las Vegas.

Chapter Three

Iris McGillis, despite all advice to the contrary, was in the habit of sleeping in the same bed as her lions, which meant that—besides having the remarkable ability to suffer through terrible clouds of bad breath and flatulence—she was an impossible person to wake or speak to, especially when she wanted to be left alone. Something her friends respected almost too well.

She blamed the new environment for her current insomnia—easier than confronting old nightmares. Too many unfamiliar noises, too much city in the desert air that should have been clear and clean, full of nothing heavier than starlight. Except here, buried in concrete, the Las Vegas smog clung like smoke in her nose, as did the remnants of tar and stale sweat and the burn of hot earth, scorched grass. It did not matter that a quiet wilderness lay only minutes away by fast car. Here in the city the crush was inescapable; scents crept through her rattling air conditioner, through the crack under the old thin door of her RV that required masking tape and the clever use of paper clips to keep closed.

It was night. Past dinnertime. The scents of barbecue and microwave dinners had folded, drifted, faded. Now, dessert. Guitars strumming. Iris could hear her friends and coworkers moving through the semipermanent camp, their voices a lyric of jumbled languages: Russian, Chinese, English, and Spanish. She picked up a word here and there, but nothing solid. She did not try very hard. It was enough to piggyback on other lives while she lay in darkness, buried in sleek fur and bone and thick mane. Petro and Lila were finally quiet, and Iris—though she was having trouble drifting to sleep—found herself enjoying the warm solitude, the protective cocoon.

Not so alone, she thought, and flinched as the wiry thatch of Petro's tail slapped hard against her face. Iris spit out thick hairs, which was enough to wake Lila, whose paws flexed. Iris watched, wary. The bed was too small, and the lioness had a thing for kneading Iris's body—or pummeling it. In her teens Iris had gone head to head with a visiting sumo wrestler; the sensation was very much the same.

Not that she was ready to change her sleeping arrangements. Petro and Lila needed her. Unlike the small towns and cities where Reilly's Circus had once made camp, Las Vegas was big, booming, a constant rush of sound and movement. Wild times for wild cats, and it was making them nervous, anxious. The regulations—those hard-nosed son of a bitch regulations—did not help, either. According to the inspectors who had come crawling out of the woodwork, wild animals were not allowed near human living areas, including RVs. Big cats had to live apart. Safer for the people.

Iris did not agree, but then, she cared less about people and more about her cats. And her cats—her *family*—did not like being separated from her. Lions were such babies.

So her RV was now a dorm for two emotionally needy four-hundred-pound cats. Her mattress would never be the same—not to mention she was breaking the law—but hell, a girl had to be a rebel sometimes. And besides, it was just Petro and Lila. The others were doing just fine in their pen, though Iris missed being able to look out her window and see them sleeping. Not like the good old days, just three months past. Poor as a church mouse, but footloose and fancy-free.

Iris held up her hand, watching as golden light shimmered from the tips of her fingers. Claws glinted, fur riding soft and speckled down her slender wrists.

Fancy-free, she thought. *What a joke.*

Iris heard movement outside the RV; her stomach turned sour and her hand dropped to her side. She held her breath, listening, and recognized the tread, the soft-soled shoes shuffling on gravel.

Keep on walking. Just keep on, please.

But the feet stopped and a fist knocked hard on her door, a jackhammer *bam bam bam* that made her grit her teeth in panic, frustration. Petro and Lila lurched, ears flat against their massive heads, and she felt the entire RV rock on its wheels with that one fast movement. Any desire to play dumb, pretend she was not home, flew up in smoke. After a brief pause the racket began again.

The lions growled. Iris grabbed the ruffs of their necks, pushing her thoughts into their heads, pleading with them. After a moment their bodies relaxed. Iris forced herself to do the same, but it was difficult; her mouth felt full of teeth, and her skin . . . there was still too much fur—

Swearing, she rolled forward off the bed, landing lightly on her feet. The door rattled; the paper-clip lock was coming loose. A few more good hits and the man standing outside would get an eyeful.

You and your shitty control, Iris thought, running to the kitchenette. She grabbed a bottle of water and upended it over her head, drenching herself. The cold splash did the trick; humanity returned in an instant. Iris stuck her fingers in her mouth to test her teeth, also checking herself in the mirror on the wall. Red hair streaked with blond, pale skin, no spots . . .

"Hello?" called a familiar male voice. "Iris? Please, wake up!"

Fully human, she did not bother being careful; she yanked open the door and paper clips flew, duct tape ripping like large Band-Aids. Some of the cheap wood paneling came off the wall and almost hit her head.

"What?" Iris snapped, trying to maintain her dignity, her ire, in front of the very handsome man who stood on her stoop dressed in nothing more than a tight tank and loose sweatpants.

Danny Perry, with his all-American good looks and broad shoulders, his clear gaze and those sexy glasses that fueled the hot-professor fantasy of every woman in his immediate vicinity, was another up-and-coming performer, six months new and Pete's lucky find—and he was, officially, the hottest thing Riley's Circus currently had to offer.

And he liked her. Iris could smell it on him every time he got close. Even now. Unfortunately, she had no idea what to do about it.

But Danny had stopped talking, simply stood staring. And Iris suddenly realized that she was wearing nothing but a thin camisole and teeny-tiny hip-huggers, and that the front of her body was completely soaked with water.

Shit. Iris tried to cover up, turning to look for a robe. Danny said, "Wait."

"Right." She glanced over her shoulder. "I bet you want me to wait."

Danny did not smile. "Please, Iris. It's about Con and Boudicca."

Iris froze. "What?"

He said nothing else. Merely pointed in the direction of the holding pens. Iris stared, focusing her hearing . . .

. . . and heard shouts. A wild throaty scream that was animal and angry, and that made her blood run so cold she gasped.

Iris leapt from her trailer. She heard a roar behind her, Danny's startled shout, but she did not look, did not tell Petro and Lila to hold back. No time—no time—and *God,* all this crap was supposed to have stopped, gotten better, gotten *gone.*

She did not care that people called her name. She did not

care that she was half-naked, running through the unlit obstacle course of the circus camp, which was filled with RVs, cozy fires, parked motorcycles, cars, trampolines. Her eyes snapped into focus and her muscles pumped power into legs that looked too human for what she was doing. Too much speed, too much agility—she vaulted over a stack of unpacked crates, landing lightly on her feet—and then again, dancing weightless through a spilled collection of poles that were rusty and broken and sharp. Petro and Lila closed ranks around her, large and strong, and for a moment it was the old times again, and Iris imagined her mother's cool presence, racing and racing like a shadow in the sun.

But it was dark, hot, a Las Vegas night with the city lights a close rainbow on her left, and Iris bent her will on the sounds ahead, on the cries and shouts, fighting for control, fighting with all her might not to slip into her secret second body.

On the other side of the cargo trucks the holding pens appeared: large circular cages made of a strong, stable mesh, covered by a wire roof. The structure was stable, but easily flexible due to a series of interlocking pins and hinges. It was her mother's design, a way to create variation while on the road.

But one of the walls was down—as was the jaguar crumpled on the dry grass. The tiger standing nearby was not doing much better. Iris saw a splash of blue in his shoulder. A tranquilizer dart.

She tasted blood in her mouth—her teeth growing, sharpening—but she slammed her fist against her stomach, swallowed hard, and pulled it together. There were people all around—friends, strangers—all of them fighting. The crowd just outside the broken pen surged and rolled, bodies moving against one another in something that looked like a very angry orgy.

"Iris!" Pete Reilly broke from the fray. The old man was short and round, like a pink, sweaty egg draped in a nightshirt. The fight got quiet when he said her name—fast, in the span of just one breath. Iris felt the collective sigh as bodies stopped moving, pounding, ducking. Everyone stared, and for once Iris did not care. Petro and Lila pushed close against her sides, and she draped her hands in the ruffs of their enormous necks.

Quiet now, she told them. *No blood.*

"Iris," Pete said again, hushed. She found him looking at the lions, indecision painted on his face. Iris let him hang. She loved the old man, but she was not going to play this one safe. Family was hurt. Family was down. And he, better than anyone, should realize what that meant to her.

The crowd moved apart. She recognized her friends and coworkers, but kept her gaze locked on the four individuals being held beside the pen. Tranquilizer guns lay on the ground in front of them; just beyond, the tiger staggered.

"Con," Iris murmured, and patted Petro's shoulder. *Go to him.*

He did, without hesitation, and she did not miss the glint in the eyes of the people around her, the silent approval and admiration. The circus always appreciated a good trick.

If only they knew the truth.

Lila stayed pressed against her hip; Iris felt the hunt enter her body as she moved with the lioness, turning her muscles liquid, warm. She glided over the ground with her head tucked down, staring and staring at the three men and the woman who peered at her with a mixture of surprise and righteousness. They wore black militia-type uniforms, with ski masks askew on their heads. One of the old riggers waved at Iris and held up a digital video camera. Pete moved close.

"Billy got it from the woman," he told her quietly. "They documented everything. Brought a trailer, too. They were just waiting for Con to go down before they started moving them. Don't know what they were thinking, trying to sneak into the middle of this crowd, but I guess they got arrogant. Or desperate."

"Same old routine." Iris cracked her knuckles. "Which cell are they from?"

"No identifying markers, but it's either the Animal Liberation Front or that Earth First group."

"Fucking eco-terrorists. Self-righteous sons of bitches. I hate this, Pete. I hate *them.*"

"I've called the police. Same with that FBI contact. We're supposed to sit tight until they arrive."

Iris didn't care if the entire army drove out. All she could think about was Boudicca and Con—how she had failed to protect them. She missed her mother at times like this. Talk about sweet revenge; Serena McGillis was a master of retribution.

"So you're Iris," drawled one of the men. Young, tall, blond; frat boy cover model. Cocky enough to hide his unease, though his scent did not lie. All four of them smelled angry, scared. Yuppies out to save the world and ready to shit themselves because of it.

The young man, however, still had guts enough to rake his gaze over her body, lingering openly on her poorly concealed breasts. Iris wanted to bash in his head, do a tap dance on his crotch.

He licked his lips and sneered. "I get it now. You think you're a regular little Sheena of the jungle with your big cat show. Standing there so pretty, so tit-happy, with a lion at your side. Makes me sick. You're nothing but a lie. If people really knew what you did to these cats, what you've done to make them so *pliant* and *obedient*—"

She tuned him out. Same old bullshit, though she had to struggle like hell not to go for his throat. Control, control—good God, she needed to work on her control. Fear alone was not the trick, and neither was guilt. It was going on seven years since she had drawn a man's blood, and despite all the heartache that had caused, she still had trouble fighting herself when emotions ran high.

Danny reached for her and she stepped away from his hand, a move that brought her closer to the eco-asshole, who was still running on at the mouth like some verbal laxative had been shoved down his throat. He leaned so close some of the riggers grabbed him around the shoulders, but the young man ignored them, his fear-scent fading into something darker. His breath hissed. "You treat these cats like whores, you little cocktease. You profit from their misery and exploitation, and until they're liberated from your fucking abuse—"

Iris punched him. She did not mean to—his rhetoric was old hat, familiar as a lullaby—but her arm started moving faster than her brain and wow, there was a fist attached, and bam—he went down hard, blood spurting from his nose. He screamed, his companions screamed, and suddenly the fight began all over again, except this time Iris was in the middle of it, feeling stupid.

"Iris!" Danny shouted, but three of the tumblers—brothers from Mexico—knocked him aside with giant grins as they flung themselves with terrible accuracy upon the squirming pile of bodies heaving in front of Iris.

Lila slipped away. Iris followed, grabbing the lioness's thick tail, allowing herself to be led from the fight—which was rapidly becoming a wild experiment in how long four people could keep breathing with an entire circus performing gymnastics on top of them.

The skirmish, thankfully, stopped just at the entrance of the holding pen. Iris bent down on her hands and knees, crawling through the brittle yellow grass to Boudicca and Con. Petro hunkered over them both, panting in great huffs that sent a wash of hot meaty breath over Iris's face.

The tranquilizers were still in their shoulders. Iris yanked out the darts, tossing them aside. She pressed her ear to both their chests, one after the other, listening to their hearts beat. Behind her, the free-for-all began to quiet, grunts and shouts dissolving into strained laughter.

Iris stood, swayed. Too much stress, too much heartache, too much struggle to hold herself in check. Any more, and—The hairs on the back of her neck shivered. Instinct crawled. Somewhere near, above, Iris heard an odd click.

Something large suddenly collided with her body. The air cracked, popped—a sound she recognized from the firing range—and she hit the ground hard enough to have the wind knocked out of her. Iris fought the weight on her chest, tried to breathe, but then her vision cleared and she forgot everything—air, lungs, movement—because all she could do was stare into a pair of the warmest brown eyes she had ever seen in her entire life.

She was dimly aware of a very heavy body pressed atop hers, tight between her thighs, and though a tiny voice was screaming that he was a stranger, a danger, it was those eyes, those wonderful hot eyes, that made her forget that she should be frightened. Her aversion to human touch, gone. She tried to say something to those eyes, tried to give them a word, but all she could do was squeak.

And then that warmth—that remarkable far-seeing gaze—disappeared into a very large cat's mouth filled with very long white teeth. Petro. Iris, horrified, heard a muffled voice from within, deep and masculine and wry.

"Ouch," said the man.

"Oh, God." Iris grabbed Petro's thick mane. *Let him go. Now.*

The lion did not want to. His protective instincts were a scream inside her mind, but she screamed back, pushing her thoughts hard against his, begging him to release the man. Lila watched, tail lashing.

No blood, she told Petro, envisioning him opening his jaw. *Please, no blood.*

The lion hesitated. Iris, staring into his golden eyes, felt a slight tremor run through the man above. Her left hand dropped from mane to the rough edge of a beard. His neck was warm; his pulse beat wildly.

"Petro," she whispered. *He is not hurting me.*

A low growl rumbled from the lion's chest, but a moment later his jaw loosened. The man, showing a remarkable amount of control, did not move a muscle until Petro gently disengaged and took a step back. Iris closed her eyes, wondering what kind of mess it would make if her heart exploded from her chest; the pounding rattled her ribs.

The man stirred. "Hey. You okay?"

Iris bit back a startled laugh and opened her eyes. Her breath caught again—that damn gaze of his—but she sewed up her control and leaned into his body, pressing so close she could see herself reflected in his dark eyes. She studied his face, pretending cold clinical scrutiny.

"No broken skin," she said, and then shocked herself by touching him, her fingers grazing his high cheekbone. Her nose was full of his scent, which was like the air before a summer thunderstorm—as though he carried a charge, something electric and hot. Teasing, exhilarating; like a high wind sweeping through her brain. She wanted to put her nose to his skin and drink him in, soak up that heady scent.

The man cleared his throat. Iris's hand flew away, tingling. "Your lion was gentle with me, all things considering."

"He's not my lion," Iris said, berating herself for being so stupid and flustered. Her face felt red as sun-burned metal, and just as stiff. She pushed on the man's chest and he made a low sound, almost embarrassed. He scrambled off her body, color rising in his own cheeks. Iris had never seen a man blush like that—it made her heart feel funny. Worse, when he held out his hand, his fingers were long and strong, his skin as deeply golden as the rest of him.

Iris stood on her own. "Petro is my friend. I don't own him."

"Friends are worse than a leash," said the man, smiling crookedly. He wiped his face with the back of his sleeve. "Not that it's anything to complain about."

Her mental cylinders refused to cooperate with a snappy response, so she settled for silence. The fight had died down outside the holding pen; she felt Pete watching her, but did not see Daniel. No sign, either, of the people who had attacked her cats, but Jose and his two brothers were sitting at the top of a colorful human pile. They grinned at her, thumbs up.

"Are you all right?" asked the man again. He was dressed all in black like Johnny Cash, and his face had the same angular intensity. Handsome, striking, with a wave of black hair brushing over his eyebrows.

"I'm not the one who got chewed on by a lion," Iris reminded him. "Besides, all you did was knock me down. *Hard.*"

His expression darkened. "Someone shot a gun at you."

"Impossible," Iris said, but her memory echoed—the air, cracking. Her heart, which had just begun to slow, resumed its thunder.

The man crouched in the dry grass. She leaned over his shoulder and saw a funnel of dirt like a comet trail; at the heart of it metal, glinting. A sick ache spread through her stomach; her head hurt.

"A bullet," he said. "Just one. It hit about a foot from where you were standing."

Too much to take in; more insanity she did not need. Before Iris could say anything, though, she heard the high wail of sirens. Pete jogged toward her, stomach jiggling beneath his nightshirt.

"Iris," he called. "Police."

"Okay," she replied, and turned back to the stranger. He had moved in those few seconds of distraction, put some distance between them, almost to the point of escape. She had never seen anyone move quite that fast—no one except her mother—and it startled her.

"We need to talk," she protested.

"Yes," he replied, but before she could say another word he closed the space between them and touched her cheek. The contact was unexpected, as was the spark—a shock of electricity from his fingers. They both flinched, and it was a toss-up as to what startled Iris more: his touch or her reaction, which left her breathless, stunned. Iris did not touch people. She did not like to be touched. But with him she could not help herself . . . and his hand . . .

He stared, and in a ragged voice whispered, "Be careful."

Careful of what? Iris wondered, because right then, the

only thing that felt dangerous was him. So dangerous, so distracting, she could barely remember the violence behind her.

The man dragged his gaze from her face, turned on his heel, and walked away. Iris began to go after him, but Pete caught her arm and dragged her back.

She saw uniforms swarming through the circus folk, bathed in the flicker of red and blue. Unease filled her. It didn't matter that the cops had been called to help—her mother's paranoia still lingered. Men and women in positions of power were never to be trusted; anything could make them turn against you, and then . . . disaster.

Petro rumbled, tail lashing. Iris struggled to control herself; it was no good letting her fear-scent infect her cats. She had to be stronger than that, tougher. Again, Iris looked at where the man had disappeared, but it was all shadows and light now, and he was gone, nothing but a memory of warm brown eyes.

"Iris," Pete said.

"Help me put up the wall," she muttered, disgusted with herself. The two of them quickly hefted the wire, swinging it into place. It was an imperfect fix, but Petro and Lila made no effort to escape, simply hunched down in front of Con and Boudicca, watching the commotion with careful hooded eyes. Observant. Protective.

Not normal, Iris remembered others saying. *Not normal that big cats act that way, even out of the wild. Different species behaving like pride, a family.*

Yeah, well. Like she was the poster child for normal.

Iris felt heat against her back, the crush of bodies drawing near. Voices cut through her hearing. She swallowed down a deep breath, steeled herself for a mess, and glanced at Pete.

His mouth quirked. "Just like the old days."

"Don't remind me," she replied, and set her jaw into a grim smile. Time to meet the cavalry, a time-honored tradition in her life, which seemed to attract enough crazies to fill its own little Arkham Asylum. Men and women who refused to believe that Iris was anything but a whip-cracking animal abuser who got her jollies by torturing cats into performing menial tricks.

The Las Vegas police, however, were far more genial than she expected. All the cops were men. And she was wet and half-naked—a match made in Heaven.

Still, she lost track of time. Too many people wanted a piece of her, with too many questions that she could not answer. Miracle's hotel management was no help, either: pale narrow men in suits who were more concerned about press control and Iris's ability to perform than the fact that she was scared as shit. Another wake-up call about the new world she had entered—one where the bottom line mattered more than flesh and blood.

But she managed. As always. And between the talk—and the very satisfying moment when the police loaded the four sullen interlopers into the back of a van—her friends lingered, offering the kind of silent support that was all the sweeter because it respected her distance. Present, accounted for, and ready to help—that was the unspoken message. Circus family was a strong family, right up until the bitter end.

God, she was happy for it. Especially as her last interviewer drew near and flashed a badge from the FBI.

"This is the first incident of ecoterrorism we've had here in almost six months," said the agent after a brief introduction. He called himself Fred. No last name, which seemed at odds with typical FBI professionalism. Iris could not recall seeing a last name during her brief glance at his badge. Not that she particularly cared. One fed was like any other, after a while.

"It isn't *my* first incident," she remarked sourly, more than a little irritated that she had heard something similar all night long. Six months without incident. Violence was a rarity. Not much in this town bothered the environmental extremists anymore.

Until you, they implied. *Fine, dandy.* How wonderful.

Iris, wrapped in a threadbare blanket Pete had brought her, scanned the crowd and found the old man talking to some of the riggers. Danny was gone, and had been for quite some time. Poof, like smoke. Just like that stranger.

Mr. Nice Eyes, she called him, and then Fred said something and she answered, "My mom and I have always been targets. Animal rights activists—the extremists, anyway—never seem able to reconcile the idea that our cats are well cared for *and* part of a circus environment. We've been dodging their interference for years now." Years of other cops in other cities, other federal agents, all of them nodding their heads and writing reports and doing jack-shit to help.

"Your mom," Fred said. "Is she here?"

"No," Iris told him firmly, and before he could ask where or why, she said, "What about the gun? The person who shot at me?"

"We've recovered the bullet, but not the weapon or the shooter. We assume, though, that he was working with Kevin Cray—the man you punched—and the rest of his crew."

"Which extremist group are they with?"

"Hard to tell at this point. We need to talk to them some more. But don't worry." Fred clapped his hand on her shoulder. "We'll take good care of you."

Iris decided it would be unwise to roll her eyes. "Are we done here, Agent . . . Fred? I need to check on my cats."

"Sure. Before you go, though, can you tell me what happened to the gentleman who saved you from the gunman? I'd like to talk to him, too."

"He disappeared," Iris said. Then she turned and did the same.

The police left. So did Fred. The only people who stuck around were circus folk, and after a brief impromptu display of fire-eating and tumbling and yodeling—all meant to cheer her spirits—most everyone drifted away. Tomorrow was a performance day, with both a matinee and an evening show scheduled at the Miracle. People needed their rest.

Iris stood against the wire, savoring the quiet—the stillness—and felt a relief so strong she wanted to cry. Instead she went to Pete. He did not try to hug her, though part of her wished he would—that his big, thick arms would work themselves up into a protest against her usual standoffishness and just haul her in for a bone-crunching hug. She needed to be held. So very badly.

But Iris did not move and neither did Pete, though his eyes were kind.

"There, there," he murmured, still in his nightshirt, but now with a pipe in hand. He smelled like coffee and cherry tobacco. "You're okay, and the cats are fine. Just sleeping. Nothing to be upset about."

"Except for the part where you got shot at," rumbled a familiar accented voice. Samuel, coming up behind them, sleepily rubbed his massive arms and ribs. The tall German looked like he belonged in a maximum-security prison—all hard lines and hard muscle—but oh, what a sweetheart, a circus strongman who doubled as a clown.

Pete gave him a dirty look. "We don't need to talk about that right now, *Sammy*. Iris has been through enough tonight."

"That's okay, Pete. I can handle this." Whatever *this* was. An attempt on her life? A warning? But what could she do? There was no way she could stop working with the cats, not unless Petro and the others told her it was time. And so far they seemed to be enjoying the high life of stage and spotlight and applause.

"Iris," Pete said. "I want you to sleep in my office tonight. Tomorrow we'll move you to the hotel. Management is offering you a penthouse suite, with round-the-clock security."

"Not interested."

"Iris—"

"*So* not interested, Pete. What, and they'll let me take the cats, too?" Iris shook her head. "I'm right where I should be. Safe, too. We might be open territory, but strangers stand out." She glanced around. "Speaking of which, did you see what became of that guy who knocked me down? You know, the one with the beard?"

"Ah," Samuel said. "The *wunderschön* one."

"Um, yes," Iris said. "Him."

Samuel scratched his ribs. "I do not think he wanted to talk to the police."

"Join the club," Iris said. "But I wanted to ... thank him."

Pete tried to smile, but it looked more like a nervous tick. "I'm sure you'll get your chance. In the meantime, you're coming with me."

"No way. I'm staying with the cats tonight. Petro and Lila are already upset, and if I'm not here when Con and Boudicca wake up, I can't imagine how they'll react. You know how high-strung they are, Pete. And after tonight? If I can't calm them down there might not be a show tomorrow. Really."

Calculated words. Above all else, the show had to go on. No matter what. Pete narrowed his eyes. "You're spinning, Iris. Don't do that to me."

"It's the truth," she insisted, though inside her head she was crossing her fingers. "Besides, I doubt our ecoterrorist gunslinger will be back tonight. Too much heat."

Pete closed his eyes. "If your mother was here—"

"She's not," Iris said in a sharp voice. "And don't you use her against me. You might have been close, but I knew her better than anyone. And she wouldn't leave the cats right now, either."

"I know," Pete said quietly. "And it breaks my heart."

It broke Iris's heart, too. Because she knew how much her mother had treasured her life and her daughter, and if she hadn't come back after all this time ...

She swallowed hard and looked away at Samuel, whose hooded gaze flicked between her and Pete. She patted his thick arm.

"G'night, bad boy."

"*Gute Nacht*," he replied solemnly. "But if you like—"

Iris shook her head. "I'll see you both in the morning."

Pete did not say anything. He turned on his heel and walked off. The tails of his nightshirt flapped. Samuel hesitated, then shocked Iris by reaching over to wrap her in a quick, fierce hug that felt like a cocoon of rock and steel. Tears sprang to her eyes, and she was thankful that Samuel did not look at her—just ducked his head, mumbling something in German before shoving his hands deep into his pockets and rushing off after the elderly circus owner.

Iris sighed, watching them go. Finally alone. Stupid, maybe, but alone.

She pulled aside the wire gate and entered the pen. Petro greeted her with a loud moan, rolling on his back. Lila lay nearby, sprawled on top of Boudicca, who still lay very still. Con slept. Iris curled close, right into the center of their warm pile, pushing gentle thoughts of love and bonding into all their minds. She closed her eyes, reminding herself that this—*here*—was home. A home she had to protect no matter what. Even if sitting out, exposed, creeped the hell out of her.

Slowly, though, she relaxed into a doze, drifting into a sleep deep enough to dream, to float on spotted clouds, to run and run on endless roads that brought her into a wood and a boy and his screams and blood ...

Iris opened her eyes. Her heart pounded, but she swallowed down the old memories, focusing on the here and now, the sounds of a large camp shifting restless in sleep. Her instincts tickled; she felt a change in the air. A presence.

Iris sat up. The world felt darker than she remembered, but her eyes snapped into focus, and the rest of her senses compensated with sharp immediacy. She inhaled, testing the air, and caught a familiar scent.

"You always like to spy on girls while they sleep?" Iris asked the darkness, studying an area of deep shadow near one of the cargo trucks. The shadow moved and walked toward the pen, becoming a man.

Iris joined him. The chain link did not feel like much of a barrier; his eyes made her feel exposed, naked. She clutched Pete's blanket even tighter around her body as he watched her, and she did the same to him, pretending to be unabashed, bold, when in truth she simply did not have the strength to look away.

The man was lean, with broad shoulders and narrow hips, his body garbed in clothes with dark, clean lines and that looked highly tailored and expensive. Good taste, if nothing else. A man primed and ready for a night in a high-end yuppie club, a martini—shaken, not stirred—in his large, elegant hand.

Money, Iris thought when she looked at him. *Born to it, bred to it, or married to it.* Of course, that was an image completely at odds with his presence and his behavior. Men like him did not wander into the private domain of itinerant circus folk—even a circus parked on some dusty abandoned lot behind a glittering hotel on the Las Vegas Strip. They did not save women from snipers.

"You shouldn't be here," Iris said to him. He folded his arms over his chest, expression darkening.

"Funny. I was just thinking the same thing about you."

Iris frowned. "My camp, my territory."

"Doesn't mean this place is safe. You were shot at, and what? You decide to stay out in the open where you'll make another target? Bad idea."

"Of course it's a bad idea," Iris snapped, irritated that a stranger was giving her this lecture. "That's not the point. I can't move the cats while they're passed out, and I refuse to leave them while they're vulnerable. Especially if someone is running around with a gun in hand."

"So instead you gamble with your life."

"Cut the melodrama. I can take care of myself. Besides, I'm betting whoever shot at me missed on purpose. Probably a friend of those assholes who went after the cats. Those types like to scare, but they're too chicken for murder."

"You sure about that?"

"Yes," Iris lied. "Anyway, what does it matter to you? You're not my protector."

He said nothing. Iris moved closer to the fence. His eyes

were lost in shadow, but she imagined they looked the same: rich and brown and full of something . . . warm.

"Why didn't you want to talk to the police?" Iris asked him, proud her voice did not shake, that she sounded so strong and calm and easy.

His jaw tightened. "I wanted to see if I could find the shooter. I thought that would be more useful than standing around trying to explain the happy coincidence of how I happened to be there just when a gun went off."

"Right. I could use that explanation."

"You could use a bulletproof vest or a roof over your head."

"Or some straight answers. Give me your name."

He hesitated. "My friends call me Blue."

"And your enemies?"

"They don't worry about names."

"I don't find that particularly comforting."

His mouth crooked into a smile. "What's your name?"

"Iris," she said slowly, not quite certain why she was being so forthcoming, why she was unable to help herself. She did not like strangers—not usually, anyway—but there was something about this man that was utterly compelling. It frightened her, just how compelling.

He stepped closer, reaching out to lace his fingers through the chain link. "Iris, maybe you should think about spending the night somewhere else. I'll walk you home. Or not, if it makes you uncomfortable. But this isn't safe."

Iris clutched her blanket closer. Behind, Lila yawned, teeth flashing long and white beneath the sparse campground lights. The air felt very still, though she could hear the wind-up music and distant chime of the Strip. No escaping the concrete jungle; no peace, anywhere.

"Why are you doing this?" she asked him, studying his eyes, drinking in his clean scent. "Why are you here?"

"Why not?" he replied, voice rumbling low and soft. "Why wouldn't I help you?"

"Because people don't. Not like this."

His fingers tightened around the chain link. A big man,

broad and tall, he made Iris feel small, almost delicate. She did not lean away, but stepped closer, inhaling him, drinking in his gaze. Dangerous—this was so dangerous; her mother would be ashamed—but she could not help herself. Even the leopard called to him; she could feel her other half rolling through her chest, stirring to life.

"You need to meet better people," he said, glancing at her mouth. Her pulse quickened, heart jumping with a tiny ache that made her remember older days, older pain; why this was bad, dangerous. Iris forced herself to lean away, but as she did, she caught a new scent in the air and stopped moving, tilting her head and glancing left into the dark shadows. The man—Blue—followed her gaze.

"What is it?" he asked.

Iris could not answer him. No way to explain how she knew someone was coming.

Careful now. You have to be careful. Though of what, she could not say. Good hearing in itself was not enough, in this day and age, to declare a person inhuman. Even if that was the case.

She heard her mother's voice, chiding her, that old faint whisper of: *Better to be safe than sorry, Iris. Be ever vigilant, because the moment you are not, an accident will occur. You will be caught off guard. Your true nature will emerge, and you cannot let that happen. You cannot. The world is too dangerous for those like us, and we are alone. We are alone, and all we have is each other. . . .*

And now all Iris had was herself. She glanced at the man—Blue—and found him studying her. The attention, the intensity, made her nervous.

"What do you want?" she asked him, ignoring for a moment the scent on the wind, the steady approach of footsteps. None of that mattered compared to what was going on inside this man's head.

Blue's gaze faltered. He touched the wire separating them and opened his mouth. Iris leaned forward.

Before he could speak, though, a wavering light cut through the darkness on their left. She turned. It was Danny, walking with a flashlight. Blue moved—she half expected him to run—but when she glanced at him she found that he had only shifted position, standing so that it would be easy for Danny to see him.

And Danny saw, and stopped walking. Stumbled, actually, though he caught himself so easily Iris almost missed it. She was used to his grace, though, his abilities as a dancer, and the misstep was glaring. His scent changed, too. It became acrid, bitter, his unease incomprehensible. Blue, too, smelled nervous.

"Iris," he said in a low voice. "Are you okay?"

"I'm fine," she said slowly, looking between the two men. "This is the person who saved me from being shot. His name is Blue."

Danny said nothing. He studied Blue, shining the flashlight directly into Blue's face. It must have been uncomfortable, but Blue did not protest. Just stood there, letting Danny get his fill. Neither of them spoke or moved. Iris found it all rather creepy. And confusing.

"Do you know each other?" she asked.

"No," said both men, in unison. Iris rubbed her forehead.

"Right. Okay, then. Danny, get that flashlight off his face. You're blinding him."

"Good." His voice was unfriendly, eyes hard as flint behind his glasses. "I want to know why he's here."

"Just passing through," Blue told him, and if Iris thought his gaze was intense before, it was nothing compared to what passed through his face when he looked at Danny. The intimacy of it made her uncomfortable, but only because Danny's eyes shared the same raw focus. Iris thought of lions, males meeting on pride land, ready to fight for the right to hunt, to mate.

"Hey," she said, and then again, louder. Both men looked at her, cheeks flushed, scents so prickly she wanted to shake them both and then run like hell. Danny's throat worked; the flashlight wavered from Blue's face.

"Iris," he said. "I went by your trailer to make sure you were okay. You weren't there. I got worried."

"I'm fine." She glanced at Blue. "Really."

"It's not safe for you here."

"So everyone keeps reminding me. The frost in her voice was nothing but a mask for a sudden case of bone-deep weariness. She might not be alone, but she wanted to be—alone except for the company of her cats. Humans, be gone. Her heart ached.

"I'm not leaving this holding pen," she told the men, and it was a surreal sensation, feeling like she had to defend herself for doing the right thing. "Not until Con and Boudicca are awake and I know they're calm. So both of you can go away now. Go beat each other up. Work out whatever it is that has you both so riled."

Iris turned her back and lay down between Con and Petro. Lila threw herself on the grass at her feet and began licking Iris's calves. Her tongue felt like sandpaper.

The men did not move for a very long time. Iris felt ridiculous ignoring them, but the alternative was involvement and she did not have the energy. She was confused enough, and exhausted. She simply lay on her side, curled into a ball, listening to the men size each other up. Their scents continued to bother her. Not because they were entirely unpleasant, but because it was suddenly difficult to tell them apart. Danny's scent did not carry the same electricity as Blue's—his was more rain than thunder—but there was an underlying quality that was undeniably similar.

Almost like they're family, she thought, chewing on that possibility for only a moment before discarding it. Too unlikely. Besides, both men had said they did not know each other, and she chose to take that as the truth.

Iris closed her eyes. She heard cloth rustle and joints pop. A very quiet grunt of pain. She thought it was Blue and wanted to roll over, but she made herself lie still, and every sound and scent felt clear and new and sharp. She listened to him lie down in the grass outside the holding pen and could not fathom why this man, a stranger, would go to so much trouble for her. She wanted to feel suspicious, wanted to chalk up his astonishing behavior to ulterior motives, but his scent was beginning to clear and calm, and she could not argue with that. Nor did she want to.

"You can't stay here," Danny murmured.

"Then call the cops," Blue said.

Silence. A moment later Iris heard more movement, another body settling on the ground.

"Don't try anything," Danny said.

"Okay," Blue replied, and that was the last thing Iris heard him say for the rest of the night.

She went to sleep.

Chapter Four

Against his better judgment—because, in his experience, being unconscious was usually better than the alternative—Blue woke the next morning with a crick in his neck and a boot in his crotch. He was not sure which was worse, although he thought the very large half-naked man staring down at him with a cleaver in his hand might trump them both.

"Hello," Blue said.

"*Guten Morgen*," said the man, with a smile that was almost as violently cheerful as the giant yellow happy face tattooed on his massive chest. "I think you are very *wunderschön*, but if you hurt my friends, I will cut you. Okay?"

"Okay," Blue said, hoping to God that was the right answer.

Apparently it was. The man turned and walked to the holding pen, which Blue was almost as surprised to see as daylight or that cleaver. He had not meant to sleep. Not with his brother hunkered close in the darkness, no doubt waiting for an opportunity to smother him. Although, given that Blue was still alive—sans wounds—he figured common sense had won out. Maybe even common decency. Though he doubted it. Daniel, quite obviously, knew who he was. And that was just great.

He sat up. His body ached, and when he leaned forward he noticed the dusty stamp of a great big boot on the crotch of his black pants. Just what he needed; Blue wondered if it was a portent of things to come.

He glanced at the holding pen and met the collective golden gazes of four very large cats, all of whom studied him with the kind of intense concentration that Blue usually reserved for shooting people. Iris, however, was not with them. Her absence bothered him—a lot—and he tried to stand. His right leg gave out at the last moment, sending him back down to the ground. Hard. He swore, rubbing his knee.

"Trouble?" asked the tattooed German. Blue found him crouched over an extremely large side of beef. He began hacking at it with the cleaver. The cats ignored him, still staring at Blue.

"Recent injury," Blue told him, more than a little disturbed that he was more interesting than a slab of raw meat. "I don't think sleeping on the ground helped much."

"You should have asked for a bed," came the reply, as though strangers requesting a place to sleep was a common practice, the easiest thing in the world. He took one long step and held out his hand. "My name is Samuel. You need room? Come to me."

Blue grabbed his hand and the man yanked him off the ground with enough force to almost send him back down again, this time flat on his face. He teetered. Samuel steadied him.

"Thanks," Blue said. "I appreciate it."

The German smiled and went back to cutting meat, attacking it with a ferocity that made the intense unerring scrutiny of the cats even more eerie. Blue moved a safe distance away. "I don't suppose you know where Iris is, do you? Or Daniel?"

The man grunted. "Today is a show day. Everyone is practicing. Or should be."

"Can you tell me where?"

"Not far. Just on the other side of the camp. We practice, and then go to the Miracle for our performance."

"Ah." Blue hesitated. "And what do *you* do?"

The man's smile widened. "I am a clown."

Right. Blue hobbled away. Quickly.

Las Vegas in the daytime was ugly as sin. At least, the part he was in. Forty minutes out was another matter entirely, but unfortunately, the Valley of Fire and all of Nevada's other natural wonders were not on his list of things to do or see. Here, in the ass-end of a resort and hotel, the world was made of concrete and scrub grass, large trucks and RVs. Everything bordering the back lot and the camp looked cheap and old, worn down like a yellow tooth.

And the city—the city! Even with his eyes closed, it was nothing but a scream inside his mind. It perched on the edge of forever, like he stood in the center of a glass bubble, and all around him water, the deepest ocean where monsters swam. Blue had been to Las Vegas only twice before, and never for long. The city consumed a colossal amount of electricity, and though Blue had been in other urban areas where the power use was similar, Las Vegas was unique in that all major use concentrated over a relatively small area. He could feel it in his teeth, on the tingling skin of his hands. Power rose like a heat mirage over his body.

The sun was bright. Not a cloud in the hazy sky; it was going to be a hot day. Blue's stomach growled. His clothes were wrinkled and dusty. He wanted a shower and thought—very briefly—about trying to find a room at the Miracle, about maybe buying himself breakfast and a quick change of clothes. Forty minutes tops, and no one the wiser.

But then, through a maze of RVs, Blue glimpsed a very familiar head of red hair, and the idea of leaving the camp suddenly did not seem all that attractive.

Iris McGillis. Shape-shifter.

Golden eyes. Fire in her gaze, a subtle glow. A trick of light to anyone else, but to Blue a call of magic. Mystery and science, myths walking tall in golden light. Crows, tigers, cheetahs, dolphins, dragons—and God only knew what else.

And now Iris. Iris, whom Blue had known was not human even before he had gotten close, before—*she's under me, I'm crushing her, but oh, God, those eyes, those beautiful, lovely, eyes*—she pressed against him nose-to-nose, sharing his breath.

He had seen her in the darkness of the camp. Less than an hour in the city, with Dean on the cell phone giving him instructions, descriptions, leading him to another world—a sprawling camp sheltered and removed in the middle of Las Vegas—and there . . . there . . . a slender body had raced past him with lions at her feet, wild and impossibly graceful. Like some myth—a huntress, a goddess thrown down from heaven. And even now Blue wanted to wax lyrical thinking about her. Even now his heart wanted to jump out of his chest and race alongside her. She was nothing less than incredible.

Plus, she had a mean right hook, a sharp tongue, and a stare to kill for. None of which, unfortunately, was any defense at all against someone with a gun.

Someone with a gun who knew what they were doing.

Very unsettling. In the moments before the actual shot, Blue had felt the electrical signature of a battery-operated power scope, the trail of a subvocal walkie-talkie, and those two things alone implied a more elaborate setup than just ecoterrorists out for a night of vandalism. Not to mention Iris was right: The shooter *had* missed on purpose. Blue was certain of it.

Enough. You came here to do a job. To find your brother, which you did. And now . . .

Now, nothing. Blue had no idea what to do. Roland had suggested he find out what the hell Daniel had that made him so important to their father, but seeing his brother in the flesh, hearing him speak, resting close for an entire night listening to Daniel listen to *him*?

God Almighty.

Despite Samuel's claim that the morning was supposed to be spent in practice, Blue saw a lot of people sitting around their RVs, eating breakfast, talking, and laughing. He recognized quite a few languages, but didn't understand much of what was being said. Although he knew well enough what it meant when his presence created waves of silence. He endured the quiet, the hard stares, and kept moving. He did not want any trouble, although the irony suited him. For the first time in a long while, Blue felt like a complete and utter trespasser—but for different reasons than usual, reasons that had nothing to do with his abilities as an electrokinetic, and everything to do with simply being unknown.

He found Iris standing outside a beat-up brown RV that held a closer resemblance to a battering ram than a so-called recreational vehicle. A relic from the early nineties, maybe, tottering on its wheels like an elephant on roller-skates.

Iris seemed very much at home. She had a barbecue going, the grill covered in sausages and bacon. The side gas burner held a large skillet filled with half-cooked eggs that she stirred with a spatula. Her hair was down, her skin fair and rosy, and she wore a thin lavender robe that did nothing to disguise her figure. A figure that was, and forever would be, emblazoned upon Blue's memory in all its soft, lithe glory.

Iris blinked when she saw him, but he was gratified to see a smile touch her mouth. "Mornin', stranger."

"Good morning," he said, more pleased than he would care to admit that she was actually talking to him. And with a sense of humor, no less.

Iris pointed to the smoking bacon and sausages. "I was going to bring you something. Clearly, though, you have an excellent nose."

Blue did not know if she was telling the truth about her plan to deliver breakfast, but there was a clear honesty about her gaze that seemed sincere.

"Thanks," he said. "You didn't have to. I'm not completely down on my luck."

"I didn't think you were," she said tartly, making an open examination of his clothes.

Her scrutiny made him self-conscious, though Samuel's footprint at least had been brushed away. Blue moved a little closer, keeping the barbecue between them. "How are your cats? Con and ... Boudicca? I thought they looked more alert this morning."

"Yes," Iris said, still studying him. Blue wondered if she could see through the eyes of her cats—and if she could, what that had told her about him. "The tranquilizer wore off in the middle of the night. They were a little unsettled, but it was nothing a few calm words couldn't take care of."

From anyone else it would have been an understatement, perhaps even a lie, but Blue had seen the way the cats responded to Iris, and knowing what he did about her secret heritage he suspected that words were indeed enough. Maybe not even that much.

"You have a connection with them," he said carefully. "I don't think I've ever seen anything like it."

Iris turned and flipped the bacon. "How much do you want?"

Hello, sore spot. "I only meant it as a compliment."

"I get a lot of compliments. How much bacon?"

Blue hesitated. "Three pieces. Please."

Iris grabbed a paper plate and slapped on the bacon, as well as a couple sausages and a pile of eggs. She dug inside a nearby bag for a plastic fork, and then practically threw him his breakfast. Watching her carefully, Blue settled down on the ground and began eating. Iris joined him.

"I'm sorry," he said.

Iris picked up a piece of bacon. "Don't be. I get a lot of people hounding me, wanting things. Outsiders, not the circus. So compliments don't mean much anymore."

"You think it's all fake. You believe there's a motive."

Iris shrugged. "Why are you here talking to me?"

"Why are *you* talking to *me*? Why feed me, if you think I'm some loser groupie?"

"You helped me. And you're ... alone."

Blue tried not to smile. "I did not know who you were when I helped you last night. And I *still* don't know anything about you except for the fact that you get on extraordinarily well with four very wild cats."

"And the magical coincidence of your arrival last night?"

"An accident. All I saw leading up to that moment was a fight, a gun, and a target. I removed the target."

"And then you decided to hang around."

Blue set down his plate. "Have I asked you for anything, Iris? Other than bacon?"

"Not yet," she muttered.

"Then until I do, cut me some slack." He shoved eggs into his mouth, and around them mumbled, "Thanks for the meal."

"Thanks for saving my life," she said quietly, and shot him a look that was so distracting he temporarily forgot how to chew and breathe at the same time. He started coughing. Iris shook her head, biting her bottom lip.

Footsteps, the hard plod of soles on pavement and gravel. Low male voices. Daniel and an older man appeared around the end of Iris's RV. They stopped when they saw him and Iris sitting together, and Blue struggled to regain control over his lungs. It was easier than he thought it would be. Looking at his brother—*my brother*—made everything slow down. Made the world narrow in the same way it did when he looked at Iris. Only Daniel inspired less ... affection.

He looks like our father, Blue thought again, still taken by the resemblance. Daniel was the spitting image of Felix Perrineau Senior—as the old man had been, once upon a time. And with luck, Daniel would age exactly the same way. Slowly, and with elegance. Whether or not the personality would reflect the appearance remained to be seen. So far, Blue was not impressed.

"Iris," Daniel said. It was difficult for Blue to stay steady in front of that piercing gaze. Too many memories, too many questions—and his reasons for being here did not make things any easier.

You are here to betray him. You are here to betray your brother.

Brother. *Shit.* This was really his brother. Living, breathing, dreaming—

"Danny." Iris glanced between him and Blue. "Would you and Pete like something to eat?"

Pete shook his head, openly studying Blue. "I'm fine, Iris. But I, uh, just received a call from the local police that I think you should know about. Kevin Cray is out on bail. They set the bond at two hundred thousand, and someone coughed up the money early this morning."

Iris closed her eyes. Blue set aside his plate.

"That's a lot of money," he said. "Why would a rich kid go to all the trouble of hurting Iris and her cats?"

Pete frowned. "And you are . . . ?"

He held out his hand. "You can call me Blue."

"Blue." Pete had a firm grip. "You saved Iris last night, didn't you?"

"That's up for debate," he replied, glancing sideways at the young woman. Her mouth twitched into the ghost of a smile. Daniel's frown deepened.

Pete cleared his throat. "Folks like Kevin Cray are part of an advanced animal activist group. Extremists. Some of them believe keeping house pets goes against the laws of nature, so using big cats in a circus atmosphere makes them see red. Most members are young college types. Good schools, good families, lots of money. Members work in cells, get guidance from the Internet. There's no real leader—just so-called heroes—which is why law enforcement finds these groups hard to track. They don't have a structure."

"*You* could be one of them," Daniel suggested. Easy, simple—it was one of those floating accusations that was impossible to prove and even more difficult to shake. Blue wanted to punch the son of a bitch. To wipe that bellicose look right off his face.

He glanced at Iris instead. "Going to judge me now?" he asked her grimly.

"Already did," she shot back. "You think I would have left you alone with my cats otherwise?"

Blue fought down a smile. "Based on what I saw last night, I think you could kick my ass and then some if I tried anything to your cats. Speaking of which, do you think there's any danger of retaliation from Kevin and his friends?"

"Probably," Pete said, a furrow digging deep between his eyes. Daniel looked just as concerned—and what a surprise to see that his brother was human, that he was not some cold paternal replica, after all.

And you didn't know that already? The fact he ran away didn't clue you in at all? Maybe, but Blue trusted nothing when it came to Daniel. Not even himself. He looked at Iris. "You won't be safe here."

"You're a broken record."

"And you're too stubborn for your own good."

"Like you aren't. One save and you're suddenly an expert on my safety? You don't even belong here."

Blue gritted his teeth. "I'm looking for work, Pete. Who would I talk to about that?"

Iris went very still, as did Daniel. Pete glanced at them both. "That would be me. I'm the Reilly in Reilly's Circus."

"I'm an electrician," Blue told him, which was enough of the truth that he did not feel at all guilty about lying. "And I'm very good."

"So good you're looking for work with the circus?" Daniel shook his head. "You dress better than most of the people who come to our shows."

"Any law against that?" Blue's voice slipped into something hard. "Any law against wanting to try another life on for size?"

Daniel's jaw tightened. Pete tilted his head, reaching into his shirt pocket for a pipe. "No law against either one of those things. But I'm careful about the people I bring into the family. Not just anyone will do. I hire only the best. Best in skills and best in temperament. Because, son, we're *all* outsiders here. We all had to run away from someplace. But in my circus we're not outsiders to one another, and if we're runaways, then we ran away to home. My home. This home. So if you join us, then by God, you better have the heart for it, because I promise you won't last long, otherwise."

You don't have to last long, a tiny voice whispered, but it was a bad thought, a poor tribute to what Pete had just said, which was something that Blue understood all too well.

"You sound like some of my friends," he said quietly.

Pete grunted. "You worked for the circus before?"

"No. I was a … tech specialist for the navy. Spec ops, mostly."

"Ah," said the old man, as if that answered something for him. His gaze flicked to Iris.

Blue held out his hand, pressing his advantage. "Give me a chance. Let me do some work for you. Don't pay me. Just see what I'm capable of."

And see if I can protect Iris, Blue thought, knowing that mattered more to Pete than wires and currents. He could see it in the old man's eyes.

"Pete," Daniel said. Iris looked like she wanted to protest, too. But the circus owner shook his head and grabbed Blue's hand.

"One day. Just one day. You screw up, I'll let Iris's cats have you for dinner."

"Meow," she snapped, leaving them for her trailer. She slammed the door—a gesture made less effective by the fact that it didn't actually stay shut. The lock was clearly broken, and the hinges …

"I'm fixing that first," Blue said.

"Electrician?" Daniel reminded him. He looked unhappy.

"Jack-of-all-trades." Blue said, pasting a smile on his face. It probably looked as fake as he felt, but Pete clapped a hand on his shoulder. The grip was surprisingly strong.

"Danny will show you where the tools are kept. Introduce you to everyone, too. Hell, the two of you will have to bunk together until we can find you a place to stay."

Blue wondered if the old man was a mind reader or just flat-out maniacal. Daniel began to protest. Pete held up his hand. "You're the newest guy on the block, kid, and when you came here you had to do the exact same thing. Just because you're getting successful doesn't mean I cut you any breaks. So go. *Now*."

Much to Blue's surprise—because obedience was most definitely *not* the Perrineau way—Daniel clamped his mouth shut and nodded with a sharp jerk of his head that looked more like whiplash than acquiescence. He turned and walked away, spine so straight it looked like he had an arrow up his ass. Blue stared. Pete shrugged.

"Growing pains," the old man said, as if that explained everything. Blue was not so optimistic. Daniel was twenty-seven years old, fully formed and of a decidedly unique upbringing. Hell might freeze over before anything could change that.

Pete, however, gave him a suspiciously serene smile, and walked the short distance to Iris's door. Rapped his knuckles on the side of it. Iris said something too muffled to hear, and Pete went in.

"Are you coming?" Daniel called. Blue glanced at him, surprised he was still there. Surprised, too, that he was talking to him of his own free will.

Blue did not reply. His mouth and brain refused to cooperate, and besides, this was Daniel's turf, Daniel who was his brother. He did not feel like rocking the boat just for the sheer hell of it. Maybe later, though.

Walking with him was a very strange experience, though Blue did not make small talk. Daniel did not encourage him, which was fine. Being with him was too surreal—for a variety of reasons—though first and foremost was the fact that Blue was pretty damn certain his brother knew who he was, and it made him uneasy that Daniel had chosen not to say anything. He was an unknown quantity, a variation on the old theme of his father. Blue did not know what to expect.

Try fear, he told himself. *If you had tried to outrace the old man and your long lost brother suddenly showed up on your doorstep, you would do a hell of a lot more than mince words.*

Run or fight. Neither of which had happened yet.

Daniel's gaze slid sideways. "I don't have much time to spend with you. I have to prepare for my show."

Blue tried to imagine Felix Perrineau's son performing in the circus and it made his head hurt. Or maybe that was the bright sun or the old bomb blast still echoing hard in his skull. The air felt too warm. Blue unbuttoned the top of his shirt and rolled up his sleeves.

All those art degrees, he reminded himself. *Juilliard, Harvard ... but there was that master's in education, too. Daniel was a teacher, once upon a time. And now ...*

"What do you do?" he asked.

"I'm an escape artist."

How appropriate. Blue almost laughed. "Where did you pick that up?"

The corner of Daniel's mouth curved. "Life."

Life. Yes. How appropriate. Blue tried not to let anything more than polite curiosity show on his face, unable to decide if he should press—or whether it mattered, even, that he hear the story behind that one word. What was he doing, anyway? If Roland and the others could not find a way around his father, if the threat still held true, then the choice was clear: For his mother and friends, he would have to turn over this man, his brother. Getting to know him better would just make it harder.

But who are you kidding? You think you can do this and stay cold? You think you can look this man in the eyes and not feel anything?

Apparently not, because if the guilt in his gut was any indication, he was doing a pretty lousy job of it already.

"How long have you been here?" Blue asked. They passed two young and impossibly skinny Chinese women—twins—who giggled and smiled when they saw Daniel. He waved at them but did not stop to introduce Blue, who jumped aside as a pair of men racing inside a giant wheel rolled past. A dark-skinned woman leaped and danced above, keeping perfect balance on top of the quickly moving metal surface. Blue tried not to stare.

Daniel did not spare the acrobats a second glance. "Three months. I arrived just before Reilly got the offer from Miracle—this hotel where we're performing. I started out at the bottom, working as crew. And then I got a chance to try my own thing."

"And you like it?"

"Wouldn't give it up for the world," Daniel said, which was probably a more literal statement than anyone would believe. As Felix Perrineau's heir, Daniel really could have the world. Maybe just not the one he wanted. Assuming, of course, that he was behaving genuinely and not just blowing smoke.

Blue heard shouts, commands in Spanish. Men and women, standing a good distance apart, climbing upon shoulders and flinging themselves at one another like living torpedoes. Daniel led Blue right between them—bodies hurtling merrily above their heads—and pointed at a white moving truck. On its side was a painting of a clown, a big top, tigers and lions and a lithe woman with short red hair, arms outstretched, posed for conquest. She looked very familiar.

Daniel popped open the back doors while Blue studied the painting.

"Iris?" he asked.

"Her mother." Daniel pointed. "There. Tools."

Many tools. The entire interior of the truck looked like a portable workshop, complete with overhead lights, workstation, racks filled with gear wisely strapped against the wall. There was even equipment for welding. Everything a man needed to fix a problem under the big top. Or in this case, the auditorium in a Las Vegas hotel.

"Who's your current handyman?" Blue asked. "I don't want to step on any toes."

Daniel grunted. "The only reason Pete agreed to a trial run is that our last guy got lured away by Cirque du Soleil. No big deal, though. The Miracle has its own people. You're not needed here. At all."

"Apparently not wanted, either," Blue remarked. "Especially by you. I'd like to know why. I haven't done anything."

"Not yet," Daniel replied, folding his arms over his chest. "But I know how it works. I know it's all about timing and patience and that final cut, and if it were just me, fine. I can handle it, I've been expecting it. But if you go after Iris, after the rest of these people—"

"Stop." Blue leaned in, looking him hard in the eyes, guilt and anger burning in his gut, frustration building to a scream. "You have no idea how close you are to getting your ass handed to you. No idea at all."

"Oh," Daniel whispered, something equally terribly moving through his gaze. "Oh, you'd be surprised at what I know."

"Then tell me," Blue said, all that rage creeping and dying. "Tell me why I'm here, *Danny*. Tell me why a man like me would go to all the trouble of playing drifter in some circus on the edge of nothing and nowhere. Tell me why you hate me."

Daniel's jaw tightened. "You want something."

Tell him, Blue thought. *Tell him now. Give him the truth and let the dice fall. He already knows. Don't string it along; don't fuck it up.*

He never got the chance. Daniel backed away, shaking his head. He looked like he was in pain—his mouth tight, his eyes a little too bright—and he turned hard on his heel and walked away. Ran, almost. Blue followed him.

"Wait," he called out. His brother did not respond. Hesitating, torn between forcing the issue and just letting him go, Blue glimpsed something large and dark move fast off to their left—furtive, skirting the RVs, sweeping between. A chill raced down Blue's spine and he reached out with his mind. The city overwhelmed, but he picked up the threads of bioelectricity, the pulse of heartbeats. Three of them, keeping pace with his brother.

Circus folk, he told himself, but that was not good enough. Not until he was sure. Blue reached for his brother's arm. Daniel glanced back at him, eyes narrowed. He raised his hand.

Bodies slammed out of the narrow spaces between the RVs, colliding against the two Perrineaus. Blue was ready; he spun with the impact, turning the force of one assailant's momentum against him by grabbing a thick arm and throwing the man headfirst into some metal siding. Daniel went down, but only for a moment. He rolled, barely missing the boot clomping toward his chest, and in a move too fast for Blue to see, found his feet and his fists, striking out with two quick punches that sent the man in front of him straight into the ground.

One man left. Gunmetal glinted, but the draw was not fast enough; Blue got to the weapon first, grabbing the wrist and arm holding it, twisting the joints with enough force to make the man scream and drop the gun into his hand. Daniel marched up, his face twisted with rage. He grabbed the man's throat, forcing him to the ground. Blue backed away, clicking off the gun's safety.

Daniel looked at him. "You plan this?"

"No," Blue said, trying to catch his breath. "And I'm not pointing this gun at you."

His brother's mouth tightened. He looked back at the man, who was big and broad, his blond hair pressed flat against his head. Muscles bulged in his arms and chest. He was almost twice the size of Daniel, but Daniel never budged an inch as the man bucked and writhed, clawing at his hand, gasping for air.

"You're killing him." Blue glanced at the other men sprawled out on the grass. They were not quite unconscious enough for his liking. He patted them down and found two more guns.

"Maybe," Daniel said calmly. "Does that bother you?"

"Yes." Blue glimpsed movement just on his brother's right. "And you've got witnesses."

Daniel looked up. A little boy leaned against the corner of an RV, watching them. His eyes were huge. He looked too scared to move, and he stared like Daniel was the main attraction of some terrible monster flick.

The distress that passed over his brother's face was so fleeting Blue almost convinced himself that he imagined it, but then he saw it again; horror running through Daniel's expression like a deep fracture. He let go of the man, who fell back on the ground, scrabbling at his neck, face beet red as he coughed and wept. He appeared just as frightened as the little boy when he looked up at Daniel, who stood there for all the world like nothing more than some mild-mannered professor. Blue did not know whether to clap his hands in admiration or make some serious use of the gun in his hand.

Daniel took a step toward the child, who shied away from him, trembling. Blue watched his brother's face break just a little more. "Philippe," he said quietly, crouching so they were at eye-level. *"Você vai para casa.* I'll be there in a moment to speak with your poppa and momma, *sim?"*

The boy nodded, scampering away, and when his footsteps were nothing but a distant whisper Blue sidled close to his brother, careful not to spook him as he continued to crouch in the dusty grass. The men behind them were just beginning to struggle to their feet, dark clothes covered in dust. Blue aimed his confiscated gun at the nearest one.

"Daniel? What do you want to do about these guys?"

Daniel's fingers trailed through the grass. "Let them go."

"No police?"

Daniel shot him a hard look. Blue sighed. He studied the men—all of them muscle, hard-nosed types with flint for eyes. They looked wary, though; they were smart enough for that, at least.

"Who sent you?" asked Blue. The men glanced at each

other, tightlipped. He'd expected nothing less, nor did he really need an answer. He knew the truth. Only one person wanted Daniel Perrineau, and somehow, despite all his precautions, Blue had led these men right to him.

Daniel stood, turning on them. "Get out of here. Don't come back. If you do, I will kill you."

Blue was not entirely certain if Daniel was telling the truth, but the look on his face was enough to convince the men. That, and Blue was the one with all the guns. They shuffled backward, and then broke into a quick run into the maze of RVs. Blue tracked them briefly with his mind. Their heartbeats were fast—pulses continuing away and away. They were not being paid enough, apparently, for a second quick ambush.

Blue held the guns out to Daniel. His brother stared at them. The two men stood like that for a long minute, silently weighing each other.

"I don't want those," Daniel finally said.

"Then give them to someone who's responsible. I don't want them, either."

"You're probably already armed."

"I won't be if you just take these damn things."

"And if I shoot you with them?"

"Why shoot if you can strangle? You seem pretty good at that sort of thing. Practice much?"

Daniel's expression darkened. He took the guns, checking the safeties before tucking them in the band of his jeans, beneath his t-shirt.

"Iris isn't the only one who isn't safe here," Blue said.

"Stay away from her," Daniel replied. "Stay away from *me*. You get the fuck out of this place."

"And what will you do? Stick your head in the sand? Those men weren't here for me, Daniel."

His brother said nothing. No acknowledgment, no confession, no nothing. Just stared at Blue like he was taking his measure, and finding it wanting. The silence stung like hell.

"I'm not who you think I am," Blue protested, knowing very well it was a lie, but unable to speak the truth, to say out loud the words both of them already knew.

We are brothers. We are strangers and we are family.

Daniel walked away. This time, Blue did not follow. He would have preferred being a man of action—running after his brother, grabbing his arm, confessing the truth and then battling it out with guns or electricity or whatever the hell made them both feel better—but preferences were not the same as will or reality, and all Blue wanted to do right now was run, run and hide and lick wounds that should never have existed.

Blue walked back to the tool trailer, grabbed a tool belt, and locked up the doors. He did not have to think about his destination.

Pete was gone. Iris stood outside her RV, messing around with her door. She wore tight white shorts and a low-cut tank that showed off a mile of perfect cleavage, partially hidden beneath tendrils of red hair streaked with blonde. She glowed—from the sun, nothing otherworldly—but he felt the heat, imagined gold sleeping just beneath the sheen of her skin. He breathed easier, seeing her, and he realized that despite the violence that had just occurred, he worried more about Iris than he did his own brother. Good or bad, Blue did not know. Nor did he care.

He had no chance to simply stand and stare, though. Iris tilted her head and without turning said, "That was a fast tour. Daniel didn't abandon you, did he?"

"Not quite." Blue watched her bend large paperclips into makeshift hooks. One of them had already been anchored with duct tape. It took him a moment to fully grasp what she was trying to do, and even then he could not believe it. He bit back a laugh and gently shouldered her aside.

"Hey," she protested.

"Hey, yourself. This tool belt is here for a reason."

"Then let me use it. I can fix this door by myself."

"I know," he said, gazing into her eyes. "But let me do it for you."

Iris hesitated. Blue leaned in, the heat of her body making his heart jump, his brain go soft. He did not speak, just moved and moved, so tight and close he felt certain his mouth was going to make contact with her lips—but she moved aside at the last moment, making room for him, and he covered by crouching over the door's one floppy hinge. Two bad screws and a thin piece of metal were making the bottom corner of her door jut at an angle that made it impossible to meet the lock—which also needed some WD-40 to grease the mechanism.

He forced himself to focus on the work, making no quips as he fixed the bad hinge. There was something about the way Iris had fussed with those paperclips and duct tape that spoke more about her pride than anything else. He did not want to offend her.

You should not be doing a lot of things, a tiny voice warned. *You're not safe.*

Blue pushed aside the thought. It had been a long time since being around him meant the possibility of death. A long time since his lack of control had resulted in obituaries and hospital visits. He did not need to be scared of love anymore. The people he loved did not need to be scared of him.

Iris sat down on the step and wrapped her arms around her knees. She turned her head just enough so that he could see her profile, but her eyes were distant. Blue heard bangs and shouts and music playing; a child crying. He wondered how much more she could hear. Shape-shifter senses went beyond the pale.

"So I guess you're not all hot air," she suddenly said, glancing at his work. "Thank you."

"My pleasure," he said, wrestling with a screw. "I don't want any crazies invading your personal property while you're out."

"A lock won't stop someone who really wants to get in."

"Better than the alternative."

"Maybe."

"Maybe?" Blue stopped working. "You'd prefer an open door policy? Hello, strangers?"

"I'd prefer to be left alone."

"Fame and fortune not what you thought it'd be?"

"Do I look famous or rich?"

"Seems to me you've got the same problems."

"I don't like to talk about it. I feel like a whiner."

Blue bit back a laugh. "I've seen grown men piss and moan their lives away over nothing more serious than a bad case of beer, but you are the *first* person I have ever met who worried about complaining too much after getting *shot* at."

Her cheeks flushed. "Circus folk have to be tough, and my mother raised me not to complain. She said it was a waste of time."

"Why talk when you can act, right?"

"Something like that." Iris hugged her knees. "She's … gone now."

Blue thought of her mother's picture on the side of the trailer. "Did she pass away?"

"That would be easier," Iris said, and tension suddenly rolled off her body like a whip crack. She swallowed hard, turning her startled gaze on Blue. "I'm sorry. I didn't mean to say that."

He almost responded with something flippant, but stopped himself at the last moment. Iris seemed truly distressed. Blue set down his screwdriver and scooted close.

"It's okay," he said in a low voice. Iris shook her head, looking away from him.

"I love my mother. I don't want her to be dead."

"Of course not. But she's gone?"

"Two years. She … left a note."

"Ouch."

"Understatement. She said she needed to get away for a while. And she has. For a while."

"With you left behind trying to pick up the pieces."

"It wasn't like I was a kid. But she was—still is—my best friend. It hurt."

Hurt like hell if the tremor in her voice was any indication. Blue nudged her with his elbow. "You want to ditch this place and take a walk?"

Iris smiled, rubbing her eyes. "What about my door?"

"Almost done. Just give me a minute."

It took five. Blue kept expecting Iris to make some excuse to run from him. She had guts, but there was still something about her that was skittish. Too many secrets, something he understood all too well. But when he finished she was still there. Painfully quiet, but ready for a stroll.

"I'm all yours," he said. Iris smiled, tucking her hair behind her ears.

They walked through the camp. They did not talk, but unlike with Daniel the silence was comfortable, easy. Blue kept his mind open, scouting ahead and around them. He did not expect an ambush, but there was no guarantee those three men had completely left the camp—or that there were no others lurking about. Though after catching a glimpse of how the circus had banded together last night, he did not think any stranger, let alone a group of them, could wander around here for long without being noticed.

Don't underestimate your father. If he's even responsible.

Because the old man was right. A rich man's son was never safe. The son of Felix Perrineau even less so. His father, despite his reputation for being a good Samaritan, probably had more enemies than a dog with rabies.

The sun was hot. Blue unbuttoned his shirt a little more, noting with some interest how Iris pretended very hard not to watch him. He walked just a little closer and she did not move away.

"So," he said. "Where's the big top?"

"Stashed in a truck," she said. "It was a sight to behold. Big and blue—pardon the use of your name—with room enough to sit up to sixteen hundred people once we put in the bleachers. Back-breaking work to get it up, though. All of us had to pitch in."

"Full house every night with roaring crowds?"

"I wish. In some towns we were lucky to attract even a tenth of our capacity. You don't work in the circus to get rich. Out on the road you need to train twenty-five hours a day. Wake up yesterday and work again. Circus skills aren't easy, although I think the trapeze artists and tumblers have it worst. They're always trying to come up with something new and better, and that's dangerous work. Sergei, one of our boys from Russia, broke his spine last year. He can still use his legs, but Pete had to send him up to Toronto to recover in Cirque du Soleil's rehabilitation center."

"Sounds expensive."

"It is. Pete had to call in a favor." Iris smiled sadly. "Sergei still plans on walking the wire again."

"Call me stupid, but don't call me a coward?"

A quiet laugh escaped her. "Yes. That about sums up all of us."

"How long have you been with the circus?'

"Years. Since I was sixteen. My mom was the one who brought me into it. Before that we lived on a ranch in Montana. A big cat preserve for animals that have been abused, or raised in a domestic setting. Lions, tigers, leopards—many of them born into captivity and then sold out of vans or on private internet auctions. Con? He was kept in a closet when he was a cub, and when he got bigger his owner chained him up in the garage. No fresh air, no heat in the winter, filthy conditions. He was a mess when we got him."

"I thought there were laws against that sort of thing."

"It's up to the states. Enforcement is a joke."

"So people like you and your mom clean up the mess."

"We used to, but the preserve got too expensive to run. We had to give most of the cats to other rescue centers. Petro, Lila, Con, and Boudicca were the only ones we couldn't part with. That, and they're good performers."

They reached the holding pen, a large circle of chain link. Someone, maybe Samuel, had thrown in some hay and a children's swimming pool. The tiger lounged in the water, while the other three cats slept in a loose pile, tails flicking lazily against the flies. All of them stood, though, when Iris appeared. Her face lit up into something rosy and lovely, eyes flashing light as she stretched out her arms and greeted them. Not a shred of fear; she unlocked the gate, swinging it wide as she stepped inside. Blue hung back, watching as the cats buffeted Iris with their heads and shoulders, rubbing against her with their eyes half closed and full of pleasure. She ran her fingers through their thick coats, winding herself around them with boneless grace. Blue forgot how to breathe.

Iris smiled at him. "You can come closer."

Blue would if he could make his legs begin working again. He tried to remember what it felt like to be cool and collected, but being around Iris made him feel like he was sixteen, so painfully awkward he wanted to scream. He did, however, manage to lurch into the holding pen. Five pairs of eyes watched him, but the only face that mattered was Iris and that delicate wistful smile on her mouth.

"You look like you're afraid of being bitten," she said.

"There's precedent," he said wryly. Iris beckoned him closer and Blue waded into the tangle of fur and muscle, marveling at the twists of his life that could have him chasing human traffickers one day, helping his father in the next, and mixing with lions, tigers, and shape-shifters in all the same breath.

"This is incredible," Blue murmured.

"They're family," Iris said, staggering as the lioness leaned hard against her knees. "Those assholes who tried to take them don't understand that. They think they have a right to pass judgment on me, or rip us all apart because it's not what they think is ... is *moral*. I just want us to be left alone, Blue. I want to be who I am."

She stopped, looking down. He could feel her uncertainty, her embarrassment, and it pained him because he was still a stranger to her and she had no right to trust him.

"People judge," he said. "That's just the way it is. It's power, control, and suddenly they're better than the person standing next to them because their skin is dark, or their religion is different, or because they perform in a Las Vegas show with lions and tigers and—"

"No bears," Iris said, mouth quirking.

"No bears," Blue agreed, smiling.

"So what's your hang-up?" Iris tucked a strand of hair behind her ear. "What gets stuck in your craw? Makes *you* pass judgment?"

"Too many people," he said, trying to keep it light. "I don't like crowds and I don't like cities."

"Really. Seems you're in the wrong place, then."

"I could say the same about you."

Iris gazed at the sea of RVs surrounding them; farther, even, to the looming walls and palms of the Miracle. "It would be nice. One day. But this is home—wherever I am—and until I get some money together ..." She stopped and looked at him again, smiling ruefully. "I guess we all have dreams of making it, right?"

"And you aren't?"

Iris smiled, and it was breathtaking. Blue swayed forward, unable to help himself. He was dimly aware of some large body pushing between them, but he could have been standing in a pit of vipers for all that he cared. Nor did Iris pull away. She stared into his eyes, sweet as a sunrise, and his hand reached out to touch her.

On the periphery of his mind he felt an electric tickle that was not a cell phone or television; instead it was small and individual, moving briskly in their direction. Blue faltered. Iris seemed to sense the change and turned from him, looking toward the RVs. So much for privacy. Her smile faded.

A man appeared. He wore a brown suit that complemented his brown hair and brown eyes, creating an effect that was pleasant and professional and wholly unremarkable. Iris left the holding pen; Blue followed, moving just enough to put himself between the man and Iris. He heard the gate lock behind them.

"Agent Fred," she said, stepping sideways, out of Blue's shadow. "I didn't expect to see you here again so soon."

FBI. Blue tried not to react. Dirk & Steele was well-known within law enforcement circles; the agency had an international reputation for solving crimes deemed too cold or politically sensitive to handle. A fact that did not always rub the police, the feds, or certain other government agencies the right way.

Blue did not recognize this particular agent—this Fred—but that was no guarantee of safety. Because if the man recognized him ...

Fred stuck out his hand. "I don't think we've been introduced."

"That's right," Blue said, shaking his hand. He did not offer his name.

Fred's smiled thinned. "You fit the description of the man who spotted the shooter last night. I wanted to talk to you about that."

"There's not much to say. I saw the gun and I acted."

"And did you see the shooter?"

"It was dark."

"Not too dark to see a gun, though."

"I believe there was a mask."

Fred studied Blue's face. "Those do come in handy, don't they?"

Iris brushed up against Blue. "I need to finish preparing the cats for their transport to the hotel. Was there something you wanted, or can this wait?"

Fred looked at the two of them standing so close, and even Blue wished he could see the picture they made. Iris did not strike him as the touchy-feely type at all, so even her touching his sleeve felt startling. And good.

"I just wanted to let you know about Kevin Cray." Fred held up his hand. "I know. I saw Mr. Reilly on my way in, and he said he already informed you about the release. Don't worry, Ms. McGillis. We're keeping an eye on him. He won't be coming here again."

"Forgive me if I'm not reassured," Iris drawled, swaying even closer. Blue took the opportunity offered—knowing full well he would probably pay for it later—and put his arm around her waist. Tension rattled up her spine, but he did not let go and she did not move. Her body was warm and soft, slender without being skinny. All woman.

"I thought the two of you were strangers," Fred said mildly.

"Oh, there's no bond like danger." Iris smiled. "But if that's all you wanted to tell me, I think you should go. I'm very busy." No apologies, no hesitation. Just balls and brass and catch-me-if-you-can. Blue bit back a smirk.

Fred's eyes narrowed. "I'll be in touch, Ms. McGillis. And with you as well."

"Of course," Blue said easily. *But not in this lifetime.*

Fred walked away. Iris remained inside the circle of Blue's arm until the slender FBI agent was out of sight, and then she stepped forward, turning to face him with her hands on her hips. Blue smiled. "Sorry."

Iris's mouth twitched. "Liar."

"Yes," he said, watching her expression shift from amusement to sadness, all in the blink of an eye. He wondered, briefly, if he really had done something wrong by touching her, but Iris surprised him by reaching out and lightly brushing some imaginary dust off his shirt. Blue captured her hand, rubbing his thumb over her palm. The sadness in her eyes only grew deeper.

"Iris," he murmured. "What is it?"

"Nothing I want to talk about," she whispered, tugging back her hand. "Come on, Blue. We have work to do."

He did not press her, nor complain. He followed her lead in silence, lending muscle and an extra set of hands. But as they worked to brush down the cats and play with them—a relaxation technique, Iris told him—he could not stop thinking about that look in her eyes, which was so unbearably sad. His fault, perhaps. Touching her like that had brought back old memories, most certainly painful. It made him feel like crap.

You thought lying to your brother was bad. You stick around and things are going to get worse.

Because spinning lies to this woman was no way to start something, not anything that could last; and it was stupid to even consider the possibility of a relationship, terrible to dream, the worst thing he could do. . . .

But you want her. You want her badly.

That scared him to death.

CHAPTER FIVE

The Miracle Hotel and Casino was less than a year old—a brand-new gleaming white lily of a baby that was banking its success less on spectacle than on the promise of a luxurious oasis within the hard-boiled heat and grit of the strip. Class and dignity, a center of refinement for those with tastes that ran more to spa treatments than showgirls. Even the casino was smaller, tucked off to the side, almost an afterthought.

Which was why, at first, Iris thought that Reilly's Circus seemed like an odd fit. Popcorn, clowns, and tightrope walkers did not normally move in the same circles as afternoon tea or concerts starring Yo-Yo Ma and James Galway. Then again, Vegas was a city of surprises, and the Miracle was no different. Hotel management wanted entertainment friendly to children, something better than regular big-top fare, but nothing quite so artsy as Cirque du Soleil—which, Iris had to confess, she absolutely loved.

So, Reilly. No one, not even Pete, was quite certain how or why his circus had come to the attention of the Miracle management—especially given the small crowds they gathered on the road. Regardless, the call had come during a summer spot in Oregon, and the entire troupe had rolled on down to Nevada for a brief session of tryouts.

Leading to now. A lucky break. Private dressing rooms. Air-conditioned practice space and a permanent parking spot in a city that never slept. Some of the trapeze artists were talking about looking for apartments. Buying minivans. Going cold turkey into the settled life.

Not me, Iris thought, walking down the narrow backstage hall at the Miracle, straight from where she had left her cats—all safe inside the holding pen in the hotel loading bay. The Miracle had begun to discuss building alternative arrangements—a prelude to an offer of something more permanent, Iris suspected—but both she and on-site inspectors from the USDA had checked the temporary holding site and found it acceptable for performance times, especially given that all the employees had, with some small exceptions, honored Iris's request that no one visit the cats but her prior to a performance. The hotel had erected a breezy silken pavilion around the cage, which completely hid it from prying eyes inside the loading bay. They had also given her cats a nice little sound system that continually played Kitaro and Ravi Shankar and—at Iris's request—the Rolling Stones. It was an attempt at the Siegfried and Roy treatment, for sure.

Natalya, one of the Russian contortionists, passed Iris in the hall and waved a sinewy hand. "You have many flowers in dressing room, Iris. Again."

Iris sighed. "You want some of them?"

Natalya snorted, mouth curving. "What I do with other woman's flowers? Like borrowing paper with love letter written on it, yes?"

"Da," Iris said, which got a full smile out of the smaller woman, who paused in the hall to look her up and down, lips pursed, eyes critical.

"You must take lover," Natalya concluded, with the same sensibility that would have accompanied an order of caviar or wine. "With good man in your bed, you can laugh at flowers. Turn them into nice joke. Otherwise, now? They make you feel lonely."

"I don't feel lonely," Iris said.

Natayla smiled slyly. "Then you are stronger than me. But maybe not too strong to refuse Danny, yes? Or new man with beard? The one you came to hotel with?"

Iris's cheeks reddened. Natalya laughed and walked away. "Silly girl! Take them both! Or *I* will!"

Iris glared at the Russian woman's back, wishing she could come up with an appropriately scathing response. Instead, all she felt inside her head was dead air and simmering resentment. Why was it that most if not all of the women in the circus felt the urge to give advice on her love life? Did they really think she didn't know how to get a man? Did they think she spent her evenings depressed and pathetic, just because there wasn't someone tall and broad and male snuggled up beside her?

Well, yes. Apparently they did. And, frankly, there was some truth to it. It had been a long time since she had even tried to be with someone, and that had ended in disaster.

And now? You think you can keep going down this road with Blue without ending up in that same deep shit?

Iris swallowed hard, trying not to think about his warm hard body pressed against her side, the weight of his strong arm around her waist. His touch had been a shock, but only because it felt so good. Made her feel safe and protected in ways she had never imagined. Like a drug she wanted more—more than was safe to have in her life. More than was safe for him.

Entering her small dressing room was like stepping into a celebrity greenhouse filled with a cornucopia of flowers: extravagant displays of roses, lilies, orchids, the occasional daisy or curling twig. But mostly, overwhelmingly, the small space was kept supplied with a daily arrangement of large, fat, verdant ... irises. Purple irises, to be exact. Giant baskets and bouquets of them, pressed against the wall, blooms jutting out like spikes or spears or swords.

Oh, the collective imagination of my admirers, Iris thought. There were some cards on her makeup table. One in particular caught her eye. She recognized the handwriting, the richness of the paper, which looked almost as soft as skin.

My love, she read. *I will make you mine.*

The end. No signature. No method of replying. Just seven words that were blunt and to the point. Iris could almost imagine the writer thumping his chest and preparing his big wooden club.

Yeah. Good luck, pervert. Try to take me anywhere and you'll get the surprise of your life.

Iris tossed the note into her garbage can. Third time was always the charm. Maybe her admirer would stop after this. Either way, all the attention was embarrassing—and disquieting. Iris did not like being singled out. Onstage it was inevitable, part of the job. But in her private time the intrusion was more than a nuisance. It felt like a threat. Because if anyone got too close . . .

Old lessons die hard. Mom made you paranoid.

"But the paranoid are the ones who survive," Iris murmured, echoing her mother's voice. Although if her mother had really followed her own advice . . .

You wouldn't have been born. Which was not, when Iris thought about it, such great evidence of her mother's hypocrisy. After all, Iris had no idea who her father was. Probably a one-night-stand John Doe. A safe bet, too, that he was human, someone her mother had *not* been in love with. According to her, a shape-shifter who gave her heart gave it forever. No going back, not ever.

Which frightened the hell out of Iris. This was the twenty-first century, after all. People got divorced left and right. Cheating on spouses (if one watched Oprah) was practically a national pastime.

You were a romantic, once upon a time. Once, long ago, in another life. Before reality had stripped away all her notions of happily-ever-after and the old cliché of one love to last a lifetime.

More like one love to kill.

Yeah. She had issues. And even if she didn't, the rest of her life did not allow for any more mistakes. Finding a good man was not the problem—finding a man who could keep and handle her secrets, on the other hand . . .

I am a shape-shifter, Iris thought, gazing into the mirror. Her eyes flashed golden, and for the first time outside her RV she let the leopard rise within her, rolling and rolling to curl against her heart. She watched herself shift, forced herself to swallow down the reflection of light and fur, and it was difficult, so difficult, like observing a live sex act, intimate and strange.

Her face transformed. Her jaw grew more pointed, her forehead receding as fur poured through her skin, swallowing up the human hair that disappeared quickly into her scalp. There was no pain. No prick or break of bone. Just warmth, a hot rush that wiggled through her body like the flush after an orgasm.

You are beautiful, she remembered her mother saying. *You are so lovely in your skin.*

And there was a part of Iris that agreed. Though she had been forced to alienate herself from the world because of her difference, she loved it all the same. Give up the leopard, her ability to transform into another being? Never.

But regret the losses it caused? Fear herself, even? Maybe, just a little.

Iris studied her reflection, trying to imagine someone sharing this moment with her, someone who would love her for it, who would not be afraid. She tried to imagine a man who would see the woman before the magic, the woman beneath the fur—who would be everything for her and more.

She found herself imagining Blue. His face rose unbidden in her mind, and she thought of him behind her, hands loose and open at his sides, the collar of his dusty black shirt unbuttoned at his throat, his body lean and tall and strong, face hidden behind that mask of beard while his eyes—those eyes—watched her from beneath a sweeping edge of shining black hair, hot and hungry and unafraid.

Breathless. She felt breathless thinking of him.

And he doesn't make you nervous. He doesn't scare you.

Or rather, he did—but in a different way from other men. He scared her because she was actually comfortable with him. He scared her because she could actually see herself doing something with him. Because she *wanted* to do something, and to hell with the risks.

Iris heard movement outside her door. She sucked in her breath, fighting for control, watching the mirror as fur bled into pale hairless skin, her face reforming, sliding into its humanity.

Get thee gone, cat.

Someone knocked. Iris swallowed hard. "Come in."

Danny pushed open the door. He was already in costume: an elaborately decorated bodysuit that showed off every hard line of his perfect body. Scales and feathers had been painted on the fabric—a shining chimera in spandex—and he wore a hood that covered most of his head except for his face, which was covered by an elaborately painted mask that was an extension of his outfit. He looked wild, fantastic—and every time she saw him she wanted to laugh, because it was so different from the man he seemed to be.

"There's a camera crew down the hall," Danny said, slipping into the dressing room. "Someone from channel five. They want to know about the attack on you and the cats."

Iris briefly closed her eyes. "I won't talk to them. I just won't, Danny."

"I know." He crouched beside her, fingering one of the roses. "Pete is taking care of it."

"Good," she said, uneasy. Danny smelled nervous. More nervous than he usually did before a show, and more nervous than having a camera crew down the hall should warrant. She watched him fuss with the flower, and his silence was yet another punctuation point.

"Is there something wrong?" Iris asked.

Danny shook his head. "Just have a lot on my mind."

"You want to talk?"

"Not really." He gave her a grim smile. "But thank you, Iris.

You've been good to me since the first time we met. A real friend when I didn't have anyone at all. I won't ever forget that."

"Sounds ominous. You going somewhere, Danny?"

He looked away from her. "No."

"Danny."

"This is my home," he said, almost to himself. "My real home, Iris. The one I left behind … it was a bad place. Bad people."

Wow. Danny was actually talking about himself. Really talking, and not just about art or television or books. That never happened—or if it did, not with her. But here, now— *bad people*—and she did not know how to respond, how to handle the scent that hit her: tension, fear. It bewildered her, made her want to reach out and touch him. She did not, though. That much, she could not bring herself to do, even if she had already broken her own rules with Blue.

"Has your family contacted you?" Iris asked him. "Do they want you to leave us?"

He laughed, sharp. "Something like that."

"Well, that's ridiculous. No one can force you to go home, Danny. You're a grown man."

"It's not that easy. My family isn't the kind you run from."

"You make them sound like the mob." Iris shook her head. "Whatever. You've made a life for yourself. No one helped you. No one gave you anything. You did this on your own, and unless you really do want to leave, I suggest you stop acting all gloom and doom and just tell your family to back the hell off."

"Never give up, never surrender?" His mouth settled into something gentler, more like the man she knew. "You really believe that, Iris?"

"I think you believe it," she said. "I don't think you would have found the circus if you didn't. And I sure as hell don't think you get up on that stage each night for any reason other than pure love. If that's not something worth fighting for, then I don't know what is."

He closed his eyes. The paint on his face glimmered metallic; glitter danced across his cheeks, fading like stars into the sheen of his suit. He was very large and very near, and Iris thought again about touching him, just to see if it felt different from Blue, if that rush of warmth and protection was something any man could give her, or just one.

You want perfection, but there's no such thing. You want trust, but that's impossible to find. You want love, true love, but all that brings is blood. Just give it up. Run, cat, run.

Iris heard voices outside her dressing room: Pete, sounding angry. He was coming here, would walk through that door at any moment—and that would be fine, great, a wonderful interruption to something that had suddenly become too heavy.

Danny opened his eyes. The look he gave her was creepy, almost as though he had heard her thoughts, and he said, "Will you go out with me, Iris? Tonight?"

She stared, unable to find her voice. This was her fantasy and her worst nightmare all rolled into one.

"I've been wanting to ask you for a long time," he said, grave. "But if I don't bring it up now, I might not get another chance."

Iris licked her lips. "Danny—"

"Please."

She hesitated. The sadness, the hunger of his gaze, was too much, and a little voice whispered, *Be a normal woman, just this once. One date won't kill you.* Even if she wished a different man was doing the asking.

"Okay," she said. Danny smiled, which only made the butterflies in her stomach turn into bumblebees. He began to lean in. Close.

She was saved by Pete's arrival. Iris could hear him muttering on the other side of the door, and stood up before he started knocking.

"Come in," she called out, trying not to look at Danny.

Pete opened the door. Blue was with him. He had traded the sleek black button-up and trim slacks for a plain white

T-shirt and khakis. The tool belt was still slung loosely around his hips. He looked good. His eyes were warm when he gazed at her, though she didn't miss the way he took in Danny still crouched beside her chair. The ache in her heart got worse.

Pete sighed, rubbing his belly. "Danny told you about the reporters, right? They're gone for now but they'll be back. You and your show are hot stuff on the strip right now, Iris. An attack is big news."

"They can find some other piece of 'hot stuff' to report a story on. Anyone but me."

Pete frowned. "Not that I want to capitalize on your tragedy and misfortune, but even a little interview would be good advertisement for us, Iris. *All* of us."

She didn't have to hide her expression; she was used to this by now. "You know I'm not trying to be selfish, Pete. You *know* that, so don't try to make me feel guilty."

"I don't need guilt. You're too smart for that. But please, kid. The old days are over, and if you want to keep playing with the big boys, you'll have to go the extra mile on the publicity front. If not for me, then for Miracle's management. They might not have said anything to you yet, but they've been pressuring me to get you on board. You, too, Danny." He shook his head, running his round hands over his thinning hair. "I love you both, but I just don't get why you're so press-shy. Not when you both get onstage every night easy as breathing."

"That's different," Iris protested. "Less personal."

Less personal was good, her mother had always said. Less personal meant fewer chances of discovery. Because even though being a performer, living briefly in the public eye, was a form of exposure, it was also a mask. A way of hiding in plain sight, of being just slightly peculiar in ways that no one would ever question. Because circus performers were supposed to be odd, a little bit more than human. The key was never to let anyone look too deep.

And one interview is deep? One interview and boom, freak-show central?

Iris glanced at Blue. He didn't have much of an expression on his face, but she thought he looked at her with a hint of concern—even, maybe, understanding. She tore her gaze away. "Fine, Pete. But you tell Miracle that they'd better make it count—choose the right station or magazine, or whatever. Because I won't be doing another interview, not for a long time."

Pete closed his eyes and smiled. "Thank you, Iris. I know this isn't easy for you."

That was an understatement. Of course, she seemed to be agreeing a lot of things tonight that weren't easy for her. She was getting weak. Or just desperate.

"Lights go down in ten," Pete said. "Danny, I need you out there now for the initial lineup. Iris, do your thing."

Which meant putting on loads of makeup, getting dressed, and then running out to the loading bay to get Petro and the others prepped.

Danny stood, still looking at Blue. "What about him?"

Pete frowned. "Worry about yourself, kid."

"I'm worried about Iris. We don't know this man. We don't know what he'll try if he's alone with her."

His bluntness took Iris off guard, as did the implied accusation. She struggled for a reply—glanced at Blue—and found all her words dead as ash in her mouth. He had a look on his face that was pure anger—a quiet, terrible anger—and though he stood very still, she could feel energy pouring off his body, waves of power washing over her skin like the echo of some awful rattling thunder. The lights in her dressing room flickered.

"I would never hurt Iris," Blue said. *"Never."*

"Never?" Danny echoed. His hands curled into fists. Air stirred over Iris's skin; flowers wavered, the mirror frame shivered. Blue narrowed his eyes. Pete, glancing between the two men, cleared his throat.

"Sons," he said, but his voice did nothing to cut the tension, the electricity building and building. Iris wanted to scream at them, rake her nails through the air. Her skin crawled.

"I don't want to fight you," Blue whispered.

"Then don't," Danny said. "Just go. *Leave.*"

"No," Blue murmured. His gaze flickered to Iris. "No, I won't do that."

It was the way he looked at her that finally made her lurch forward, putting herself between the two men. She raised her hands—it felt like they were attached to wings in quicksand—and touched both their chests at the same time. Sparks flew off her fingertips; bolts of baby lightning. She jerked back, gasping. Daniel tried to reach out but she shied away, holding her hands. Blue did not move. He did not talk. He looked at her, and his eyes were impossibly grim.

"Stop this," she said to them, finally finding her voice. "Whatever both of you are doing, stop it now."

Before someone gets hurt. she wanted to say.

Pete moved. He took up Iris's place between the men and looked at them with stern disapproval—and even a little wildness in his eyes. Iris understood.

"I feel as though," he said, very slowly, "I just watched two men come to blows without ever touching each other. And while part of me is horribly intrigued by that, the rest of me is even more horribly disturbed. Because frankly, I can't see one good reason why it should have come to that. And why"—Pete fixed Daniel with a very hard glare—"you would level accusations of poor character upon a man you don't even know. Unless you *do* know him?"

"No," Daniel said, after a moment's hesitation. "I don't."

"Then let it go, son. I know you care about Iris—we all do—but making this man feel unwelcome isn't any cure to what's ailing you. Besides, who are *you* to talk about trust? You're still new, green. If I were an ungenerous man, I could lobby the same insult. But I won't. I give people a chance in my outfit."

No one said a word. Iris found herself still rubbing her

hands, and stopped. She watched Blue stare at Daniel—
watched Daniel stare back—and felt the pressure in the room
ease and ease, like an awful shrinking bubble. Daniel—and
Iris realized that she had suddenly started thinking of him as
Daniel, and not Danny—slowly unclenched his hands and
pressed them loose and flat against his thighs. Blue took a
deep breath.

"Good," Pete said, and opened the dressing room door.
"Danny, you go on now. You have a show to do."

Iris expected him to argue. Fire still ran through his eyes,
the lines of his body tense and hard. He was a mirror of Blue,
who continued to stare at him like he expected a blow and
was prepared to return one in full. *Danger, danger, danger.*

Daniel edged backward to the door, and ended the staring
contest by looking at Iris.

"Later," he said, very quiet, very gentle. Iris nodded, well
aware of the way Blue looked at her, the way he measured
her response. All she wanted to do was turn her head and return his gaze, get her fill of him—to tell him it was okay, she
wasn't scared of him, not like that—and she felt like a traitor
to both herself and Daniel for that desire, for the wanting of it.

You're just going on a date with Daniel. It's not marriage.

But he was standing right there, and Iris liked him too
much—and had more class—than to coo over Blue in his
presence. Or maybe that was just sneakiness talking, and not
loyalty. It felt like a fine line.

Daniel left. Pete said, "You, too, Blue. Iris needs to unwind."

"In a minute," Iris said. The old man gave her a long hard
look, but he left. Not far, but enough.

As soon as Pete disappeared into the hall, Blue stepped in
close and covered Iris's hands. His intensity startled her; she
had no time to move away, and that was another shock—her
reflexes were usually better than that.

Blue's grip was loose, warm. "Are you hurt? Did that shock
hurt you?"

"No," she said, bewildered by his question, the passion of
it. "You?"

A short laugh escaped him and he shook his head. "I'm sorry, Iris. For all of this, I'm sorry."

She wanted to ask him why he was sorry—and why Daniel seemed to know him, why he would lie about that—but Pete poked his head back into the room, looked at their joined hands, and without missing a beat said, "Come on, son. Let's give Iris some peace."

Blue nodded, turning his body slightly so that only Iris could see his face. She was almost as tall as him, but he felt much larger, like a giant when he stood so close to her, and she forgot how to breathe as his thumbs caressed, much too briefly, the backs of her hands. His gaze was quiet, steady, all the anger flushed away by heartbreaking warmth, and Iris found herself swaying close, unable to help herself, as if the world were leaning beneath her feet.

Blue looked at her mouth—stared, hungry—and Iris was unprepared for what that did to her, for the ache that spread through her body. She thought, *Please do it. Please, I want to taste you.*

But Pete cleared his throat, and even though the intensity of Blue's gaze did not fade, he let go of her hands and stepped away. Stepped back like his legs were caught in quicksand, his body trapped; she could smell his arousal, the wildness in his blood, and it made her physically weak.

He turned and left, almost at a run. Iris stared, battling the urge to follow.

Pete shook his head. "Your mother warned me about this before she left."

"About what?" she asked, distant.

"Men," he said.

Iris tried not to smile. "And?"

"And nothing. You're twenty-four years old, which is old enough to know your own mind. Just be careful, Iris. Danny's right. We don't know him."

You don't even know me, she thought as he shut the door behind him. *You don't know what I really am.*

And Blue? Daniel? What about them? How much truth did

a person need to know another? How much truth did a person need before it was safe to fall in love?

Iris returned to her chair, but just before sitting down she felt a presence rub—in her gut, in her heart, in her head—and for a moment it was like being with her mother again, as though Serena McGillis was there with her. Close. It was a shape-shifter call, from one animal to another, an unforgettable sensation that had not filled her in years.

Iris ran to the door and yanked it open, throwing herself into the hall. Nothing. It was empty. She ran down the corridor, testing the air, breathing in every scent, but all she found was the lingering taste of perfume, something her mother abhorred.

No, Iris told herself. *No, don't. This is just your imagination. It has to be. You get stressed and she's the first person you turn to.*

Mommy, oh, mommy.

Disgusted with herself, Iris returned to her dressing room and slammed shut the door.

CHAPTER SIX

Blue managed to avoid Daniel after he left Iris. Pete was to blame for that. The old man led him on a circuitous path through the upper backstage levels, an area inhabited only by plainclothes workmen, the occasional guy in a suit, and a couple of harried-looking women hauling costumes in their arms.

A chime rang once.

"First warning," Pete explained. "It means that everyone who's performing in the first half had better be in their proper places."

"You're not in the show?"

"Used to be. When we were on the road, for sure. Ringmaster, son. Nothing like it in the world. But here in Vegas? This is more of a young man's game."

Pete said it with a smile, a hop in his step, but Blue had an ear for bitterness, and he tasted the edge of it in the old man's voice.

"It wasn't your choice," he guessed, quiet. "Management told you to step down, didn't they?"

Pete faltered, but only for a moment. He schooled his features into a better mask. "The money is good and the job is stable."

"But you miss it."

Pete gave him a long, hard look. "A man has to make sacrifices sometimes. Give up one love for another love. Regrets are for sissies."

Which was an effective way of telling Blue to shut up.

Another chime rang, this one longer. Pete picked up the pace and pushed open a heavy white door. On the other side, darkness, the scent of piped-in air and smoke and perfume. A low buzz filled the air—chatter, the rattle of paper. Pete tugged on Blue's sleeve and led him onto a narrow catwalk. Just two steps and the stage appeared, spreading in front of Blue like a great wild expanse of props and people. He stood at eye level with the trapeze. The platform hung a good ten feet away.

Blue glanced down. He saw Daniel speaking to some women who were dressed in a similar fashion to him: elaborate bodysuits, heavy makeup that did an impressive job of making them unrecognizable. No one, not even their father, would recognize Daniel in full costume.

Hiding in plain sight. Soon to be one of the richest men in the world, playing in the circus.

That alone might be enough to kill their father. If, in fact, he was really dying.

"You sit here," ordered Pete, showing Blue a solitary wooden chair perched on the catwalk. "Observe, enjoy, think about ways you can improve or fix things. Afterward, I'll ask you questions."

"Am I going to have to write a paper, too?"

"Don't be a smart aleck with me, son. Not now."

"I apologize," Blue murmured. Pete frowned, glancing down at Daniel.

"You two," he said quietly. "You know each other. Don't bother denying it. There's history when you look at each other. Something deep."

Blue said nothing. He knew Daniel, yes. But there was no way Daniel should know him. Not on sight, and probably not even by name. In his father's ideal world, Blue would never have been born. To speak of him, to acknowledge his existence to the only son he considered *legitimate* ...

No. Not possible. Nor did he think his father would have gone to such lengths to ask for his help if there was a chance that Daniel knew who he was. Too much risk of spooking the young man, making him run.

But there was no denying the fact that Daniel seemed to know the truth. And if he did, especially after that ambush in the circus camp Blue could not understand why he hadn't started running.

Iris. It's because of Iris.

Maybe. Probably. If he were in Daniel's shoes, it would take more than his father to tear him away from a woman like her. And he had seen the way his brother looked at Iris— heart in his eyes.

Blue pressed his palms against his thighs. Calm, calm—he was usually the calm one—but not this time. Not about her.

Pete still gazed at the stage. "Were you telling the truth about your military experience?"

The question took him off guard. "Yes."

"And do you really care about Iris? Really care, with the heart and head, and not just your dick?"

"Yes," Blue said, taking a wild guess as to where this was leading.

But after a moment of contemplative silence, all Pete said was, "Enjoy the show, son. Take care not to fall."

He left. And like magic the lights went down.

The darkness was absolute, but Blue stretched out with his mind and found the world alive with electricity, sizzling and jumping through a maze of wires. He followed the trails, traveling them, flying quick as light through the Miracle hotel, coming home full circle to his body just as the music began to play.

It was ambient, classical, perhaps just slightly New Age with a soft-voiced choir that chanted words in a language that might have been Latin—or pure fantasy—and Blue found himself leaning forward as a blue light filled the stage and bodies moved into place, striking poses.

The curtains pulled apart. Blue could not see the audience, but he heard the low murmur of appreciation, and thought that whatever he was seeing up here must be twice as impressive at floor level.

But for the next hour, Blue found himself drawn in, entranced, mesmerized, as every person who entered the stage performed some impossible act of human agility, some dance through the air that required nothing but the focus of an incredibly strong body and spirit. Stories played out, told only in movement and music, a shifting play of light and curtains across the stage, and he found himself thinking that all his gifts, his power, meant nothing in the face of such breathless beauty. He could turn off a lightbulb with his mind, but big deal—the men and women below him could *fly*.

He thought he recognized Samuel, who emerged off stage left; a clown, yes, but a giant who carried at least six delicate young women on his shoulders and arms, holding them up with nothing but sheer brute strength. He threw them all into the air, light and easy, and they floated away like butterflies trailing wings and ribbons. Attached to wires, yes, but that did not kill the magic.

And then Daniel appeared, and gave Blue the shock of his life.

It was not the fact that he dressed like some demonic peacock—Blue had gotten over that particular marvel in Iris's dressing room—or that he moved with a grace and speed that implied years of dance, hard training. Nor was it the fact that he seemed born to the stage and spotlight, that he had the charisma to reach beyond both and pull in his audience. That was natural, blood, all from their father.

No, what surprised Blue, what hit him hard in the gut, was the pure, unadulterated passion Daniel exuded, the unabashed freedom that carried him, marked him like a brand of light. It was infectious, it was astonishing, and Blue found himself marveling that this was his brother, his own flesh and blood—the product of a man who had never, in Blue's limited experience, expressed any kind of joy, no love, nothing that could touch the presence that danced across the stage.

Daniel won't leave this, Blue realized. *Daniel* can't *leave this.*

The two women he had seen earlier ran on, leaping and pirouetting, trailing ropes and ribbons. In the center of the stage a trapdoor fell away, and Blue felt the groan of hydraulics inside his head as a glass cage rose slowly from beneath the floor, the solid walls broken only by two large hoses running up from beneath the stage. Inside the cage was another structure, narrow and clear. Like a coffin in the shape of a man, replete with spaces for the arms and legs. It hung from the cage's ceiling by a chain.

Blue heard a creaking sound beside him. He glanced up and saw Samuel walking quickly up the catwalk.

"Ah," whispered the big man, his face covered in swirls of white and black. "You have my seat."

Blue began to stand, but the man touched his shoulder and shook his head. Together they watched as Daniel opened up the door of the cage and stepped lightly inside. The women joined him, lifting away the clear cover of the spinning coffin. Daniel placed one foot inside and twisted around like a man on some odd swing until—in a movement too fast to follow—he slammed himself backward, sliding into the spinning coffin with astonishing agility. It was difficult to see from above, but it looked as though the structure had been custom-made for his body; there was barely any room between his skin and the interior, which molded to him like a sleeve, trapping his legs and arms in individual columns. The women slowed his spin and in one smooth motion replaced the clear cover, locking him in.

Daniel's hands were restrained by the shape of the plastic, his arms held separate from the rest of his body. The front of the panel fit him perfectly; looking down from above, Blue could see that he filled it out, pressed against the interior even. No wiggle room.

"He can't move," Blue murmured. "There's no way."

"Ja." came the soft reply. "Daniel is in deep shit."

"But you've seen him do this before."

"Nein. This is new. First time. The girls said he refused to practice the actual escape because he was afraid someone watching would ruin *das Überraschung*—the surprise. Pete doesn't know that part. Daniel has been rehearsing something safer in front of him. More routine."

Oh, man. Blue leaned over the edge of the catwalk for a better look. The women, with two great heaves, set the coffin spinning on its chain—a motion that seemed to grow faster and faster all on its own, casting Daniel's body into a blur. The women leaped out of the glass cage. One of them ran offstage and returned moments later with something large and red.

A gasoline canister.

The crowd began to murmur. The woman unscrewed the lid and began splashing the interior of the cage with gas. Blue knew it was the real thing within moments; he could smell the fumes. So could the audience.

Daniel still spun inside his coffin. Spinning himself into unconsciousness, if he wasn't careful. The human brain could take only so much centrifugal force. Torture, self-imposed. The women replaced the cage wall, locking it from the outside with padlocks that they tugged and yanked.

The woman who had not handled the actual gasoline pulled a matchbook from her sleeve. She held it up to the audience, ripped out a match, and struck it. Fire blossomed. Her partner slid aside a panel in the glass that Blue had not noticed.

Dead silence, breathless.

The girl tossed in the match. Fire exploded. The audience screamed.

"Shit," Blue muttered, standing. The man beside him grabbed his arm and pulled him back down.

"Nein," he said. "Wait."

"Wait for what?" Blue snapped, but he looked back at the cage and stared, helpless, as his brother spun inside the fire, still locked within his coffin. The heat had to be intense, too much to bear, and even if he did escape there was still the rest of the cage to contend with. A cage locked from the *outside*—

He heard gagging sounds in the audience, cries for help, the police, 911. But no one ran on stage. *Amazing.* Blue was ready to do some running of his own—anything to stop this—when suddenly he noted a change within the cage, a jerk in the tension of the chain.

The lid exploded off the spinning coffin, ricocheting off the interior wall with a deafening bang. Inside, still trapped within the flames, Daniel shot out an arm and grabbed the chain above him. He swung out, legs moving through fire.

The padlocks fell off the exterior of the cage. Simply opened by themselves and dropped away like magic, like fingers plucking and prying, and the moment the locks hit the ground, Daniel kicked off the opposing wall and slammed into the clear door. It flew open with a bang and he let go of the chain, tumbling to the stage in a controlled roll that brought him to his feet in a breath, a heartbeat that felt stolen from Blue's own life, because, God Almighty, he had *never* seen anything so horrifying.

Smoke curled from the surface of Daniel's body, his costume singed and torn, and in the perfect silence—because someone, at some point, had turned off the music—Blue could hear the hard rasp of his brother's breathing. Behind him, water poured into the cage via the hoses attached to the fiberglass. The fire hissed, went out.

The audience remained silent—dead, broken, frozen in their seats. Kind of like Blue, who wanted to have a nervous breakdown, staring at his brother. He wanted to commit some selective swearing, too, when Daniel straightened, lifting up his chin as he stared at the men and women seated in front of him. Defiant almost, with a real *fuck you all* that enveloped his body as he threw up his arms and swept down low into a cocky bow.

For one breathless moment it was anyone's guess what the audience would do, but Blue heard the first clap, and then another and another, and within seconds the auditorium was roaring so fiercely his body shook with the sound. Pleased as punch, Blue thought. Or pissed off and hiding it very, very, well. Daniel bowed again, gathered his helpers close, and ran off the stage. Still smoking.

"Well," Samuel said mildly. "That was entertaining, *ja?*"

Blue sat down hard. The crowd cheered, still with so much thunder in their clapping hands that the catwalk trembled, his heart drowning in the rumble. As the glass cage, sloshing and stained black with smoke and ash, sank beneath the stage, acrobats ran out to fling themselves in somersaults, great leaps and twirls. A distraction, perhaps, as curtains descended—great swaths of fabric painted like a jungle— ropes decorated like vines and flowers tumbling from the upper catwalks directly above the stage. As the applause died, Blue heard birdsong, the rush of a waterfall.

But the fire still haunted him. The fire and padlocks.

Samuel stood and stretched. "I am needed for the next act. You want to join me?"

"No," Blue said, distant, staring at the stage. "But thanks."

The big man sauntered away. Blue closed his eyes, pushing deep, sinking below the stage to the cage. He found gears, the water valve, the mechanism that had lifted the structure—but everything else was dead inside his head. No sparks, no flickers of electric life.

Which meant that nothing man-made had been involved with the release of those locks. No remote trigger. No one on the outside who had pushed a button to help Daniel escape. He had done it on his own.

Blue buried his head in his hands. This was no case of Houdini. There was only one way a man could simultaneously unlock a handful of padlocks all at once without touching them. Without the use of modern technology. And that was with the mind.

Ridiculous. Just because you're psychic doesn't mean he is. He might have found a way to do it—an ingenious, normal, human way. You're jumping to conclusions.

Maybe, but everything inside of Blue was screaming, *Freak.* He put his head between his knees and breathed very deep, forcing himself to go calm, to go easy on his aching head. Memory surfaced—standing inside Iris's dressing room, feeling the air move, the floor vibrate.

And now he knew why. His brother was a telekinetic. A very powerful, very public telekinetic.

"Shit," he muttered. Now what was he supposed to do? Roland was going to piss dandelions when he heard about this.

The lights dimmed around him; birdsong swelled. The audience fell into a reluctant hush, and for a moment Blue put aside thoughts of his brother as he glimpsed movement through the willowy darkness of the stage. Somewhere, very near, a lion roared.

The sound was loud, thrilling, and, unlike the birdsong, undeniably real. Gasps came from the audience, followed by nervous titters. Blue suspected everyone was still on edge from Daniel's performance, himself included. But when he saw movement in the black shadows masking the stage—human bodies furtive, darting—and heard the cry of another wild cat, the sounds and sights curled through him, preparing, warning him—only, not enough, not nearly enough—and he felt a cut like a lightning strike when a spotlight suddenly flicked on. It was blinding, one narrow beam of golden light shining down like a glow from heaven, and in the center of it, face upturned, stood Iris.

Her red hair hung loose; her perfect body was clad in only the lightest of simple dresses. Silk, maybe, the color of shell. Her feet were bare. She wore no jewelry. She looked breathtakingly sweet—and desperately alone.

There was movement outside the circle of light, stripes and spots and glimpses of golden fur treading lightly around the solitary woman, skirting the edge of sight. If it had not been for the fact that Blue had already seen Iris around her cats, he might have been scared for her—nervous, at the very least—but he *had* seen, and he knew that the fragility she presented was nothing but an act.

Roars and rumbles and low moans filled the air with another kind of thunder, restless and wild and deeply sensual. Iris swayed within the spotlight until—quite suddenly—she disappeared into darkness. Pulled away. A tiger slipped into the light, taking her place, and against the tiger a jaguar pushed close, butting her head under his great striped chin. Lions passed in front and behind, curling close, rubbing and stroking until it was difficult to tell where one cat began and another ended, so tightly were they bound together.

Beneath the birdsong came the hint of a drumbeat, a slow rhythm gathering strength like some ominous song, and Blue was so busy looking for Iris outside the spotlight that he almost missed the pale hand that emerged from within the writhing bodies curled on the ground. A hand, a flash of red, half of a face that looked at the audience with a hunger that Blue felt hot in his gut.

Good-bye, sweet little innocent.

He heard a creak on the catwalk behind him. Samuel probably, or Pete, coming back to check on him. Blue did not care. He could not tear his gaze from Iris, who emerged from within the pile of cats, rolling over their bodies to slink low to the ground, boneless and supple, as if her body were made of lava, one touch a burn. He expected to see scorch marks on the stage.

The catwalk creaked again; Blue smelled heavy perfume. His nostrils itched from the scent, but still he did not turn. The stage around Iris had begun to move; large objects shaped like boulders and cliffs rolled forward. Offstage, close, Blue heard the recorded sounds of shouts, gunfire.

Iris froze, as did the cats. All of them turned as one to look in the direction of those sounds. Iris's movements were so attuned, so perfect, that for a moment it was impossible not to imagine that she was one of the cats, that her human skin was nothing but illusion and that beneath, skimming blood and bone, was a creature of fur and claw.

The shouts offstage grew louder, drowning out the drums, the floating lilt of bamboo flutes. The audience stirred uneasily. Boots slammed; Blue heard the pump action of rifles and flinched.

Iris did not cringe. She ran, and the cats ran with her. They were an explosive blur of fur and skin moving as one tight group across the stage at impossible, desperate speeds through lights that cast the world in shades of red—until Iris suddenly left the path and leaped upon the fake boulders, scrabbling, swinging. The audience gasped, lost within her terrible desperation. The tiger followed immediately, and then the lions and jaguar, all of them climbing higher and higher off the stage, finding trails on an uneven surface that made Blue ache with worry.

But Iris led them back down—safe, quick—and again they ran circles and circles around the stage.

A net fell. Unfurling from above, hanging like a wall in front of Iris and her cats. Behind them another net tumbled, and then another and another, until they were completely trapped. Blue leaned forward, peering up. He saw another catwalk, and on it stood Mr. Cleaver and several other men, holding on to the ropes upon which the nets hung.

All pretend, utterly fake, but Iris … Iris stood surrounded by the milling cats with a look on her face that broke Blue's heart, that made him want to stand up and rage, to fight for her—and if the shouts from the audience were any indication, he was not the only one who felt that way. It was like watching the slow desecration of freedom, the terrible decay of the most perfect essence of wild, unflinching joy. Like watching the death of dreams and wonder.

This is what terrifies her, Blue realized. *Being caught, trapped. Hunted.*

And he understood. Completely.

The scent of perfume still lingered. Blue heard the rustle of cloth, felt the hint of warm breath against his neck. Annoyed, he began to look—and felt something cold and hard press against the back of his head. A gun. He sat very still. Below him, Iris raged.

A hand touched his shoulder. Against his ear a soft voice whispered, "My, my, my. This is quite a surprise."

The voice was too familiar; impossible, even. The entire right side of Blue's body ached in sympathetic echo as he turned his head and glimpsed a sharp chin, the rim of sunglasses. Blond hair peeked out from beneath a baseball cap.

The woman from the Jakarta market. The woman who had given him a bomb. The woman who worked for Santoso Rahardjo.

"No," Blue murmured. "No, you can't be here."

Her mouth curved. She backed away, just one step, enough to reveal a tight white tank top and loose tan slacks. A messenger bag hung against her hip.

"A beard," said the woman. "A mask. Not good enough to hide from me. And, unfortunately, not sufficient disguise against the interests of anyone else who might know you."

Below, Iris had escaped; the audience sat, rapt, as she tried to rescue her cats. Blue wondered how much noise he could make without ruining her performance; how far he would make himself go to end this. The final step, the final drop of his shield and will ... and nightmares forever after.

"What do you want?" Blue asked the woman. "Why are you here? Did you follow me?"

"Do not flatter yourself," she replied, the irritation in her voice a surprise. "You are startled to see me? Imagine how I feel. Your presence here is more unfortunate than you know. It would mean my death if you are discovered by my employer's men."

"Because you were supposed to kill me."

"Because they think I did." She tilted her head, studying

him. "You must have angels on your shoulders to heal so quickly. I thought I did a very good job of crippling you."

"You did," he said, feeling the torrent of Iris's music in his bones, in his furious heart. He rose from his chair, unmindful of the gun, and took a step toward the woman.

"Stay," she said.

"No," he replied.

"I won't warn you again."

"Then shoot me. Do it right this time. Otherwise I might just owe you for *almost* killing me—or maybe just for making me lose the trail of a mass murderer when I was so close to finding him. Nice. So very nice."

The woman sneered. "You were never close. You were not even in the same part of the world. All you had were breadcrumbs, and that is what you would have died for. *Nothing.* Just pieces of a puzzle that were, and still are, too big for you to comprehend."

"So you throw a bomb into my lap. What a wonderful solution to life's little problems."

The woman said nothing, but her head turned just slightly, and Blue followed her gaze down to the stage. Iris had freed her cats. The nets were gone. The lights had turned up enough for the audience to appreciate her intricate dance as she flew on light feet between and around the cats, all of whom flowed with her, the interaction seamless and perfect. There was no such thing as tricks or artifice; Iris was no cat trainer making her animals roll in circles or jump through hoops. What Blue saw below was pure, wild, straight from her heart.

"You need to go," said the woman, tearing her gaze from Iris. "Leave this city now."

"He's here, isn't he? Santoso is *here.*"

"It would be unwise for you to look for him, *Mr. Perrineau.*"

Her use of his name caught him off guard, but only for a moment. Someone had sent Roland a message telling him of his accident, and Blue had the sudden sinking suspicion that this woman was the person responsible. And if she had known to contact Dirk & Steele, it only made sense that somehow she would know some of the more personal details of his life.

But how much more is the question. Your secrets are less of a concern than the agency's, after all. If she's *seen past the cover to its true face—the psychics, shapeshifters, magic …*

That meant there was yet another weakness in the agency's security, another sore spot to line up against the one his father had created.

The problem was how; a mole was impossible. Roland had placed telepathic safeguards inside the mind of every agent, and if one word of Dirk & Steele's secrets passed though protected lips, Roland would know. The safeguard was infallible.

"I'm not going anywhere," Blue said to the woman. "I have a job to do."

"As do I. And believe me when I say that any impediments to the completion of that job will not be tolerated."

"Let me guess. You have another bomb tucked away somewhere."

The woman smiled. "No explosions this time. Bullets, however? A definite possibility."

"Then why are you waiting?" Blue moved close, watching her face. "Why are you holding back? Why bother saving my life when you should have killed me?"

"Perhaps I am a good woman." Her smile changed, becoming softer, more sensual. "Perhaps I think you are a good man."

Blue narrowed his eyes. "I think you're a liar."

"Lies are nothing but stories we tell to survive. But I think you know all about that, Mr. Perrineau. I think you might be an expert."

She stood directly in front of him. He was not stupid enough to try to take her gun; he trusted her reflexes more than he trusted his. Instead, Blue remained very still, waiting to see what she would do—and it was not until the last moment that he truly understood.

The woman leaned into his body, pressing herself against him with the gun digging into his chest, and Blue held his breath as she rose on her toes, free hand tracing a path along his ribs. She kissed his mouth, slow and easy.

Blue did not kiss her back. She was warm and dangerous and beautiful, but he felt nothing but profound unease when she touched him. All around, music—drums and flutes and now violins—and he glimpsed Iris below, dancing across the stage with incredible power and grace, her feet barely touching the ground. He wanted to be with her. He wanted her to be the one in front of him, touching his body.

The woman broke off the kiss and followed his gaze. She studied Iris for a long moment, then said, "She *is* beautiful, isn't she? Everything a woman should be and so rarely is."

Fear cut through Blue, but only for a moment; he studied the woman, and though he could not see much of her face, he felt nothing of a threat in her body, in the line of her mouth. Just something tired, almost wistful.

"You talk like you know her," he said carefully.

"I talk like a woman who was once just like her."

Again, that odd melancholy. Blue looked at her. Really stared, wishing he could see her eyes.

The woman smiled. "Look hard, look deep, Mr. Perrineau. You will never know me. Never."

"Does anyone know you?" he asked softly.

Her smile turned brittle. She jabbed the gun against his chest.

"Remember what I said. Leave. Or else I *will* kill you."

Blue shook his head. "Why are you doing this? Why work for a man like Santoso?"

"Who says I am working *only* for Santoso?" She sidled backward, deeper into shadow. Blue began to follow, but she shook her head, still pointing her gun.

"Remember," she said again, and then she left through the heavy door beside the catwalk. Blue went after her, but she was too fast—by the time he reached the hall she was completely gone, without a trace. Behind him, through the wall, he heard thunderous applause.

Blue got out his cell phone and called Roland.

CHAPTER SEVEN

Iris did not return to her dressing room after the show was over. She tried to, but the memory of that siren shape-shifter call still lingered, and the pain it caused made her walk in the opposite direction. It was a gift, her mother had once told her, that shape-shifters could feel when another was near. A gift in this modern age when their kind were so few.

Iris had felt the call before, but only with her mother. This time, she knew it was her imagination. There were no other shape-shifters flitting about—she had resigned herself long ago to the idea that she just might be one of the last—and she refused to believe her mother might have come so near without revealing herself.

Still, it made Iris uneasy. She fled to the loading bay where the incongruous presence of the silk pavilion fluttered like a ruby amidst concrete and trucks, men in hardhats unloading construction materials; or restaurant assistants hauling giant boxes of newly delivered fruits and vegetables.

The circus had constructed a small warm-up space in the loading bay, well out of the way of most traffic but still within clear sight of all the Miracle's employees, who occasionally gathered to watch the tumblers bounce and twirl upon the massive trampoline stationed less than twenty feet from the artfully hidden holding pen. The theatre itself was very close, the backstage doors only steps away from what had become the circus's unofficial green room. One of the Miracle's handymen had set up a small television with a live feed of the stage; anyone not performing could sit on the edge of the trampoline to watch the show.

Thus, everyone knew about Daniel's performance. Iris, being the act after his, had watched it just offstage. She could still smell the smoke and gasoline, would never forget the look on his face as he ran from the roaring audience. His eyes had been filled with pure joy.

The crew was still talking about it when she slipped into the pavilion, pulling the silk drapes behind her so that she was encased in a red cocoon of perfect privacy. Giant pillows lay strewn inside and around the holding pen, and the Kitaro music she had tuned earlier still played on repeat.

The cats were lounging inside their holding pen: relaxed, eyes half-closed, giant paws twitching. Iris wished she could let them out, but this was not Montana or some quiet remote town. The circus would understand a tiger roaming about, but not anyone else.

Iris heard shouts; Pete, calling out for Daniel. Iris rolled off her pillows, crawling to the edge of the pavilion curtain. Cheek pressed to the ground, she pulled up the fabric just enough to peer out. She saw Daniel jog across the loading bay to greet the old man, who leaned against the trampoline with one hand on his belly. His face was red, mouth turned down into a very deep frown.

"I hope you're happy," Pete said.

"Well, I *was*," Daniel said. "What's wrong? The audience loved that act."

"Of course they loved it. You almost killed yourself. Death, danger, and mayhem are what make the masses happy. Unfortunately, hotel management does not share their sentiments. They are *furious,* Danny. So furious, they are officially canceling tonight's show and deducting the ticket costs from our salaries."

Ka-thunk Iris could have heard a pin drop. Everything outside the pavilion went silent.

"Pete," Daniel said weakly. "Pete, I just wanted—"

"To do something great. Memorable. Death defying." The old man sighed, rubbing his face. "Son, there is a reason everyone goes through me when they are preparing a new act. There is a *reason* I have to approve these things. And yes, if we were still on the road it would be another matter entirely. But we aren't, kid, and the rules are different here. There are codes and laws and men in suits, and they don't like surprises. At all. Surprises mean lawsuits and injuries and bad press." Pete reached up and placed his hands on Daniel's shoulders. "Son, you set yourself on fire. You almost set the *stage* on fire. You practically screamed fire in a room full of people, many of whom were children. One man called 911 on his cell phone. An elderly woman complained of chest pains. Which, I want to emphasize, you should *not* feel guilty about. It is, however, the reason the hotel is making us call it quits for the night. They want to get everything sorted out with the fire marshal. And the lawyers."

Daniel closed his eyes. "I'm sorry, Pete."

"I'm sorry, too," he said. "Best night of your life, one of the finest acts I've ever seen, and I have to rain all over your parade. But that's the way it is in this business. Now, maybe you'll get lucky. Management might come back singing your praises as the best thing since Houdini. If so, everyone's going to be patting you on the back, telling you that you're some genius. Fantastic. But if that does happen, don't you forget the flip side. Don't you dare forget the price we *all* could have paid for that arrogance. Because success is great, kid, but only as great as the person handling it."

Iris glimpsed movement to the left of the men: Blue. He stared at them like he had heard every word, which was likely—everyone in the loading bay had stopped work to listen. This was big news, the kind that would get Daniel treated like shit until the future cleared. Screw the famous bond of the circus family; this was the gig of a lifetime for almost everyone on the crew, including herself, and Daniel had just cost them money—and maybe their jobs.

Pete waved Blue over. "Funny thing, you two. A little bird told me you both had a scuffle earlier today. Not with each other, but some strangers who wandered into the camp. Men with guns?" His voice dropped to a whisper, but that was no bar to Iris's ears. Shock willied down her spine, along with a good dose of fear.

The tension on Danny's face intensified. "We took care of it."

"And the men left," Blue said, his expression also closed, hard.

"They left," Pete agreed, "but someone else has been asking questions. About Daniel. This isn't the first time, either. I got wind of it a couple weeks ago, but didn't take it seriously. Now I do. And I want you to tell me why you're so special that some private goons want to rough you up."

Neither Blue nor Daniel said a word, though the two men shared a long measuring look that was becoming typical of all their encounters. Iris was not quite sure what it meant when men stared at each other, unblinking, for such long periods of time—although it was beginning to seem a tad more significant than the typical pissing contest.

Pete blew out his breath. "Fine. Be like this. But if I hear of another incident, you're both out, and I won't be counting any losses." He waited a moment, staring, then made a shooing motion with his hands. "Danny, go. Keep your head down. Blue, stay. We need to talk."

Daniel looked like he wanted to protest—he certainly sucked in enough air to do so—but Pete stood his ground, chin tucked, eyes hard, and the young man lost his nerve. Or maybe shame kicked in. Either way, Iris breathed her own sigh of relief when he turned on his heel and walked away. His shoulders and spine were a little bent—certainly charred as all hell—but it was nothing a little determination could not cure. If he still had enough fire in his gut to keep on fighting.

Iris glanced back at Blue and Pete. To her shock she found

Blue staring at her, head tilted, expression inscrutable. Iris, cheeks hot, let the curtain fall and scooted backward into the shadowed safety of the pavilion. The warmth of his gaze haunted her, as did the memory of his hands, his voice, his *Did I hurt you?*—and she wanted to pull aside the curtain; she wanted to walk out there and stand at his side and *touch* him.

Petro rumbled; all the cats watched her with wise eyes, and she felt their contentment inside her head, the warmth, and she thought about fleeing—not to Blue, but into the pen. She needed a hug.

A moment later, though, she heard a deep cough outside the pavilion; not random, most definitely an announcement. She caught a whiff of cigar smoke and flowers. Of money smells, rich man smells.

Iris stood just as the curtain was pushed aside. A man entered. He held a bouquet of purple irises. He was short, narrow, and impeccably dressed. Brown skin, black hair, with Asian features that had enough of something else in them to keep him from being completely ordinary. The man smiled when he saw Iris—smiled like he was used to being complimented on his very white teeth.

But he did not speak, and neither did Iris. She could not. All the hairs on her arms were standing on end, and in her head, the only thing she could hear was a scream. She had some experience with fans—years' worth—and she knew the signs, the differences between the ones who were true admirers, and those who wanted something—usually a quick fuck. Either way, there was always a smell, an energy, a way they looked her in the eye—or did not look at her at all.

The man in front of her was easy to read. He smelled like blood and sex. Bad, like the edge of murder.

His smile widened. "You look strong, up close. I like that."

"You won't like it when I kick you in the balls," Iris said. "I don't know who you are, but you don't belong here. Get out. Now."

He laughed and tossed the bouquet at her feet. Petals broke, scattered. Con and Boudicca sat up; Petro and Lila began pacing against the bars, lashing their tails, lips curled back over their teeth. Iris took a step toward them; the man did not move, but he watched her, his eyes undressing her body like he owned it: flesh and blood, thigh and breast. His intensity went beyond invasive; Iris imagined knives sharpening in his gaze, in the dart of his tongue against his thin lips.

The man pulled something small from his breast pocket: a notecard. He flung it at Iris and she caught it out of the air, recognizing the soft paper the moment she touched it. Dread spilled low into her gut.

My love, she read, and stopped.

The man smiled—again, that awful smile. "I am an artist, too, you know. I have an eye for beautiful things. Like you."

"I don't consider myself a thing."

"Ah. Fine. A *woman,* then. You are a *woman.* Does that make you happy now? Yes? I want to make you happy, *Iris.*" He looked at Con and the others. "Do you see that paper you are holding? I made it for you. I made it with my own two hands. Very special, very rare. I think you might appreciate the source material."

There was something about his voice, the way he looked at the cats, that made her skin want to shrivel right off her bones. Iris stroked the paper, found it still soft, but this time instead of letting her fingers do the work she raised it to her nose and inhaled deeply. She smelled flesh.

The paper fluttered to the ground; dark lights swam at the corners of her vision. Petro snarled, raking the ground with his claws, while the other cats put back their ears, slinking low. She felt their concern echo in her head and thought, *No, quiet. Walk quiet now.*

Walk quiet around danger, her mother had said once upon a time. *Walk careful.*

Iris curled her fingers; a claw broke through against her palm. The sleeping leopard inside her body began to wake, unfurling like a bud in a seed, pushing, pushing, pushing into a rage. Iris kept the beast in check, sweating with the effort.

The man's smile turned knowing. *"Layak,"* he whispered. *"Layak,* I know what you are."

She did not know what that meant, but a chill shuddered through her, a sense of even worse mojo, and she stepped toward the man, intent on beating the living crap out of him. He did not move away, but his eyes turned so mean Iris found herself faltering.

"You are mine," he whispered. "You are already mine."

"I'll kill you first," she told him. "I'll cut your throat with my bare hands."

"And I will thank you for the pain," he said, gliding backward, slipping past the curtain, disappearing from sight. Iris stared and stared at the spot he had just left, heart pounding so hard she felt lightheaded with it, breathless. The cats pushed up against the bars, moaning, but Iris could not comfort them. All she could look at was the note on the floor— and try to imagine what life had been sacrificed for it.

He can't hurt you, she tried to reassure herself. *But you can hurt him.*

Or at least gets the cops breathing down his ass. Iris shoving aside the pavilion curtains and raced into the loading bay. The man was gone.

Yet his scent—the sex, the blood—still lingered. Iris let it wash over her and felt her teeth sharpen, the leopard stir. She bit her tongue, tasted her own blood, and the rush that filled her rustled warm and deep inside her stomach. There was movement behind her, coming around from the other side of the pavilion: Blue and Pete, still talking. She glanced over her shoulder just as they appeared—caught Blue's eyes, watched them widen—but before he could say a word she began to run.

She did not worry about what people would say, how they would react; for once, drawing attention to herself did not matter. The man somewhere in front of her, the man getting away, needed to be stopped. Stopped cold, stopped dead.

The loading bay was large, cavernous, the air filled with musty mechanical scents that made the man's trail stand out like blood on snow, blood on skin, blood on pale paper made of flesh.

Iris heard her name—Blue, running after her—but she ignored him, following the scent through the double bay doors. She squinted at the sun, sucking in a quick breath as a hot wave of air rolled over her body, scorching her skin. But there—*there*—she glimpsed the man a short distance away, climbing into the backseat of a slick black Mercedes. The windows were tinted, the driver unseen. No license plate. A black van was parked behind him.

Iris shouted. The man turned to look at her, flashed white teeth, and yelled back a word that was definitely not English—and, she realized, not for her. The van doors slid open. Four men in dark clothing poured out. Big men. Big muscle.

But the one she wanted—Mr. Crazy—slid into the backseat of his Mercedes, which pulled away before his door fully closed. The engine roared, and within seconds the car disappeared around a lush stand of palm trees.

Leaving her alone with the goon squad. Thick faces, red cheeks, brown hair, sunglasses. Broad chests, and arms so thick they almost couldn't bend properly.

"Ma'am," said one of them, in a surprisingly high voice that made him sound like Baby Huey on steroids. "You need to come with us."

"Like hell," she said, backing away. The men followed. They looked bored, unconcerned for their safety. Iris did not feel sorry for them. Again, she heard her name called, louder this time—Blue, finally catching up—but she could not afford to glance back at him because the men shared a look ... and lunged.

Iris sprang back on light feet, bouncing on her toes as she slipped and danced just out of reach of their hands. Her fingernails lengthened subtly, and when Baby Huey got too close she lashed out and caught him across his forehead, knocking his sunglasses askew. Blood ran into his eyes; he shouted, clutching his face. All that boredom disappeared;

the other men hesitated, startled. One of them reached under his jacket. Iris glimpsed dark metal.

And then Blue was there and his fists were a blur, cracking like rock against bone as he threw himself against the men surrounding Iris. His face was terrible to look at—his eyes black with rage—and he was relentless, quiet, deadly—breathtaking—as he spun on his heel like a dancer, fighting as if his life depended on it, fighting for *her*.

But that man was still reaching for his gun, and Iris darted around Blue's back, claws again lengthening in a glimmer of gold as she struck him hard in the gut, cutting fat and muscle, ripping him deep enough to cripple. He stared at her, pure astonishment passing over his face, and it was easy to take his gun, to break his wrist for it, and he shouted in pain, shouted even more when she kicked out the back of his knee, driving him hard into the ground.

An arm curled around her neck, hauling her backward. Iris smelled garlic, mints, whiskey—and she slammed her elbow into a hard gut. Nothing, just a grunt, no loosening of that grip, and she raked her claws across the thick forearm, going so deep she scraped bone.

Obscenities poured from his mouth, but the man did not let go, taking Iris off her feet and spinning her around until she saw Blue again. Blood ran from his chest; the man across from him had a switchblade. Iris heard shouts, men and women running from the loading bay, shock on their faces. Some of the circus crew was with them—Samuel ran into the fray, pale and huge, his shirt half-unbuttoned with its happy-face tattoo covered in sweat. He tackled Baby Huey, who had finally collected himself enough to get back into the fight, and the two men rolled until Samuel ended up on top, fists making bloody meat of the other's face.

"Come on, bitch," muttered the thug holding Iris. "Stop squirming."

"Fuck you," she said, pouring power into her muscles. She stepped back, bent over in one violent motion, and flipped the man over her shoulder, driving him hard into the cement.

She kicked him in the head, his ribs, and suddenly the Mexican tumblers were there and they pushed Iris aside as some of them flipped the groaning man over on his stomach and yanked back his arms.

"Blue," Iris shouted, heart in her throat as she watched him block a knife strike to his chest. All the other thugs were down, but the last … the last looked wary, like he wanted to run but knew Blue would catch him before he reached the van. Iris could see a driver through the window; he watched the fight with a grim expression on his face and a cell phone pressed to his ear. He looked at Iris, Iris looked at him, and his window suddenly rolled down. He held the phone out to her.

Iris hesitated. Daniel appeared from the loading bay; she saw him look at Blue, look hard at the man holding a knife on him—and suddenly that knife was gone, flying, skittering across the pavement a good twenty feet away. And not just a drop or a slip.

The driver of the van still had the phone extended. Iris moved to take it, but Blue appeared at her side and grabbed her arm, holding her back. The driver looked at him—looked very hard—and his green eyes narrowed.

"You're dead," he said quietly, staring at Blue. Daniel slipped close, standing on Iris's other side. The driver looked at him, too, and his gaze changed, flickered. Daniel went very still.

The van's engine cut out. The driver turned the key, but the vehicle refused to start. The cell phone sparked and he swore, dropping it. Somewhere distant, Iris heard sirens.

"You should have gotten out of here when you still had the chance," Blue said to the man.

"I had my orders," said the driver grimly, looking at Iris. But then he focused on Daniel and Blue, and his expression turned sly. "Both of you … both of you are so fucked."

"You first," Daniel said, and smiled.

The police came. Iris answered questions. Blue stayed with her, as did Daniel, listening with grim concentration as she told the entire sordid story. Their previous aversion to the cops seemed to be gone, though Iris smelled a wave of tension when they were asked to give their names. Which they did, with enough reluctance that the cops very nearly arrested them on principle. Iris was not entirely certain what the men were hiding, but she had a very terrible suspicion that it involved them both.

Strangers, my ass, she thought, though whatever animosity they shared seemed to disappear when they looked at Baby Huey and the rest of her attackers, sitting on the hard concrete awaiting medical attention. Blue and Daniel watched those men with peculiar gravity, giving each other a knowing glance and nod. Iris recalled, with glittering clarity, Pete's brief discussion with them outside her pavilion walls.

"Jesus," she said. "You know those guys, don't you?"

Blue hesitated. "We might have seen some of them earlier."

"And taken their guns?"

Daniel frowned. "You heard."

"You bet your fire retardant ass I heard. And these bozos have been asking questions about *you*?"

"Yes," Blue said flatly. "That *is* odd."

A paramedic strolled up and clicked her fingers at him. "Sir, come with me. Your chest is bleeding."

"It's nothing," Blue said, but Iris clicked her own fingers and pointed at the ambulance. Both men stared, though only Blue bit back a laugh. Daniel looked downright disturbed. She couldn't really blame him.

Pete appeared some distance away, just inside the doors of the loading bay. He waved at them and Daniel cleared his throat, eyes darting between Blue and Iris. "I'll ... take care of this." And before Iris could say a word to him, he jogged away. She watched him go, feeling unaccountably guilty.

"Huh," Blue said, also watching him. "I don't think he wants to kill me anymore."

"I know," Iris replied. "That doesn't seem right."

The paramedic beckoned once again; Blue and Iris followed her to the ambulance. Up until that moment she had not gotten too close to him, but as they walked Iris dared to brush up against his arm—and she smelled perfume. The same perfume had doused the hall outside her dressing room. It was faint—she blamed it on his mere passage through that scented cloud—but still, it made her think of her mother all over again.

"You might need stitches," said the paramedic, who rather gleefully forced Blue's shirt from his very nice, very muscular body. She quickly cleaned away the blood and taped a white bandage over his wound.

"I'll be fine," he insisted. He sat down on the back end of the ambulance, his hands balled into fists, knuckles pressed into the hard metal beneath him. "It's Iris you should be looking at. She's the one who was attacked."

The paramedic made a humming noise and glanced at Baby Huey and his three cohorts, who were finally being loaded onto separate ambulances. Their wounds were not terribly serious, but Iris's bloody fingers and her very blunt nails had certainly raised eyebrows.

"I think your friend is fine," said the paramedic, somewhat snidely. Blue narrowed his eyes and very gently pushed the woman's hands away from his chest. Iris tried not to smile. Blue reached for his shirt and pulled it over his head. Iris—who, up until then had tried desperately to be polite—sneaked a look at his body.

Hard chest. Hard, rippling stomach. Smooth golden skin that looked soft and warm and utterly delicious. His head poked through the neck of the shirt; Iris glanced away, right at the paramedic—who gave her an immensely dirty look, ripping off her latex gloves with enough force to tear the material.

No matter; Blue jumped off the back of the ambulance, immediately reaching for Iris's hand. She gave it to him without thinking—a shock, a jolt to her sensibilities because it felt so natural and that was wrong, wrong, wrong—but when she tried to pull away, Blue refused to let her go. He just stroked his thumb over the back of her hand and said, "Are you okay, Iris?"

She did not immediately answer, and instead found herself wishing he would touch more than her hand, that he would wrap his arms around her so she could be recaptured by the warmth and safety she had felt so strongly at his side.

And maybe her face revealed her heart, because she did not need to ask or wish for long. Blue murmured her name and pulled her close into the curve of his body, holding her so gently she felt tears spring to her eyes. Her throat felt full, her heart dull with a soft ache that spread through her entire body.

"No," she whispered, her face pressed against his bristly neck. "I'm not okay, Blue."

"Then we'll make you okay," he rumbled. "I promise."

Can you promise not to break my heart? Iris wanted to ask. *I can handle the rest of this if you just don't break my heart.*

And if she could forget the last man she had loved—the last boy—and the horror in his eyes and the blood on his body, and oh—oh—his screams as he had seen her true face . . .

Iris pulled away. Blue let go, his fingers trailing along the edge of her jaw.

Behind, footsteps. She glanced over her shoulder and found Pete approaching. Samuel loomed over his shoulder, mouth turned down into a frown that was the perfect antithesis to the happy-face tattooed on his chest. Daniel walked with them, his expression troubled as he looked at Iris and Blue.

She expected questions from Pete, a hug, some outburst of concern. Instead, the old man rubbed a hand over his sweaty scalp and said, "You need to get out of here, Iris. Right now. News crews are coming. Hotel management is planning on milking this attack for all it's worth."

"Shit. How much advance warning did you have?"

"One of the crew saw the vans pull up outside the Miracle's front doors and overheard your name. We put two and two together."

"Bastards. They weren't even going to warn me." Iris cracked her knuckles. "And the cats?"

"The transport truck is here. You shouldn't wait, though. Not unless you really do want to talk to the press."

"Funny. And no, I'm not leaving without the cats. I won't take any chances with their safety, not after today." She glanced over her shoulder as she walked back to the loading bay; Blue and Daniel were following, trailed by Samuel, who kept studying both their backs with a very confused expression on his face.

"Hey," he called out to the men. "*Nanu!* Did you know that from behind you both look like *eineiige Zwillinge*?"

Daniel stumbled. Blue said, "What?"

"Twins," Daniel muttered.

Blue grimaced. "Fuck."

Whatever, Iris thought. Those two had way more problems with each other than she had time for.

Pete shooed her with his hands. "Go, Iris. Run ahead."

And she did, no questions asked. The transport truck, on loan from the MGM's lion exhibit, was already in place. The driver had pulled aside the pavilion curtains and was angling the ramp against the mouth of the holding pen. The ramp itself had its own collapsible chain-link walls attached to its sides—forming a tunnel from truck to pen—but Iris didn't need that, and the driver knew it. She waved at him, he stood back, and she opened the holding pen door.

The cats, however, did not immediately run up the ramp. They swarmed her, smelling her clothing, rubbing close, and Iris dropped to her knees, letting them have at her.

"Ms. McGillis," said the driver. Barry, she remembered. Blond, in his mid-twenties. "Mr. Reilly warned me about the time constraints. I think we ought to go."

"Yeah," she murmured, but it wasn't easy finding her feet. She swayed, sinking her hand into the ruff of Petro's neck, and glanced left. The note was gone. One of the police officers had mentioned that a crime-scene investigator would be stopping by to collect it. She hoped they had. Hoped that no one else had taken it.

"Go on," she murmured to Petro, shoving him toward the ramp. There was another cage in the interior, which was climate-controlled and filled with hay. The lion moved without hesitation, and Lila, Con, and Boudicca quickly followed. Barry shook his head.

"I see it every time and I still can't believe it. I'm sure you already know this, Ms. McGillis, but cats like this—different species, I mean—just don't get along the way these do. And I've seen your show...." He stopped, smiling shyly. "I like it a lot."

"That's sweet of you," Iris said. "Thank you, Barry."

Thank you for being normal and nice, the perfect fan, and not in the slightest bit psycho.

Psycho like what, though? Because the man who had threatened her was not *just* crazy. How many people, after all, had their own goons for hire? And how many people could get those goons to stick around, even when they were losing the fight? That kind of thing took money, power... or fear.

"Ms. McGillis," Barry whispered urgently.

Iris peered around the truck. She saw suits, bright lights, cameras—all moving fast in her direction. She did not think any of them had seen her yet, but they were definitely eyeing the pavilion.

"Lock me in," she told Barry, and jumped into the truck with the cats. He nodded, began closing the door—but before he shut it completely she heard a scuffle, a low argument. Blue climbed in after her.

"Hey," he said, smiling.

"Ma'am?" Barry asked.

"We're cool," she told him.

The young man locked the doors. Darkness swallowed them. Outside the van Iris heard chatter, fast questions about her whereabouts, about the attack—why and how and who was hurt, whether or not it was true that she had been visited by a man who wanted to pay her for sex, whether she had been paid for sex, whether she was being kidnapped for sex, who the men in suits were, if it was a sex deal gone wrong— Mafia, extortion—and would the hotel condone such a thing, was the hotel getting a cut, was it running a brothel?

Iris pushed her nails into her palms, using the pain to keep tight rein on her anger. *What a bunch of assholes.*

A roar surrounded them as Barry started the engine; the walls and floor vibrated. Blue began crawling across the hay-strewn truck bed to sit by her. Some light crept in from beneath the large doors; not enough for him to see by, but plenty for her night vision to kick in. She saw Blue on his hands and knees, watched how he bumped into Lila's hindquarters and froze.

"Move to your right a couple inches," Iris murmured, not thinking until it was too late how odd it might seem that she could see so well in the dark.

But all Blue did was whisper his thanks, and in moments he hit the wall and slouched at her side.

"So," he said quietly, as the van bumped and rumbled.

"Yeah," Iris replied, just as quietly. She felt greasy, sweaty, and for a moment all the lingering adrenaline seemed to rush away, flush down to her gut She fought for control over her body, though she was too far gone to stop the tremor that pulsed through her. Con pushed close and she slung her arm over his thick neck, savoring his musky scent, the clean sweetness of hay. Blue pulled her against him. She sighed, unable to bring herself to protest. It just felt too good. Too right.

"I don't like to be touched," she confessed. "But with you, I seem to keep making exceptions."

"Forgive me if I totally don't complain."

"So you like this, huh? Riding in old semis with wild animals and a girl who just keeps drawing crazy?"

"No better way to live." Blue shifted, unbending his right leg with the slow careful movements of a man in pain.

"Did they hurt you?"

"Just my chest. The leg is part of an older injury. If that hadn't been sore, I might not have gotten cut"

"Used to fighting?"

"A bit. You?"

"No, but I've picked things up over the years. Circus folk are always good in a brawl, and my mother taught me some tricks."

"I can only imagine." Blue fell silent for a moment, and then, quiet: "Tell me about the man who visited you."

Sickness curled through her stomach. "I already told the police. You heard the whole thing."

"You gave them the dry version. I want to know how the bastard made you feel. What your instincts told you. Please, Iris."

It was the *please* that made his request impossible to ignore. He said it gently, without any pretense or arrogance, as though he really, truly cared.

"He terrified me," she said. "Scared me shitless. He acted like he owned me, said I was already his. And he smelled like death."

The last detail was something Iris knew she should not say, but the desire to tell was so strong she could not help herself. Blue's arm tightened. "What else?"

Iris thought for a moment. "He called me something. A word I didn't recognize. *Layak,* I think. Do you know what that means?"

"No," Blue said, his scent spiking with tension. "But it sounds . . . Indonesian. I . . . had to spend some time there not long ago."

"Really. You travel a lot?"

"It's part of the job. Doesn't give me much of a life, though. I broke up with my last girlfriend because of it, although in all fairness, she traveled a lot, too."

Iris's heart sank a little. "Business-type?"

"No. Musician. I always seem to end up with the artists." His lips brushed the crown of her head, sending sparks through her body. "You were remarkable tonight, Iris. Not just the way you handled yourself with those men, but your performance on stage. It was nothing like what I expected."

She smiled, scratching behind Con's ears. "I don't do parlor tricks or gimmicks."

"No," Blue said quietly. "You tell stories. You take people to other places. You make magic, Iris."

She bit back laughter, knowing it would sound bitter. She did not want to feel bitter. She appreciated the compliment—chose to believe it was sincere. But to show him that would be too much.

"All I do is get myself attention I don't want, Blue. Psychos and love letters, thugs who cut you and want to drag me off to God knows where. Animal activists who want to take my cats and ... and give them to some pseudo-sanctuary where everyone will pretend they're fat and happy and loved." Iris shook her head. "And I can't stop. I can't stop because this is all I have, and even if I didn't need the money I would still be here. For Pete, the cats, everyone. The old place, the ranch, wouldn't be home anymore. And I'm not made for a nine-to-five job."

"Is anyone?"

"Not you," she said without thinking. "I can't imagine you sitting at a desk, or working customer service."

He laughed, low. "I cleaned toilets when I was thirteen, Iris. Bagged groceries, stocked cans, swept floors. I was washing dishes in a restaurant by the time I was sixteen, moved up to busboy not long after, and at nineteen I joined the military so I could finish paying for college, get some life experience. But you're right. Never a desk job."

Iris wished she could see his face, but settled for being bold, reaching out to touch his jaw, his cheek. His beard was soft, though it seemed too hot for the desert; she wondered what he looked like beneath it, why a man as handsome as him would grow facial hair in the first place. "Sounds like you grew up as poor as I did."

"My mom was—still is—a lawyer, but she was young when she had me, just barely out of school. It was hard for her. Being a woman and an immigrant also made it more difficult. People didn't trust her."

"Where's she from?"

"Afghanistan. She got out in the seventies, before the country went to hell. Came to America as a student and never left."

"And your dad?"

"Not in the picture."

Ah. A pain she understood all too well. It didn't make it any easier to talk about, though. "My dad wasn't around, either."

"You miss him?"

"I never knew him. I figure, though, that if he was worth knowing, my mom would have kept him." Iris hesitated. "You never told me what you do for a living."

"I'm not sure I should."

"International Man of Mystery," she countered. "You must be a spy. That, or an accountant."

He grunted. "Close, actually. I'm a detective."

"Seriously? A real detective? A Magnum P.I.?"

"I don't drive a Ferrari, but yeah, I'm for real."

"Huh," Iris said. How ... unsurprising. Because if she really had to choose a profession for Blue, detective fit the bill just perfectly. Or at least, the movie star version. He had the look, he had the moves, and he had enough sincerity to kill a goat.

But it bothered her. She just couldn't explain how.

"That's why you came to Las Vegas," Iris said slowly. "You're on a case."

"I am," he said. "Or rather, I was."

"So is the person you're looking for here? In this circus?"

Blue hesitated. "I can't say."

"You can't or you won't?"

"It's not like that. The question can't be answered in a straight way, Iris."

"What does *that* mean?"

"It means what I told you. Circumstances have changed."

"They can't have changed that much. You're still here."

"A lion tried to swallow me. I fell in love."

"Smart ass. Besides, Petro's too nice for you."

"I know. And his mother is scary."

"Terrifying," Iris said, and she felt his lips touch her cheek, his strong hand smooth back her hair with such gentleness that once again, heat suffused her face, tears burned her eyes. Her reaction terrified her, but there was no help for it. She could not bring herself to pull away.

The truck rumbled, bouncing over the uneven ground of the back lot. The cats yawned and groaned, shuffling and turning in the darkness. Blue, so quiet she could barely hear him, said, "I was standing right there, Iris. Just on the other side of that tent. And he walked right in without anyone noticing and threatened you. He *threatened* you."

"I let him. I could have fought him, subdued him, but at the moment when I was going to do it, he just ... looked at me. I froze."

"There's no shame in that."

"There is if he managed to hurt me or the cats. As it stands, I just feel ... dirty."

Blue fumbled for her hand and kissed it. Iris forgot how to breathe, how to talk. "Don't," he whispered, his breath hot against her wrist. "You did the right thing. You have to trust your instincts."

"Sometimes my instincts are wrong."

"No. You have to trust yourself, Iris. You have to trust your mistakes. Even the bad times teach us things."

"What have they taught you?"

He laid her hand on his chest, against his heart. "That being alone is too easy, and that I'm a lazy person."

"I'd almost say we're two of a kind, then."

"You're not lazy."

"No," she agreed. "I'm just frightened."

Blue sighed. The truck began to slow, and Iris was sorry for it. She wanted to stay here, like this, forced to commune with Blue in the darkness. She did not want to let go, and her hand on his chest as she savored the slow rise and fall of his warm breath. She felt the bandage, too, and remembered him fighting, the look on his face. "I'm sorry you got hurt, Blue. I'm so sorry. But thank you for helping me."

"I would have done more if I could have."

"I'm glad you didn't have to," she said quietly. "I'm glad that's all there was."

The truck stopped. Blue did not let go of her hand, and she let him help her stand. Barry opened the doors. The holding pen was right in front of them, and next to that . . .

"My RV," Iris said. "Someone moved the pen to the living area?"

Barry shrugged. "I just went where Mr. Reilly told me to go."

"It makes sense." Blue jumped out of the truck. He winced, favoring his right leg. "Your neighbors can watch you, and you can watch your cats."

"And if the on-site inspectors come?"

"So what? The worst they'll do is fine you."

"And I suppose you'll pay for that?"

"I dress well for a reason," he said.

She hopped down and Barry pulled out the ramp. The desert furnace surrounded her; she smelled exhaust, sweat, some distant greasy kitchen. Fading perfume. The sun was so hot it hurt.

Petro led the march from the van. He moaned, lashing his tail as he walked slowly down the ramp. Someone had set up their swimming pool; above it, tied from one side of the wire to the other, stretched a blue plastic tarp. All the cats headed for the shady spot. Con went directly into the water. Boudicca and Lila flopped down. Petro rolled on his back.

Barry closed up the van. "I'll see you tonight, Ms. McGillis?"

"No. Tonight's show has been cancelled. I'll give you a call tomorrow afternoon and let you know the revised schedule."

That was good enough for Barry. He smiled, waved good-bye, and less than a minute later the truck rumbled away. Dust and dried grass kicked into the air. Iris coughed.

"They won't cancel the show permanently," Blue said. His chest was one big red spot.

Iris grunted, not ready to agree or disagree with him. "Your shirt is ruined."

"I'll get another."

"You bring luggage?"

"Not really, no. Pete commandeered these clothes from Daniel."

"Ah. Your soul mate."

Blue's expression soured. "That's not funny."

"Nothing about the way you two act toward each other is funny. Especially because I can't understand it. One thing I *do* know, though, is that you definitely aren't strangers."

Blue grunted. "I've seen the way he looks at you. Were you ever ... close?"

"No," she said, somewhat amused by his question. "But I had a crush on him not so long ago. I'd also like to think he's my friend."

Another grunt. "Escape artist. I've never seen anything like it. The cage, the fire ... I thought he was going to die."

"He must be one of the best in the world. The things he could do, right from the beginning, shouldn't have been possible. No one's ever been able to figure him out. And if he keeps it up, if he doesn't get sacked, he could receive his own show. It might happen anyway, even if the Miracle does get rid of him."

"The same is true for you. You're one of the stars."

Iris shrugged, leaning against the holding pen. "I do my thing, I enjoy it, but I'm no better than the rest of the performers."

"But if the hotel—if *anyone*—gave you the opportunity, you'd say yes, right?"

Yes to fame and fortune, yes to glory, yes to newspapers and cameras and the city? Yes to a life of illusion.

"I don't know," Iris said. "The money would be good, but I'd have to leave everyone behind. Not physically, but it would still be a separation. Reilly's Circus is all I've known for such a long time. How do you leave family, Blue?"

He smiled sadly. "You don't, Iris. Not ever."

"Some help you are." Then, because she was already on a roll with the truth, she added, "I wish I could run away, Blue."

She had an image in her head like some old cartoon: a stick over her shoulder with a packed red bandana swinging, and around her the cats, ranging wild and free down the open road. Or forget the bandana, forget humanity; she could travel into the hills and mountains, the old places people didn't ever go, and just ... be something else for awhile. Let the leopard be her pilot, her skin—let the human woman sleep for a day or a month or a year until humanity, until this life, was nothing more than some distant dying memory.

"Running away sounds like a good idea to me too," Blue said. "Excellent, in fact. It's not safe for you here, Iris."

"I have obligations, though."

"You have a more important obligation to stay alive. Someone shot at you last night, in case you've forgotten. And today? That was attempted kidnapping, and as far as I'm concerned, emotional assault."

"I told you—"

"Yes, obligations. I do respect that, you know. I understand it, too."

Iris turned away and walked to her RV. Blue joined her at the door, grazing her arm with his fingers before she could—what a novelty—unlock it with the key.

"Let me," he said, and made her stand outside the RV while he entered first. *Scouting out the premises,* she said to herself, wondering if he had ever worked as a bodyguard, in addition to being a detective.

"You know," she said to his back, as he disappeared into the dark interior of her tiny home. "Despite the way I froze against that little psycho, I *can* defend myself. I did fine against those goons today."

"And if they had managed to pull a gun? Maybe the same kind of gun that was used against you last night?" Blue's voice was muffled. Iris heard a rustling noise and peered into the RV. He was in her nearly non-existent bedroom, checking out her very narrow closet.

"Excuse me," she said, entering her home. "But I can barely hang a shirt in there, let alone an entire man."

"Uh-huh," he said, glancing at the clothes scattered on her floor. Iris scowled, marching into the room—which involved less actual marching than squeezing between the wall and the mattress. The air smelled somewhat stale, like lion and old carpet, but at least it was home. There was so much crazy outside the walls of her battered RV, but here she could let her mind rest from the stress of facing the world, and she could be herself in all her furry splendor. It felt strange to have that territory invaded, however temporarily, by another person.

"I'm not going to take anything," Blue said mildly, glancing over his shoulder.

Her cheeks warmed. "I didn't think you would. Not that I have anything worth taking."

"Oh, I don't know." Blue held up a pair of rhinestone-studded four-inch stilettos. "These are nifty."

"You can have them. They'll do wonders for your legs."

He laughed quietly. Iris leaned against the wall, reining herself in, trying to control her emotions. She wanted him again, and the attraction, emotional and physical, made her head all tangled and twisted.

"I'm safe," she said, fighting for her voice. "You can go now."

He stopped. "Do you want me to leave?"

"You shouldn't feel obligated to protect me."

"I'm here because I want to be. Obligation has nothing to do with it." He frowned, stepping close. "I like you, Iris. Hasn't anyone ever done anything for you, just because they like you?"

"Of course."

"But this is different for you." His gaze sharpened. *"We're* different."

"I don't want to talk about this." She backed out of the bedroom, trying to stay strong as Blue followed, his expression concerned.

"You really are scared," he said. "Iris, you don't have to be."

"Easy for you to say." She grabbed a water bottle from the kitchenette counter and twisted off the lid. Blue reached out and covered her hand. His skin was dark against her own, the bones of his wrist strong and large. His touch made her go soft on the inside, and she hated herself for it. Surely she had learned her lesson. Surely she could resist this man.

Iris backed away. She needed distance, separation, anything but Blue, who despite her best intentions brought her too close to the edge, making her forget all the lessons that had kept her alive and safe. Secrets and lies, masks and illusions—her life, one unending performance.

Your humanity is not a lie. You are just like everyone else.

Except, she wasn't. Not entirely. And it was that other half—the leopard, the predator—which was going to get her into deep trouble, if she was not careful.

But Iris made the mistake of looking into Blue's eyes, and the warmth she found echoed low and sweet. She wanted to lick her lips but did not dare; his gaze drifted to her mouth and he moved toward her with slow deliberation, time slowing into an ache that pooled inside her heart.

Electricity filled the air, a pressure that felt like wind and lightning, a fast run in a dark wood with clouds rolling through the sky. She inhaled, filling her lungs with that unbearably wild scent, which curled through her body, wrapping around the leopard sleeping inside her chest. Iris felt the cat stir, felt the light and heat grow beneath her skin, but even as she fought it down, fought to stay human, she thought, *I want to be me. I want to let you see.*

Blue touched her face, caressing her cheeks, her throat, running his fingers through her hair. "Go out with me, Iris. Let me take you to dinner. If you don't like dinner, then lunch. You don't like lunch, we'll do coffee. But let me take you somewhere. I want to do something with you. I've been wanting to do something since the first time I saw you."

God help her, but Iris wanted to do something, too. But instead of saying yes, instead of leaning in and in and in, she opened her mouth—fought like hell with herself—and said, "I have a date with Daniel tonight."

Blue stared, his hands going still. "You're going on a date with my—Daniel?"

"Yes," she said, but it sounded more like a question. He frowned, stepping even closer, stealing her personal space until their bodies were separated by a hairsbreadth, a whisper.

"Yes?" he asked softly. "Or *yes?*"

Iris swallowed hard. Blue moved slowly, giving her time to stop him, but she said nothing as his hands drifted down her bare arms to her waist. His touch shot electricity through her body, a tingling flush flowing from sternum to groin, hot as his breath on her cheek, hot enough to taste. It was a struggle not to move, not to rub her legs together, to rub against him. She gave in, pushing her aching breasts against his chest, sidling against his body. The sound of his breath catching made her want to throw back her head and laugh. God, this was good.

Blue's grip tightened on her waist and Iris gasped as her feet left the floor. She found herself sitting on top of the kitchenette counter, breathless—close to crying out as Blue pushed himself between her legs, his hands traveling to her thighs. He touched her skin, fingertips riding up beneath her shorts, moving higher, higher, hesitating only once at the place where there should have been a panty line.

"I don't like underwear," Iris murmured.

Blue swallowed hard. His fingers pushed deeper into her shorts. Iris shuddered, closing her eyes. It was the first time she had ever been touched like that, and she savored it, holding her breath.

But his hands were large and the clothing trapped them. She felt Blue hesitate, and then his fingers were back at her waist, rimming the edge of the button, the fly. Iris forced herself not to question it. She wanted to be touched; she wanted so much to let go. Just once. She was older now, stronger. Surely she could do this without losing control.

Iris touched him back, savoring the hard waist beneath her hands, the flat stomach and taut chest that flexed beneath her palms as her hands moved over his T-shirt up to his neck. His quickening breath stirred her hair—his scent, everywhere, drowning her—and the leopard stirred again, rolling hot as his fingers wound into her hair, tugging just slightly so that her face turned up toward his.

Blue kissed her. His mouth was hot and hard and Iris thought she must be hallucinating, dreaming, because kisses could not possibly feel this good, could not possibly be real, because there was sunlight in his lips, sunlight in her skin, sunlight rolling in her heart, pouring through every muscle, pouring like …

Fur! She felt fur on her arms.

Iris shoved Blue away, pushing so hard he slammed against the wall. Sparks shot from the socket next to him.

Her violence was shocking, shameful—a nightmarish echo of another boy. Teeth cut her mouth, the taste of blood strong and bitter, and though she wanted to go to Blue, her fear won out, terror and horror destroying every shred of confidence and hope she had painstakingly rebuilt. Iris ran fast, throwing herself into her bedroom, pushing up hard against the wall out of Blue's sight. She huddled there like a child.

Iris heard a low groan and bit down on her lip. Her teeth had receded, as had the spotted hair on her arms, but she could not go to him. Not after what she had just done. He would never understand.

"Iris," Blue called softly.

"Go away," she said, fighting back tears. "I'm sorry, Blue, but *please,* just go."

She heard a rustling sound, and then, "Don't hide. Iris. Please, not from me. You don't have to hi—"

His voice broke off. Sudden, punctuated by pure silence.

Iris hesitated, but the quiet was unnatural. She uncurled from the floor and slowly, carefully, peered around the doorframe.

Blue stood with his back to her. He stared at the fire alarm attached to her ceiling.

"Oh, my God," he said. Iris wiped her face and joined him. He did not react to her presence, showed no sign he noticed her at all. She peered up at the small white alarm. It did not appear any different than she remembered, but Blue reached out with one long arm, fingers dancing over its surface, and sucked in his breath.

"Hey," she whispered, and then bit back a gasp as sparks spat from the dark gills of the alarm. Blue did not flinch. He did not act surprised at all as he dug his fingers under the edge of white plastic, grunting as he pried it off the ceiling. Iris did not bother trying to stop him. He was too intense, too focused. She wanted to know why—why *this* was suddenly more important than what she had just done to him.

Blue pulled a screwdriver from the tool belt still slung around his hips and began opening the alarm. He did it quickly, silently, and when he pulled off the covering and the components lay exposed, he touched Iris's arm and drew her close.

"Look," he said, pointing at a rectangular piece of black plastic soldered onto the guts of the device. A thick wire curled, stretching to the dome, where it had been glued into place. At the very tip was something shiny, like glass. A lens?

"What," Iris said slowly, "is that?"

"A remote transmitter," Blue said grimly. "A camera."

"Oh," she said. "Shit."

CHAPTER EIGHT

If seeing Iris attacked and nearly kidnapped had not already been enough to make Blue crazy, then finding a hidden camera in her fire alarm was more than enough to make him start bleeding from his ears and speaking in tongues. *God Almighty.* What a terrible day.

He sat on Iris's stoop, safe in the shade, keeping company with the cats. Sweat rolled down his face; the bottle of water beside him was almost empty. Early evening was drawing on, but the heat had not lessened; he was just getting better at enduring.

Iris was inside her RV. He did not know what she was doing, but he suspected it involved the fetal position. Or not. He wished he could join her, but he was trying to be a gentleman and give her space—even though what he really wanted was to curl around her body. Hell, he needed to be held, too.

No police, though. Iris did not want to talk to them. Under different circumstances, Blue would have forced her to call, but this situation was different. Painfully so.

Blue cradled the fire alarm in his hands. The crackling of the hidden camera still felt sharp in his mind. It was a complicated piece of technology, far more complex than it appeared. It was military grade, the kind that could transmit images over a good long distance, and to nothing more simple than a laptop. This was not the work of an amateur.

The problem was, he had no way of knowing just how long the camera had been in Iris's home. From the look on her face, though—and knowing what he did about her secrets—any amount of time was too much. The damage—real damage, shape-shifter damage—might already be done.

Like when we kissed, he thought, remembering the feel of Iris's body, her incredible warmth, the golden light that had streamed from her eyes. Her arms, soft with sleek fur that had felt like silk beneath his fingers. He loved the sensation, the wildness of it, could not imagine Iris any other way. Blue had wondered, though, just how deep she would go, how far she would trust him.

Apparently, just about as far as she could throw him. Not that he could blame her. He understood her fear. Given his past, it was foolish of him to get involved as well. If *he* ever hurt her ...

Blue resisted the urge to rub his back. The cut in his chest throbbed. His knee was killing him and those stars were back in his vision, competing with the glare of the desert sun. Iris packed a punch.

But the pain was nothing at all to his fear. Bone-deep, chilling, fear.

Santoso Rahardjo. Fate had a terrible sense of humor. That, or the bomb blast had made Blue clinically insane. A distinct possibility—he might be wrong, overreacting, going over the deep end into some crack den nightmare—because what were the odds? What was the chance that Blue would find himself in the same place as Santoso Rahardjo? *Again?*

And yet, his instincts were screaming, and so were the coincidences. That blonde woman, Santoso's employee, appearing at the Miracle? A man dropping words of Indonesian appearing with notecards made of flesh? That same man having enough money to retain an army of goons to do his dirty work? Goons who had also gone after Daniel?

Right. *That* part did not make sense, but as for the rest, Blue could pretend that he was not crazy. And, pretending he was not crazy, he allowed himself to tackle the very real possibility that Santoso was in town. The question was, why Iris—and why Las Vegas?

Business, he answered himself. Regardless of Santoso's tastes in women, he was first and foremost an entrepreneur—and anything *but* business would be a waste. Crime lords, in Blue's experience, were always workaholics. Nothing like the possibility of losing power to keep a man in shape.

So there's a deal going down. Something big. It has to be. Santoso rarely visits the States. Too many people looking for him.

But was Iris nothing more than a side interest? Something to keep Santoso occupied between business dealings? And if she was, then how did that explain the hidden camera, the attempted kidnapping, the personal visit and notes?

My love. I will make you mine. That sounded a hell of a lot more involved than a man looking for some entertainment.

His cell phone buzzed. Con and Lila raised their heads and looked at him, their beauty sleep interrupted. Petro yawned, showing off the inside of his massive mouth. *Hello again, teeth.*

The cell phone's screen identified the caller as Roland. Blue, still looking at the lion, answered, "You'd better have some good news for me, man. The shit I mentioned to you earlier? It just got deeper. I am now officially screwed."

"Really," said a familiar voice, which was female, brusque, and most definitely *not* Roland. "Is your situation so terrible, *Felix,* that your entire conversation must begin with profanities? Is it?"

Blue froze. "Mom? What are you doing with Roland's phone?"

"I am in his office in San Francisco," she replied curtly. "Brandon and I arrived less than thirty minutes ago. Your father's men found us and were being . . . difficult."

"Difficult? What do you mean, *difficult?* Did they try to hurt you?"

"They tried to bring me back to your father. No doubt for another round of threats." He heard papers rustling; in the background, Roland rumbled something. His mother added, "Your employer assures me that no one will be able to retrieve us in this place."

"Did you find anything that can help us?"

"Most of your father's illegal dealings have been in cash. Everything else has been conducted through businesses with enough fronts in place that even his employees have no idea who they are really working for. Fortunately, I am quite familiar with one of those business chains. Your father has probably cleaned up most of his paperwork by now, but I managed to take what I have from my office safe and place it in a safety-deposit box."

"So you have proof."

"What proof is there against a dead man? No, Felix. None of what I have is enough. Not if he remains dead."

"He doesn't have to. We could expose him. Get a camera crew up there, swamp the place with journalists."

"And then what? Yes, he would be shown as a liar, but you know him. He will spin the truth, he will claim temporary insanity, he will beg his friends in the Department of Justice for favors, and he will still be *rich*. Rich and angry. He will hurt your friends, Felix."

Roland said something else, and Mahasti said, "You do not understand this man at all." And then Blue heard another rumble, another voice that sounded surprisingly like his father's. His mother made a clicking sound with her tongue. "Brandon believes we are risking your friends by even being here. Your father must know by now that we have come to ... Dirk and Steele."

Blue could almost feel her cringe when she said the agency name; it was far too tacky for her sensibilities.

He heard yet more voices in the background and said, "About you and Brandon ... "

"He is my friend," Mahasti said firmly. "And has been for some time. That is all I will say on the matter, Felix. At least until all of this has passed. Now, wait. Roland wants to speak to you."

How convenient. She did not even give him a chance to say good-bye before Roland coughed his way onto the line.

"I have more news," Blue said, and told Roland what had transpired in the few hours since their last conversation. He tried to keep his voice low; he was not entirely certain Iris would approve of him sharing her story.

Roland made a humming sound. "You are one unlucky son of a bitch, man. You sure it's Santoso?"

"I'd rather be paranoid than dead."

"I'd rather be having a Swedish massage with some naked blondes, but life just isn't fair that way. Speaking of which, you can't complain too much. I looked that Iris McGillis up on the internet. The Miracle has a website with pictures. Those are her cats in front of you, right?"

Good old clairvoyant vision. Roland was a master of remote viewing. Blue said, "Yes."

"You sure she's a shape-shifter?"

"Yes."

"A hot shape-shifter."

"Yes."

"And if I make a dirty joke about her right now, you'll fry the electrical grid of my—"

"Yes," Blue interrupted smoothly. "Oh, yes."

Roland sighed. "I don't know what to tell you about Santoso. *If* it's him. And if it is ... God, just do what you can. Don't forget your priorities, though. You've got Iris now, but also your brother to deal with. Don't lose sight of that, Blue. He needs your help, too. We all do, because if we can't find out where your father is storing that information, his back-ups, how to access them ... "

"I know," Blue said.

"No, you don't. We'll find another way, I promise. Problem

is, we might need Daniel's help. At the very least, it'll get fucking messy."

"You just used a bad word in front of my mom," Blue said.

"Tell me about it. I've had to be a monk in front of her. But I'm all done with that now. This is *my* office, and— *Shit*. I have to go. Your mother's staring at me. I think she's got powers. She's looks at you funny and you can almost feel your balls ripping off."

Blue heard a low, sharp voice. Roland said, "Your backup should be there soon," and then the connection went dead.

He stared at the darkened screen for a moment, contemplated calling back so he could reassure himself that his mother was fine—and to tell Roland that he did *not* need backup—but he felt on the edge of his mind the approach of a car and looked up in time to see a dark green sedan pull into an open spot several RVs away. Agent Fred jumped out, his cheap suit wrinkled, his brown hair pressed flat against his head. Blue set the fire alarm on the ground and pushed it under the stairs behind his feet.

"Long time, no ... Oh, never mind." Fred shrugged. "I think I should begin chaining myself to Ms. McGillis's leg. It would save me some gas."

Blue did not find that particularly funny. "Why are you here?"

Fred's brow crinkled. "I'm an FBI agent assigned to an existing case involving Ms. McGillis, and I get a call about an attempted kidnapping? You bet I'll come out to ask some questions."

"I don't think it's related," Blue found himself saying— knowing he should shut up, that the more he talked the worse this would get. "The men who attacked her today were not ecoterrorists."

"And how vitally important your opinion is to me," Fred said sarcastically. "But you *are* right. In fact, according to the initial findings, the men arrested belong to a who's-who list of ex-cons and escaped felons. Real celebrities, in their circle.

Thing is, none of them are giving names, addresses, anything that can lead us to the person who hired them. I've never seen a group of men more tightlipped than these five. I'd call it loyalty, but I don't think they're capable."

"So call it what it is, then. Call it money. Fear."

Fred smiled. "I've got the strangest feeling that you're an expert on these kinds of things. There's definitely more cooking inside your head than what you show the world. Or would you disagree?"

Blue said nothing. There was a gleam in Fred's eye that bothered him. No way to explain exactly how, just that … something did not seem quite right. He was too talkative, too willing to share information with a total stranger. No sense, definitely stupid. Straying miles from typical FBI procedure.

So the next time you call the office, ask for a background check. Easy, simple. Except—

"What's your last name?" Blue asked.

"Wilhelm. But when people call me that I feel like a prick." Fred's smile stretched even wider. "You know, we never did talk about you and that shooter. Or why you're here with the circus."

"I'm just passing through," Blue said.

"And making sweet memories while you're at it. Very sweet, if what I saw this morning is any indication. I assume, of course, that Ms. McGillis knows that you don't plan on lingering."

"I don't think what goes on between myself and Iris is any of your business. You should be more concerned about the psycho stalking her."

"We'll handle him. But you, on the other hand … *you* are a conundrum. A problem."

"I can't imagine why. I haven't done anything wrong." Except lie his ass off to Iris and his brother.

And if you had *told her the truth? If you had shown her what you were, right from the beginning? You know you could have trusted her.*

Maybe. But old habits died hard.

The door opened behind Blue. Iris peered out. She looked tired, exasperated, far too pale—and when she saw Agent Fred her expression did not improve.

"All of you are useless," she said to him without any kind of greeting or hesitation. "Absolutely useless. Frighteningly incompetent—or maybe just frightening."

"I won't be giving you any job approval surveys to fill out," Fred said, squinting against the sun. "Care to answer some of my questions about what happened?"

"No," she said. "I already gave my statement to the police. I didn't leave anything out."

"Do you mind if I take a look inside your home?"

Iris gave him a dirty look but stepped aside, gesturing to her door. Fred smiled and entered the RV. Instead of following him, as Blue expected she would, Iris plopped down on the step. He looked at her, eyebrow raised.

"Small spaces with strangers aren't my thing," she said.

"Ah," he replied, deciding not to remind her that she had done quite well with him in that same space. Mostly, anyway. "Are you okay?"

"No," she snapped, but then she seemed to catch herself, softening just slightly, softening even more as a furrow appeared between her golden eyes. "How's your back?"

He thought about lying to her, saying he felt fine, but he couldn't bring himself to do it; too many lies and omissions already. "A little sore. Remember that old injury I told you about?"

Iris closed her eyes. "I'm so sorry, Blue."

"You were scared. I scared you, and I'm sorry for that."

It would have been easy for her to take his opening, to place the blame on him—easy because Blue expected it, did not mind at all—but instead Iris surprised him by vehemently shaking her head.

"You didn't scare me," she insisted, then lowered her voice as Fred rattled something near the door. "What we were doing was … was really good. I just … got scared. I had a bad experience once."

She did not look at him as she spoke, and that alone would have been enough to make the alarms start clanging. But her voice—the tremor in it—made him sit up and start sharpening his mental knives.

"Did someone hurt you?" *And where is that someone, so I can go beat the crap out of him?*

Iris sighed, still not looking at him. "More like the other way around, though I suppose the pain was mutual."

Blue slid his hand along her cheek, turning her head, forcing her to look at him. Her eyes were so pained. He battled for words—the right words—because Iris was a private woman, and he could not imagine what it was costing her to tell him this.

"Next time," he said gently, "all you need to say is no."

"Next time? You're actually going to let me near you again?"

Blue laughed. He couldn't help himself. The idea was too ridiculous.

A flush crept up Iris's neck—again, he wondered if he had stepped wrong—but then her mouth twitched, the uncertainty in her eyes began to fade, and the shift was so lovely, so unexpected, Blue stopped laughing and whispered, "Goddamn, you're beautiful."

Her breath hitched, but she did not say anything, just stared at him as if it were the first time she had ever received a nice word about anything—and he wanted to kiss her so badly he thought his heart would explode.

But Iris relaxed, her mouth curved into a smile, and she very quietly said, "Compliments will get you everywhere, Blue."

"They don't get *me* everywhere," Fred said, rejoining them. "Your home checks out. I noticed you're missing a fire alarm, though. You ought to get that replaced. It's not safe being without one."

Blue glanced at Iris, waiting for her lead, but all she did was look Fred in the eye and say, "Thanks."

"Sure," he said, but that weird look was back, and Blue did not like it at all. It occurred to him, too, that Fred had never asked for his name. Not once.

"You're an odd FBI agent," Blue said.

"And you've got too many opinions."

"Yeah. Like instead of talking to us, you should be out trying to find the little psycho who threatened Iris."

"Maybe you would care to help? Since you're so … invested in all of this?"

"You're the FBI. I'm a lowly electrician. I think you'll manage, regardless."

Fred smiled, but it didn't reach his eyes. "You and I. Later." Whatever that meant.

The FBI agent walked away. Iris asked, "Is it just me, or do all men hate you?"

Blue laughed. "Only the special ones. I'm a natural asshole repellant."

Iris grinned. A small grin, sweet.

Blue said, "Good. That's good, Iris. You're ready to fight again."

"Is that what a smile means?"

"Sometimes. In my experience people don't smile unless they have something to live for. And I'm talking real smiles, not that fake crap your Agent *Fred* was giving us."

"He did seem a bit plastic this time around." Iris watched the FBI agent start his car and drive away. "Do you think I should have told him about the hidden camera?"

"I think you did just fine."

"There are things I wouldn't want anyone to see."

"I know."

"And if the FBI or police were to find the person who set that camera, if there were tapes, recordings …"

"Yes," Blue said. "You don't want those to get out. You don't have to tell me any more."

"I don't, do I?" Iris's voice was soft, almost wondering. She searched his face. "Why is that, Blue? Aren't you curious?"

"Yes," he said.

"And?"

"And nothing. You'll tell me when you're ready."

Her expression sharpened. Indecision, maybe. Blue sighed. "Iris, you have better things to worry about."

"Yeah." She dug her nails into her palm, pushing and pushing until Blue was afraid she would make herself bleed. "So what do I do? How do I fix this?"

"You don't." Blue took her hand and uncurled her fingers. He rubbed her palm, smoothing out the deep crescent marks her nails had left. "*We* fix it, Iris. Together. I'm a detective, remember? So I'll detect. I'll protect you. I'll help you keep your life the way you want it."

He was afraid to look at her face, to see what was in her eyes, but she was silent for such a long time that he didn't have a choice. He found her staring at him, wide-eyed, her golden gaze glimmering with a soft light.

"I'm afraid to trust you," she said. "I'm afraid you aren't real."

A mask, an illusion—being nice only because he wanted something—that later when the mood struck he would become another man. Weak, petty, hurtful . . .

"I'm not perfect," Blue said. "But I told you, Iris. I like you."

"You like me," she said. "How much do you like me?"

He wanted to laugh again. "I like you enough not to care if you trust me—but I also like you enough to wish that you would."

"You make it sound easy."

"It's not."

"It feels strange. Like I'm doing something dangerous."

"Because you are."

"The most dangerous thing I'll ever do, huh?"

"Maybe. But can you think of the alternative?"

Iris surprised him by laughing. "Not sharing my high heels with you? Sole possession of my closet?"

"What closet?" he asked, grinning. "Personally, I'd like to check that kitchen out again."

Iris ducked her head. "I don't know if that's a good idea, Blue. You know, for us to be together like that."

"I think it's a fantastic idea," he said, touching her chin. "Besides, I'm tough. I bounce."

"Maybe that time," she murmured, then straightened up, looking left. Her eyes grew distant. "Someone's coming. Pete and Daniel."

"Ah," Blue said, wondering if she realized how much she had just given away with that little display of sensational hearing. "Are you getting tired of all the company?"

"Depends." Iris eyed him, and he thought, *Yes, she realizes what she did.*

"Iris," he said, but when he tried to keep going, the words froze in his mouth. What was he going to say? The truth? That he knew what she was? That he had friends who were shape-shifters, that his own humanity stretched a gene or two past the norm? Hell, he hadn't even been able to tell Daniel that they were brothers. This was worse.

"What?" she asked, frowning. "Blue?"

"You're not alone," he said.

She frowned, peering into his eyes. "I know."

"No," he replied. "You really don't."

Pete rounded the corner, Daniel close on his heels. Blue stopped talking. Iris's frown deepened, but when she looked at the newcomers her expression darkened even more.

"Something's wrong," she murmured. "Pete doesn't look happy."

She was right. Pete had a grimace on his face made more pronounced by his sagging jowls, tucked head, and hunched shoulders.

Daniel was far less demonstrative, but there was still a hardness to his face, a cold light in his eyes, that was pure effortless Perrineau. He turned his gaze on Blue, but it was not in the least bit intimidating—no more so than Blue's own face. Blood, after all, was blood. Only, he did not want to think about how much the two of them resembled their father.

Daniel's expression changed when he looked at Iris, softening into concern, melancholy, something that was, to his credit, almost sweet. "Iris," he murmured, but she shook her head, quieting him.

"I'm fine," she said. "How was the press?"

Pete said grimly, "The hotel is furious that you dodged those journalists. They're threatening to dock your pay if you don't play to the rags and cameras, just like we discussed."

"They can dock me all the way to hell, for all I care. I'll quit before they push me around like that."

"They won't fire you and you won't quit," Pete said firmly. "You need the money and they need you. But they can still make you miserable. Better to cooperate a little, soothe the wild beast, if you will. Then negotiate."

"That's not in my vocabulary."

"Liar."

"Hey," Iris protested, and Blue moved close, touching the small of her back.

Pete and Daniel both noticed, and the look Blue's brother gave him was indescribable. Hurt—it hurt Blue's heart so badly he almost winced, and he felt caught up in the surprise that emotion gave him. Surprise that he should feel guilty, as though having his heart full of Iris was committing an act of betrayal.

Pete set his jaw. "Son, I also came here to talk to you, too."

"Something wrong?" Blue asked.

"You could say that." The old man sighed, rubbing his face. "I need you to go. Right now."

Blue stared. "You promised me a day."

"And the day is up. Sun is going down in an hour."

"Pete Reilly," Iris murmured in a hard voice. "What is going on?"

"Business," he said. "*My* business, Iris. And Blue can't be part of it."

His stomach felt hollow, as did his heart. He listened to Pete's words rattle through his head, words that did not match the old man's eyes, which seemed to tell a different story, like *stay*.

Someone got to him. This isn't right. Blue glanced at his brother, but Daniel was also staring at Pete, and he looked just as surprised. Even alarmed.

"You can't fire him," Iris said, and there was a touch of desperation in her voice that Blue did not want to hear, not even for him. "After everything that happened today? The way he helped me? That's ridiculous."

"This is not open for discussion, Iris. He has to go. Don't make it any harder than it has to be."

She began to argue, but Blue touched her shoulder. "Don't beg. Don't. Not for me."

Her eyes flashed with light—quick, breathtaking, a trick of the sun to anyone but Blue—and though she did not kiss him, did not hold him, he felt her spirit lean and lean, as though her shadow were made of electricity, hot, and it was almost too much, more than he could bear.

I want you, he thought, trying to speak with his eyes. *I think I love you.*

"Blue," Pete said. Inexplicable, mysterious Pete, who still looked at him with those soft, sad eyes so at odds with that hard mouth, that cold voice.

"This isn't over," Blue said quietly, but he spoke to Iris, only to Iris, as though nothing existed but her. She nodded grimly, hands rolled into fists. Daniel also watched her.

Blue grabbed the front of his brother's shirt and dragged him close, staring hard into his eyes. "You were right, Daniel. You don't really know me. Not in the slightest. But you take care of her. *You take care of her.* Or else I swear to God I *will* do whatever it is you think I'm capable of—*and I will terrify you.*"

Daniel did not flinch. His gaze did not waver. He nodded once, jaw set, and Blue let him go with a shove.

Everything, gone to hell. That was the story of his life.

Blue looked at Iris. "Kiss Petro for me."

She choked back a laugh, her eyes far too bright. He didn't give her a chance to say anything; his heart couldn't take it. Blue got out of there, fast.

CHAPTER NINE

It was evening in the human desert—this place where hot earth was covered in concrete, steel—and the last blush of day was flung sweetly across the horizon. Iris thought about taking her RV, loading the cats inside—however ill sized it was for them—and rumbling out of town. Going, going, gone. Straight into the sunset, burning up in the sun.

Pete was gone. Back to the hotel, back to some hole, back to a cave where she decided he belonged. No more words. Not to him, ever. He'd refused to give her reasons, refused to say anything at all, and his scent—so tired, sad, and *pained,* so completely at odds with his demeanor—made no sense at all.

Made no sense, like the ache in her heart for a man she barely knew.

This isn't over. Blue's voice was still strong inside her head, strong like the sound of his heartbeat, the lightning in his scent.

She lay flat on her back in the cats' holding pen. Con's head rested heavy on her stomach, while Boudicca curled around her head. Petro lay against her, with Lila draped over his back, eyes half-closed in sleep. *Lazy lions.*

Iris heard a low sigh. Daniel. He sat cross-legged outside

the holding pen, his back against the wire. He hadn't said a word since Blue walked away, just followed her, silent, like a ghost, blue eyes watching her every move. She was too tired, too upset to tell him to go.

But now he sighed again, and very quietly said, "You could have gone with him, Iris."

Easy to say, and thoughtless. Iris could not have just simply left. Blue had known that. He had told her as much—*this isn't over*—and for Daniel to say those words, say them and believe them ...

"You don't know me," she told him. "You don't know me at all."

"I seem to be getting a lot of that. Much more and I could become insecure."

"Don't let Pete know. He might fire you."

"He might anyway. I'm in trouble, Iris."

"You're arrogant," she accused, staring at the darkening sky, the deep blue hue. "That's what your brand of trouble is called."

"Arrogant," Daniel echoed softly. "Yes."

"Yes," she murmured, and then, "Why don't you like Blue, Danny?"

He did not answer. The silence stretched. Iris waited.

"You want dinner?" Daniel finally asked.

Iris almost sat up to look at him. "Danny."

"No," he said firmly. "I don't want to talk about him. Not now. I'm hungry. You must be hungry."

"Danny—"

"It doesn't have to be a date, Iris. I'm not that stupid."

Iris closed her eyes. "You act different, Danny. You're not the same man you were this morning."

He laughed, low. It was not at all humorous. "Danny. You've always called me Danny. But Danny is someone else. Quiet, with a flair for the dramatic. You're talking to Daniel now."

She agreed. But she had to ask: "And who's Daniel?"

"Another question." He said it softly, and the holding pen

creaked as he leaned away and stood. Iris sat up. Con rolled free of her.

Iris looked at Daniel. His face was drawn, tired.

"Dinner?" he asked again, and Iris remembered, very briefly, that she had crushed hard on this man, that she had wanted him once upon a time, and that here, now, he might still be a friend.

"Okay," she said.

Walking through the Miracle hotel—through most hotels in Vegas—made Iris feel like an actress on a movie set. Big decorations, wild lights, flash and glitter and overdone glamour—all wrapped up in elaborate facades hiding cheap construction that was good for nothing but show. Not that anything built on the Strip was meant to last. Not even her, though it was interesting seeing her face—and the cats—on a poster near the front of the lobby. Interesting and disconcerting; her mother had always warned about publicity photos. Disdained them. Iris had never been entirely certain why.

She did a lot of things you didn't understand. Like leaving.

Leaving, leaving, two years gone. Gone, taking none of her clothes, no money—nothing at all—with only a note to mark her passing, and no good explanation. Out for a long run, a hunt, time spent in another body.

The wild is calling, her mother had written. *The wild is calling and I must go.*

Crap. All crap. Iris did not understand it and never would. Only, she remembered that her mother had seemed restless in those weeks building up to her departure; there had been an edge in her eyes every time she looked at Iris. As if she were measuring her, taking stock, identifying and cataloging every strength and weakness with the cold precision that had marked all her mother's actions.

She and Daniel hit the street, the crowds, the stink. Prostitutes crowded the corner, big hair whipped up by the racing cars; around them small, sweaty men aggressively passed out handbills and brochures covered with pictures of naked women. The sidewalk was also plastered in paper, along with whole catalogs and baseball-sized cards: wallpaper, skin paper, sex, sex, sex. Iris thought about the love letter written on flesh, and she gritted her teeth.

People swarmed. The air was dusty, dry. Daniel walked, Iris following. She found herself buffeted, touched, penned in by men and women—entire families with wide-eyed children in tow—assaulted by sights and sounds that overwhelmed her eyes and ears.

There's a reason you never leave the Miracle's premises, Iris reminded herself, and grabbed Daniel's sleeve. "Do we have to walk far?"

Daniel hesitated, studying her face. Without a word he moved to the edge of the sidewalk and hailed a cab. Iris sighed.

The air inside the car smelled like cigarettes and air freshener and cheap cologne. The seats were plastic, sticky. The leopard stirred within her chest, dreaming of the open desert, the mountains, the forests. Of running and running.

Iris did not talk to Daniel as the cab crept through the heavy traffic along the Strip. She thought about Blue and watched the sidewalk, scanning the faces of the men who drifted like ghosts in the neon machine, searching for magic in the cooling night. Hard faces, soft faces, tired faces—all of them dreaming of a good time, a little risk, a piece of something hot to hold and take home.

Never leave Las Vegas empty-handed. Isn't that the whole point?

But when Iris left this place, what was *she* going to take with her? Fame, glory, money? None of that mattered. None of it would last.

And you think Blue will? You think Blue will stick around longer than a bank account full of cash? You think he'll last past the final clap of hands, be willing to go to bed with a woman and wake up with a leopard?

Iris remembered his eyes, the heat of his large hands. The intensity, the passion that had rolled off him like quiet

thunder, clear lightning, surrounding and lifting and drawing
her near.

"We're here," Daniel said. All Iris could see of him was his
profile, standing out strong against flashing red and gold. For
a moment his nose and forehead reminded her of Blue, and
she forced herself to take a deep breath. Not that it helped.
Daniel's scent reminded her of him, too.

God, she was pathetic.

Fremont Street. The entertainment had already started. For
a moment she and Daniel stood like zombies, mouths hanging open as they craned their necks to stare at the light show
exploding against the giant screen suspended above their
heads. Electric lava poured and sizzled, exploding into fireworks, shadows, bursts of night and cosmic rainbow. Music
roared; Iris's hands crept to her ears. She gave up pride and
covered them, wincing. Daniel noticed. They started walking
again.

The casinos and hotels turned off their neon during the
show; the entire street was lit only by the wild lights raging
from ninety feet above. Iris, glancing down at her arms, at the
faces around her, felt bathed in fire.

Restaurants lined the street, but Daniel did not take her
into any of them, instead leading her to the Golden Nugget
Casino. There was a crowd out front; Iris and Daniel had to
push to get through. For a moment she panicked. If she
shifted, if the fur ran wild over her body where everyone
could see ...

"How did you find this place?" Iris asked him.

"Natalya told me about it. She said the steaks are good."

Iris had kept herself sheltered; the Golden Nugget was only
the second hotel and casino she had found herself in since ar-
riving in Las Vegas. The lobby was pale, made of marble—
not quite as grand as the Miracle's. Daniel led her into the
casino, down a carpeted path that followed the edge of the
gambling pit.

The casino looked as though it had been designed for
someone with the tacky taste of a crow: all cheap glitter, gild-

ing and lights, a lure for the eyes and heart, whispering, *Come to me, come to me,* to all the men and women living and dying by the dollar sign. Iris could not understand the attraction of games of chance, the kinds of risks people took with their livelihoods. Money, which was already so hard to earn, was thrown away in bits and pieces and chunks, tossed on tables or into slot machines like lifelines to a sinking ship, lines that would only drag them down and under, them and everyone else who depended on that cold, hard cash.

Daniel did not ask if she wanted to try her hand. That was a point for him, although she was not entirely certain his silence had anything to do with understanding her. He smelled nervous. His eyes kept moving—to the people, the security monitors, the security guards.

"You okay?" she asked him.

"Fine, though I'm beginning to think this was a stupid idea."

"We should be safe here. It's crowded."

"That's part of the problem." He gave her sharp look. "I'm sorry, Iris. I forgot how much you dislike these places. We can go if you want."

She sighed. "We're here. Let's just try and make the best of it."

But by the time they reached the restaurant, nestled on the other end of a long and rambling walk through a ringing casino maze, Iris was not in the mood to eat. Daniel was still too quiet, the discordance of his scent putting her on edge. She also missed Blue.

You still don't know him. Not really.

And yet, he always smelled the same as his words. Scents never lied, while it amazed her just how many people did, and over the smallest things. Blue, however, had never shown one side of his face and then exuded another—no wolf in sheep's clothing was he. He was holding back, yes— she could read that as easy as breathing—but the irony of it was that in his own way he was still straightforward. Even if most of his life was still a mystery, he made her feel as though she knew him better than almost anyone—a heart knowl-edge, a gut instinct, a tiny voice whispering *yes, he's the one.*

Iris knew she had a funny way of showing that. Knocking him across the room, running away to have a nervous break-down? Acting like a terrified idiot, because she really was just that frightened?

Very romantic. A sure sign you guys will last.

The Golden Nugget's restaurant had nice clean lines and dark wood details, neutrals everywhere—probably to make up for the crass exterior.

Iris had her own deal with the Miracle management when it came to her food: meal tickets for the buffet anytime she wanted to eat there, fresh fruits and vegetables from the chefs themselves at the restaurants. It wasn't just charity; there was simply too much food.

The air smelled like grease and beer. The line to get in was long, and even though Daniel had reservations, the hostess directed them to the bar to wait while a table was found and cleaned for them. The bar was not Iris's idea of predinner re-laxation. Too many people, and the air was hot. Men jostled her, covered her in their scents. Gazes dipped to her breasts. Mouths smiled.

Iris managed not to kick anyone in the testicles. Daniel gave her the only seat available, angling in beside her so that he could lean against the slick counter. There was a TV above the bar. CNN was on, which did not seem like good television to get drunk by, though Iris knew she wasn't much of an ex-pert on the subject. Everyone else appeared to be enjoying themselves.

"What would you like?" Daniel signaled the bartender.

"A Coke would be fine. Nothing special in it." A drunk shape-shifter, after all, was not a smart shape-shifter. She had enough trouble controlling herself when she got excited.

Daniel ordered himself a beer. He traced circles in the pol-ished countertop while they waited for their drinks. Outside, slot machines dinged in discordant symphony while the low murmur of voices, drunk and sober, rose and fell, rose and fell—that was the heartbeat of the city, which also had a scent: cash, excitement, arousal, desperation. Harsh, rough smells—they would never get prettier or gentler, no matter how nicely Las Vegas dazzled her eyes.

"You get out often?" Iris asked Daniel, unsure what else to say, knowing only that the silence was heavy, awkward. This was not supposed to be a date, but it sure as hell felt like one. Not that she had any experience. *Face it. You're twenty-four years old and you might as well have been raised in a nunnery.*

Yeah, some nun.

"This is the first time I've been away from the circus since we got here," Daniel said.

"It's been months, Danny. You're worse than I am."

He smiled, still tracing circles. "I was just getting my feet under me. I had a lot to think about. I didn't much feel like exploring."

Their drinks arrived in glass steins large enough to drown in. Iris hefted her Coke and toasted him. "Here's to getting out and getting a life."

"How about just keeping the life we've got?" Daniel smiled, rueful. "I'd give a lot just for that."

"Things change," she said, thinking about her own life. "Maybe you don't want them to, but that's the way it is."

Daniel sipped his beer, watching her over the rim of his glass. Iris felt uneasy meeting his eyes—too intense, too much scrutiny.

"You're in love with him," he said. "Blue."

Iris shook her head, cheeks flaming. "No."

A sad smile tugged on his mouth. "It's okay if you are."

"This from the person who hated Blue from the very beginning."

"Yes," he agreed. "I hated him. I'm not sure what I feel anymore, though. Jealous, maybe?"

Iris shook her head. "It's no secret you both know each other. Care to explain?"

"He didn't tell you?"

"I didn't press. And I'm not going to press you, either."

"You're too nice, Iris."

"Not particularly." She smiled and sipped her soda. "So, Blue?"

"We're strangers," Daniel said. "And that *is* the truth. I just . . . happened to know *of* him, that's all."

"His reputation precedes him?"

"Something like that."

"He told me he's a detective."

Daniel nodded, his scent spiking with tension. "I knew that."

Iris stared, clarity hitting her so hard she almost gasped. "Oh, my. He was looking for you, wasn't he? He was sent here for *you*. That's why you started talking about your family."

Daniel grimaced. "Iris . . . he *is* my family."

She almost dropped her glass. Daniel's hand shot out, steadying it, but soda still sloshed over both their wrists. She tried to talk, but her voice would not work. Daniel's face reddened. He grabbed some napkins and dabbed her hand.

"Sorry," he muttered. "I should have guessed that would take you off guard."

"No shit," she snapped. "What are you? Brothers?"

"Half-brothers." Daniel shrugged, not meeting her eyes. "This is the first time we've ever been within spitting range of each other."

Iris slumped against the bar counter. "I can't believe this."

"I couldn't believe it when I saw him," Daniel muttered darkly. "The only reason I recognized Blue is that our father likes keeping pictures of him around to taunt me."

Iris raised her eyebrows. "Taunt you?"

"It's a game my father plays. He likes to make people feel like shit."

"And pictures of Blue would do that?"

"It's not the pictures. It's the fact that my father uses them as a constant reminder of my . . . inferiorities."

She needed something stronger than soda. "What is *that* supposed to mean?"

"Everything, anything." Daniel shrugged, shoving his glasses up his nose. "I don't think Blue has any idea. As far as I know, the old man never had anything to do with him."

Iris closed her eyes. Brothers. Daniel and Blue were brothers. Which . . . made sense, in an odd sort of way. Or at least, it explained the similarities of their scents, and how every now and then she thought they resembled one another.

"Wow," she breathed. "How much weirder is this day going to get?"

Daniel bit back a short laugh. "I'm afraid to find out."

So was Iris. "Have you talked to Blue about this?"

"No. We've been . . . dancing around each other."

"More like ripping each other to pieces."

"Given our family, you don't know how appropriate that really is."

"O-kay," Iris said. "Do you at least know *why* he's here?"

"I thought I did. Now I'm not so sure. He's not what I expected."

"No," she murmured. "He's not."

That same sad smile flitted over his face. "Again, love."

"I don't love him. I barely know him."

"I've watched you for months, Iris. You're funny, sweet, probably the most delightful, talented, woman I've ever met, but you don't go out, you don't have any close friends, and you never *touch* anyone. Never, not even by accident."

"I'm not the huggy-feely type. So sue me."

"This goes beyond huggy-feely, Iris. At first I thought you had a phobia, but after awhile I realized that you were just . . . closed off. So used to being alone you couldn't even think of the alternative. Not that I'm criticizing you. I'm the same way. Just . . . not quite as extreme."

"Thanks," she said dryly.

Daniel shrugged. "Types like us . . . it takes something special to bring us out of our shells. We're too used to being on our own. Maybe too afraid of what will happen if we're not.

So when I see you with Blue, touching *him,* letting him touch *you . . ."* He looked at her, eyebrows raised. "Red flag, Iris. Big screaming red flag."

"You make it sound as though I'm doing something wrong."

"No." He shook his head. "Not wrong. What's wrong is that you can't even admit out loud that you like him."

"I *do* like him. I probably like him more than you do."

"Probably," Daniel muttered. "Question is, what are you going to do about it? What are you going to give yourself *permission* to do?"

Iris narrowed her eyes. "I don't like it when people psychoanalyze me, Danny. It requires a level of arrogance that I don't much appreciate. And, frankly, my feelings toward Blue are none of your business. *Really."*

"Arrogant is my middle name, Iris. And I'm not psychoanalyzing you. I'm just thinking out loud."

"For your benefit or mine?"

"Both."

"So we have issues. We have trouble trusting people. Big deal, Danny. Why are we even talking about this?"

"Because Blue is the one person we both can't stop thinking about." His mouth curved, bitter and wry. "The one person we can't ignore. And if neither of us can scratch together the balls to confront what his presence does to us, then we're both screwed."

Iris looked down at her drink. "You're being melodramatic."

"I'm feeling melodramatic." Daniel slid his empty beer bottle away from him. "But I'm right and you know it. I was raised to hate him, and the fact that I don't, not anymore, feels wrong. Like I can't trust myself."

"Because you're afraid he'll hurt you," she said. "Or that you'll hurt him. And you don't know whether or not to trust the way you've been raised, or what your heart is telling you."

"Poetic." Daniel's hand inched toward hers. "You can never plan the future by the past."

"And why would you want to?" Iris added, hesitating for

one long moment before patting his hand. The contact was brief, his answering smile soft.

"I waited too long to ask you out," he said. "But even if I had, you probably would have said no."

"Hard to say," Iris told him. "And I'm still not convinced about Blue."

"Neither am I. Our father has enough charm to convince angels they should be devils, and if Blue is anything like *him*, he'll get what he came for and then leave you. Build you up and tear you down until all that's left is a shell, until even your memories of the life you had before will hurt so bad you might just take a razor to your wrists rather than deal with the living anymore. Men like him—like our father—do that to women like you. They do *not* know how to love."

"Jesus." Iris looked at him, horrified. "Take some happy pills, will you?"

"Sorry. I'm just saying, that's all."

"Right." Iris pushed her drink away. "Thanks for the lovely night. I think I'll skip dinner."

"Wuss," he said, but that was all. His gaze, already roving everywhere but her, settled on the television—and froze.

Iris turned to look. All she saw was a photograph, the face of a man who, even aged and weathered, was strikingly handsome. He had a strong gaze, deep-set eyes that were piercing and blue. Beneath his picture was a date of death, a headline that mentioned heart failure and loss and how the world would grieve.

Maybe some parts of the world. Not the one Iris was from. She had no idea who that man was.

But Daniel did. She could see it in his face. His expression was terrible, awful—shell-shocked and twisted and pale.

"Danny," she murmured, but he did not seem to hear. On the television a journalist appeared. She said a name—Felix Perrineau—and spoke about a funeral that had taken place just yesterday, rattling off an impressive list of attendees that included celebrities, business moguls, and one former president. More talking heads appeared, commentators, all of whom smiled like nasty little sharks as they began the distasteful discussion of the old man's wealth, how Mr. Perrineau's considerable estate would be distributed, and how all those assets were destined to fall upon the young shoulders of his only child, a son only recently discovered, a son that no one knew about, and who could not be reached for comment.

None of which explained why Daniel seemed so torn up over some dead rich guy. But as she watched the television, marveling at CNN's bombastic journalism (wondering, too, what those talking heads would think of *her* secrets), the network showed a photograph of Felix Perrineau's son and heir ... and he looked exactly like Daniel. *Exactly* like him.

"Oh," Iris breathed. "Oh, my God."

"Shit," Daniel said. *"Shit."*

He looked stricken, horrified. Iris tried to reach out to him, but this time he was the one who flinched, shying away like a child expecting a hard blow. He hunched his shoulders, his glasses sliding down his nose, trying to hide, to become less of himself.

He smelled like fear. He smelled like pain. He smelled like all those things that would have sent Iris running had it been any other man. Breakdown coming, crazy on the street. Not good. Not good at all.

Speak of the devil, Iris thought, recalling all they had just discussed. What terrible timing.

"I'm sorry," Daniel mumbled, still staring at the television. "I haven't watched the news. I haven't read any papers...." He stopped, looking at Iris. "My father is dead. I can't believe it. That son of a bitch is gone."

"Danny," she murmured, but he squeezed shut his eyes and shook his head. His shoulders shuddered. *Tears,* thought Iris, and Daniel did begin to cry. But instead of sobs—instead of something broken—

He began to laugh.

It took a moment for Iris's brain to register the truth. It was too unexpected, utterly bizarre. Daniel clapped his hands over his mouth, and still he could not swallow the sound that bubbled out of his throat. Hysterical—he was close to hysterics—but the laughter was real. Painfully, astonishingly real.

Iris said his name. Daniel stumbled away. People were watching them now. Iris wondered whether, if everyone recognized him, that would be a bad thing.

She tried to follow, but Daniel shook his head. His hands fell away from his mouth, clenching into fists that he jammed against his stomach. Beneath her the floor began to vibrate— the glasses on the counter rattled. Iris braced herself as the shaking worsened. People cried out, afraid.

Iris was not afraid. She watched Daniel, a vein standing out on his forehead as he stared into her eyes. She felt as if she were observing a ceiling descend upon him—a great crushing pressure.

Slowly, slowly, the tremors eased.

"I'm sorry," Daniel whispered hoarsely. "I'm so sorry, Iris."

"No," she said, but it was too late. He turned and ran, barreling his way through the crowd; reckless, almost violent. Iris tried to follow—made it as far as the slot machines—but a strong hand shot out of nowhere and fastened around her arm, hauling back so hard she staggered. Breathless, startled by the strength of that grip, Iris turned.

The man holding her was small, dark, and very familiar.

"My love," he said, smiling. "It is time."

CHAPTER TEN

Las Vegas, burning in neon. Blue's brain felt as if it were on fire as he leaned against a narrow strip of wall beneath the striped turquoise awning and facade of the Horseshoe Casino. His right leg buckled—just slightly—and he slid down into a loose crouch that offered more psychological rest than anything real. Blue wanted to stretch on the sidewalk, cool his body and aching head, but this was Fremont Street, downtown, not as free or gritty as the Strip, and he could already feel the nearby police watching him from the corners of their eyes.

So he just sat, head down, surveying from under his eyelashes the crowded entrance of the Golden Nugget, situated in all its brass glory directly across from him on the other side of the packed pedestrian walkway. He tried not to think about how much he needed a soft bed, some shut-eye—a good long rest away from anything more powerful than a battery.

You stay here much longer and your shields will buckle.

Tough luck. Two weeks ago, before the bomb, this wouldn't have been a problem. But that blast, the lingering pain inside his head . . .

Iris.

Blue gritted his teeth. He could barely see the Golden

Nugget's doors through the crowds, most of whom were waiting for the light show to begin again on the Viva! Vision screen arched above them. Twelve million lights, hundreds of thousands of watts, all pounding like jackhammers against his skull. The casinos were little better; the Horseshoe and the Golden Nugget felt like volcanoes ready to explode: fire into electricity, electricity into the inferno, burning, burning.

The power spoke to him; just one touch, one whisper of desire. One thought, and the world would go dark. Las Vegas, dead.

Do it. Do it and see what it feels like to bring a city to its knees.

Blue shifted uncomfortably. A nearby elderly couple glanced at him, gazes turning uneasy before they looked away and pushed through the crowd. He wondered what they saw in his face, and decided that he didn't want to know. There was a darkness in him tonight, a hard edge that had been getting sharper and sharper ever since he'd left Iris, and he could taste its bitterness on his tongue like blood.

No, he told himself, battling the old edge of temptation. *You have to keep others safe. Above all else, do that.*

Because he did not want to live with the price of his self-indulgence, did not want to be a person who felt entitled to wreak havoc simply because he could. Great power, great responsibility, and all that crap. Nor did he want to waste a lifetime cultivating his control, only to give it up because … because …

You want to know what it's like to be your father. Ruthless, without conscience. A perfect cunning ego. If he had your gifts …

God help them all. Disgusted, Blue pushed away that thought and focused on the Golden Nugget. He wondered if he should go in. Iris and Daniel had recently disappeared inside that place, and though he knew his brother was certainly capable of protecting her—and that she was more than able to take care of herself—not being able to see Iris was beginning to drive him a little bit crazy. It had been hard enough getting his cabdriver to follow them in the heavy traffic on the Strip—hard, too, for Blue to keep his distance when trailing them both on foot—but this, now, being so close …

He had set out to catch Santoso if he returned to the Miracle, and what he had caught instead was Daniel and Iris. Going out on that date she had told him about.

And so what if she is? You don't have any say over her life.

Maybe not, but he had a say over his own—and at the moment, it was completely devoted to keeping her safe.

As for his brother …

The crowd surged; cameras flashed, and tourists craned their necks, chatting in different languages as they continued to stare at the darkened screen, waiting. Blue heard the faint ding of slot machines, the tinkle of some carousel melody, and above that, closer, he also heard someone playing the guitar: a rendition of an old Elvis song, the music delicately plucked and drifting lightly through the air. Sweet notes on a hard street.

He smelled perfume, too. A very familiar perfume.

A gun pressed hard and cold behind Blue's head, while a long golden thigh pushed tight against his shoulder. Pressing his body into the wall. Hiding the weapon.

"You are such an odd man," said a familiar voice. "So very odd."

"No odder than you," Blue replied, slowly tilting his head. The woman standing beside him had changed her appearance; she had long, dark hair now, scraggly, which fell over a loose wrinkled T-shirt covered in old stains. Her shorts were baggy, her tennis shoes well-used. She wore a black fanny pack. And, of course, sunglasses.

"Nice disguise," Blue said.

"I'm a wanted woman," she replied. "One of Santoso's men recognized you today and placed a phone call from the jail. I barely escaped with my life."

"And yet you're still here."

The gun pushed harder against his skull. "Maybe I wanted to punish you for coming between me and my job."

"If your job is to be an assassin, you're lousy at it."

"And you are terrible at small talk." The woman sighed. "And at running."

"I don't give up."

"No," she murmured. "None of you do."

"And what does *that* mean?"

"It means that you and your ... agency ... have a reputation, Mr. Perrineau. Not a bad reputation by any means, but one that demonstrates a certain degree of ... naïveté."

"Naïveté." Blue shook his head, smiling grimly. "You seem to know quite a bit about everything, don't you?"

"I make it my business."

"And is it your business to spy on men like Santoso?"

The woman did not reply. Her body still shielded the gun pressed to his head; cops stood nearby, but Blue had no intention of asking for their help. He was too intrigued. He said, "If you know about the agency, if you know anything about me, then you must be aware of the fact that we don't hurt people. You can trust us. You can trust me. We can work together."

"You're a fool," said the woman, though not unkindly. "A fool to say such things and believe them. You know nothing about your agency."

"Then enlighten me," he said, anger creeping up his throat. "Throw me a line, a word, something that would be helpful. Give me your name, even, instead of acting so goddamn superior about everything you know that I don't."

"Temper," she murmured, but her hand shifted and the gun disappeared. She leaned close, the tips of her dark synthetic hair brushing the top of his head. "You want Santoso, but he is nothing but a cog in a machine, and like a machine, he was made to order. Everything he is, all that he has become, was given to him. He has earned *nothing*."

"You're saying he's just a figurehead?"

"A very dangerous figurehead. He has come to the United States with orders to expand his operation, to find new ... investors."

"And has he?"

"Yes," said the woman quietly. "Oh, yes."

Blue studied her mouth, the curve of her jaw. Everything else was hidden by hair and sunglasses. "You were sent to find out who he works for, weren't you?"

"It took me years to earn his trust," she said softly. "Many sacrifices. And because of you . . ."

She stopped. Blue said, "You could have let me die."

"Yes," she replied, and looked away toward the Golden Nugget. Her shoulders stiffened. "Stand up. Now, Mr. Perrineau."

Blue did as she asked, following the line of her sight. He bit back a shout when he saw Daniel standing in front of the casino, shoulders hunched, face red, looking as lost as a little boy.

Iris was not with him.

"Fuck," he muttered, and began to move. The woman grabbed his arm. Her fingers felt like steel; her grip hurt.

"Why is he there?" she whispered harshly. "Did he go alone?"

"No," Blue said grimly, still watching his brother. "No, he brought a friend."

The woman made a low sound, almost a groan, and it was so unlike her polished, deadly poise, Blue turned his head to stare. She was looking away from him, at Daniel, and something came over him—screaming instinct. He reached out and ripped off her sunglasses.

The woman flinched, meeting his gaze. Her eyes were the color of gold. Not even human, but cut with split irises. Cat eyes.

"Oh," Blue breathed, and then he saw more than her eyes: the curve of her face, the height of her cheekbones, and he remembered, too, the way she had stared at Iris as she danced on that stage.

Her mouth pressed into a hard white line—a stubborn expression, identical to one Blue had already seen on a much younger woman. She held out her hand. Blue dropped the sunglasses into her palm and she slid them slowly over her eyes.

Cold, quiet, she said, "Santoso is in the Golden Nugget. I followed him here. And you say Daniel brought a *friend*?"

Again Blue tried to move. The woman's grip did not weaken, but she leaned close and in a voice so deadly it made the hairs on his neck curl, she said, "Take care of your brother. Iris is mine."

And then she was gone, running light as air through the crowds, straight toward the entrance of the Golden Nugget. Blue followed her, watching as she reached Daniel and grabbed the front of his shirt. The young man had no time to react—she was too fast, swinging him around like a broom twirling on its bristles, throwing him hard and fast into Blue's arms.

The two men went down, crashing into tourists, spilling themselves and everyone around them onto the hard ground. Blue's body screamed—fireworks exploded in his vision— but he tried to stand and found his brother still sprawled on top of him.

"You son of a bitch," Blue growled, kicking Daniel away. "You *left* her."

But that was all he had time for. Men in suits appeared outside the Golden Nugget; one look was enough to tell Blue that they weren't just local security. They had the same cold eyes as the men who had ambushed Daniel and tried to take Iris—the same uniform, the same bodies. Thugs, picked with image and temperament in mind, like warhorses or hunting dogs. They smiled when they saw Blue and Daniel, like they were sniffing a prize.

Blue clambered to his feet. He saw police pushing through the crowd; Santoso's men saw them, too. They edged sideways, fingers flexing. Around them music boomed; the Viva! Vision screen flickered to life over their heads, colors dancing. Daniel also stood, staring at the men.

"Hey," said one of the thugs, ambling close, unmindful of

the approaching police, the people around them. "Hey, rich boy. You going to come easy?"

"Um, *no.*" Daniel's cheeks were wet: tears, maybe. He glanced at Blue. "This isn't your doing, is it?"

"We're on the same side, you asshole."

"Right. Like you can blame me for asking."

"Hey," said the thug.

"Of course I can blame you," Blue snapped. "Have I done *anything* to hurt you? Anything at all?"

"Not yet," Daniel muttered.

The thug rolled his eyes. "Fine, bullets."

"Whatever," Blue said. The men in suits began closing in, hands reaching under their jackets for guns. The police were not far behind them, but apparently, no one cared. This was going to get very ugly.

"Daniel." Blue steadied himself "Do you feel like saving yourself?"

"I love these trick questions. What do you need me to do?"

"Push." Blue said, and dropped his shields.

The lights went out.

If Iris had not been standing in the middle of a gaming pit filled to the brim with an unending array of security cameras and regular people just out for a night of fun, she might have thrown caution to the wind, given the leopard screaming inside her chest a chance at blood, and taken the drastic measure of ripping out the heart of the man in front of her and shoving it down his throat.

Unfortunately, the timing was off. Her entire life was swirling down the drain.

"We really need to stop meeting like this," she said. "I'm going to start thinking that you're stalking me."

The man's grip tightened. "Stalking is an ugly word. I prefer to call this … an acquisition."

"That's not much better," Iris said. "Really."

The man smiled. "The disquieting future. It is the same for

us all, I assure you. The unknown can be such a ... startling thing."

The crowd momentarily thinned. The casino floor stretched in every direction, glittering with golden chandeliers and neon. In front of the slot machines, women lounged on their animal-print stools, hair limp and eyes bleary. Behind them, ranged in a loose circle, stood men in suits. They smelled like cigarettes and dirty underwear, and their eyes were dark and cold.

"Making a scene would be a poor idea," said the man. "You would like to scream, I know that. Scream and cry foul and bring security upon all our heads."

"Is there a reason I shouldn't?"

"Of course." He snapped his fingers, and one of his thugs stepped forward with a very large briefcase in his hands; black, leather, and boxy. Iris was surprised that no one had stopped them to make certain there wasn't a bomb inside. The case smelled odd, too. Like blood.

The crowd was still thin; no one was near them. The rest of the suited men stepped close, forming a lose circle as the lid popped open with a click. The scent that rushed over Iris made her gag; she turned her head, but the case followed her, begging for a look.

She saw a head. Human, blond, familiar ... and very detached.

"Kevin Cray." The man drew out the name, tasting it. "My sources discovered that he was going to sue you for assault. I thought I would ... head him off ... before he caused you any trouble."

The briefcase lid slammed shut. Iris snarled, wrenching her arm away. The man let go, but only just; she felt movement all around her, a wall closing in, a living cage. The scents of filth and smoke overwhelmed, along with something colder, like bleach, and the leopard uncurled inside her chest, whispering *fight*.

"Tell me your name," she said to the man, feeling her body shift inside her: a shift of spirit but not flesh, quiet and invisible.

"Only for you, *Layak*," he said softly. "My name is Santoso."

"Santoso," she murmured. "You are a very bad man."

"I know," he said, swaying close. "Oh, I know."

It was the Golden Nugget casino; a public place, filled with people, security, cameras. Iris opened her mouth to scream—

—and saw a woman pass beneath the arch from the lobby. A woman with long dark hair, sunglasses, a baggy shirt, a sharp jaw, long, tanned legs—and Iris felt inside her body a pulse like the boom of thunder, a boom without sound that rippled through her bones like water. Everything around her stopped. Santoso stopped. The men behind him stopped. The casino froze in midglitter, cutting dry and silent inside her head. The world, gone gray to ash, and the only thing that existed was that woman, who slowly, slowly removed her glasses.

Mom, Iris thought, heart pounding. *Mommy.*

Time kicked in—color, movement—and Iris, stunned and breathless, watched as Serena McGillis ran straight toward her, full-tilt, high-speed, a leopard racing, into thin air.

Santoso turned, began to say a word—

—and the lights went out. Screams filled the air, cries of confusion, but Iris's night vision kicked in, and she slammed a fist into Santoso's face, knocking him flat on his ass. He cried out, rolling, but when Iris tried to jump over his body he shocked her by grabbing her ankle and holding on tight.

She tried to shake him loose, was ready to take off his hand if she had to—but Iris suddenly smelled perfume, familiar, and a warm body pressed close. Tears burned her eyes.

"Baby," murmured her mother. Iris heard a ripping sound and Santoso cried out, letting go of her ankle. Her mother grabbed her hand, pulled ...

The air cracked with gunfire. Serena fell. Iris screamed—a silent, hissing scream, because her throat locked up—like a child too terrified to cry out, to squeak—and something sharp pierced her neck. Heat rolled down her spine. She turned and lost her balance, staggering to one knee. Iris smelled blood, perfume, saw her mother lying very still on the casino carpet.

Iris crumpled, fell, and she could smell her mother beneath the perfume, warm and real and soft as sun and honey.

A boot slammed into Iris's shoulder. Hot breath whistled against her ear.

"You are mine," Santoso whispered.

Iris felt another prick, this time in her arm, and the world disappeared.

Downtown Las Vegas was a beautiful place when all the lights were off. The world fell silent inside Blue's head—a sweet silence, punctuated by very human screams and gasps—and though his eyes were blind, inside his mind he felt a soaring rush that brought him higher and higher, light enough to fly.

"Daniel," Blue said, and a moment later he heard a series of hard grunts and thuds. His vision began to adjust; he felt his brother beside him.

"Done," Daniel said breathlessly. "Those men are down."

"Good," Blue replied, listening to the police shout orders to stay calm. Flashlights blinked to life, but he let them stay on. He wanted the cover of darkness, but it was unnecessary to be completely medieval.

He ran toward the hotel, sending his mind ahead of him, flicking on a light here, there, enough to travel by. He heard his name, and a moment later Daniel appeared at his side.

"What the hell is going on?" Daniel asked as they careened through the Golden Nugget's darkened marble lobby, side-stepping disoriented and frightened men and women.

"Iris," Blue said. "You left her alone inside a nest of vipers."

"She was in a public place."

"Public doesn't mean shit to the man stalking her. I *told* you to take care of her." Blue swung around, grabbing the front of Daniel's shirt. The moment he touched his brother the air around him thickened; his grip weakened and his fingers were forced away.

"Don't touch me," Daniel whispered. "Don't you ever raise a hand to me. I was patient the first time, but I swear to God I'll break your bones if you do it again. Even if we are family."

"You know who I am." Blue gritted his teeth. "You knew the first time you saw me. And you didn't say a word."

"Neither did you."

"I had my reasons."

"So did I. Because I knew you were here to hurt me, to take me home. But I was wrong, wasn't I? He's dead. He's dead and I didn't know. I just found out—"

"No," Blue interrupted, because the truth was out—and he was not going to betray his brother. He was not going to lie. "No, Daniel. He's not dead. Not even close."

Daniel stared, confusion quickly transforming into a narrow, biting rage that turned the blue of his eyes unfathomably cold. "Son of a bitch. That bastard set me up."

"He set us both up," Blue said. He heard sirens outside the lobby, flinched, remembering Iris, and found himself able to move again.

He and Daniel ran into the casino. Nothing but chaos remained, shouts and cries and whimpers. Most of the people inside the Golden Nugget had been at the slot machines or tables when the lights went off; those trying to get out had succeeded only in trampling one another.

Guilt was a bitch. Blue turned on some more lights.

But when he did, the first thing his saw made his balls shrivel and his vision blur: a woman on the floor, a woman with long dark hair and red staining the front of her shirt. Her sunglasses were gone.

Blue raced to her side, falling hard on one knee. Pain radiated up his leg, but he swallowed it down and felt for a pulse. He found one, strong and steady, and the woman's eyes fluttered open, catlike and golden.

"Iris," she said.

"Daniel," Blue snapped. "Help me get her out of here."

"Iris," she said again, trying to sit up. "Santoso took her."

"Don't move," he growled, trying to hold her down. "Daniel!"

"Go to hell," she muttered, and slammed the heel of her palm into his face. Blue tumbled backward and she sprang away from him, staggering into a run. Daniel chased her— and Blue, feeling as if he were going to vomit, did the same.

The woman headed away from the main lobby, racing the gauntlet of people and machines, moving like a dancer as she dodged fights that spilled out in front of her. The gaming tables were a mess; chips had been looted during the blackout, and hotel security was playing cops and robbers—too busy protecting money to notice that a woman had been shot and another kidnapped.

Iris's mother, Blue thought, watching blood fleck to the dark carpet as she sprinted across the casino. Iris's mother, the shape-shifter. Who had been hired to spy on and infiltrate Santoso Rahardjo's business. Who had blown Blue up in an Indonesian slum. Who had stuck a gun in his face and kissed him.

Shit.

He sent his mind ahead, looking for watches, phones— any self-contained group traveling in a tight pack. Nothing notable. There were too many people packed into a very small space, and his luck did not change as he followed the buzz of currents beyond the confines of the casino, out into the street.

Police raced past. Sirens wailed. Iris's mother ran to the very edge of the sidewalk, looking as if she were going to throw herself under the wheels of a car. Daniel reached out to pull her back, but Iris's mother stopped before he could touch her. Blue heard his brother bite back a gasp as she turned and fixed him with a cold, inhuman stare.

"You lost my daughter," she whispered. "You left her."

Blue stepped in front of Daniel. "He couldn't have known. If anyone deserves the blame, it's me."

The woman's lips pulled back in snarl, but she whipped away from them and yanked off her wig, dropping it to the ground. Her short blond hair was sweat-soaked, plastered to her head, and she ran her fingers through it as she crouched low to the sidewalk, taking a few steps and then coming back.

"The scent ends here," she said, and there was a break in her voice, a cut, as though something other than her body were bleeding out, and though Blue saw nothing of that emotion in her face he could see her body quiver, the fight go out, and he knew that she was dying on the inside.

"You need a hospital," Daniel said to her, unable to stop staring at her eyes.

"No hospital." Her fingers fluttered over her wound, which was drawing considerable attention from passersby. "My blood."

Daniel frowned, but Blue understood. Shape-shifter blood could not possibly be the same as human, and if anyone examined her, even looked into her eyes, which seemed unable to shift to human ...

Blue hailed a cab. As the car pulled up, Iris's mother moved back from the road and shook her head.

"I have no time for this," she said, and began walking down the sidewalk, moving quickly though not very steadily.

"Daniel," Blue said. "We need her with us. Now."

"I wish I knew why," he muttered, but a moment later Iris's mother stopped and turned. Her movements were jerky—like a robot or a zombie—and it was clear she was doing her best to fight, because when she finally took a step her entire body leaned backward at an impossible angle: a limbo queen on the streets of Las Vegas, lurch, lurch, lurching her way right back to them. Her face screwed up into a snarl. She looked crazy, dangerous, and the blood covering her did nothing to help. People shied away. Some of them reached for their cell phones. Blue shut those off.

"You and I need to talk about this," Daniel said, voice strained.

"Now isn't the time."

"It sure as hell is. What is going on?"

"I have a better question. Why aren't you surprised that I know you're a telekinetic?"

"I don't know what you're talking about," he muttered darkly.

"Funny. I suppose you're going to tell me you *aren't* forcing a woman to walk to us against her will, using nothing but your fucking mind. Or maybe you would care to explain why you didn't hesitate to use that mind—with me, with her, with those thugs out on Fremont Street, *or* in front of hundreds of people *on a goddamn stage*. Those are some balls you've got there, Daniel. Or trust."

"It's not trust," Daniel said, glancing at him. "I just don't give a shit."

The cab was still waiting. Iris's mother finally rejoined them, mouth curled in a snarl. Blue leaned close, savoring for one moment her helplessness, her immobility—because yes, whatever her reasons or relations, payback was a bitch—and said, "I am going to find your daughter or die trying, and if I have to play dirty to get you to help me, then by God, I will. So don't you fucking mess with me, Ms. McGillis, or I will pull a bomb out of my ass and take you apart, just like you did to me. You got that?"

"I have it," she said in hard voice. "Just as you have the knowledge that if we fail, I *will* take your life."

Blue clenched his jaw so tight he thought his teeth would explode through his nose. "Fine, I agree. Now get in the cab."

"Make me," she said.

So he did—with Daniel's help—unceremoniously dumping her stiff body into the backseat of the taxi. The driver ignored them, staring resolutely at his battered wheel. *No trouble here, no sirree.*

"Ms. McGillis?" Daniel hissed, but Blue pointed and his brother shut his mouth, dodging traffic to climb in on the other side of the car. Blue jumped in on the woman's right. "Where would Santuso take her?"

She bared her teeth. "We are not equipped to fight them."

"We can get equipped." Blue reached for his cell phone. "Tell me where."

"No. You want my help, we do this my way."

"Now who's wasting time?"

"Do you want to live or die?" She stared hard into his eyes. "The question is easy, Mr. Perrineau. What do you value more? Your life, or death by pride?"

"Blue," Daniel said. "How does she know—"

"You are a fool," she snapped at Daniel. "Both of you brothers, and fools." She slid down the seat and stared at the cabdriver. Her body smelled like blood; her T-shirt glistened with it, clinging to her lean body. She pressed her palm over the wound.

"Tell him to take us to the airport," she breathed. "I have a car there, waiting."

"And then?" Blue asked, sinking into the dark place, old memories resurrecting like zombies to kiss his soul.

She bared her teeth. "We kill."

Chapter Eleven

Iris lost herself in blood, inside a dream of darkness where her mother lay dead and decayed, a river pouring from her chest into a wood where leopards ran. Blue was there, running beside her in the darkness, his heartbeat making thunder without sound, and there was fire all around, burning, bound, holding her tight—

Iris opened her eyes. It took a moment to remember herself; the world was hazy, full of shadows cut by candlelight, the air heavy with the scent of beeswax, marijuana, cigarette smoke. Beneath her, silk. She tried to move, but her body refused. Not weariness, but tight bands around her ankles and wrists. She smelled iron. Listened to the clink of metal.

Chains. She was wearing chains. Large chains, shining, heavy as sin. But for a moment it did not matter. All Iris could think about was her mother, and the memory was a nightmare, an endless roll of sight and sound, the tactile impression of her mother's hand on her wrist, her voice saying, *Baby,* and the crack of that gun. The smell of blood.

Not dead. She can't be dead.

Iris refused to believe it. Her mother was a fighter—strong, fast—and a bullet, one bullet, would not be enough to stop her.

But if that's the case, then she might be nearby. Santoso might have taken her, too.

Iris raised her head, wiping her eyes. Movement flickered on her right; she turned her head and saw a diaphanous curtain, sheer fabric billowing as it was pushed aside.

A woman appeared. Iris thought she might be young, but it was hard to tell. Twenty going on forty, perhaps. Her eyebrows were nothing but lines, her skin heavy with a thick foundation that only made black eyeliner and bright red lipstick look cheap, tired, and old. The girl had stringy brown hair, a lazy gaze, and a lazy smile. She held a joint in one hand.

She was also naked. Glitter dusted her entire body.

"Hey," she said softly. "Hey, you finally woke up."

Iris yanked on the chains. "What the hell is this? Where am I?"

"King's palace." The girl started laughing. "God, yeah. Hail to the fucking king."

Iris looked past her and saw other women through a haze of shadow and smoke. Black women, Asian women, Caucasian women—all lounging on the floor, curling against embroidered pillows and soft blankets. No one seemed even vaguely conscious, but Iris saw syringes and smelled something bitter beneath the marijuana. Heroin, maybe.

Iris was also the only one still wearing clothes. Everyone else was adorned in only jewelry; diamonds glittered against throats and wrists.

She pushed herself up on her knees and tried to see more. Mosaics decorated the walls in intricate gleaming patterns, lit by thick candles impaled upon golden sconces. Carved pillars broke up the room in chunks, along with curtains like the one surrounding Iris's small space. Large bowls of fruit had been left on the floor between the drugged women. Most looked untouched.

She did not see a door, but there was a curtain in her way. On the other side, maybe.

Breathe, she told herself. *You breathe in and out and keep yourself calm.*

Right. Holy fucking shit. She was in a harem.

Iris tugged on the chains. The links were strong, the cuffs pressing hard against her skin. Tight, very tight. If she shifted shape she might be able to slip free—but a quick glance at the ceiling and corners of the room revealed two cameras. Both of them trained on her.

Fuck the consequences. This is about survival now.

Tempting. But if a recording was used against others of her kind? Iris looked at the girl, who swayed on her feet, humming to herself. Her eyes were glazed; one hand rubbed her lower belly in a slow, wide circle. Iris snapped her fingers. "Hey! Hey, you! We need to talk."

The girl kept swaying and smiled. "Hey, hey. I want to dance. You want to dance with me? Mmm-bop, yeah. Like, oh! J-Lo!"

Iris took another deep breath, the leopard burning inside her chest, growling, growling so loud, and she realized the sound was not in her head, but in her throat. Her skin itched; her fingernails ached. She forced herself again to breathe. If she lost it now she would lose it all, and she thought of her mother—her mother in a disguise, her mother running, her mother at her side—*Baby, baby*—her mother shot and bleeding and lying so still—no time to say *Hello* or *Good-bye* or *I love you ...*

"Hey," Iris said hoarsely, softer this time, inching forward on her pillows. Her arms ached; the chains did not let her move far. "Hey, kid. Sweetheart. I want to dance. But I'm all tied up, see?"

"All tied up," sang the girl. "The king turned the key."

"The king," Iris repeated. "Santoso? Is that who you're talking about?"

The girl smiled and dropped on her knees in front of Iris, peering deeply into her face.

"You have pretty eyes," she said lazily. "That must be why he took you."

"Did he take anyone else? Was I alone?"

"All alone," the girl drawled. "Just you and him. Another queen to his crown."

The girl was this close to lucid, but even closer to batshit crazy. *Damn.* Iris leaned forward, pulling on the chains. "And you? Are you another of his ... queens?"

"A queen," she murmured. "Oh, yes. I was special."

"Why?" Iris pressed. "Why were you special?"

The girl laughed again, only this time it was edged with bitterness, something sharp, dangerous. She tucked her chin to her chest, hands playing in front of her with the delicate gestures of a dancer, and Iris almost expected a pirouette, a twirl, some lazy dance, but the girl suddenly stopped fussing, stopped moving, stopped everything at all ... and she began to sing. One high trill that was so lovely and sweet, so unexpected, it stole Iris's breath away. Pure notes skipped from her throat, staccato—and her control, the way she carried herself, screamed training and money and a good, soft life.

This girl has a family somewhere, Iris thought. *This girl was* taken.

Just like Iris. Probably like those women sleeping off their fixes.

The girl stopped singing. Her eyes were bright. Iris noticed track marks on her pale, slender arms.

"Songbird," she said, still with the melody in her voice. "The king calls me Songbird."

Iris brushed her fingertips over the girl's face. Up close her cheeks looked hollow; shadows stretched wide beneath her eyes. The girl let herself be touched, but after a moment frowned and swayed away.

"What's your real name?" Iris asked softly.

"Songbird," the girl muttered, pressing the heel of her palm against her forehead. "Songbird is it."

Iris sat back, looking past her at the other women. She counted at least fifteen, but had a bad feeling there might be more stashed away, perhaps in other rooms. She thought of her mother and tried to imagine her nearby, in chains. All she could see in her head, though, was the memory of her body on the floor of the casino, the pop of the gun—and more, other moments, just a child curled in her arms, a kit to her cat, running wild and wilder still with the wind and moon in their blood—

Fear cut to her heart, but Iris stuffed it down; there was no room for it. Not here, not now. She had to be strong. She had to fight.

"Songbird," Iris said, catching the girl's eye. "How long have I been here?"

"Awhile," she murmured.

"And you?"

"Awhile," she said again, which Iris knew could mean anything from hours to days to weeks. The girl was too stoned. Probably for a good reason.

Iris followed the chains to a ring in the wall. She placed her feet on either side and pulled back hard, straining until she cried out. She felt a budge, a slight give, and stopped. The camera was still watching. Even that much effort might draw too much attention. If Santoso wanted her ...

I'll rip his balls off, Iris thought, feeling the leopard rise within her. *I'll make him bleed to death from his dick.*

Good plan. As long as he didn't drug her again.

She heard a rattling sound. Voices. Men. Songbird did not appear to notice, but then there was click, the ring of a delicate bell, and she flinched. The lazy smile disappeared—no more dancing queen—and in her eyes the haze began to fade.

"Come here," Iris said, and the girl pushed in close behind her, huddling against the wall.

The curtain was ajar; men entered the room, proving correct Iris's suspicion that the door was on the other side.

One of the newcomers was blond and tall. He wore a suit. The other two men who followed in his wake also wore suits, but they were older, shorter, and spoke Japanese to each other in soft voices.

"Broker," Songbird murmured, looking at the blond man. "That's Broker."

Broker had good hearing; he glanced over his shoulder at Iris and his eyes were cold, hard. He looked at her for only a moment, right before saying something quick and fluent to the Japanese men. They nodded, smiling, and Broker gestured at the prone women with a wide sweep of his hands Some of the women had begun to stir—several waved and smiled weakly—but most were still too drugged out to do anything at all.

The men began walking, and it was clear what this was, what they had come to do. Iris wanted to vomit as they stepped over legs and arms and heads, reaching down to pinch breasts, pat hips, finger pubic hair. Meat market, sex market, bodies for sale. Songbird shivered.

One of the men looked up and saw Iris. He pointed and said something to Broker, who merely shook his head.

Off-limits. Iris did not need to understand the language to know what that meant—and she was glad for it. Desperately so.

The men finally chose their women, both of them blond and leggy and utterly stoned. Broker reached into the inner pocket of his jacket and removed two gold bracelets that chimed like small bells. He handed one to each man, and they squatted beside the women and carefully attached the jewelry to their limp wrists. Symbolic, maybe, a way for those loser perverts to say, *I give you this,* or *I own you.* The cuffs around Iris's own wrists chafed; her chains felt the same as those bracelets.

Broker held a cell phone to his ear and said, "We're ready for the team."

Ready and waiting for liftoff. Iris could smell the two men: their arousal, their excitement. One of them had to adjust his trousers, while the other went so far as to touch himself, stroke himself, eyes fluttering closed as if he were ready to get down and dirty right in front of them all.

Broker put away the phone and gestured toward the door,

speaking quietly in Japanese. The two men did not look very happy, but they nodded, bowed, and quickly left.

Broker did not follow. He turned in a slow circle and looked at Iris. His cheekbones were high, his mouth firm. A handsome man, maybe. Iris wanted to kill him.

"For your benefit," he said quietly. "Santoso wanted you to know how it could be."

"Could be," Iris repeated, trying not to think of those men touching her, slobbering over her, sticking their dicks into her. "But if I behave?"

Broker's mouth curved. "You will serve only one man. Like Songbird serves."

"Well," Iris said. "I suppose that's a deal I just can't pass up."

Movement. Four men appeared behind Broker; they carried stretchers and quickly, silently, loaded up the women who had been chosen.

"Wake them, but not too much," Broker instructed. "Our guests want them pliable, not engaging."

"God forbid a woman who engages," Iris said loudly. "Might be too much excitement for such limp dicks."

One of men snorted; Broker shot him a chilling look and then turned back to Iris. He walked to her and she straightened against her restraints, mustering all the stubborn defiance still left inside her battered, frightened heart.

Broker studied her face, his gaze lingering on her eyes. "Enjoy yourself while you can. Santoso has plans for you, and what he wants, he always gets."

"He might be disappointed this time," Iris told him, fighting to keep her voice from quaking. "He might have just bitten off more than he can chew."

"Perhaps," Broker said, surprising her. "But Santoso's plans are my plans, and I can assure you that I know *exactly* where you stand."

A chill raced through her. Broker smiled and left. As soon as the door clicked, Songbird uncurled, crawling on all fours until she crouched in front of Iris. She still had her joint; it flip-flopped between her lips and then dropped to the floor with a very soft thud.

"Broker is a bad man," Songbird murmured. "He makes things happen."

"He sells women."

"He does other things." The girl's shoulders quivered as she peered past the curtain. "He wants your eyes. The king, I mean. I heard him tell Broker that he wants your eyes. He wants your body, too."

"He can't have it," Iris told the girl. "I won't let him."

"Maybe," she said softly, picking up the joint. Her hand shook. "But he's not the one in chains."

Rest was impossible. Iris lay on her pillows, Songbird curled nearby, and simply filled her head with all kinds of motivational speeches—*kick, bite, fight, kill*—as she waited for the next twist in her life to unfold.

She thought about her mother, too. About why now—why her mother had come home just at that moment, and it was a safer train of thought than all the others—*gun, blood, body*—because anything else filled her with a hurt too terrible to bear, the kind of thing that would kill hope if she dwelled on it too long.

Knocked unconscious, that's all. No need for tears, no need to fear, no need at all to be blue—

Blue. She wanted to see him almost as much as she wanted her mother—and that was a shock. What was the old test of love? Hang a person over the edge of a volcano and see who they cry for?

Well, now Iris knew. Although love was not something she wanted to think about right now. Not her love, and not his. *If* he felt anything for her. And really, why would he? He had known her for only a day.

Not that it matters. Even if he does care, he won't find me. He might try, but the only way I'm getting out of here is on my own. I can't depend on anyone else.

Because even if she could rely on her friends or the police

to help her—even if there was the possibility of rescue—it was too dangerous to lull herself into believing it would happen. Complacency was the devil. She might as well sign away her life if she stopped taking responsibility for herself, just give up, play dumb, pick up a needle and start shooting away her mind so that whatever happened next just wouldn't matter.

Right. Like that's your style. Give me a break.

She heard movement outside the room; beyond the curtain, the door opened. The two women who had been taken away appeared, still naked, but slightly more alert. They settled immediately on the pillows they had vacated and began munching on some grapes in the bowl beside them. They did not look at Iris. They did not look anywhere but down—down at the food, their hands.

Santoso appeared behind them, accompanied by three of the same men who had been with him at the casino. Songbird rose to her feet.

"You may go," he said to her. "Take a shower. Your hair's dirty."

"Yes," she said, and ran out without a second glance at Iris.

"I hope you don't expect me to be that well trained," Iris said to him. "It's not my style."

"No. I can see that." Santoso removed a set of keys from his pocket. "I'm going to unlock you now. I'm sure you'll see this as an opportunity to escape, but that would be unwise. My men will shoot you."

"I'm a patient woman," Iris said.

"Yes," Santoso agreed. "But then, you're not really a woman."

Iris frowned. Santoso walked around her and unlocked the main chain from the ring in the wall, the one upon which all the others were linked. He held the steel in his hands and jingled it like a leash.

"Go on, now," he said. "Up."

Iris thought about barking like a dog, but was afraid that might be a turn-on for him. She stood. Her body ached, her legs felt weak, but the leopard unfurled and her muscles reacted. Good as new in seconds. She imagined snapping Santoso's neck—and really, who would have thought she could possibly be so bloodthirsty?—but she glanced at the men, saw that all of them now had guns in their hands, and thought, *Later, save it for later when he makes a mistake.*

Santoso made Iris walk in front of him. It was not easy; her ankles were still bound, and she kept feeling as though she would trip as she stepped over the resting women. With one man preceding her, and the other two following Santoso, she left the modern man's version of Harems-R-Us ... and entered the cover of an *Architectural Digest.*

The spacious area was a waiting room—she saw that instantly—covered in gleaming hardwood floors polished to a mirror shine. Archways floated above her head, delicately carved with trees and birds, and indeed, piped into the background, Iris heard a New Age chorus of pipes and drums. The theme was delicate, neutral—most definitely woodland chic—and the immense bronze pots brimming with rich ferns and orchids served only to heighten the sensation of nature, artificial privacy. Brown leather chairs dotted the edges of the room; men in suits occupied them. They sipped drinks and read magazines and seemed so perfectly normal that Iris wanted to rage and scream when they looked at her with nothing more than mild interest. As though seeing a young woman in chains were nothing. As though seeing, as they must have, those women carted out on stretchers were as normal as apple pie.

There was a refreshment center; a young woman in a modest black uniform poured coffee for an elderly man leaning on the counter in front of her. In another corner was a large desk that held a computer and telephone. Another woman manned it, also in uniform. Iris heard her mention a time, a date, a session with a therapist—oh, how delightfully *not* funny that was—and Iris looked at Santoso and said, "What the hell is this place?"

"An empire, *Layak*," Santoso said. "Or rather, the future of it."

"And it's yours?" she asked, thinking of how Songbird had called him king. "You're responsible for this?" This cruelty, this perversion, this display of refinement and wealth that was nothing more than a mask for slavery and degradation and God only knew what other horrors.

Santoso looked at her. Studied her eyes in the same way Broker had, as if he were trying to dive right down into them. It made her insecure, as though there were something wrong with her, something terrible that could be revealed just by looking into her face. Iris wished she had a mirror so that she could see her eyes, which made her think of her mother, who always wore dark sunglasses to keep people from seeing her deformity: cat eyes, slit irises—caught permanently in a bad shift.

Santoso never answered her question. He pointed to a hall on the other side of the receptionist desk. Iris almost refused him—wanted to see what kind of rise she could get out of those other perverts sitting so calm and rich with their eyes on her body—but she calmed herself and walked, chains heavy and clinking. Broker appeared from another hall, glanced in her direction, then introduced himself to a gray-haired man in a green shirt. He said something in French, and pointed to another set of doors near those Iris had just walked through.

"More sex?" Iris asked Santoso.

"This wing is devoted to sex," he replied, as though it were the most natural thing in the world. "Were you expecting something primitive? That is unnecessary, you know. There is no reason at all why sex—or anything the world finds distasteful—cannot be negotiated with class and dignity."

"Ah, right. Because kidnapping women and forcing them into sexual slavery ranks right up there with high tea or Sunday dinner. Fuck you, Santoso."

"You think to insult me?" He smiled. "We are all slaves, Iris. The fight of one's life, the only fight, is to become the master."

"Then I expect we will have a very exciting relationship," Iris said, tugging on her chains.

They walked. The halls were wide and beautifully decorated. No windows. It was impossible to tell whether or not it was night or day. The air smelled like flowers, undercut with the odors of bleach and other cleaning fluids. She did not know how the men in the waiting room had entered the building; she saw nothing that looked like an exit, and no one else who could be a guest.

But the scents changed; she began to smell blood, though she did not know from where. She also smelled sickness, death, and dying.

"We're in a different wing," she said without thinking, and glanced over her shoulder at Santoso.

"Yes," he said, tilting his head to study her. "We do not sell sex here."

"And?"

"And we are a corporation, a diverse business. You will see."

And, apparently, everyone else would see her see. There were cameras embedded in the walls, in the ceiling—and near the base of the floor she noted tiny silver markers that were, no doubt, motion sensors. If she changed shape, if she slashed her fingernails across Santoso's throat, someone would see her do it. Someone would record it. And then what? Proof for the masses? Or worse, motivation for some underground party like Santoso to try to sell her as a freak of nature, prime for perverts or scientists?

One thing at a time. One step, one breath, one action. Live in the moment. That's all you have.

All she had, and it was so terrifying she wanted to crawl out of her body with a scream on her lips, because the nets were down and the wildness was gone. Collared and chained, a slave to flesh, and the more she walked, the stronger the sensation, so overwhelming that it was all she could do not to give up her life in one burst of light; give up the human ghost even if it meant bullets and the betrayal of her kind. She could not take this. She could not.

But Iris pressed her sharpening teeth into her tongue and tasted blood; she pressed her nails into her palm and bit flesh; she fed the leopard her physical pain and said, *Rest awhile longer. Sleep. Sleep and dream.*

Dream a way to escape. Dream a destiny that involved more than being Santoso's sex slave.

They stopped walking in front of a wide set of ornately carved double doors, and on the other side of those doors Iris found a very plain room. A long table took up most of the space, and a large plasma screen television hung on the wall.

"Our specialists hold conferences here," Santoso said. "You may sit wherever you like."

Iris took the chair nearest the entrance. She felt one of the men take up guard directly behind her. She smelled his sweat, his aftershave, the metal of his gun. Her chains dangled to the floor, clanking. Her wrists and ankles hurt.

"Are these really necessary?" She pointed at her restraints. "Surely you all outnumber me."

Santoso smiled, gesturing at the man standing near him, who opened a small cabinet in the wall and revealed a tiny refrigerator. He pulled out two bottles of water, the first of which he gave to Santoso. He opened the second and handed it to Iris. She hesitated, battling pride, but her tongue suddenly felt thick, her mouth dry, and she took the water. The cool bottle felt delicious against her skin; she drank deeply, heavily. Iris knew Santoso watched her, but she did not care. She had to stay strong.

"The chains," Santoso said slowly, "are an experiment."

"In perversion?"

"In resourcefulness and desperation. I want to know what it will take for you to release yourself. How far you are willing to go."

"You act as though I could just slip free of these restraints anytime I want."

"Can't you?" Again he smiled, but this time it chilled Iris to the bone. His expression was knowing, sly, and she reminded herself that this was the man who made notes from flesh, who had shot her mother—*no, don't think of that, not now*—and that despite the veneer of civility, he was exactly the same as the business he ran: dirty, sick, and violent, with absolutely no respect for the dignity and freedom of others.

In other words, one dangerous bastard.

Santoso pressed the table; Iris saw buttons inlaid into the wood. The television set flickered to life.

"I noticed you some time ago," Santoso said. "An acquaintance introduced me to your show, and while the other acts were tolerable, yours …" He stopped, and for the first time his smile seemed genuine. "You, Iris, were beautiful. Free, powerful, full of youth. In other words, perfection. I have not missed a performance since."

"And so you decided to kidnap me? You didn't think that would draw attention to you, that I would be missed?"

Santoso laughed; the sound was unpleasant and it did not reach his eyes, which glittered black and small. He pressed another button. A picture flickered to life on the screen.

It was her dressing room at the Miracle.

"My plans were simple," he said quietly, as Iris—horrified—watched herself enter the room. It had to be a tape from just that morning; the clothes were the same, and her actions, the way she paused at the flowers and then threw herself down at the makeup table …

"So simple," he said. "I would make you my woman. I would make you perform for me, and me alone. My dancer, my lovely, the Catwoman to my Songbird. Such a good plan. So perfect. And then … yes. Here."

Iris could not look away. She knew what was coming, she remembered, but still, watching that shift come over her face, the fur and the light, the ripple of her skin as the cat pressed up and up through her flesh—it was beautiful and terrible, disturbing beyond words because she could see in that moment how far removed she was from the rest of the world. How *inhuman* she truly was. And for this man to see it, too . . .

Iris looked at Santoso and found him watching her, drinking in her reaction. She schooled her face into something flat and hard, and he smiled, whispering, "No, you cannot hide from me, Iris McGillis. I have seen what you are, and it is beautiful. You are *Layak*. A shape-shifter."

Iris battled nausea. "What do you want from me, Santoso?"

He pointed at the screen. "That. I want that. Give me *that*."

"You want to see me shift."

"Not just that, but yes. First, you will shift for me."

And what then? Iris wondered, but she did not dare ask. Not now. Not with that look in his eyes that was both hungry and aroused. He smelled excited. His men smelled scared.

Yes. Be scared. Here there be monsters.

"I won't do it," Iris said. "And you won't kill me. So that leaves us with a problem."

"Your problem. Not mine." Santoso looked at the man nearest him, and he left the room. Only for a moment, though. He returned with Songbird. Her hair and skin were wet. Pulled out of a shower, and with no towel to cover or dry her body. Iris wondered how long she had been kept out there, waiting for this moment.

The man pushed Songbird against the wall and pinned her there. She was very small compared to him, small and wan and pale, and his companion drew a long knife from his jacket that made the girl whimper—not just with fear, but recognition. Her eyes were clearer now, the drugs wearing off; Iris could smell her terror and it was horrifying, awful.

"I suppose this is another experiment," Santoso said calmly, as the man with the knife stepped close to the cowering girl. "An experiment in compassion. Not mine, of course. Do *not* think for a moment that I will not hurt you if I must, Iris McGillis. If you were any other woman, I would not hold back. I would break you. I would have you pinned and pissed upon and raped, again and again, by every man in this facility, if it would make you say yes. Unfortunately, I am afraid of what that would do to your physiology, and I just cannot risk your body being sullied. Not when I have other uses for it."

"You're an animal," Iris murmured. "You're an animal, and I'm going to kill you."

"No," he said. "You're going to save me. So shift. You shift, right now. Or I will have that man cut off her breast."

Iris hesitated. The man pressed the tip of the knife beneath Songbird's breast and slowly, slowly pushed upward. The girl flinched, crying out. Blood trickled.

"Stop," Iris said. "Stop, please."

"Show me your other form. Show me."

Songbird wailed, twisting against the hands holding her. The knife pressed deeper. Iris stepped forward—found a gun pointed at her face—and snarled. Her fingernails shimmered; nails disappeared beneath claws, pale skin overcome by sleek fur and spots.

"You want to be entertained?" Iris held up her hands before Santoso's wide eyes, shoving them near his face, and though she hated it with every fiber of her being—exposed and violated, forced to rape herself for his pleasure—she let the leopard rise in a burst of golden light, a roar of fur that poured down her body, rippling like water through her bones. She tore away her tank top, ripped off her shorts, her underwear—and the nudity was nothing, nothing, because she was already worse than naked, stripped down to her soul, and nothing could change that now. All she could do was ride the shame and turn it into power; give herself something in return for what she was giving away.

Iris bared her teeth and screamed; her voice was inhuman, wild. Santoso laughed, and though she was close enough to do it, she did not kill him. She felt the guns pointed at her head, saw Songbird still with a knife to her breast—but the fear, the fear she smelled was so damn good, and she rode it, drinking in the scent of piss and sweat as her face began its final shift, elongating, ears expanding as her hair receded into her scalp, swallowed whole by fur. Her spine changed, grew more fluid; she sank to all fours and stepped out of her restraints. A tail poured from the base of her spine. One of the men behind her vomited. Songbird screamed like a banshee, though her voice cut out after a moment. Iris looked; the girl hung limp, knocked out.

Santoso was the only one who betrayed no fear. In fact, the expression on his face was one of pure delight.

"Wonderful," he said, eyes shining. "Beautiful."

But she barely heard him. It had been a long time since Iris had committed to a full shift; she was unused to the sensation, the raw quality of her senses streaming the world into her head. And this body was so different—liquid and strong, long with the leanness of an arrow bolt. She wondered how she had gone so many years without *this*, how she could have forgotten what it felt like.

Santoso rolled up his sleeves and knelt before her. Her tail lashed the air; she wanted to pounce, to fasten her teeth and kill. She almost did, too, except for the guns—those awful guns. Santoso might not want her dead, but no one else would care. They'd skin her and hang the fur on the wall, whispering, "This was a human once. A fairy tale. And we killed her."

Santoso stared into her eyes, still smiling, still smelling like happiness on legs, and it struck Iris as highly ironic that the one man on earth who could look at her and not run screaming was also a raging lunatic. Just her luck.

He placed his arm under her nose. His skin smelled bitter. Iris growled.

"Sir," said one of his men, but Santoso shook his head, his gaze never leaving Iris.

"Your eyes," he whispered. "Your eyes give you away, you know. They are the gold of heaven and you are its magic, everything a man dreams of as a child, but can never attain because the sky is too high, too fanciful, too much a dream.

But I have you. I have you, Iris, and I will have my dream. I will take my magic. I will take it all."

Santos pressed his arm even closer, right up against her mouth.

"Bite me," he said. Totally serious, extremely earnest.

Bite me. Right. Good one. Thank you, God.

And Iris almost did—because really, he was asking for it. Literally.

But at the last moment she held back, kept herself in check. Something was wrong—a lot of things were wrong—but Santoso's asking her to bite his arm was wrong in a very specific way that she did not understand, and as there were several guns trained on her head, she wanted to know exactly what that was before she got a taste of his blood—and maybe a bullet.

Iris reverted shape, but only enough so that she could talk. She remained on the floor, tail lashing, and her voice was rough and raw as she said, "The hell you mean, you want me to bite you?"

"I want to be like you. I want you to give me your gift."

"Give you . . ." Iris stopped, choking down a laugh. Santoso had been watching too many movies. He thought that if she bit him, he would gain her abilities. What a joke.

So what? You tell him the truth? How smart would that be?

Because he would either think she was lying—resulting in some bad consequences for her—or that she was honest, therefore making her very, very useless. Either way she was screwed.

Santoso still held out his arm, but his gaze was changing, turning cold and dark, ready to dish out the hurt. *Aw, hell.* "I can bite you, but there's no guarantee that you'll become like me. None at all. It doesn't work for everyone. And not always right away. This is a change that occurs on a genetic level. It takes time."

Yes, time. And she was the biggest bullshitter of her generation.

Santoso's eyes narrowed. "If you're lying to me . . ."

"My paw to God. Why would I lie?"

"I can think of numerous reasons," he said dryly. "Fortunately, I already have a contingency plan in place."

Really. Iris could not possibly imagine the kind of contingency plan that would be sufficient to turn a human man into a shape-shifter, but if it bought her time and kept Santoso happy . . .

He thrust his arm into her face. "Do it."

Iris shifted shape, sliding back into the full leopard. She sniffed Santoso's arm—hoped her gag reflex did not kick in—and bit down slowly. She could have done it fast, hard, but she knew how powerful her jaws were, and though it would not pain her greatly, she did not want to take Santoso's arm off. Her teeth pressed and pressed—Santoso paled, jaw flexing—and Iris suddenly felt the break in his skin like a popped bubble. Blood filled her mouth—hot, metallic, a rush that ran down her throat like a drug.

Human blood. She had never tasted human blood. It had been almost a decade since she had swallowed any blood at all, but human—human was not elk, it was not sheep, it was not anything of the wood or mountain. It was sexy. It made the leopard hungry.

Her jaw tightened; Santoso squirmed and cried out. She felt a blow across her shoulders and growled, tightening her grip. Another blow, another, and Santoso shouted, pulling back. Iris let go. She did not want to, but she remembered— *Human, I am human*—and the leopard gave way to the woman.

She heard shouts, smelled pain; she shifted shape, fur receding into pink skin, spine shrinking as her tail burrowed into her back. *Slide human, slide fast,* Iris told herself, but halfway there the metallic taste in her mouth changed with her body. The blood no longer tasted so good. Iris leaned forward and vomited. A foot landed hard in her ribs.

"You tried to hurt me," Santoso said. His voice shook; from

anger or pain, Iris could not be sure. One of the men had dragged out a first-aid kit and was wrapping up his arm with careful, almost tender movements.

Money or fear. Iris still did not know what inspired that kind of loyalty.

"You asked me to bite you," Iris said weakly. Her ribs hurt and her mouth tasted like a rotting carcass. She could almost see the flies buzzing around her teeth. "What did you expect? A joyride?"

Santoso sucked in his breath. "You are enjoying this."

Iris smiled. "Don't *you* get off on pain? Isn't that why you do this? Don't tell me it's just the money. That's never enough. Not for what I've seen."

She heard a knock and turned. Broker stood in the doorway. He looked down at her, and then Santoso. He appeared amused, though Iris did not know why; surely it was something his boss would not appreciate.

Iris rose to her feet as Broker entered. Songbird was still mostly unconscious. She groaned, fingers twitching.

"The Russians are here," Broker said. "Nikolai Petrovona is waiting in your office."

Santoso's face hardened. "He is early."

"And he says you are late with the merchandise. *And* that this facility is a waste of money."

The man finished wrapping his arm, Santoso pulled down his sleeve and glanced at Iris. "I want her placed in the hold. Do not give her clothes, no food or water. And tell the doctors to prepare the medical bay."

"Medical bay," Iris said. "What does that—"

"I was going to fuck you," Santoso interrupted coldly. "Before I knew what you were, I was going to keep you naked and on a leash, never allowed to stand higher than your knees. But I have many women for sex, and you can offer me more. You *are* more. And I will make you part of me, forever."

"Nice speech," Iris said. "You son of a—"

Santoso backhanded her. Iris almost went down to her knees, but she caught her footing and felt a fierce smile rise up her throat, let loose with a low laugh that made all the men stare.

"I am not impressed with your attempts at foreplay," Iris said, touching her stinging cheek. "Not at all, Santoso."

The man raised his fist. Broker said, "Sir, you really don't have time for this."

Maybe not, but he hit her anyway. Or tried to. Iris blocked his blow, grabbing his wrist and twisting it back until she drove him into the ground. Santoso cried out. The cold muzzle of a gun touched Iris's temple. She did not let go. Her gaze slid sideways to Broker. A fast draw; she never even saw him move.

"I hate your guts," she told him. "All of you people are too sick to live."

"But you aren't," Broker said, gun hand steady, unwavering. "So why don't you prolong your life just a little longer, and let go of my employer?"

Iris glanced down at Santoso, at the base of his neck, his greasy black hair, and felt something suck on her eyeballs as she examined the man—knew with a cold, hard certainty that she was watching a transformation occur. Not to cat, not to something more than human, but rather, a devolution into a creature small and ineffectual. A tiny man with a tinier heart. And there was part of her that could taste that weakness—taste, in contrast, her own power—and she knew that if she turned Santoso around she would be able to peel through the mask of his face and see the ghost beneath; an expensive shell that was fragile, screaming.

Fear left her; uncertainty died. Iris spit on the back of his head and turned him loose, throwing him away with a hard shove. Santoso snarled. Broker stepped between them both.

"The Russians," he said in a firm voice, and much to Iris's shock, Santoso listened. Shaking with anger—shuddering, almost—he walked past Iris, trying to stare her down. Iris matched his gaze and, at the very last moment, just before he entered the hall, he raised a shaky hand and pointed at her.

"You and I," he said, and touched the corner of his eye. "Together."

Which was appropriately enigmatic, given everything else he had said to her. Santoso disappeared. Two of his men followed, but the last hesitated, looking between Broker and Iris.

"Go," Broker said, gun still drawn. "I can handle her."

The look on the man's face clearly begged to differ, but he followed orders and left, dragging Songbird away with him.

Alone at last. Iris took a step back and studied Broker. He returned her stare, examining her body with a clinical detachment that might have frightened her thirty minutes ago, but was now just par for the course.

Yes, look at my breasts, asshole. They're the same breasts half the people in this world have, and if you try to touch them, so help me God I will take off your hand and shove it up your ass.

"You would do well here," Broker said, finally looking at her face. "Ah, well." He glanced down at the discarded chains, but made no move to pick them up or restrain her. He pointed at the door and held up his gun. "Walk with me."

Anything that let Iris see more of this place was fine by her, though his equanimity made her suspicious. Broker led Iris down a wide, elegantly decorated hall that continued to smell of blood and antiseptic. She saw no other people, but on several occasions heard low voices, one of which was discussing white-blood-cell counts.

"So," she said to Broker. "Where are you taking me?"

"I'm not sure it matters. Where do you think you are?"

Iris thought about wrestling him for the gun. "I think I am in a place where anything can be bought, and where very bad people can pretend to act civilized while doing terrible things." She looked him in the eye. "You know what I am."

"That you can change your shape?" Broker smiled. "Yes."

"You don't act surprised."

"Act surprised and do what I do? Act surprised, and yet still fulfill the requests of the men and women who do business here? Oh, no. A shape-shifter is nothing compared to that. Almost, I would say, *mundane*."

"But you work here anyway."

Broker's smile widened. "I like making people happy."

Iris dropped low, kicking out the back of his knee. Broker went down, but instead of staying there, he rolled, grabbing her ankle and twisting. Iris didn't fall, only staggered—but all her plans of sending him flat and taking away that gun went to hell. He shot up, body a blur, and pressed cold steel against her forehead. Iris froze.

"Bang," Broker whispered.

"Bang," Iris echoed softly, watching his eyes: cold gray, storm gray, bone gray.

Broker moved slowly away, gun held steady. "You tried. I admire that. Would you have killed me?"

"Maybe," Iris said.

"Maybe." Broker tilted his head, amused. "You have never taken a life. I can see it in your eyes. Don't start now, Iris."

"Dirty times, dirty measures. I want to live, Broker."

"Then live," he said, and gestured for her to stand. "Hurry."

Frowning, Iris followed the man as he pushed open a set of doors that led into a room filled with medical equipment—a surgical table, tools, lights, monitors, and a counter filled with odd metallic canisters.

"Santoso thinks he can be more than human," Broker said, his voice echoing gently. "He thinks he can stop being the prey if he is the hunter."

"Prey to what? As far as I can see, he answers to no one." Iris shook her head. "Fine. So he sees I'm a shape-shifter and thinks that will give him an advantage. He has no idea of the price."

"No one ever does." Broker leaned close, eyes intense. "He wants your body, Iris. He wants your blood. You see this room? This is where it will happen. Everything is prepared— the finest doctors available. What he does for others, he will do for himself, even though he is healthy. He will strip you,

Iris. He will take you apart and put you back together inside himself." His mouth curved into a grim smile. "And I think he will start with your eyes."

Iris hesitated. "You can't be serious."

"We both know the bite will do nothing for him."

"Neither will giving him my body parts." Iris looked for a weapon, for anything. Enough of this shit; a bullet would be better than what that operating table promised.

But Broker aimed the gun at her head, walked slowly around her, and pointed at another set of doors right off the medical bay. "Open those. Now."

"Another surprise?"

"Yes," Broker said. "Do it."

The doors were heavy; rubber seals coated the edges, making them airtight. She pulled hard and, as the seal parted, Iris smelled dirt, fresh clean air. Her hair stirred away from her face, and she threw back her head as she pushed open the doors and found the desert before her.

Broker stepped close. "As I'm sure you've surmised, this facility is not just a brothel. We also provide services of a medical nature, and this is the direct entrance for our more critical patients. The ambulance drives right up to the door."

Iris wanted to scream. "Why are you doing this? Are you going to shoot me when I run?"

"No." Broker put away the gun. "But I won't promise not to chase you, either."

Iris edged through the doorway; her bare feet touched dirt and it felt like silk. She glanced back over her shoulder. "Was I brought here alone, Broker? Was there another woman?"

A smile played over his lips. "There was no one but you, Iris."

"And I should trust you about that? About anything you've told me? I thought you said Santoso's plans were your plans."

"I said that. But I received some curious news ... and I am allowed to be flexible."

"I doubt your boss would feel that way."

"Ah," he said, smiling. "But which boss are you referring to?" He pointed at the desert. "You have five minutes. Use them well."

The night called; the wind was sweet, the moon bright and cold as a diamond.

Iris ran.

CHAPTER TWELVE

Much later, when asked to recall the events that took place in the hours following Iris's kidnapping, Blue found his memory selective, without details, so that all his recollections of the past consisted only of the strong and vibrant: snatches of conversation, a stream of neon reflected in his brother's glasses, the heat and scent of the woman bleeding from the gunshot wound beside him. Hard memories, sharp—like his heart, aching like a scream inside his chest.

"You're Iris's mother," Daniel said during that taxi ride. "Serena McGillis."

"Serena," Blue said softly. "Oh, Serena."

"Do not speak of it," she rasped at him. "Do not use that name."

"And what name should we use?" Blue asked, but Serena did not answer him, and all he could do was listen to her harsh breathing, each swallow of her pain.

True to her word, she had a car at the airport—a black Humvee that took up two parking spaces and that looked spacious enough for Iris and a whole troop of cats to live inside.

"Here." Serena pushed keys into Blue's hand. They were sticky with blood.

"You need a doctor," he said to her, but she had already turned and was crawling into the backseat of the car. Daniel closed the door behind her and looked at Blue with an expression that was pure *What the fuck?*

Blue shrugged. No way was he going to explain how he knew Serena, not unless she began talking first. Daniel might not give a shit about his secrets, but Blue was more of a professional than that. For the most part.

The two men got into the car. Serena gave Blue directions on which freeway to take, and with the city still buzzing on the edge of his mind, he steered them into the desert, where the moon was just beginning to rise over the mountains, casting a cold light that looked good enough to drink.

Blue heard cloth tear, grunts and whistles, all kinds of sounds indicating discomfort, pain. He and Daniel shared a brief glance, Blue looked into the rearview mirror, saw nothing but shadow, and said, "Are you sure you don't need help?"

The barrel of a gun pressed against his head. "I am certain. Do not look in that mirror again."

Blue cleared his throat. "Sorry."

A low grunt. The gun tapped his head. "Take this. Daniel, here's another."

Blue reached back and took the gun. His brother did the same. Daniel held the weapon easily, as though he knew how to use it.

"Where's Iris?" Blue asked Serena. "Will we catch up to them on this road?"

"No," Serena said, and her voice was rough, weary. "Santoso would have gone immediately to the airport and taken his helicopter to the facility. There is a good chance Iris has already been secured."

"What does that mean?" Daniel asked. "Who the hell are these people, and what do they want with Iris?"

"Santoso Rahardjo wants Iris for the same reason he ever wants anything beautiful," Serena said in a hard voice. "To use it."

"He's a flesh peddler," Blue told his brother. "The supposed head of a global operation that specializes in black-market human organs: hearts, livers, corneas, bones. Anything and everything. His people take what they want by force, and if they do pay, it's only in pennies or livestock."

"Your view of the situation is limited." Serena's voice floated sharply from the shadows. "All you have seen is the medical aspect of his trade. The operation is much bigger than that. Santoso is a human trafficker in the purest sense of the word. Flesh in all its forms. His presence is very strong in the international sex trade, for both women and children, and he is about to strike a deal with the Russians for skin and weapons."

"And this guy has Iris? Jesus," Daniel muttered.

Blue unclenched his jaw. "Will he sell her?"

"No. He is enamored with her. Ever since he came to this city he has not missed a performance. All the time, he is at the hotel. He sent her notes."

"Yes," Blue said in a flat voice. "So I've heard."

"Love letters. Obscene love letters. When I discovered what he was doing ..." Her voice trailed off. Blue could not help himself.

"You kept silent. You let him continue. You didn't protect your daughter. You fed her to the wolf. You didn't even tell her you were alive." Easy words, true words, and each one he spoke made his anger grow, his rage deepen. Hold up a mirror, he knew, and that anger would look like fear—but that was okay. Fear was a good thing. Fear for Iris would keep him from failing.

But all that emotion made his head ache, and the pain pushed against his shields. Blue forced himself to breathe, to relax. This was all about control now, all about keeping himself together, and the anger was good, great, fine, but he had to move past it into something constructive, had to transform it, had to soothe it before he did anything stup—

Blue punched the dashboard. He punched the wheel. He punched the ceiling of the car so hard he split his knuckles, and still he wanted more. He wanted to beat the crap out of something and see it bleed.

"Christ," Daniel said.

"Do you feel better?" Serena asked softly. "Would you like to stop the car and do that to me?"

Cold washed through him. "That's not funny."

"No," she agreed. "It's not."

Blue looked at Daniel, expecting some similar condemnation, but his brother was staring at his own hands, his expression haunted.

"Goddamn," he murmured. "We're just like our father."

Blue's coldness turned to ice. "What does that mean?"

Daniel closed his eyes. "Dumb question, Blue."

And he was right. It was a dumb question, but it was the only thing Blue could say. He could not bring himself to speak anything else, because the idea of being like his father—with that temper, that abuse—made him want to die.

"I'm sorry," Blue said. He thought about saying more, but kept his mouth shut. Excuses were useless. It did not matter how rarely he lost his temper; one time was all it took, one act of violence, and that was something that could never be taken back.

He waited for a response, but all he received was a low sigh from Daniel, who folded his arms across his chest and leaned back in his seat. "I want to know where we're going."

Blue heard shuffling from the backseat, followed by a grunt, another tearing sound. "Santoso has built a state-of-the-art facility out in the desert. On paper it is called a private residence, and on the outside it looks like one, but the facility stretches underground and is immense, both in size and execution. It provides in one location all the services he peddles elsewhere in the world. On-site organ transplants and postsurgical care, along with sex, illegal adoptions, drugs, weapons ... everything and anything, as long as clients have money to pay."

Blue's knuckles hurt. "And Iris?"

"Santoso is immensely proud of the facility, and the security is excellent. I am certain she is there."

There, alone, with a psychopath. Blue pressed harder on the accelerator. The Humvee roared. Daniel stroked the gun in his hand.

"He taught you how to shoot," Blue said, recalling, long ago, a brief vision of a gun room in his father's mountain home: rows upon rows of firearms, some mounted on the wall, others under glass.

"One of the bodyguards taught me on the sly. He worried I would get into situations, that people would try to hurt me. Funny, that. The only person who ever tried to abuse me was him."

Him. Father.

Blue knew that Serena was listening, but he did not care. He looked at his brother and said, "He faked his death to draw you out, and when that didn't work he got desperate. Blackmailed me on two fronts to bring you home. Threatened my mother and my friends."

"And you're going to do it."

"I considered the option. I'll find another way."

"And you expect me to believe that?"

"Believe anything you want."

"But do not be stupid about it," Serena rasped. "As difficult as that might be for you."

"Listen," Daniel said, but as he turned in his seat, something hard flew out of the darkness and hit him on the head. Blue heard a very loud gasp, almost a shout, followed by, "Fuck, you tossed a grenade at me."

"You might need it later," Serena said. "And don't look at me."

"God help me if I try." Daniel cradled the grenade in his hands, staring helplessly at it.

"Glove compartment," Blue suggested.

"Oh, sure," he muttered, and then, quieter: "I'm not going back to him, Blue. I won't do it."

"Okay."

Daniel gave him a hard look. "No, not okay. I have a life here, Blue. I made it for myself, with nothing at all but my own hard work. And even if you don't rat me out, those goons who ambushed me obviously work for someone who knows my secret."

"Santoso. What could he possibly want with you?"

"Ransom?"

Blue frowned. "What do you know about this, Serena?"

"Nothing. Which I find odd. Are you certain Santoso's men pursued Daniel?"

"It happened this morning. The same bastards tried to take Iris several hours later."

"That still doesn't explain our father's motives," Daniel said.

"Any idea why he would go to that much trouble?"

"I'm done guessing what goes on in his mind. There might be something genuine about his desperation. I doubt it."

"Which means you have something he wants."

Daniel sighed. "I was in New Orleans right after Katrina hit, working with the Red Cross. It was easy to slip away in the chaos. But all I took was cash and some clothes. I hadn't even been back to the old home in months. There's no way I took anything he values."

Unless you're the prize, Blue thought. "And the circus? How did that happen?"

"Crossed paths. Or rather, I saw Iris at a diner and followed her back to the big top."

Blue gave him a dirty look. Daniel shrugged. "Anyway, the circus was just what I needed. Off the grid, constant movement, dirt-poor. The last place anyone would expect me to be."

"And a place where you could practice your telekinesis," Serena added from the shadows of the backseat. "Ah, well. How unfortunate you have your father's pride. You brought too much attention to yourself today."

Again, Daniel began to turn—stopped himself at the last moment—and said, "How do you know our father?"

"He used to work for my employer. My *other* employer."

Blue hit the brakes and swerved to the side of the road. Horns blared. Daniel slammed his hand against the dashboard, and behind him a low, feminine grunt of pain filled the darkness.

"Tell me," Blue said.

"There is nothing to tell," Serena replied coldly. "He conducted business on behalf of my employers. *Legal* business. He was very good at it, too."

"Does he still work for them?"

"No. He cut ties several months ago. He cited illness as the cause, and we were able to confirm that."

"What kind of illness?"

"Cancer. Aggressive."

"Fuck," Blue muttered.

Daniel pressed his forehead against the dash. "Who do you work for, Serena?"

"None of your business. And frankly, not at all important to the task of rescuing my daughter."

Blue pulled back on the freeway and gunned the engine. "So our father worked for your people until he got too sick. I suppose you know about his personality problems, his other not-so-legal dealings."

"Of course, but as long as it did not intrude on the business he conducted on our behalf ..." Her voice trailed off, but the message was clear. *Scratch my back, and I'll scratch yours. No questions asked.*

"That still doesn't explain why he wants Daniel," Blue said.

His brother snorted. "Jealous?"

"Fuck you."

"Maybe you want his money. Maybe that's why you really caved to help him. Maybe you lied about the blackmail and this is all part of some elaborate scheme to kiss his wrinkled white—"

Blue's hand shot out. He remembered Daniel's warning, but it was too late to stop. He grabbed his brother's collar and twisted. The air quivered. Blue felt pressure on his throat, digging and digging. The car swerved, but he steadied the wheel, one eye on the road and the other on his brother.

"You let go of me," Daniel said quietly. "Right fucking now."

"Let go?" Blue bit back a sharp laugh, coughing as the pressure increased. "You first, *Danny*. Let go of that attitude, let go of the baggage, and don't you ever fucking say anything like that to me again. You have *no idea* what that man did to me and my mother."

"Oh," Daniel breathed. "So we're going to compare sob stories? You think you got it bad? Go to hell, Blue."

Blue pushed him away. "Goddamn you, Daniel. You think you were the only one who got screwed over by him? You think he didn't make my life miserable, just because I wasn't in the picture?"

Daniel shook his head, taking off his glasses and rubbing his eyes. "I would have taken your life over mine in a heartbeat, Blue, no questions asked."

"Enough," Serena said, finally leaning forward. She was naked except for a tight bandage wrapped around her shoulder. Fur covered the injured side of her body; leopard spots rolled thick and soft over her breasts and arm.

"The bullet isn't still in there, is it?" Blue asked, trying to keep his eyes on the road. Daniel stared outright.

Serena leaned forward and slapped him hard enough to draw blood from his lip. "What did I say?"

Daniel slumped against the door. "I'm sorry."

Serena remained silent. A moment later her hand appeared beside Blue's face and he got a good luck at the slug. It—and her hands—were still covered in her blood.

"You have some balls," Blue said.

"Yes," Serena replied. "And I am extremely grateful I have only one child. Your father should have thrown the two of you into a pit when you were young. Let nature take its course."

"I suppose that's what you did with Iris," Blue said, unable to help himself. "Or Is Santoso your version of the pit? Survival of the fittest?"

"Be more worried about yourself," Serena answered coldly. "I have a gun pointed at the base of your neck. I could paralyze you. Condemn you to a life of diapers and bedsores and amputations as your limbs rot off your body from disuse. Do you want that, Mr. Perrineau?"

"I want your daughter. After she's safe, you can do whatever the hell you want to me."

"Oh, promises," Serena said, but she leaned away from him, and Blue slowly exhaled.

The silence continued. Daniel rested his head against the window and closed his eyes. Serena brooded. Blue drove. He thought about Iris as his headlights cut through road and desert. Iris and his father, but mostly just her. He tried not to think about the danger she was in, what already might have been done to her. He remembered her on stage, caught in that net, and the pain that streaked through his heart almost made him breathless.

Daniel's breathing deepened. Serena leaned forward, fingers waving over his still face.

"Remarkable," she whispered. "I can hardly believe he is your brother."

"You don't know him," Blue said.

"Your family loyalty is admirable, but misplaced. He lost my daughter. I cannot forgive him for that."

"And me?"

"That remains to be seen. You are both like your father."

"I don't believe that."

"Then you are naïve. All men are products of their fathers. It is inevitable. You, Blue, carry the old man inside you. The way you talk, the way you walk, the way you look a person in the eye. It is him. All him."

"You sound as though you know him well."

"Business."

"Right." Blue sighed. "So you're a shape-shifter. Do your employers know that?"

"Do yours know that you are an electrokinetic?"

Blue frowned. "I hate it when you do that."

"I cannot help that Dirk and Steele's intelligence is so poor."

"And what about Iris? Does she know all of this?"

Serena hesitated. "No. I never told her."

"So you just left her. For years. Did you ever stop to consider how that made her feel? What she thought about your disappearance?"

"Of course," Serena snapped. "But I had no choice. Would you prefer that men like Santoso walk free?"

"He was walking free when you were spying on him. I don't see that you did much except his dirty work."

"Cut off the leg of a dog, and the dog can still walk. Cut off his tail and he can still run. Cut off his head and he is dead and gone. Santoso was nothing but a limb. I needed something more permanent. Which, I say again, you ruined."

"Sticks and stones may break my bones, but bombs will never hurt me."

Daniel still slept. Serena drifted closer to Blue; her breath tickled his ear, and in a whisper she said, "You were wrong about me. I did help my daughter, as much as I could, though she might not have felt my presence in her life. With Santoso so close, I could not be obvious. I had to tread lightly."

"She misses you. I haven't known her long, but I've seen that much."

"You think you love her."

"Yes," Blue said, unable to say that he did not just think it, but that he knew it, felt it, down in his gut. "I don't know how she feels about me, though."

"Are you having sex?"

Blue tore his gaze from the road and turned his head, forcing himself to look her straight in the eyes. Golden light flashed. He smelled the old traces of fading perfume. "Not yet."

"Not yet," Serena murmured, and then: "My daughter has never been with a man. You must be careful with her."

"Okay," he said, trying not to let his face reveal just how much this conversation unnerved him. *Of course* he would be careful, but having Serena say as much made him feel like a pervert for wanting her daughter.

He cleared his throat. "So, Santoso. What can we expect in terms of firepower?"

"Overwhelming force. The facility is the largest stationary operation of its kind in the world. It is not a backwater hack job."

"Someone in the FBI or CIA must know about this."

"No. And those who have gotten close are now either very rich or very dead. The stakes are too high for anything else. The money he makes worldwide is already in the billions, and after this facility becomes more established, after he builds his network of them, he stands to gain even more."

"That kind of money, he must have an army at his disposal."

"Yes."

"We need help."

"Absolutely not. The three of us are enough. Too many people increase the chances of someone getting hurt."

"I think the opposite is true."

"This is nonnegotiable."

Blue bit the inside of his cheek. "Fine. I suppose you know what you're doing."

Serena did not answer that. She pointed and said, "Do you see that turnoff? Take it."

Blue did, the Humvee lurched, and Daniel woke up with a long snort and a cough. Serena grumbled something under her breath and retreated deeper into the shadows of the backseat. Blue, taking pity on his brother, handed him a bottle of water that had been stashed between them.

"Thanks," Daniel mumbled.

"Why'd you run?" Blue asked him. No warning. Point-blank.

Daniel paused in the middle of drinking his water. "Because he killed my mother."

Blue felt the air go very still inside the car. "He *killed* her?"

"Not with a bullet or poison. But he did murder her, sure as I'm sitting here. Talked her to death with his meanness. Hit her, too, but the physical wasn't as bad as the mind games." Daniel stared down at his hands, the water bottle. "My mother was the only good thing about my life, growing up."

Blue thought of his own mother. "She didn't leave him?"

"Not for lack of trying on my part. She just wouldn't do it. She was afraid of him, afraid for me … and she wanted to make sure I got my … birthright." Daniel said the word as if it were made of nails. "She never said so, but I also think she had been abused before, and in her mind being rich and in trouble was a lot better than the opposite."

"When did she die?"

"A year ago. She cut her wrists."

The car swerved just slightly; Blue looked at his brother, at his slack, cold profile, and his dull voice rang again inside Blue's head with those four matter-of-fact words.

"I'm sorry," Blue murmured.

"Our father was in Jordan at the time," Daniel explained, still quiet, still under control. "He didn't come home and he didn't tell me. The housekeeper let me know, and I was lucky I got to see her body, because the old man had her cremated almost immediately. If I hadn't gotten there so quickly I would never have found out what happened."

Blue chewed the inside of his cheek, wondering how much to say, wondering if there were any words that would not be offensive in some way. Finally he gave what he thought might be the easiest, and said, "The old man mentioned your mother when he first told me to find you. He said she was … beautiful. A good woman."

Daniel shot him a hard look. "Is that supposed to be a consolation?"

"It's not supposed to be anything. I just wasn't sure you knew." Or if it would matter.

Serena tapped Blue's shoulder. "There's another road ahead. Take it."

Blue tapped on the brakes. All he saw was a dirt track leading into the desert, but Serena gave no other instructions, and so he pulled onto it. The Humvee bounced and growled. Its headlights cut into a world of rock and brush and cacti. The moon had risen higher; the light glimmered against the mountains.

After several miles, Blue felt yet another tap on his shoulder and Serena said, "Stop the car."

He did, cutting the lights so that the world swallowed them up in darkness. Serena opened her door and slid out; Blue shared a quick glance with his brother and did the same, taking the gun she had given him and slipping it into the back of his jeans.

The air smelled good and was cooler than in the city. Blue turned in a wide circle and saw a glow against the horizon; Las Vegas beating out the stars.

"Now what?" Daniel asked, his voice dropping to a whisper on the second word. The air was very still; even the crunch of dirt beneath their shoes sounded too loud.

Serena snapped her fingers. Blue felt like doing the same right back at her, but restrained himself and went to see what she wanted. She was still naked, standing at the back of the Humvee, hand pressed on the bandage over her blood-stained shoulder. Fur continued to cover the injured part of her body; her eyes glowed.

"There is equipment in the back of this car," she told him quietly. "Weapons, water, food. You and your brother need to take as much as you can carry."

"How far to Iris?"

"The distance is not the issue." Serena raised her head for a moment, sniffing the air. "The problem is what will happen after we retrieve her. Returning here may not be an option."

Daniel joined them. Blue opened up the back of the Humvee and found stack after stack of bottled water, along with boxes of PowerBars, trail mix, jerky, and other lightweight, nonperishable foods. Several backpacks had been crammed in the corner, along with piles of folded material that looked like aluminum, but was soft as silk.

"Sleep sacks," Serena said. Her voice was rough; Blue imagined a slight sway in her posture. "Waterproof, and they can also double as tents. It's a new fabric, similar to what some militaries use, but more refined."

"Courtesy of your employers?"

She was silent, which was answer enough.

Daniel and Blue began filling backpacks. Serena opened a crate, revealing guns, grenades, Tasers—even a box of carefully packed syringes.

"Sedatives," she said.

"Huh." Daniel chewed his lip. "What did you say you did again?"

Serena's mouth curved. "I believe that should be self-evident by now."

"No," he said, looking her straight in the eye. "It really isn't. Two years ago you performed in the circus. That's not the kind of place where you learn how to lob grenades. Or spy. Or ... whatever."

Serena said nothing, simply stared at him. Blue wondered if she was thinking about all the different ways she could kill him or blow him up or stick his head in a toilet. Not too concerned about any of those options, Blue slid into a lightweight mesh holster and began packing on the guns. "We need to go. How far is it, Serena?"

"Four miles. There are motion sensors along the property line. I do not think those will be a problem."

Blue smiled briefly. "We could still drive in, then."

"This road narrows into nothing but a footpath for more than a mile. After that, the land levels out into something suitable for vehicles, but ours would never make it that far, and there is no other way in. Do you really wish to risk our only mode of transportation?"

"And you?" Daniel asked. "What about your injury? You were shot."

"I will manage." Her eyes glowed, but this time the light

trickled down, caressing her throat, her breasts, her sinewy torso and narrow hips. Daniel made a guttural sound, low, sick, but Blue did not look at him, did not tear his gaze from Serena as fur poured through her skin, her body stretching and widening, muscles thickening, joints popping until she went down on all fours—and it happened so fast that all of it became a blur in his mind the moment the light died. In Serena's place was a leopard, watching them with unnatural eyes.

Yeah. Blue never got tired of seeing that.

Serena padded past them, a slight limp in her gait— nothing else that would indicate a gunshot wound. She stopped just beyond the car and looked over her shoulder.

Blue handed Daniel his backpack. His brother took it, but his grip was weak; the bag slid out of his hand. He made no move to pick it up, only continuing to stare at Serena. Even in just the moonlight the whites of his eyes were bright and huge.

Blue sighed and shut the car door. Daniel jumped as the door slammed; he clutched his chest as though shot. No words, though—no sound at all. Just more staring. Blue waited a moment, giving him a chance, but when Serena began slipping away he gave up and jogged after her. His knee hurt, but he thought of Iris and swallowed down the pain.

Dirt scuffed; Blue glanced over his shoulder and saw Daniel running after them, backpack swinging from one hand as he tried to put it on without slowing. He caught up quickly, still looking shell-shocked. Blue thought about talking to him, making certain he was all right, but Daniel was on his feet, moving, and what the hell—if and when his brother wanted to share, he would.

Serena moved quickly; the only way Blue could track her in the darkness was to focus on the faint electrical hum of her heart. The moonlight helped, but only enough to show him that they traveled on a narrow track that cut a swath through the desert. A road, maybe. Blue had no idea where they were. The night was very still, the air comfortably cool.

He patted his pocket—cheap reassurance that his cell phone was still there. Roland had promised backup, but that was hours—and a lifetime—ago. No way for his friends to find him now, not unless Dean was on board; and even if they were looking, he doubted they would arrive in time to help break Iris free.

Forget Serena and her rules. Contact Roland.

But he did not. He pulled out his phone and turned it off. Daniel watched. He was a loud walker; his breath hissed, his jeans rubbed.

"You planning on making a call?" His voice dropped to a whisper.

"No. We're on our own."

Somewhere distant, a coyote howled. "You said you were in the military, right?"

"More as a tech guy, but I did my share."

"That's deliberately vague."

"It has to be. Some of what I did is still classified."

Daniel grunted. "So you think you're qualified to storm the castle and rescue the princess?"

"Don't you?"

That earned him a small smile. "Answer something for me."

"If I want to."

"Fuck you."

"Not between brothers, please."

Daniel let out his breath in a slow hiss. "You weren't surprised by my ... abilities. I want to know why."

"How did you know who I was the first time you saw me?"

"My question first."

"Maybe later, then," Blue said, and moved from a fast walk into a run. His body protested, but he fought to stay steady, to manage the pain. Daniel kept up easily with him. He asked no more questions, just tucked his chin, gaze fixed on the path ahead of them.

Serena was a flicker in the moonlight; a shadow sliding from one patch of darkness to another. Watching her, Blue pushed out with his mind, stretching to the limits of his gifts.

Without a current to ride upon, his range was limited. In cities there was power everywhere—he could follow the lines, could lose himself in individual electromagnetic threads, his own private labyrinth. But here, nothing.

Until, quite suddenly, something sharp tapped against his shields, a staccato dance, and Blue called out a warning even as he dropped his mind into the middle of a grid. He found electricity running beneath the ground directly ahead of them, fueling a network of sensors.

Blue turned them off. Easy as thinking about it, using his instincts to feel where the current should be broken, and—there. Done.

"What happened?" Daniel asked, as Serena appeared. Still a leopard, still on all fours. Blue ignored them both, riding the current, the wires, trying to push all the way to the source, searching for anything else that could harm them. Nothing—nothing—and he had almost reached his physical limit when something else tickled, something large, moving fast.

Cars. Heading straight toward them. He could hear the vehicles in his head, buzzing like bees, and it was only when Daniel stirred and said, "Something's coming," that Blue realized the buzzing was not just inside his mind, but in his ears, as well. Engines whining.

A gunshot split the air. Daniel flinched. Serena went very still, head raised, ears swiveled. Her eyes glowed.

"No," Blue said, but it was too late. Serena ran.

"Shit," Daniel muttered, but that was because Blue followed her, throwing himself into a long, lunging run that made his bones scream and his breath whistle in his lungs. Hell week, he reminded himself. Basic training, all over again. Except he was thirty-two and injured, *and* he was trying to keep up with a goddamn leopard. In the desert. At night.

Serena left the path, and the ground turned uneven, filled with sharp rocks and sharper plants. Blue pushed past his shields, splitting his focus, letting his body take over the running while his thoughts rode the underground grid below him. A split-second journey; his mind came up directly beneath the cars, sending him right into their metal hearts, the pulse of currents leading from the batteries. Blue entered them, one after another, disrupting the flow of power.

Silence. Blue tracked the buzz of radios and shorted those as well. He heard a faint shout, another crack of gunfire. He pushed himself harder, wishing for that Humvee as he made his way up a low ridge. His foot snagged painfully on a heap of sharp rocks—he almost went down—but Daniel was suddenly there with a hand under his arm, hauling him up and forward.

They reached the top of the ridge. Below, another spread of desert. Moonlight revealed the dark glint of cars, scattered and still. Flashlights swept the ground. Blue heard more shouts, doors slamming. Behind them, in the distance, headlights bounced—and beyond that Blue saw yet more light—from a building that, even at this considerable distance, appeared large. The facility was outside of Blue's range, as were the cars driving from it. Soon, though.

He and Daniel were too far up the ridge to be seen, but Serena had already veered to the right and was headed directly toward the men. Desperate, reckless. Not at all concerned with staying hidden. Almost as if she were trying to draw attention to herself . . . to protect someone.

"What's she doing?" Daniel asked, but Blue caught sight of new movement at the base of the ridge, a long, dark body racing low to the ground, shadow to shadow, and he did not think, he did not plan, he scrabbled down with the same wild abandon, falling hard on his hip and sliding most of the way with one hand braced against the rough ground as he tore a path to the flatland below. Ugly, loud noises. He kept expecting gunfire, shouts, a crotch full of cactus—

The air zinged; a bullet slammed into the ground beside him. A near miss, but he kept moving, finally finding his feet and cutting sideways in a zigzag pattern. He looked back over his shoulder just once; Daniel was behind him, moving far more gracefully. *Careful*, Blue thought, but that was all the concern he could spare his brother. He had almost reached bottom, and the men were running now. Blue cut out their flashlights. He thought about doing more, if he could get close enough—one thought, ten heart attacks—but held himself back. If he slipped, if he lost control—

You're older now. You know what you're doing.

Maybe, maybe not. Killing a person with his mind was a hell of a lot different from shutting off a toaster.

Blue reached the base of the ridge; Serena had already begun to draw fire, though the sounds that alternated in his ears were a mixture of bullets and something softer, like the beat of a wing, or a slap. A tranquilizer gun, maybe. Bullets to herd, sedatives to take down? Which made Blue wonder if the men really knew what they were hunting—woman or leopard ... or both. Because that was Iris down there—he knew it, felt it in his gut and in the way Serena was acting— but if Santoso knew it, too ...

The moon was too bright; there was no such thing as true cover. Taking away the flashlights had not slowed the men at all, which also said something about their training.

"Can you get rid of their guns?" Blue called back to his brother.

Daniel slid close. "Too far. My range is limited. I bet Serena could outrun those assholes, though. She needs to be moving away, *not* toward."

Blue said nothing. He knew why she was drawing attention to herself, and his suspicion was confirmed when he heard a high, wild scream split the air that was definitely *not* from Serena.

Damn. Blue reached for his gun. More than three hundred yards of rock and scrub separated him from his enemies, who had spread out from the three stalled vehicles in a diamond pattern. Blue began running just as a long, dark body hurtled across the ground toward Serena—who suddenly exploded from the scrub, trailing golden light. She threw herself at one of the gunmen, and though it was too dark for details, Blue heard the man scream like his balls were being ripped off. She was fast, brutal, left the man in the dirt and then went for another, and her body rippled as she moved, still surrounded in light, until suddenly she was on two feet instead of four, dancing like a gymnast: raking faces, bodies, shimmering like some specter of death.

Blue stopped, aiming, but there was no clear shot, nothing that might not clip Serena as the men themselves struggled to shoot her with a tranquilizer. She was too fast for them, too slippery, gunshot wound be damned.

The other leopard was almost there, a blur in the moonlight. Blue found himself running after her, shouting her name, shouting *"Iris,"* and the cat faltered, looking at him. Eyes glowed, illuminating her face, and for a moment Blue could see the woman inside the leopard, could trace the lines of her cheeks to a gaze that was so human, so startled, that it seemed to Blue there was no such thing as fur or claw or tail. Just Iris. Just her.

"Stay back!" Blue shouted at her, but Serena screamed—this time in pain—and Iris turned away and threw herself into the fight.

"Iris?" Daniel murmured, but there was no time. The two brothers ran, and this time Blue fired shots—wild, meant to miss—trying to create a distraction, trying to draw the fire away from Iris and Serena as those two shape-shifters tore into Santoso's men. The darkness was saving them, but Blue knew that would last only so long. Serena, he thought, was not moving quite as fast.

And those cars were still coming, still out of range. Blue could see the dots of their headlights getting larger. *Soon, soon, soon.*

Santoso's men began to return fire; Blue dropped to the ground, dragging Daniel with him. Some of them were stupid enough to break away from the others; Blue shot them down.

"Close enough?" Blue asked his brother.

Daniel grimaced, and began crawling on his stomach toward the fight. Blue followed him, giving cover, still trying to draw attention away from Iris and her mother. Both were in leopard form now, impossible to tell apart, but Blue saw a rifle butt slam into a spotted back, and felt the answering cry reach down into his chest and squeeze.

He almost killed that man. Almost used his mind to reach out and cut the electricity around his heart.

And if you make a mistake? If Iris catches the wave? If her mother does, or Daniel?

Fuck. And fuck sitting here while they were in the middle of it. Blue shot to his feet and started running. Daniel called his name, but there was no such thing as turning back. He shouted at Santoso's men, waving his arms, feeling like a crazy man and not caring as more of them broke away, raising their guns. Blue had the faster trigger, but even as he fired, even as the men fell down, he felt something tickle the edge of his shields, a low hum that was not strong enough to be a car but that had a similar mass. Or rather, enough numbers crowded close to feel like a mass.

People. A lot of them.

Cold sank into his heart; he pushed harder and felt no cars behind that group, no radios within it. Nothing electronic. Close now. Traveling upwind. A group of ten—ten hearts, charged—and not one of them wearing so much as a watch. They had to be pressed together, tight—the electrical charges were too faint to catch on their own, if spaced out. Not unless he knew what he was looking for.

How could they know? Blue thought, numb. *How could they know how to hide, unless ... unless ...*

"Iris!" Blue roared, but it was too late. He saw movement less than a hundred yards away at the base of the ridge, deep within a jumble of large rocks that were only steps from one of the stalled cars.

He ran. He ran straight toward Iris—Iris fighting, her jaws clamped around a man's throat, rolling and rolling with her back feet raking his gut—and felt bullets whistle past his head as he looked down the barrel of a gun aimed directly at his face, moonlight glinting on the barrel.

The weapon never fired. It was there and gone—torn away and flying through the night to skitter across the rocks. Not just one gun, but others—all of them in that small circle of violence going, going, gone—and for one brief moment Blue thought they would make it out of there, that they had a chance.

And then the reinforcements hiding in the rocks started firing, and their guns did not go away, did not stop. Serena and Iris broke from the men they had been fighting—men who flopped like broken dolls on stone—and they met no resistance from those left untouched as they raced toward Blue and Daniel.

Blue met Iris halfway, slamming up hard against her lean, long side, one hand on her furred back as he tried to provide cover against the hail of tranquilizer darts ricocheting off the ground near their feet. His aim was good; he listened to the hearts inside his head, and the darkness was no cover for that.

"Fuck is this?" Daniel shouted, still running—away, now, back to the ridge—and Blue glanced over his shoulder at the stalled cars. Too late. No way to go back for them.

"It's a trap," he snapped, pushing against Iris's shoulder, trying to get her to run faster. She stayed with him, growling, even when her mother pulled ahead for a brief moment, looking at her daughter with a snap in her eyes that was nothing less than, *Ditch these losers and follow me.* Blue could not agree more.

"Go!" he raged at Iris, trying to run faster, moving on nothing but pure desperation. If she got hurt because of him—

Too late. A dart hit her side. Iris stumbled, managed to keep going another few steps before crumpling against the rocks. Serena was there in an instant, golden light sweeping over her like a storm, and Blue heard her whisper, "Shift. Shift, Iris. Hurry."

She did—a slide from leopard to woman that her mother matched, guiding her with yet more words that Blue could not hear, but that sounded like a song.

"Mom," Iris murmured, but that was all. Her eyes fluttered shut. Serena yanked out the dart and began to lift her daughter. *Like hell.* Blue pushed her out of the way and slung Iris over his shoulder; one great heave, stifling a tremendous groan. *Oh, God.* His knee.

Serena did not revert to the cat. Only partially human—the lower half of her body covered in fur—she held her daughter's hand, steadying her as they began to run again. Blue felt their pursuers leave the rocks, join up with the other men. The headlights still bounced in the distance, in range now, and Blue shut off the engines with a thought.

"We're not going to make it to the ridge," Daniel said, pausing for a moment to sweep his hands through the air. A wall of dirt and rock kicked up behind them, a cloud that masked their movements from the pursuing men. It was only a brief comfort, though; darts still whistled, cutting far too close, and Daniel aimed blindly over his shoulder, firing his gun. Blue gritted his teeth and gave his weapon to Serena. She took it wordlessly, turned on her heel, and unloaded the clip into the cloud. Blue heard shouts, cries of pain ... and a dart thudded into her leg.

She ripped it out, but too late—swaying, swaying, she went down hard on one knee. Daniel tried to help her, but she pushed him away, snarling. He tried again and she grabbed a rock, slinging it at his crotch. Her aim was bad; it bounced off his hip, but Blue understood her reaction, could taste her fear and desperation as she tore her gaze from Daniel and stared helplessly at her daughter.

"Iris," she begged. "Please. Get her away."

"Serena," Blue protested, but she shook her head, crashing hard on her side. Her head lolled, the light in her eyes fading to ash, but her mouth still moved, and he heard her whisper her daughter's name like a prayer.

Daniel hesitated, bent over her ... and grunted. There came a bad sound—low, wet—and it seemed to Blue that the dust cloud thinned and time slowed down as his brother reached for his side and yanked out a tufted dart.

"Shit," he muttered, and Blue leaned forward as his brother staggered. Unfortunately, Iris was a deadweight on Blue's shoulder, and trying to bear up Daniel's body without collapsing was a losing battle. He let him slide to the ground.

He heard shouts, the sounds of rock crunching beneath boots. In Blue's mind, three hundred yards and closing.

"Sorry," Daniel muttered weakly.

"Don't," Blue said, voice thick. "Don't, Daniel. I'll get you out of here."

"No time, no way. You need to go, Blue. You're right. They want us alive. You go, you get help. Take Iris."

"Iris," Serena murmured.

Blue's eyes burned. Tears or anger or the goddamn dust, but he was done and desperate and fucking tired of running. *So kill them. Do it and end this. Now.*

He reached out with his mind. The men pursuing them were close enough; he found one running hard across the moonlit desert flatland. He focused, centered himself.

But he could not do it. He could not kill, not like that. Not another body and soul to add to all those memories of death, all those years and corpses left behind in the dirt when being close to him was like asking for death, and even his mother— his *mother*—had caught the brunt.

Hypocrite. You defend yourself with bullets.

But this was different. It had always been different.

A dart flew past his leg; another whispered against his ear. Hard choices, and he could not make them. *Son of a bitch.*

"Go," Daniel whispered, flopping his arm over Serena's still back. "Go, Blue."

Your friends or your family, or how about both? Whom do you betray? Who means more?

Blue felt Iris's breath on his back. He felt her heart inside his head. He felt her body on his body, in his hands, and he thought about Santoso touching her, hurting her, making her do terrible things.

Blue did not say good-bye. He did not look back. He ran and his body screamed, but he did not listen to the pain as he charged toward the ridge, scrambling to keep his footing as his knee threatened to give. He heard shouts, cries, but though he expected to feel the prick of something sharp, no more darts followed. He reached the base of the ridge and kept going, up and up, fighting the land and his own growing weakness.

Halfway to the top he stopped, glancing over his shoulder.

The men no longer pursued him. He saw them gathered around Daniel and Serena. No cars, no way to contact the facility in the distance, but he figured that would be remedied soon enough.

One of the men separated himself from the others and walked slowly toward the ridge. Even at his considerable distance, Blue could see the moonlight reflecting off blond hair, and he felt a dark gaze fix upon him, deeper shadows than the night. A quiet stare. One that tickled his shields.

Cold ran up his arms. Blue hefted Iris higher on his aching shoulder. He kept running.

CHAPTER THIRTEEN

No dream, only memory. Iris awakened to a vision of violence and sex, moonlight running cold on desert rock, and her mother—her mother alive and fighting—her mother at her side, gunshots ringing, with the taste of blood so hot in her mouth, and Blue ... Blue ...

Iris opened her eyes. Above her, rock. Below, the same. The ground she lay on was hard, uneven. Something sharp poked her shoulder. She carefully inhaled; the air smelled dry, hot, with a hint of electricity. Thunder.

Iris turned her head. Blue lay beside her. Based on the position of his legs, she thought he might have started out sitting up, and had fallen so deeply unconscious that he simply tipped over like a rag doll, complete with bruised eyes, hollow cheeks, and a gun cradled against his chest.

She almost touched him, woke him up, but at the last moment she pulled away her hand and watched him sleep. He looked like a running man, a hunted man, and she remembered his eyes in the night, his gaze cutting right through her, staring at the leopard and calling her name.

She remembered blood. She touched her lips, which were caked in it.

Iris dragged in a long breath. She was naked, with only a

thin sheet of some warm, shining material wrapped around her body. No extra clothes, either. A water bottle poked from the backpack beside her; she pulled it out, broke the seal, and took a long drink. She splashed water on her face and scrubbed her mouth.

She tried not to think about her mother, about why Serena was not with them, why there was no trace of her scent. Tried not to think about it because she knew the truth, deep in her gut, and she could not handle the idea of her mother being gone again. Alive and with Santoso. Alive and hurting. Alive and being ripped apart. Because her mother had not been careful. All those men had seen her shift. The truth was out.

Blue stirred. Slowly, at first, until his eyes snapped open. He did not move, simply stared at her. Iris said nothing. No words, no thoughts, nothing but instinct—to run, hide. Only it was too late for that. Too late for everything. Blue knew. He *knew*.

Iris held out the water bottle. Blue lay very still.

"Are you okay?" His voice was hoarse, raw, a sandpaper whisper that cut straight to her heart.

"No," she rasped softly. "But I'm going to fix that."

His jaw tightened, his eyes going dark, hard. Iris wanted to smile when she saw the shift; it was the perfect compliment to the rage inside her own heart.

I am going to kill Santoso, Iris thought. *I am going to eat him and shit him and dump his bones in the desert. I am going to wipe his existence from this planet.*

And then she was going to take care of that facility. Burn it all—and Broker—to the ground.

Blue took the water. He sat up, wincing, and when he tried to raise the bottle to his lips his hand shook so badly Iris instinctively reached out. She did not look at his face—she was afraid to be so close to his eyes, those eyes that knew her—but she placed her hand under the warm skin of his strong wrist and held him, steadied him, watched the mouth of that bottle touch his lips and swing back, the water as it ran down his chin, the bob of his throat.

"Thank you," he said. Iris nodded, still looking down. She let go of him, began to lean away, but he encircled her hand, catching her, and whispered, "Look at me."

So she did. And his eyes were still impossibly warm, so warm she wanted to cry because she was sick of being afraid, sick of this nightmare, sick of being alone, and looking at him felt like the closest thing she had to home.

Blue touched her chin, running his fingers down the line of her jaw to her throat. He did not speak, but his gaze was enough, and Iris did not pull away. This—this was the way a man should look at a woman, and it helped cleanse her mind of bad memories, of that room with Songbird and its other drugged women, of Santoso and his chains and that rape of her most secret identity, which still cut, which still made her angry and ashamed and so very afraid, because there was proof now—proof—and ... and ...

"I'm glad you're here," Iris said to him.

Blue dragged in his breath. Still silent, with that terrible gaze that was both hard and warm and infinitely weary. He began to move his arms, but Iris beat him to it, shifting close, rubbing hip-to-hip as she leaned into his body and laid her cheek against his. His beard rasped her skin, but she did not mind; for the first time in her life she was not afraid of being held, and she wanted it, needed it.

"My mother," she said softly.

"She's alive," Blue said.

"For now. When Santoso finds out what she is ..." Iris hesitated. "You know the truth."

Blue pressed his lips against her shoulder. "I knew what you were the first time I saw you."

It was not what she'd been expecting to hear. Iris pulled away, staring. "How is that possible?"

"Your eyes. Only shape-shifters have eyes that color."

Iris thought of Santoso, his *your eyes give you away, you know. They are the gold of heaven,* and her breath caught.

"You've met others?"

His smile was tired but genuine. "My friends."

Iris could not imagine. All this time, this man knowing—and for there to be others, more than one ...

Blue touched her cheek; his fingers were warm, his scent strong, wild. "We'll get your mother back, Iris."

"He'll kill her," she said. "He had a camera in my dressing room, Blue. Maybe he was responsible for that camera in my home, too. He knew what I was."

Just like Blue did. Maybe Blue put a camera in your home. Maybe there's more going on here than you think.

Or maybe she was paranoid and this was more information than she could handle. Mother. Blue. That was all. Everything else would kill her.

Blue frowned. "Santoso is a broker, Iris. You and your mother would be more valuable to him alive."

Alive. In that room, with his voice, his *I have you, Iris, and I will have my dream. I will take my magic. I will take it all.* She dug her nails into her palm, wanting the pain to take away the memory. Blue touched her wrist, but she did not stop. Just dug harder.

"This goes beyond monetary value," she told him, fighting to steady her voice. "He wants to *become* like us. He wants to *be* us. Able to shift. He made me bite him, because he thought that would infect him with my abilities." Iris laughed, but it was an ugly sound. "I bit him. I wanted to fucking kill him. I spun him some lie about how it might take a while for the change to happen, but that wasn't going to buy me any time. Not as much as I needed. He had a backup plan, you see. If the bite didn't work, he was going to strip me of my ... my vital organs. Put them in himself."

Blue's fingers tightened around her wrist. "That makes no sense. Even if his body didn't reject them outright—"

"I know. And maybe it's shit; maybe all he really wants is a lab rat. But either way, if he doesn't have me, he'll use her." Iris closed her eyes, shaking her head. "She was gone for two years, Blue. Two fucking years. And the night she comes back all this goes down."

Blue said nothing. His was an odd silence—all of this,

odd—but more so with him, because there was an element of weight to his quiet, a heaviness. As if he knew something.

And really, what kind of coincidence is it that they were both there last night?

What kind of wild dream, that she should enter the desert, pursued by Broker and his men, and find her mother, Blue, and Daniel on the other side of freedom? What kind of world was that? What kind of new normal, where talking about death and shape-shifters and men who wanted to rape and kill her was to be expected, accepted?

Iris studied Blue's face. He made no effort to hide his discomfort from her; she could see it in his gaze, smell it on his body.

"Tell me," she said.

"It's not my story to tell. You need to hear it from her."

"But you know the truth? You, a stranger?"

"I'm not a stranger to your mother," he said quietly. "Not really. But that's also part of the story I can't share. Not until she has a chance to tell you first. It wouldn't be right, Iris."

"Not right?" Iris wanted to hit him, strangle him, kiss him until he bled and then rattle his brains out his ears. "How long have you known my mother?"

Blue hesitated. "Not long. I met her once, two weeks ago. But I didn't know who she was until last night, when I encountered her again. I didn't know she was your mother, Iris."

"That's too much of a coincidence. You said you were a detective, that you were here investigating someone. I thought it was ... was someone else, but was it me after all? Did she ... did she send you?" Because why else would they have a connection? What else was there that could possibly bring two such disparate people together?

And what the hell has my mother been doing for the past two years?

Blue raked his fingers through his hair. "No," he growled, rocking his head back, closing his eyes. "No, Iris. She didn't hire me. And *yes*, this is all a coincidence, as remarkable as it might seem. I was here for someone else. My brother." He took a deep breath. "Daniel."

Iris snorted. "Old news. You can't surprise me with that."

She could have pulled a dead fish out of the air and slapped him upside the head with it, he looked so startled. "You know? How?"

"Daniel told me. Just before he found that his—your—father died."

Blue closed his eyes. "He's not. It's a lie. The old man faked it all."

Truth. His body reeked of stress, but not deception. Nothing of the kind. Iris lay back down on the hard ground and gazed past him at the desert. Their patch of shade was wide, but outside, the rock and dirt gleamed bright amongst the tangled scrub and cacti. Even farther, mountains. Clear air, clear scents.

Breathe, she told herself. *Just let it out.*

Or keep it in. She had questions—questions that would each launch a hundred more—but there was no time, no time for anything less essential than survival. Instead of entering the mess inside her head, instead of trying to solve the puzzle, she pushed it away—*selective amnesia, be a friend*—and said, "Where are we?"

"I don't know," Blue said slowly, watching her like she might bite him. "Last night was a trap, Iris. Those men hunting you knew we were coming."

"They knew," Iris echoed softly, and her expression hardened. "Son of a bitch. That's why he did it."

"What does that mean?"

Iris shook her head. "Broker. Santoso's right hand man. He let me go, Blue. Helped me escape. I thought it was because he wanted a chase, to make some kind of point, but maybe there was more at stake. You, Danny. My mother."

"Treating you like bait?" Blue's expression darkened. "You know what that implies."

"Bad things," she said. "Lots of bad things."

He stretched out beside her. Iris heard all sorts of interesting pops and cracks. "We had a car, Iris, a way out of here. But when I got close, I discovered people waiting with it. Another trap. I had to keep going, find a safe place. I walked until I couldn't go any farther. I found this spot in the rocks by accident." He turned his head and glanced out at the sky and sun. "I don't think we've been here long. Dawn was coming when I stopped."

"So you carried me. All night."

"I didn't drag you by the hair," he said, exasperated. Iris bit back a smile.

Too late. She knew he caught it because he smiled, too, and then laughed—a low, quiet rumble that was tired and sad, and that only made her want to touch him, hold him, rub away the wrinkles between his eyes.

"I'm sorry," he said. "I'm so sorry about all of this, Iris."

"I'm free and alive," she replied firmly. "Confused as hell, and more than a little angry, but that's all good. It'll help me save my mother. And Danny."

Blue frowned. "I can't imagine why Santoso would want him."

"Neither can I. Based on what I saw, Santoso doesn't need to ransom anyone. He's got plenty of money already."

"You saw his operation?"

"Some. Too much. He's a sick man, Blue. Sick as anything I ever imagined, but the worst part is that he wouldn't exist if there weren't already hundreds or thousands of people just as disgusting as he is."

"Supply and demand. I wish I could have protected you from that."

"And you think I can't protect myself?" Iris asked, though it was nothing but quiet bravado, because last night she had *not* been able to protect herself, not for all her gifts, not for all her precautions. Her life had been in the hands of others, and oh, what a failure she had been. Alive, yes. Unbroken, yes. But still in chains.

No chains now. You have your freedom.

Not really. Not until Santoso was dead. Not until she had her mother and Danny back, alive.

Iris held up her hand and slowly shifted, watching Blue's face as golden light shimmered over her fingers and wrist. Fur pushed through her skin, golden and black, sleek with round spots. Claws tore through her nails. Animal and human, together as one, and there was a part of her that watched the transformation in disbelief, even outrage, because she could not control her impulse to see Blue's reaction, to see if he truly could handle what she was without fear or the awful lust that Santoso had shown. Her heart hammered, a little voice screaming inside her head—*not right, not right*—but her life was all gone to hell, anyway, and she wanted to know how deep she could go before striking bottom. She wanted Blue to prove himself. She wanted to see his eyes.

And she did, and she watched him watch her, and she was there at the exact moment he looked away from her hand into her face, and said, "You don't scare me, Iris McGillis."

"I'm not human," she whispered, but Blue grabbed her hand, twining his fingers around her own, and he held them up—flesh against fur, palm to palm—and the sight mesmerized, terrified, exhilarated.

"I don't think I give a damn," he said. "I think I love you just the way you are."

Iris let out her breath, watching as he dragged her hand—her furred, spotted hand—to his lips. He kissed her wrist, her palm, and she fought herself, struggled against her heart, because it was too damn wonderful and right now she did not believe in dreams come true. She did not know if she could trust the possibility.

Then you'll never be satisfied. You'll have the world at your feet and you'll kick it away out of fear.

"We need to go," she said softly.

"I know." He cracked open an eye. "My cell phone doesn't work out here. We're on our own, Iris."

"You say that like it's a bad thing."

"It is for storming a castle." His mouth curved, his thoughts clearly for a moment wicked. "Or did you have something else in mind?"

Iris leaned close and kissed him. It was quick and awkward, but he did not seem to mind. He sat up when she pulled away, following her mouth with his, and she could not escape him as his free hand snaked to the back of her neck, tangling in her hair. His kiss was shockingly gentle, a light caress that was more breath than touch, but she could feel his body quake, his arms tense. Hunger, burning, and the fire in her heart swept into her stomach, pooling into an ache.

The blanket slipped; her breasts rubbed against his chest. Blue broke off the kiss. His breathing was ragged, as was hers. Both their hearts were raging like thunder, together. He held her tight, crushed her in his arms.

"Not here," he breathed in her ear. "Not like this."

Not like what? Iris wanted to ask him, because really, she had the very strong suspicion that making love with Blue would be just as fantastic on the hard ground in the middle of the desert as it would in some fancy hotel with nice clean sheets. Although a shower first might be good.

As would knowing that her mother and friend were *not* in the hands of a megalomaniacal psychotic pervert.

Blue's hand drifted from her hair down her spine, trailing lazy circles to the small of her back, lingering just above the crease of her backside. Iris swallowed hard. "I thought you said now wasn't good?"

"Give me a minute," he muttered.

Iris laughed and pushed him away, drawing the sheet up over her chest. Although, really, when she thought of it, modesty was almost ridiculous at this point.

"Walking in the desert right now is a terrible idea," she said. "The heat is bad enough in the shade."

"I think staying here might be worse." He cleared his throat, glancing out at the bright world beyond the outcropping. "Santoso's men let us go last night. I can't imagine he'll let that stand for long."

Iris thought of Broker, but said nothing. What did she have

to tell Blue? That something else was going on in that facility? A power struggle, perhaps? She stood. "If we're going, I need to shift shape. No clothes and no shoes will make for a very interesting walking experience on those rocks."

"Tell me about it," he muttered, and Iris rolled her eyes, biting back yet another smile. Blue grinned and turned around, giving her privacy.

Iris dropped the blanket. She prepared to shift, but as she did, memories racked her—of Santoso and his men, of the chains and Songbird, crying with a knife to her breast. She shivered, and maybe she made a sound, because Blue stirred, tilting his head just slightly, and said her name.

She studied the strong lines of his back, the rough edge of his dark hair brushing his shoulders. Iris thought about his eyes, what they would look like watching her body, and defiance filled her, along with a deep, quiet rage.

"Blue," she said. "Blue, turn around. Please."

He did, his gaze flickering briefly on her body before focusing on her face.

"Iris," he said. "What—"

"I want you to watch," she said. "I want you to see me shift."

He frowned. "Not that I mind, but you don't ... There's nothing to prove here, Iris."

You're wrong, she thought, but did not say that, did not answer him at all. Iris let the glow rise off her skin, body shimmering into something liquid and malleable, and she watched him watch her, fighting to fill up her mind with memories of something better—memories of Blue—before anything darker could take root.

No flinching. Not ever, not for her.

Blue did not disappoint. She looked for his fear, his disgust—wondered if she would ever stop looking—but all she saw in his eyes was desire, an acceptance that was not forced or patronizing, but sweet, almost kind.

You're a good man, she thought at him, even when his gaze slipped to her breasts, and lower. His expression darkened with another kind of heat, and Iris had to fight the urge to lick her lips, to prolong the shift. So much for testing his tolerance; this was changing into something else entirely.

"Iris," Blue said in a hard voice. "Iris, you'd better do something about this. Or *I'm* going to do something."

"Really," she said, her voice lowering as her throat shifted. Fur covered her body, a sleek coat that would thicken soon enough, but at the moment just dusted her skin. She had never delighted in the sensuality of her body, of her second self, but this ... that look in his eye ... the way his hand drifted down to his thigh ...

Iris went down on all fours, bathed in light. Her tail roped out from the base of her spine, her back arching as muscles expanded, grew long as her torso stretched and stretched— and still Blue watched, and still she felt his desire—her own, as well—and when she was finally leopard, fully cat, she padded close, moving between his legs.

Blue ran his fingers down the sides of her face, and she saw his desire become wonder. His hands felt good. Her entire body felt good. "You're so beautiful," he murmured. "I wish I could kiss you."

Iris shifted just enough so that her face was mostly human, body still sleek with fur. A difficult transformation, but she managed. Blue leaned forward, touching her face, her lips. He kissed her, slow and deep, then pressed his mouth to her ear.

"Why?" he asked, not unkindly. 'Why, Iris?"

"Because I wanted to," she whispered, curling even closer. "Because I had to. I needed you to see me. I needed ... a better memory." Because the next time she changed into a leopard, Santoso would not be the first thing she thought of. Maybe the second, but not the first—and that was all that mattered.

That, and Blue had not turned away. He had not run from her.

Blue went very still; deadly, quiet. "Santoso ... hurt you, didn't he?"

"He hurt me," Iris agreed softly, pulling back to look into his eyes. "But not like that."

He wanted to ask her. He wanted to know. She could see the struggle on his face, but he stayed silent, and Iris was glad. She would tell him one day, but not now. Not now. This was enough to dull the pain, to put her on the road to something better.

Blue pressed his lips against her temple. "Have you ever shown yourself like this to anyone else? Shifted?"

Iris nodded, closing her eyes, trying not to remember. "It was bad, Blue. It ended … bad."

He slid down beside her, pulling her body into his lap. His hands caressed her back, running down her fur, teasing warmth into her muscles. Iris clung to him, limp. "I was sixteen, still in Montana. There was a boy who hung around, a cattle rancher's son. Tommy. I really liked him. I loved him, even. I thought he loved me. And I had these romantic notions of love conquering all. I was so stupid."

"No," Blue murmured. "Different kind of love, that's all. You were young."

Iris swallowed hard, laying her cheek against his chest. "Things got heavy between us. We were out in the woods, fooling around, and I shifted. I couldn't help myself. And he … freaked out. He had a gun—he always carried a gun—and he tried to use it on me. I ran, he caught up, and I … fought back. I hurt him bad, Blue. I didn't mean to. Later, when he could talk again, he tried to tell people what happened, that I was the one who hurt him, but his wounds were from an animal and no one believed him. They put Tommy away for awhile. And my mom and I left to join the circus."

Blue's arms tightened. "And now Santoso—"

"And now *you*." She brushed her lips against his throat, tasting the salt of his skin, drawing his scent into her mouth and making it a part of her. His hands curled against the back of her head, pushing through fur, and he kissed her hard, making her dizzy as he surrounded her, spinning her into pure fire. She clung to him, desperate for the safety of his arms, his desire, fighting down the images of Santoso that suddenly flickered through her mind.

Iris broke off the kiss, gasping. "I'm sorry. I'm so sorry. I need a moment. Last night ..." She stopped, unable to finish or explain. Blue pressed his lips against her forehead. His entire body trembled.

"Iris," he said, and there was something terrible in his soft deep voice, something dark and dangerous yet infinitely gentle. "You tell me what you want, what you need, and I'll give it to you. Anything. All you have to do is ask. All you have to do is need, and I'll be there for you."

From any other man it might have sounded like a joke— *yes, need me, use me, please, oh, please*—but she knew he was offering more than just sex, and it cut her, made her heart bleed just a little, because it was too good, more than she had dreamed for herself, and it made her afraid.

"This is dangerous," she murmured, feeling the echo in her mouth, the déjà vu of a conversation some lifetime distant in her past.

The hint of a smile touched his mouth. "The most dangerous thing we'll ever do. If you trust me."

"I trust you," she breathed. "I don't think I ever had a choice but to trust you. If there had been an alternative ... "

Blue grinned. "I would have been dumped at the side of the road by now?"

Iris bit back a smile. "You got under my skin."

He laughed softly, though only for a moment. His eyes turned serious. "Maybe there's something I should tell you now. About me."

"I don't know if I like the sound of this."

"It's nothing bad. Just ... I have my own secrets. Things that I can do that aren't entirely ... normal."

She stared at him, hard. "What do you mean? You're no shifter."

"I don't have to be." He almost looked sheepish. "I'm psychic."

She would have laughed, but the expression on his face was suddenly so serious that she swallowed it down with a cough. She took a moment to stare, to think about what he was saying. To weigh it in her head with all she knew about the world. "You really mean that, don't you?"

"Don't tell me you think I'm lying."

"It's hard to believe."

"Because women don't turn into cats?" Blue gently squeezed her hand. "Or am I imagining all this fur?"

She tried to pull away, but he would not let go. Part of her was glad. The other part ... just contrary.

"Prove it," she said.

Blue snorted, laughing quietly. "God, you are stubborn."

"I'll take that as a compliment."

"Good." Blue held up his other hand and showed her his watch. The gleaming face was a mix of both standard and digital—very complicated, no doubt expensive.

"Look close," he said.

"What am I looking f—," Iris began, then shut her mouth as the watch suddenly stopped. The digital read-out was blank, the hands were no longer ticking.

"And now ..." Blue whispered, and Iris felt another tingle run up her arm as the watch blinked to life. Iris grabbed his wrist, dragging the watch so close she fogged its face with her breath.

"You turned it off with your mind?" she asked, incredulous.

"Yes. I can do that with anything that uses electricity."

"Which is almost everything.

"Almost," he agreed, watching her with such intensity that for a moment she was reminded of herself. Testing *him*, judging *him*.

Now he was doing the same thing to her.

Iris squeezed his hand. "You don't scare me, Blue. Not in the slightest."

The fleeting pain that passed over his face was not what she expected, but she chalked it up to the same old pain she lived with. Something bad had happened to him, maybe more than once. She understood.

They packed up their things and left the outcropping for the desert sun. The heat was bad in the shade, but out, exposed: terrible. Iris watched Blue walk with a water bottle in his hand, counting the number of drinks he took, reassuring herself that it was enough. In this place a man dying of thirst might never realize he was in trouble until he dropped dead.

She drank, too, coaxed by Blue into lapping water from a small cup stashed inside his backpack. Water tasted different as a leopard: richer, sharper, with nuances that she never noticed as a human. She had forgotten so much.

They traveled east, following an indirect path toward the facility. Blue found the right direction by finding underground electrical lines. A nice trick. She wondered if he was more than just a detective; there was something about the way he acted—what he could do, the fact that he knew actual shape-shifters—that made her think he might be something just a little different.

You still don't know him all that well. You don't know anything, really.

But she could live with that. For now.

Iris loped ahead of him, scenting the wind for threats. The land in this particular area was full of small hills and outcroppings made of red rock, dried riverbeds that felt like the beginnings of baby canyons. The world fluttered with sounds: insects hissing, a lone bird twittering a sparse song; the crunch of dirt beneath Blue's shoes, and the whisper of his movement in jeans. The wind murmured. The afternoon heat did not dull; it magnified everything—including the sudden crack of bone.

The sound was loud as a gunshot, and when she heard it again she could imagine the crunch of marrow, the wet sound of a tongue. It was close; she lifted her nose to the shifting wind and smelled something that was animal, and older: decay, human.

Iris snarled at Blue, raking her claws in the dirt, and when she was certain she had his attention, she moved off their chosen path, bounding around over a low rocky rise. She saw a coyote chewing furiously. On a human body. An arm. And not just one. There was a long ditch filled with badly buried bodies.

Iris charged the coyote. It ran immediately, hauling off the arm it had been eating. Plenty of torso left behind, though. Iris wondered where the vultures were, but when she got close the smell was not as strong as it could have been and the body itself was desiccated and picked over. Out for a while, then, with most of the good stuff gone.

The corpse was female and naked. Long dark hair. Hard to tell if she had been pretty, but Iris thought the answer might be yes. She was covered in dirt from the waist down. No tattoos or birthmarks. Nothing to give a name.

Iris shifted shape, going as human as she could while still retaining her sleek coat of fur. Blue joined her, and together they stared at the tangled rows of the dead. Numbers were impossible to tell, but Iris had to guess at least forty or fifty bodies.

"Mass grave," Blue murmured. "I've seen this before, Iris. In the Philippines. Santoso did something similar there, too."

It took her a moment to understand him; her mind still raged against the death in front of her. "Something similar? You ... knew about Santoso? Before all this happened, you knew he existed?"

His jaw tightened. "I've spent the past three months hunting him."

"Three months," she echoed. "I suppose that means you knew he would be in Las Vegas."

"No." Blue looked at her, eyes hard. "No, Iris. Two weeks ago I was injured and taken off the case. It was only in the past couple of days that my father asked me to find my brother. Which was I came here. The rest was ... coincidence."

"Coincidence. There's been a lot of that lately."

"If you don't believe me—"

"I believe you. But I'm beginning to feel manipulated, Blue."

"I know what you mean," he muttered, and reached for her hand. Her palm hurt, and she realized that she had been digging her claws into the skin. Blue carefully unfolded her fingers and made a hissing sound. Her palm was a mess. Her claws were sharp.

"It'll heal," she told him.

"This is a bad habit, Iris."

"You're the bad habit."

"I'll take that as a compliment."

Iris looked away from him, back at the women. She thought of Songbird, and the other girls who had lain so quietly drugged on their silk pillows—flesh for sale, for just the right price.

"You said you saw this before." Iris glanced at Blue, and then again at the corpses. "Who was buried? Women?"

"Some women, but a lot of kids and young men. Victims of Santoso's trade in human organs. Killed specifically for their hearts and kidneys and whatever else draws a high price on any particular day."

Iris briefly closed her eyes. "I'm betting the people here were slaves. Sex slaves. Santoso kept me chained up with a group of them in the beginning. To show me how it could be if I didn't cooperate. I doubt many of them survive long in that place."

Blue said nothing, but she could feel him staring. He looked furious, and his scent—when it finally rolled over her—was just as violent. Iris could not stand it and walked away, stopping when he did not follow. She watched him bend over the desiccated remains, eyes closed, whispering something so soft it was more of a breath, and she caught only one word: *promise*.

And then he rejoined her, moving at a run that sent her staggering backward. His face was terrible, dark, and he caught her in his arms, hauling her close, squeezing the life out of her in a massive hug that made tears spring to her eyes.

She returned his embrace, letting herself cry, trying not to shake as a sob tore through her chest. Blue kissed her face, her mouth, running his hands down the back of her head.

"He will never hurt you again," Blue whispered brokenly. "I promise you, Iris."

Iris believed his intentions, but not his promise, and she would have told him that, had she not suddenly heard the low drone of a car engine drifting on the wind.

"Blue." Iris tapped her ear, pointing to the south. He hesitated for only a moment, head cocked as though listening.

"Shift," he said, and she did, falling on all fours and throwing herself into the leopard. He ran and she followed, racing down the riverbed, red rock rising high, cut into ribbons and waves of vegetation and sky. The heat was terrible; she could feel Blue's strength ebbing, his breath whistling in his lungs. He favored his right leg.

The car engine got louder; Blue muttered something under his breath and the sound cut out. Which made it impossible for Iris to track the car, though Blue did not seem to share her problem. He led her on an unerring path, taking her from the riverbed on a narrow path that curved up and around a steep hill filled with loose rock.

At the top of the hill, Iris gazed down at the valley spread before them. At the bottom, like an obsidian chip, she found a black jeep parked in the dirt. Men stood beside the vehicle. One of them was tall and pale, with dark hair and dressed in a black long-sleeved shirt and gloves. Beside him stood a much shorter blond man whose hands were pressed against his chest. Thin cords bound a slender gun holster against his jean-clad thigh.

Blue joined her, squinting down into the valley. His breath caught, and a wolfish smile spread across his face. "Goddamn. Those are my friends, Iris. Come on. We're safe."

No, she thought. *We're not.*

But Iris followed him anyway, trying to battle her sense of dread. Being a leopard was no cure for nervousness; a woman still lived inside the fur, and the idea of meeting these strangers was displeasing, to say the least. Blue's friends were not necessarily her friends.

Even if those friends are shape-shifters?

Nice, fantastic, wonderful—but it was no guarantee of character, no promise of trustworthiness.

Paranoia won out. Iris veered silently into the vegetation, tracking Blue on a parallel, more protected path. She did not tell him, but he looked back once—saw she was gone—and nodded silently.

Good. He understood. Even if he did not look happy about it.

The men saw him coming; the blond let out a whoop that was friendly enough to be some small comfort, but it was the other man who made Iris's hackles rise. He did not move from his place against the jeep, just leaned, arms loose against his sides. He stared at Blue.

The blond man ran up the hill, grabbing Blue's arm for one of those loose, swinging handshakes that was pure boy: friendly and relaxed and probably the equivalent of a locker-room slap on the ass.

Crouched in the loose vegetation, Iris saw Blue grin. "Miss me, Dean?"

"Like a good fart," said the man. "Roland was whining like a baby about how you were up to your 'nads in trouble, so I volunteered to be the shit-digger who gets you out. I just didn't realize how much work it would take."

"I'm touched," Blue said, and glanced over his friend's shoulder at the second man. "What's wrong with Artur?"

Dean's smile faded. "Nothing."

What a terrible liar, Iris thought, inching closer. She watched him rub his chest like it pained him, and then the blond man glanced around the small rocky area, his gaze lingering for a moment on her hiding place.

"Dean," Blue said, frowning.

"Let it go," he replied, all his boyish charm disappearing into something tired and hard. "Please, Blue."

No, Iris thought. *Don't let it go. Something is wrong. That man—Artur—is wrong.*

But Blue said nothing and followed Dean down the hill. Iris followed, slinking through the brush, the knot in her throat growing thick and hard as the man called Artur pushed away from the jeep. He moved like a dancer, without wasted movement, elegant and deadly.

Killer, Iris thought when she looked at him. She thought Dean appeared uneasy as well. His fingers lingered near the gun strapped to his thigh.

"Artur," Blue said, holding out his hand as they got close. "How—"

No warning, no time. Artur rushed him, slamming Blue into the ground with enough force that he bounced off the rock. Iris snarled—already moving at that first touch, tearing out of hiding with enough power to rip the man in half.

She never reached him. Dean stepped in front of her, held out his hands, light pulsing just beneath his white T-shirt—

—and she suddenly stood on the hill again, almost twenty feet away.

What? she began to think, but Blue was still on the ground, and that man—that Artur—had his hands far too close to Blue's throat, and Blue was doing nothing to fight him off, was just staring up into his eyes with an expression of heart-breaking confusion. She heard him say Artur's name again and again, and then, louder, in a rough voice, "Why?"

A pure and terrible agony passed over Artur's pale face, a breathless heartbreak that made Iris wonder how the man was still standing, let alone beating the crap out of his so-called friend.

"Artur," Dean said quietly.

"Because you killed her," Artur whispered. He had a thick Russian accent. "My friend, you killed my wife."

CHAPTER FOURTEEN

You killed my wife. You killed my— Elena.

"No," Blue croaked. Impossible. Elena could not be gone, not after saving his life. Not because of him, his mind—his *motherfucking* mind with his shields torn down and his power wild, power that could not be trusted, not for anyone, not even for—*Iris, oh, Iris*—

"Artur," Dean said sharply. "Dude, enough."

"No," Artur murmured, and Blue could already feel the bullet in his brain, wondered if it was wrong to welcome it, wondered why he was not already dead.

Dean fell down on his knees beside him. "Fuck you, Artur. Blue, don't listen to him. He's exaggerating. Elena isn't dead."

Crazy. He was going crazy. Blue stared at Dean, too shaken to talk, and his friend nodded grimly. "That's right, man. She did die—that's no lie—but the doctors were able to resuscitate her."

"Two minutes," Artur whispered, still with that awful shaking voice that was murder, death, darkness all rolled into one. "Two minutes gone. And now—she is still dying, Blue. You damaged her heart in a terrible way. The doctors give her less than a month. Not even that much. Days, maybe. And she cannot ... she *cannot* heal herself."

"Artur," Blue began, but the Russian shut his eyes—too bright now, bloodshot—and sat back, large hands dangling over his knees. Blue pushed himself up, following. Not standing, though. Not ever again. His body felt like a giant fork had been pushed into his gut to stir, cut, pry his innards into nothing but liquid.

Memories filled him, not just of Elena, but of others: pets, strangers on buses and streets, his teacher, his neighbor, his *mother....*

Deaths, injuries. You're a killer. You have always been a killer. It doesn't matter if it's accidental; you have taken lives with nothing but a thought—and not even that much.

Wrong place, wrong time. A break in his shields, high emotion, stress, and there ... there ... terrible things. Broken hearts.

Blue sat in the dirt, silent. Artur and Dean did the same. All three men stared at everything but one another.

Movement. Iris. No more hiding for her. She wended her way down the hill, silent, still a leopard with those lovely golden eyes looking at nothing but him. Muscle rippled beneath the round sleek spots on her shining fur, the desert heat making her shimmer, casting shadows and light in his vision—beautiful, wild, strange, and so much like home— such an odd thing, to call a woman home—that seeing her eased for one moment the terrible scream wrapped around his heart.

There, he thought, as she stepped free of the underbrush, wholly leopard, wholly inhuman. *Right there. There's your forever. If you don't kill her.*

"Iris," he said, his voice hurt, bent, with the edge of that scream still lurking.

She hesitated, studying the other men. Artur barely looked at her; he appeared almost too exhausted to breathe. Dean only nodded briefly, which was just as well. Blue recalled a little of what he had done to Iris—teleportation, displacement.

Cold words for magic. Blue wondered what Iris made of it, though she wore the mask of the leopard with deadly calm; not a twitch or flinch.

She pushed close. Blue smelled rock and wind and heat. He touched her paw and said, "Iris, meet my friends, Dean Campbell and Artur Loginov. We ... work together."

Work together. For now, perhaps, but Blue could not expect the energy and camaraderie they had all shared over the past seven years to hold strong. Not after this. He tried to imagine leaving, resigning from the agency, going his own way into the world without friends, without the family he had made since that first invitation into the solace of Dirk & Steele.

You would survive. That's all you need to know.

As if mere survival were enough. Blue caressed Iris's paw, and she leaned into him as the wind died into a hush, heat blistering his body, cooking him into the desert rock. The world shimmered, glowed—all around him, light—and he traced the radiance to Iris, watching as gold diffused her fur, shedding tendrils of the sun as her body shifted, receded.

She did not complete the transformation. She stopped in that twilight between human and leopard, clad in sleek spotted fur, her body humanoid, shapely, but fuller around the waist and shoulders. Her face was undeniably feminine, but alien, with sleek cheekbones that lifted so high they stood out at angles. Her mouth and nose were mostly human, though more delicate, edged in black and pink, and her ears—arranged against her skull like a human's—ended in sharp tips.

Her eyes, though—her eyes were all woman. And they were only for him.

"I'm having a *Thundercats* moment," Dean said. "Someone pinch me."

Blue wondered if fur were the same as nudity. "Pinch yourself. This isn't anything you haven't seen before."

"Yes," Dean said. "But she's a chick."

"How observant," Iris rasped, her voice guttural, low as a

growl that rolled off her tongue like cream. Unbearably sexy, her vowels deeper than purrs. She glanced at Blue. "So they've seen this before, too?"

"We're certified experts in the world of weird," Dean said. "And sorry to say, darlin', but you're not even as strange as they come."

"And that's supposed to be a comfort?"

"Yes," Dean replied. "Absolutely, yes."

Iris narrowed her eyes. "So why are *you* here?"

Blue found the question unnecessary, but Dean surprised him by hesitating. "We're here to help."

Her nostrils flared. "You're lying."

Dean began to protest, but Artur held up his hand. He looked at Iris, and his eyes were black, hard, cold. "No, he is not lying. Dean is here to help. I have a different agenda."

"To hurt Blue."

"No," Artur whispered. "I want something else. I want the man you are hunting."

"Santoso?" Blue said, but even as he said the man's name all the pieces fell together. *Impossible,* he thought, but he looked into Artur's face and he knew it was the truth. He could not fathom it, could not understand why part of his mind remained unsurprised, quiet and calm, while the rest of him raged. He remembered the dead. The people cut open. Left to rot in pits and alleys.

Artur leaned forward, dark eyes burning. His lips thinned. "You know, yes? Santoso has access to human organs. I want one. For Elena. There is no time for legal channels. The doctors have told me as much."

Nightmare. This was a nightmare. "She needs a new heart, Artur."

"And he can find one. The right one. He has the resources."

"Those resources are *people.* Any donor Santoso finds will still be alive and taken unwillingly. You'd be paying for murder."

"I would be paying to save Elena. I would kill anyone to do that."

No remorse. No hint of anything close to regret. Blue felt as though he were staring into the face of a stranger, and he could not find words to respond, to argue. He looked at Dean, who stared back, his expression impossibly grim.

And you? For Iris? What would you do for her? What would you risk?

Memories flashed: moonlight and screams, guns and darts and running for his life, for Iris's life, abandoning his brother and Serena because he could not make the choice to use his gift to kill.

But a bullet would have been fine, right? A bullet to the brain, a knife to the gut, a bomb or grenade or a pit full of spikes? What the hell is the difference? Dead is dead.

Just like Elena was almost dead. Dead and dying because his mind was not as obedient or predictable as a gun. A gun could be trusted.

Iris clutched his hand and squeezed; her palm was warm, soft, sleek with fur. She looked at Artur. "You can't do this. It's wrong."

"Do not judge," Artur replied. "You have no right."

"*You* have no right," she snapped. "You have no idea who you're dealing with. That man—Santoso—kept me chained to a wall in the middle of a goddamn harem where the women were treated like meat—where *I* was meat—and the only reason I didn't get gang-raped inside the first hour was because he wanted my body clean. Merchandise whole. And *not* because he wanted to be the first to fuck me. *No.* Because he wanted to *kill* me."

Iris leaned forward, shaking. Blue watched her lovely eyes shadow with fury and fear and shame, and he found his own body quaking—with rage, a bone-deep, murderous anger. He wanted to hold her. He wanted to rip off Santoso's head.

Iris's claws crunched into stone and dirt. "Here, look at me. *Look at me.* You want a heart? You want to kill someone for your wife? You want to follow through with what Santoso was going to do? He was going to strip me for parts, you know. Trade organs. Bleed me down to God knows what, all so he could pretend to be a goddamn shape-shifter. And now he has my mother and he'll do the same to her. If he hasn't already."

Even Artur could not hold her gaze. "You seem to be under the impression that I am a man who will be moved by your story. You seem to think I care, yes?"

"Because you do," Dean muttered. "God, Artur."

"God? No." Artur gave his friend a dark look. "Compassion is irrelevant. In this I will do what needs to be done, even if the consequences are distasteful."

"And what will Elena think?" Blue leaned close, the hard knot around his heart unraveling into something wild, sick. "You know what kind of person she is. She'll hate you for this, Artur. She won't want—"

Artur slammed Blue into the rocks, landing on top of him with a grunt. He raised his gloved fists. Blue braced himself to be hit, but when those hands came down it was to punch the ground on either side of his head with bone-breaking ferocity.

Iris moved to intervene, but Dean grabbed her arm. She almost fought him—the look in her eye was terrible, fierce—but Artur stopped pounding the ground just as she pulled herself free. He swayed, gaze hollow, bleak.

"I do not hate you," he whispered to Blue. "I know you did not mean to hurt her, but *it was you* who did this. It was *you*. And if she dies . . ."

Artur did not finish. He did not need to. Tears welled up in his eyes, and he touched his forehead with his fingers, grazing his skin like it hurt so bad he could barely stand to touch it.

"I cannot hear her," he breathed. "She is so quiet, Blue. So quiet, no matter how loud I scream. I have not been separated from her for all this time, and now . . ." Artur climbed off him and lay down in the dirt, flat on his back, exhausted, almost broken. "Elena fell into a coma several days ago. Our psychic link is gone. I would not have left her, otherwise."

Blue closed his eyes against the bright blue heat of the sky.

His body baked; his heart felt as if it were on fire. *God.* The only way this could get worse was if—

Iris touched him. Her fingers clasped his wrist, and all his focus—all his fear—dropped into that one soft touch, that gentle, persistent connection.

Pull away, he told himself. *Do it now. Hurt her, refuse her, get rid of her. Before she ends up like Elena—dying or dead—and you're on the ground bleeding your soul out.*

He almost did it. He almost played the strong man, the controlled man, the cold man—a man capable of doing the right thing—but instead he opened his eyes and looked into her face and the weakness that hit him was breathless, damning. He wanted her just too damn much.

He sat up. Iris squeezed his hand, looking at him as though compassion were the same as breathing and she would breathe for him, keep him alive with only the strength of her heart.

And God help them both, Blue wanted to let her. Wanted to do the same—love her so hard she would never imagine life without him, never dream of it. Never leave him.

Dean sighed. "I hate to be the voice of reason in this party, but we need to get the hell out of here. Like, now."

"And go where?" Iris challenged. "He has my mother. He has Blue's brother."

"If they're still alive," Blue said grimly.

"I need to know. I need to save her if I can."

"We barely escaped last night, Iris. We need a plan. More people."

"And where are you going to get more people? You have some other friends stashed away in that jeep? You have an army? We don't have time to wait."

Artur stood, turning just slightly away as he removed his glove and pushed the heel of his palm into his eye, rubbing. A thread of despair touched Blue's heart, but he pushed it away and focused on Dean. "I shut off your car, but I can fix that. It's not stuck in the rocks, though, is it?"

"Nothing that a little elbow-grease can't solve." Dean

cracked his knuckles, very carefully not looking at Artur. "No cell phone reception out here, so I had to follow your vibes. Right after the tire got caught in the rocks I snared a vision of you two coming our way, and I stopped worrying that we were going to get carried off by wolves or hungry cave-women."

"You ... caught a vision?" Iris echoed slowly.

"Dean is clairvoyant," Blue told her. "A remote-viewer. Give him something of yours to hold and he'll be able to track you anywhere."

"Really," she said, giving Dean a hard look. "I seem to re-member you doing something a bit different to me."

"Sheer raw talent. I am so totally multifaceted I make my-self sick." Dean grinned, but it carried an edge. He scratched his chest, and Blue could almost make out the dark lines be-neath the thin cotton of his T-shirt: a tattoo set in red stone, red stone set in flesh.

A low drone filled the air. Blue gazed up at the sky and saw the profile of a small jet ascending. A moment later another followed, and then another. A tiny fleet of eight planes, rising from the desert. The sight made Blue's teeth hurt, the entire right side of his body ache. "Does Santoso have his own airstrip?"

Iris stared at the planes. "Don't know, but it makes sense."

Blue glanced at the jeep. "What route did you take, Dean?"

"East, in a roundabout way. Why?"

"Santoso keeps motion sensors and security cameras along the borders of his land. I turned off the ones in our path, but that was a small, localized area. If you drove in, chances are you tripped something. They'll know we're out here."

"So they'll think we're a couple of joyriders. They would have tried to stop our asses by now if they thought we were a real threat."

Blue was not comforted. "We would have been easy enough to catch last night, but they didn't follow. Doesn't make sense."

"Or maybe it does," Iris said. "There's a power struggle going on in that place. Santoso might be God inside the facility, but he's got someone to answer to. Someone he's desperate to find an edge over. He thought I was that edge, but if he has my mom, if he doesn't want me anymore ..."

Unlikely, Blue thought, recalling the note Santoso had written her, his professed love. Even the lengths he had gone to procure her, the time spent stalking her performances. The man was obsessed.

Which meant that something—or someone—was blocking him now. Running interference.

"That man who let you go. Broker," Blue said. "What about him?"

"He appears to be working for someone other than Santoso," Iris replied.

"Perhaps this boss Santoso fears," Artur rumbled, swinging around to face them. "But if that is the case, then why not simply take the man from power? Dispatch him with a bullet or some accident?"

"Because he wants something. Santoso's failure, maybe."

"Or your mother," Blue added.

"And Daniel?" Iris asked quietly. "You worried before that Santoso would find out the truth about him."

"Don't see how it matters," Dean said. "Jesus, Blue. You guys always overanalyze these things. Let's just say they're nasty fucks and get it over with. Shoot some guns, spray some blood. Give them a taste of their own medicine."

"All in a day's work, right?" Iris narrowed her eyes. "What do the three of you do, really? Blue said he's a detective, but this—"

"—is the work," Dean interrupted smoothly. "Scout's honor."

"It's the truth," Blue said. "We *do* work for a detective agency, but the organization itself is a cover. A legitimate, acceptable excuse for us to get involved in situations where as individuals we just wouldn't be welcome. It allows us to help people in public without drawing attention to our abilities."

"Psychic Boy Scouts? You make it sound like there're more of you. A lot more."

"More than even we have realized," Artur said in a chilling voice. "For good or ill, there are more."

Dean and Blue glanced at each other. Iris opened her mouth, began to ask, but Blue touched her wrist and shook his head. *Not now, not here.* There was too much to tell. Too much that was confusing and frightening—rival criminal organizations, kidnappings, torture—with nothing to show for all that violence but more mystery.

Like now.

Artur turned his gaze on the sky, the planes. "Santoso has been discovered; he knows this now. *And* you escaped. No matter how much money has been invested in his facility, a man like him will not remain, not when there is so much else at stake."

"You're saying that he's evacuating," Blue said. "Killing us would be easier. He has the manpower."

"Then I am wrong, yes?"

Iris squeezed Blue's hand. "Santoso wouldn't have gotten rid of my mother that quickly."

"So get me into a place where he's been and I can tell you where he's going," Dean said. "All I need is a taste and I'll be able to track him until kingdom come."

Artur sighed. "We must find a way inside that facility. Perhaps I will also be able to—"

Iris turned sharply. "What—" Blue began to ask, but she held up her hand, silencing him. Both Dean and Artur reached for their guns. She moved, and in less than a heartbeat managed to scale a nearby boulder. She perched at the very top on a sharp crag, supported by nothing more solid than the tips of her toes. She looked like she was floating; her balance was breathtaking, perfect. She stared at the horizon.

"Do you hear it?" she called down. "Blue, inside your head. Do you hear what's coming?"

Blue pushed past his shields, rushing over the bioelectric pulses of the three hearts around him, scanning farther in the direction Iris indicated. For a moment he found nothing—no buzz, no rattle—but then, like a door opening, he felt a rumble inside his head, something coming into range.

"Helicopters," he said, heart sinking. "Four of them flying this way. Half a mile and closing."

Dean shielded his eyes against the sun. "Direction?"

"Coming up from behind this hill."

He grunted. "Maybe they're tourists out for a Las Vegas joyride."

"Right," Iris replied. "Feel free to stay here and make a pretty picture while we go run and hide."

Dean scowled. Blue gave him a hard look. "I can take them down. I'll do it easy, just in case."

Iris looked back at the horizon, her gaze sweeping up the hill. "Make it fast. I think—"

A great boom punched the air, a sound so large Blue felt it in his chest, under his feet in the shaking earth as thunder rumbled into a deafening roar. Iris gasped, teetering, but before Blue could panic she caught her balance. Her eyes never left the horizon, the sloping edge of the rocky hill behind them. Which was completely understandable, given the thick cloud of black smoke boiling into the bright blue desert sky.

"Bozhe moj," Artur murmured. Blue jogged a short distance away, trying to see more. The smoke continued to billow and churn, the source partially obscured by the hill.

Dean followed him. "What happened? Did one of the copters go down?"

"No," Blue said grimly. "I think the facility just exploded."

Iris leaped down from the boulder. "We need to go. The helicopters are close."

Her gaze was hard, all business; her emotions were gone, hidden. Just like her mother. And then the moment passed and Blue felt a sliver of uncertainty creep into her face. Fear, maybe. He did not think it was for him.

Dean ran for the jeep, Artur close behind, keys jingling in his gloved hand. Blue stayed still, concentrating on the approaching helicopters.

Tourists, my ass.

Still, he was careful. Just in case. One little disruption from the engine to the rotor transmission—

Blue's cell phone rang. Everyone turned to stare at him.

"I thought you couldn't get cell phone reception out here," Iris said.

Artur checked his phone. "Mine is still out."

Dean shook his head. "I saw this movie, man. Real ugly ending. Don't answer the damn phone."

But it kept ringing. Blue looked at the screen. No number, just ID UNAVAILABLE. *What a surprise.*

He answered the call, putting it on speaker.

"Hello, Mr. Perrineau," said a smooth voice. Familiar, though the distortion was bad enough that Blue could not quite place it.

"Who is this?" he asked.

"You'll find out soon enough. In the meantime, I would take it as a personal favor if you did not take down those helicopters. That *was* what you were going to do, I assume."

Blue glanced at his friends, all of whom looked distinctly unsettled. Dean turned, slowly scanning the land around them. Iris joined him, eyes glowing.

"I think I have a right to protect myself and my friends," Blue said, returning his focus to the helicopters, which still were drawing near. The loud *chop-chop* of the rotors filled the air. Just one touch of his mind and—

A bullet slammed into the boulder beside Blue's head. Rock sprayed, clipping his face as he threw himself on top of Iris, taking them both to the ground. The phone clattered on the rocks, but the man speaking still came through loud and clear.

"Let's try this again, Mr. Perrineau. Don't take down the birds. If you do, I will shoot someone."

"I don't see an energy trail," Dean muttered. He and Artur lay on their stomachs. Iris's breath was hot against Blue's neck.

"You okay?" she murmured.

"That's supposed to be my line."

Her teeth touched his throat. "I'm quicker on the draw."

He pressed his lips against her forehead and pushed out beyond his shields, searching for a heartbeat, some sign of electric life. The helicopters were almost on top of them.

Another crack, another bullet in the ground by Blue's foot.

"Don't look for me," said the man.

There was obviously no need to hide his gifts. Blue said, "I could kill you faster than you can pull that trigger."

"Violence or peace. Hot or cold. You're a man of extremes, Mr. Perrineau. Just like your father. And your brother."

Dean's cell phone began to ring. Everyone stared at his hip. Blue was almost certain the man on the other end of the line had laughter in his voice when he said, "That's my associate. He also has a gun. So please, just give it up, Mr. Perrineau. This is all for your benefit, I can assure you."

Blue did not want to give it up. He wanted to find the little turd and shove that gun up his ass. Unfortunately, the decision was taken out of his hands. The helicopters roared over the hill behind them, four strong, quick and small and black. Dust kicked up, blinding, but Blue could still see clearly enough to make out men in gray bodysuits—armed with rifles—leaning out of each aircraft. Too late to crash them. The gunmen, on the other hand . . .

"Stay where you are," said the man on the phone. "I'll be there in a moment."

Blue began to sit up, but Iris grabbed the front of his shirt.

"I'm still not human," she said, and all that charm, all that easy courage she had just shown him began to fade from her golden eyes.

He gathered her close, holding her as tightly as he dared, and called out to Dean and Artur. The two men crawled close.

"Iris doesn't want all of those people to see her like this," Blue said, forced to shout over the roar of the rotor blades. "Give us cover while she shifts."

No argument, no questions; Dean and Artur arranged

themselves on either side of Blue and Iris, practically resting on top of them. Blue caught the Russian's eye; his friend nodded, expression dark, serious, sad. It made his heart hurt, because despite Artur's intentions, his anger, a good man was still in there. And he was dying right along with his wife.

Blue looked at Iris. "Okay, sweetheart. You can shift now. We've got you covered."

"Silly, huh?" Iris said, her gaze sliding sideways to Dean and Artur. "The other man . . . he must have already seen me."

Dean grinned. "Ladies are not to be questioned, darlin'."

"Only obeyed," Blue finished gently. "Go on, now. Do your thing."

And she did, fur melting into smooth, pale skin, bone and muscle flowing like water to shape the woman he remembered. Red hair tumbled around her perfect face. Iris never broke eye contact during the transformation; it was as if no one existed but her and him, no one in the world. Even the roar of the helicopters dimmed.

Then it was over, done, and he found in her gaze a breathless vulnerability, a quiet fear that made him reach out and brush her lips with his fingertips.

"Hey," he said. "Hey, now. I'm still here."

Iris closed her eyes. "Sorry. I wasn't expecting to feel quite so different outside of my other skin."

Blue glanced at his friends. Dean, for once, had no pithy remarks. He sat up, surrounded by a whirlwind of dust.

"Keep covering her," he shouted at Blue, and began peeling off his shirt. Artur reached out and stopped him. "Your chest, Dean. You have as much to hide. Let me."

Dean hesitated, but Artur had already begun unbuttoning his black shirt. He gave it to Blue, who pulled back just enough to help Iris put her arms through the sleeves. She looked very young; Blue could not help but wish it were his shirt she was wearing.

Three of the helicopters moved a short distance away and began to descend. Blue helped Iris stand, watching as the shirt fell to midthigh. She began buttoning it immediately, and glanced up at Artur. Blue saw her eyes flick over his pale chest, the thin white scars.

"Thanks," she said, but he did not reply or look at her or Blue.

The three helicopters touched down. The men did not leave the aircraft, but continued to keep their weapons trained on Blue and his friends. He thought about ending it, taking out all the people in front of him, and that shooter in the sky—but as he had the previous night, he held himself back.

See what they have to say. Find out what's going on.

Because with the facility gone, they needed another way to track Santoso.

Dean pointed. "That must be our sneaky little bastard."

Blue looked and saw a man running out of the desert. The sun was in his eyes, blinding him to details, but he listened to that heartbeat and pulse, and wondered why in the hell he had not heard it earlier.

Of course, none of that mattered the moment Blue managed to get a good look at who had pinned them.

Familiar, bland, dressed in a cheap flapping suit with a cigarette hanging from his mouth. He held a rifle, which he balanced on his shoulder.

"You," Blue said.

"*Bozhe moj,*" Artur muttered. "Bastard."

Agent Fred smiled.

CHAPTER FIFTEEN

So. Brain explosion. Iris figured she had it coming.

The helicopter interior was sparse, angular, the seat hard as rock beneath her naked backside. The sun hit her face through the tinted window, and even though the aircraft had air-conditioning, that light on her cheek was hot as hell, and there sitting in front of her was the devil himself in all his mundane glory, smiling with an unlit cigarette flopping like a toothpick between his lips.

"You are one son of a bitch," she said to Fred, for what was probably the tenth time. She had to speak through a microphone attached to the headset squashed on her ears. Not that she could complain. The roar of the rotors felt like pure pain to her eardrums; her hearing was already sensitive enough without more chainsaws going at it inside her head.

"Wasn't aware you know my mother," Fred replied. His rifle lay across his lap. Another man dressed in gray sat in the chair beside him, also armed—as were Blue, Dean, and Artur. No one had been forced to give up their weapons. Not that all those guns did anyone a bit of good; having a shootout thousands of feet aboveground in a small and highly complex machine required a level of stupidity that probably deserved a quick and fiery death.

Blue touched her hand—in warning or comfort, she was not quite certain, but it did not stop her from an indelicate snort, a rough laugh. "Funny . . . *not*. I thought you worked for the FBI."

Fred shrugged. "I have a thing for badges and damsels in distress. Occupational hazard."

"Do not listen to anything he tells you," Artur said from his cramped seat directly behind Iris. "This man is a criminal. He works for other criminals."

"You are so judgmental," Fred replied. "And completely wrong. My employers are about as far from being criminal masterminds as Anne of Green Gables."

"Aw," Dean said. "I guess she carried sniper rifles, too, huh?"

"You know your literature."

Blue twisted in his seat to look at Artur. "How, exactly, do you know him?"

"He was in Russia. He and a woman shot an associate of Beatrix Weave, the woman who founded the Consortium—a criminal organization. This man also spied on us during our journey to Moscow."

"And we saved your lives. You could try to be a bit more gracious."

"Why don't you try to shut the hell up," Dean shot back. "Unless you'd like to explain what all this is about?"

"Soon," Fred agreed, and that was all he said until the helicopters entered the urban sprawl of Las Vegas, making a beeline for the Strip.

"Are you planning on taking us gambling?" Blue peered out the window. Iris looked, too. The city felt almost as big from above as it did below; the Strip was a tangle, a jungle of people and concrete. Only from this vantage point Iris felt the chaos even more keenly—finally, the forest instead of the trees—and she wondered briefly how she had managed to last even three months in such an overwhelming environment.

And whether she would ever be able to return to that life. And her cats.

You can't leave them. No matter what happens, you need to make certain of that.

The Miracle's ivory spires loomed ahead of them; Iris spent a moment searching for the circus encampment, but the helicopter swerved left, heading directly to the tallest of the Miracle's towers. An immense green landing pad waited for them as they descended.

"You look disgruntled, Ms. McGillis," Fred said.

Iris studied his scent, which was not quite so calm or confident as his face. "This is the last place I expected you to take us."

"Small surprises are always the best."

She had a reply for that—a kick aimed specifically at his knee—but she held herself back and squeezed Blue's hand. He pressed his lips against her hair, and she felt the contact shiver through her body.

Easy affection, unembarrassed by the situation and the people around them. Possessive, even. Iris liked it. She didn't think that made her a cavegirl wannabe. After everything she and Blue had been through together, it felt right. He liked her. Really liked her. Maybe even loved her. And Iris found that it was nice to belong to someone who cared about her. More than wonderful. No words were big enough for what was in her heart. Except that she'd rather be here with him at gunpoint than anywhere else in the world.

The helicopter landed with a gentle thud, but no one moved or unbuckled themselves. Fred's hands tightened around the stock and barrel of his weapon.

"No matter how evil you might think my clutches are, please try to rein in those raging impulses to—thank you, Mr. Perrineau—kick in my skull, feed me my testicles, or do some very nasty things with my ass and this gun. You'll thank me in the long run, I promise." Fred gave Dean a rather disgruntled look. "And no chopsticks for you. Jesus, man."

Dean smirked. "That's what you get for being a mind reader, you little prick."

Mind reader. Iris stared at Fred, at Blue—who was frowning so hard it was practically an invitation to set up tent poles at the corners of his mouth—and then turned to look at Dean and Artur. Clairvoyant, electrokinetic, telepathic . . .

And one shape-shifter. God, you live in a bizarre world.

"You're not promising us much in return," Blue said.

"Not yet, anyway." Fred looked at the man beside him, who wordlessly opened the helicopter door. The rotors were already winding down to a stop. No sign of the other aircraft that had tailed them.

Fred's companion stayed at the landing pad as Iris and the others were led through an access door down several flights of stairs, which emptied directly into a short, wide corridor decorated like a marble fetishist's dream. Across from them was a pale door; Fred keyed in a sequence, the locks clicked, and through it they filed.

Penthouse suite. The kind Iris had only heard of and never seen, though she had a feeling this was far nicer than anything that ended up in some magazine spread or television documentary. A large space, decorated in varying shades of pale blue, so that the room felt like part of the sky; the outer walls were nothing but floor-to-ceiling windows.

"There are women's clothes in the back bedroom," Fred said, still holding his rifle. "You, um, can change if you like."

Iris bit back a snippy reply and began moving in the direction he indicated. Chin up, posture good, relaxed, not scared at all. *Oh, no.* He was not going to see her hesitate.

Still, when Blue joined her, she was not at all sorry.

The pair of them left the main living room via a corridor that ran parallel to the windows; it felt like walking in the air above the city, which was disconcerting at first. Iris glanced down and saw the circus encampment in the distance, just beyond the manicured edges of the Miracle's main resort.

"Petro and the others will be freaking out by now," she said to Blue.

He draped an arm around her shoulders, hugging her close. "I hate to tell you, Iris, but I think it may be a while before you're able to return to them."

"If I ever do."

"You will," he said, turning her, running his fingers lightly over her cheeks. Warmth spread through her limbs; she wanted to shut her eyes and just feel him, be with him, and so she did. *One moment,* she told herself. *Just one.*

"Come on," he murmured, voice husky. "Let's get you those clothes."

They entered the first bedroom they encountered. The closet was the size of Iris's trailer, with a digitized system designed to bring clothes to her, rather than the other way around.

Blue looked amused. "Colors?"

She smiled. "Blue."

He laughed softly and punched the appropriate button. Gears whirred, and a stream of coordinated sets flowed along a rail. She took something soft and navy and form-fitting, found a bra and underwear in a drawer farther down, and picked out a pair of running shoes.

Blue leaned against the wall, arms folded over his chest. He showed no sign of moving as she began to unbutton her shirt. Iris bit her bottom lip, trying not to smile.

"You going to watch me?"

"I'm a weak man," he said. "No self-control."

"Sounds a bit dangerous." Iris held the shirt closed, swaying toward Blue. His throat worked as she neared, his eyes growing hungry, dark. He did not reply; instead, his hands reached out, fingers pushing slowly beneath the collar of the shirt so that he touched her skin, rested his hands on her bare shoulders. His palms were large and hot, and she stood still as they traveled lower, tracing the open edges of the shirt, pulling the cloth from her hands. His fingers traced the inner edges of her breasts and moved even lower, pushing aside the shirt, pushing all the way so that it fell over her shoulders and off her arms, leaving her completely naked.

And loving it.

"You are so ..." Blue murmured, his voice trailing off into

a low rumble that was so sexy the ache between her legs pulsed.

Iris leaned toward him. "So *what*?"

His hands splayed over her waist, running down to her hips, tracing lines across her backside. "I was going to say beautiful, but it would have sounded trite." His hands found her breasts and she stifled a moan. "I've got no words for you, Iris."

She laughed softly. "I can live with that."

He pressed his mouth against her neck. "Thank God you're not fussy."

"With you, I try to be as easy as I can."

Blue laughed outright this time, and backed her up against the smooth closet wall. He kissed her lightly on the lips, but she pushed against him, and he answered back, turning his mouth into something hard and fierce, grinding into her naked body as he kissed the living hell out of her. Iris felt dizzy with it, as though her body were riding a hot, pulsing wave running from her heart to her groin, and she felt heavy there, wet, her thighs rubbing against his. She hooked a leg around his hips and drew him even tighter into her body. He groaned— deep throated, muted—and suddenly his mouth was no longer on her mouth, but on her neck, her shoulder, her breast. And while one of his hands stayed behind her head, the other trailed down her ribs to her hips, squeezing gently, before moving between her legs.

And then everything shifted and Iris found herself on her back, resting on the floor with Blue between her legs, doing things to her that made her writhe so hard he had to hold her down. She swallowed her cries, but some still leaked through her gritted teeth. Blue chuckled softly when he heard her mewls.

"Good," he murmured, and then he did something with his fingers and tongue, drawing her in with lips to suck, and Iris felt the pressure inside her snap so hard she finally did cry out—a wordless gasp that only grew louder as Blue continued to work her past that first orgasm, helping her ride the edge of it into another that was even more powerful.

Blue crawled over her body. Iris, feeling remarkably warm and lazy, reached down and touched his groin. He closed his eyes, sucked in his breath.

"You next," she whispered.

"No time," he said. "The others are waiting."

She smiled, running her tongue over her lips, loving how he watched, how he moistened his already damp mouth. Her fingers traced circles over the hard line inside his jeans.

"I'll work fast," she said. "Unless you can make that go away just by thinking about it."

"Right," he muttered. "Though one of these days we're going to find the perfect moment and I'm going to come inside you."

The idea made her breathless. "You almost make that sound like a threat."

"Depends on your definition of danger."

"You're my definition," Iris said, as he unbuttoned his jeans. "Only you."

"And if I feel the same about you?"

Iris sat up, pushing Blue onto his back, and wasted no time moving low, putting her mouth on him. She wasn't quite certain what she was doing, but practice, she figured, made perfect.

"I'd say that's entirely appropriate," Iris told him, and smiled when he called out her name.

"Did you enjoy the closet?" Fred asked Iris when she and Blue returned to the main sitting room. The men had scattered; Artur stood by the window—with a shirt—Dean had a seat near the door, and Fred was at the bar pouring himself a shot. his rifle lay on the polished countertop in front of him.

"It was a remarkable experience," Iris said. Fred smiled. Mind reader, indeed.

Blue wrapped an arm around her waist. "Enough bullshit. We're here; we're ready. What is going on?"

Fred held up his hand and knocked back the whiskey. He made a face and rubbed his chest. "Anyone want some?"

"No," they all said.

"In stereo. Very nice." Fred set down the shot glass and leaned against the counter. "So, business. First of all, I am *not* working with Santoso, and I was *not* responsible for the explosion that took out that facility. The little man ordered that himself."

Iris could still feel the explosion in her bones, the acrid scent of smoke in her nose. "There were women inside that place. God only knows who else. Did he take them out of there?"

"I doubt it. It would be cheaper to find more girls than to transport them. And he was in a rush."

"You have a spy on the inside?" Blue asked.

"We did. Two of them, actually. One is dead and the other … incommunicado."

Iris leaned against the counter. "So why all the subterfuge? Why all the attention on me? And how do you know so much about Santoso?"

Fred's gaze turned sharp. "Because I work with your mother. And your mother, Ms. McGillis, was one of those spies."

Everything inside Iris stopped; her heart, her lungs, her mind. All she could do was stare. Blue's arm tightened; she was dimly aware of Artur and Dean drawing close, but inside her head all she could see was her mother—her mother holding her, her mother cooking, her mother shifting and laughing and running and teaching her how to fight with that cold glint in her eye, and then nothing, a note, two years gone until last night, and it was not true, it could not be true—

Iris did not feel herself move, but Fred was suddenly on the ground and she was on his back, grinding his face into the hardwood floor. Blood trickled from his nose.

"Tell me the truth," she said softly, feeling something cold and hard snap into place. "Tell me how you know my mother."

"Mr. Perrineau," Fred said, his voice muffled. "I would appreciate some help here."

"Actually, I was thinking of looking for some popcorn. Guys?"

"Pretzels and beer," Dean said. "Maybe a video camera. What do you think, Artur?"

"I think I want to help," the Russian rumbled, and sat down on Fred's legs. He pulled one of his gloves off with his teeth.

"Hey," Fred said, a hint of desperation entering his voice. "Don't you dare."

Artur ignored him. He pushed up the hem of Fred's pants and placed his palm against the man's skin. Fred swore at him, thrashing. Iris held him down. Fear entered his scent.

"What's going on?" Iris asked Blue, who crouched to help.

"Artur is a psychometrist. Probably the most powerful in the world. And right now, he's getting to know our friend just a little bit better."

Artur looked rather unhappy. He replaced his glove. "It will take time to sift through my impressions, but I believe he can be trusted. For now."

"Fuck you," Fred muttered. Iris relaxed her hold on his shoulders. She could feel him trembling, and tried to stifle any and all of the little shreds of sympathy she felt for him. It was difficult. She understood what it was like to have secrets violated. She did not wish it on anyone.

"Tell me how you know my mother," she said again.

"Daniel, too," Blue added. "You obviously know about him."

"And while you're at it, you can tell us if Elvis is still alive." Dean nudged Fred with his boot.

He squeezed shut his eyes. "As far as I know, Daniel is fine. As for Serena, I already told you. I work with her."

"My mother is a circus performer."

"No, she's not. At least, not *just* that. Ask Blue if you don't believe me."

Iris remembered asking him. She remembered the discomfort in his eyes, his refusal to say anything at all. But she looked at him again, searching his gaze, and this time he simply appeared resigned.

Which scared the hell out of her.

Iris rolled off Fred's back; Artur freed his legs. The man rolled onto his side, wincing, and touched his nose.

"I should have just shot you all when I had the chance," he muttered.

"Why didn't you?" Blue asked.

"I have my orders. And then there's Serena. I don't want to think about what she'll do to me if her daughter gets hurt."

Iris forced herself to breathe. "I don't understand. Why . . . why is my mother working with you? How did this happen?"

Fred sighed, pushing his sleeve up against his bleeding nose. Dean fetched a towel from behind the bar and tossed it to him.

"I don't know the details," he said, his voice muffled. "You'll have to get those from your mother. Suffice to say, she's been at this work since before you were born, but she left when she got pregnant. Stayed away for twenty-two years until she got the call."

The call. A note. *I need to run; I need to let the wild take over.*

Lies, lies, lies. "You make it sound like the CIA."

"More like a corporation. Unlike the organization Mr. Perrineau and his friends work for, our interests are a bit more . . . monetary. But we basically have the same goals. We want to be left alone, and we want to do good work."

"Liar," Artur said, with a vehemence that surprised Iris— and, to look at Blue and Dean, his friends, as well.

Fred smiled. "Pot calling the kettle black, isn't it?"

Artur moved; Dean caught him across the chest. Blue gave both his friends a hard look and said, "So, what's your employer's interest in this? What is there to be gained?"

"A clean conscience. Santoso didn't start his empire all on his own. It was grown and consolidated by another group that I think you know."

"The Consortium," Artur whispered. "Beatrix Weave."

It got very quiet. Iris stared at the men, searching their faces—which were suddenly way too thoughtful for her comfort—and held up her hand. "For the new girl? An explanation would be nice."

"The Consortium is a criminal organization," Blue said quietly. "Mafia types, if you like. It's run by people like us. Psychics."

Iris bit back a laugh. "You're kidding me."

"I wish it were so," Artur murmured. "They took me from my home. They kidnapped my wife. They ran terrible experiments on humans and on members of your kind, and for nothing more than idle curiosity—and a drive to exploit those gifts for power and wealth. We killed their leader, but I have suspected for some time that another took her place. Power like that leaves a vacuum that must be filled."

"And it was," Fred said softly. "But we don't know by whom. What we do know is that the men and women who were under Beatrix's original mind control are working together, answering to someone new. And this individual, we're afraid, is even worse."

"Beatrix was small potatoes," Artur said distantly, as though speaking from memory. Fred looked startled but, after a moment, nodded.

"Maybe. But if that's the case, then we're all in a lot of trouble. Because she was bad as they come." Fred shook his head. "No one was surprised when they discovered what she had done. Spoiled, rotten—"

He caught himself. Iris smelled his unease. "I get the feeling this woman used to be one of you. Is that what you meant by a clean conscience?"

Fred's jaw tightened. "My employers take full responsibility for what happened—and for what continues to go on. But they're practical. They could take out the middle men like Santoso anytime they want, but it's the one pulling the strings who's the main prize. And that, Ms. McGillis, was why your mother left you. She knew the importance of the work."

"That's not enough," Iris said. "I want more."

"Then you'll have to find your mother to get it. Which is why I brought you all here. So we could work together to bring her home."

"Do you know where Santoso has taken her?"

"Santoso is a bad man, but he's a baby at heart. And what do all babies do when they're hurt or threatened?"

"They run home to their mommies."

"Exactly," Fred said. "Which means he's taking *your* mommy to the place he feels safest."

"Indonesia," Blue said, with a curious lack of emotion.

Iris frowned at him. "So we go there. Fine."

Fred shook his head. "*You're* not going anywhere. As far as I'm concerned, this is your home until we take care of Santoso."

"Like hell it is. I'm going with you."

"Listen," Fred said. "I know you don't give a rat's ass about what happens to me, but I happen to like my life. And if we get your mother back, and you end up hurt or worse? I am not kidding when I say she will do bad things to me. Very bad."

Iris tried to remember whether she had ever thought her mother capable of Very Bad Things. "Please. You almost sound scared of her."

"Terrified," Fred replied, and there was nothing lighthearted about his response. Iris swallowed hard.

Blue grunted. "Serena sent you to watch over Iris, didn't she? All that talk about being FBI was just so you could get close."

"It was part of Serena's deal. She wanted protection for her daughter."

"Shitty job you did of that."

"Shitty turn of events."

"I won't do it." Iris looked at Blue. "I won't stay here."

"Okay," he replied. There was no hesitation.

Fred made a choking sound. "You can't be serious."

Even Dean and Artur looked at him as if he were crazy. Iris

battled her own surprise; she had not expected such easy acquiescence. Blue, however, gave her a small, tired smile and
said, "Iris doesn't give up. You try to keep her here, she'll find
some different way to Indonesia. Better with us than on her
own."

"You're thinking with your dick," Fred said.

"And you'll lose yours if you keep talking like that." Blue
reached out, and Iris took his hand.

Artur swayed close. "When do we leave?"

Fred looked at Iris and shook his head. He sighed. She
thought about giving him the finger. "Anytime you want. I
have a jet waiting."

Blue nodded. "Dean, get Roland on the line. Fill him in."

"On it." Dean pulled out his cell phone and moved down
the corridor, just out of sight. Fred watched him go—a bad
man to keep secrets around.

Iris spoke up, "Santoso only recently came into my life.
What was my mother trying to protect me from before that?"

Fred dropped his bloody towel and reached for the cigarette still tucked behind his ear. He stuck it in his mouth.

"Herself," he said, and fumbled behind the bar for a
match.

CHAPTER SIXTEEN

There was no time for Iris to say good-bye to her cats, and even Blue refused to let her make a phone call to Pete. Too much risk, and too many questions that had no answers.

They took the helicopter to the airport, and boarded a sleek jet with an interior that felt more like a country estate than a BBJ 737.

"Adequate." Dean sniffed, flopping down on the soft, creamy couch bolted to the floor. He propped up his dusty shoes on the polished coffee table, which boasted a vase of fresh roses.

Fred leaned against the dark paneled wall. "Two bathrooms and two bedrooms, all down the hall. The galley is up front, and we've got a crew of two, not including the boys flying this thing. Relax, enjoy the ride, and try not to think about dying."

"Thanks," Iris said. "It was at the top of my list."

"Don't you need to see a doctor about that nose?" Blue called out to Fred, as the man disappeared down the long corridor leading to the back of the plane. Fred ignored him. The moment he was out of sight, Dean took his feet off the table and leaned close.

"You guys really think we can trust this joker?"

"Good timing," Blue said. "Wait to ask the question until *after* we're on his plane."

Dean scowled. "I'm trying to be serious here. Artur, what's your take? You got inside his head, after all."

"I already said we can trust him. At least in this. He is loyal to Serena."

"And that's it?" Blue asked after a brief silence. "You usually give us a full psychoanalysis."

"Which I'm sure he will eventually," Fred said, coming back into the lounge. He sat down in a plush armchair and pulled seat belts from beneath the cushion. His mouth twisted, bitter. "How did my mind look, Artur? Was it as good for you as it was for me?"

Artur said nothing, his face impassive. His scent, however, told another story. Conflict, unease, perhaps even a shred of fear. It made Iris wonder what he was not saying, and whether keeping quiet was an act of kindness on his part—or a betrayal.

The plane took off. Iris remained in the lounge for a time, savoring the unusual sensation of being with people she did not have to hide herself from in any way or form whatsoever. But despite their friendliness, everyone but Blue was still a stranger, and she found *that,* on top of her ordeal, exhausting enough.

Iris excused herself. It was her first time on a plane—and what a way to fly—but she found it a bit disorienting keeping her balance as she walked down the long corridor to the bedroom, which was a simpler affair than the rest of the plane. Wood paneling, a full-size bed with a thick down comforter. There was a closet and television, even a private bathroom with a large shower and a cabinet full of fluffy white towels.

Very surreal. Iris kicked off her shoes, curled into a tiny ball, and closed her eyes. She tried not to think, or remember, but it was impossible to forget everything that had crashed into her life, and she found herself trying to reconcile what had happened to her, the people she had seen, with the refinement and beauty and wealth surrounding her.

She thought of Songbird, the other women all drugged out, sprawled naked on their pillows. All gone.

Even her mother was gone; and not just her physical presence, but everything Iris thought she knew about her. Every little scrap of memory from her youth—every hug and kiss and piece of advice, those quiet moments just sitting on the porch and watching the sunset, or cooking dinner in those stupid aprons she insisted they wear, or working with the cats, *being* cats, hunting, running, living free without concern or responsibility or the rest of humanity. That woman was a lie? Everything Iris had known, nothing more than subterfuge?

You don't believe it. Not even in your gut, you don't believe it. Confused, yes. Hurt, definitely. But you know she loved you. That she still loves you.

Because Iris remembered that look in her mother's eyes when they had stood inside that casino. She remembered her mother's eyes from the dark of the desert, fighting together side by side. Whatever else had happened—the lies, the subterfuge—that much was genuine. Iris had a mother who loved her.

She heard footsteps outside the room. Blue. She was off the bed and at the door before he could knock, and she dragged him inside, wrapping her arms around his waist for a hug. No talking, just touching. She needed to be held—had years without any human contact to make up for.

Blue nudged the door shut with his foot and swung Iris up into his arms with an ease that startled her. He kissed her forehead and gently lay her down on the bed. Still no words, but he took off his shoes and spooned up behind her, cradling her body against his own, their right hands linking up while his left arm slid beneath her head. He turned her just enough to kiss, and Iris lost herself in the sensation of his mouth moving against her own. Kissing Tommy all those years ago seemed dry and clinical compared to this. At sixteen, there bad been no butterflies like the other women in the circus said they got. No sparks, no magic, no electricity.

But with Blue, Iris finally understood. Being with him, touching him, was like running in a dark wood after years of prison, with each breathless moment filled to bursting with joy—and all those doubts, all the nagging fears that had dogged her every attempt to be a normal girl with a normal man, were suddenly so far removed that Iris briefly wondered if she had ever really felt those things.

They did not talk with words, only their eyes and mouths and hands, and it was more than enough as Iris helped Blue pull off his clothes, both of them shivering as she explored his fine long muscles with her mouth and fingertips, tracing paths along his ribs, down his abdomen. She kissed his nipple, took it in her mouth to roll and tug, and she smiled at his gasp, at his low cry as her mouth moved lower and lower. Her nails bit into his thighs as she licked him.

Blue sat up, breathing hard. Iris let him undress her, loving how he peeled off her shirt and jeans with desperate urgency while lingering almost shyly over her underwear. It did not matter that he had already seen her naked—she could see the reverence in his eyes as he unhooked her bra and drew it over her arms. He straddled her, his penis rubbing against her stomach as his hands covered her aching breasts. She tried to touch him again, but he pinned her wrists above her head and kissed her so deeply she felt the rumblings of an orgasm rise and rise.

Iris tried to wrap her legs around him, but he slid away, moving down her body with a smile. She rose to meet his every touch, and when he hooked his hands into her panties and pulled down, she arched her hips, crying out when he put his mouth to her. His tongue felt so good, so wet and hot, and when he put his fingers to her, sliding inside—first one, then two—she bit back a cry as he began a slow rhythm, stretching her, pressing her. And when she was close—just a hairbreadth away, she felt something much larger rub against her, and she could not help but laugh.

"What's funny?" he growled.

Iris rubbed the crease between his eyes. "You look so serious. Scared, even."

"Because I am. I don't want to hurt you."

A sentiment she shared, but which was clearly inevitable. Iris reached down between them, and felt a moment of surprise that he had somehow managed to find and roll on a condom without her even noticing. He pushed against her hand, straining, and whispered, "Ready?"

"Stick it to me, bad boy," Iris said, and Blue stared, shoulders shaking as he choked down laughter. Just as she had planned—the shadows and worry fled his eyes, replaced by something bright, hot. Faster than she could blink he pressed flat and hard against her, so close their noses rubbed.

"I love you, Iris McGillis. I want you to know that."

Iris smiled, about to tell him the same, but he pushed inside her before she could say a word. She did feel pain—briefly—but it was nothing to the sensation of being so deliciously, astonishingly full. Blue was inside her, stretching and pressing, and when he began to move—slow, gentle—the slide of his flesh inside her body made the breath rattle in her throat.

"You okay?" he whispered. Iris nodded, still unable to speak. She could feel him shaking, and she dragged her legs over his hips, trying to match his rhythm as he increased his pace, his thrusts long and deep and so good all Iris could do was writhe beneath him, lost in the sensation. She could feel him losing control and she grabbed his buttocks, pulling him harder, urging him with her body until he held down her wrists, pinning her to the bed as his glistening body pounded her so hard and deep she came within moments, arching beneath him with a startled cry. He followed her almost immediately, his last movements wild, frenzied. Iris could only cling to him, toes and fingers tingling, the rush still pulsing through her body.

It took a long time for her heart to slow, even longer for her voice to produce something more than a whimper, and with her body still wrapped around him and his mouth pressing the occasional clumsy kiss against her cheek, she said, "Is it always that good?"

Blue laughed weakly. "God, Iris. If it is, I'm not sure I'll make it to forty."

She smacked him on the shoulder, and he rolled them over, holding her close against his body.

"No hitting," he said, kissing her throat. "You'll hurt my feelings."

Iris grinned. "Big, tough men like you actually have feelings? Be still, my heart."

His smile faded just slightly—a flash of something sad passing through his eyes—and Iris remembered too late Artur's wife, Elena.

Blue began to pull away from her, but she held on tight, clinging like a leech until he lay back down on the bed. He did not relax, though.

"I'm sorry," Iris said, her cheek pressed against his chest. She listened to his heartbeat, sure and strong.

He sighed, running his fingers through her hair. "Don't be. It just . . . reminded me of something I should have done."

"Which was?"

"Make you hate me."

"What?"

"I'm afraid of hurting you, Iris."

"Because of what happened to Artur's wife."

"It's not the first time."

Iris frowned, snuggling closer. "Tell me."

At first she thought he would not—he was quiet for such a long time—but then he cleared his throat and said, "The first time it was my dog. I was twelve and got angry. I don't remember why. But my dog fell over and died. We thought he was sick. Until the electricity started going haywire in the house, at school, in the car. Everywhere *I* was. And then other things started dying. Birds, cats. I had a mean son of a bitch for a math teacher, and one day when he started coming down hard on me for no reason, I felt something pop in my mind, and the old man started having a heart attack.

That's when I finally put it all together. Humans run on electricity, too. Bioelectric pulses that keep the heart going. I can affect those just as easily as I can a lightbulb."

"What happened to the teacher?"

"He died. Right in front of me. And I swear he knew it was my fault."

"Blue," Iris breathed. She could not imagine the pain he had endured. What a terrible burden to put on a child. She said as much, pushing even closer, trying to tell him with her body that she was not afraid. His hand crept into her hair, down her neck, trailed across her shoulders.

"I thought about killing myself," Blue said, with a simple honesty made all the more terrible because it was not idle or melodramatic. Just truth, the kind that made Iris imagine razors against her wrists or a rope wrapped around her throat. She tried not to react—was afraid of how he would take it—but she finally gave up pretending and grabbed his hand, holding it so tight she knew it must hurt. He did not complain.

"Why would you do such a thing?" she whispered.

"Easy. I couldn't live with the idea that I might hurt other people without meaning to. That just by thinking I could take another person's life."

"So what stopped you?"

He laughed, bitter. "Pure selfishness. I liked being alive more than I hated killing."

"I don't think that's selfish. That's survival."

"And if I hurt you?" Blue tilted up her chin and stared into her eyes. "What would you say then?"

"I'd say to keep on living. I'd say it was an accident and no hard feelings. And if I didn't die, but was damaged, I would say the same. And if you even contemplated something as terrible and stupid as what your friend is considering, I'd make your life a living hell."

"Ah," Blue said. "But if you were alive and healthy and making my life hell, that might just be worth it."

"Not funny."

"No," he said. "It's not. I've got better control now. Or I

thought I did. Before Elena, it had been a long time since I hurt anyone. But accidents happen."

"That's right." Iris poked his chest. "I could get hit by a car, struck by lightning, maybe, oh—find myself kidnapped by an international crime lord hell-bent on stealing my vital organs! Though I suppose that counts as murder instead of an accident. Point is, you can't control everything. Trust me, I've tried."

"And that's supposed to be comforting?"

"Well, yes. Liberating, at the very least. I think."

"Sorry," Blue said. "I missed that boat when the dog died."

Iris sighed. "What did your parents say? I know you weren't close to your father, but he must have had some kind of opinion."

"No. I never had any contact with my father. I didn't even know Daniel existed until a couple days ago."

"Huh." Iris frowned. "Based on what Daniel said, that surprises me."

"Based on what *Daniel* said? You talked about this?"

"Something … similar." Iris was not quite sure how much to tell him, but decided she had already burned her bridges by saying what she had. "According to him, you were quite the presence in his life. Your father kept pictures of you around, and used them to … make Daniel feel bad. Whatever that means."

"You're kidding me."

"That's what he said."

"That makes no sense, Iris."

"From what I've heard, it's not supposed to. Your father, apparently, is not a nice man."

"No, he's not. He's sharp, brilliant, ruthless—and his one true act of genius has been letting the world see all those qualities, while somehow convincing it that he should be loved for them. He's built his reputation around philanthropy, eradicating poverty, improving education for women and children. The perfect person. Except to his own family."

"And there's no chance of a misunderstanding?"

Blue laughed, a cold and bitter sound. "I told you my mother is from Afghanistan. She came to the United States during her country's heyday, before things got bad. She went to school here, got her law degree, and when she was still in her early twenties she found a job as an associate in a firm my father used. There was a case ... I don't know about what, but it meant my mother had to spend a lot of time with my dad. He was attracted to her, and she wasn't entirely averse to him. Things got out of hand. My mom is a traditional woman. Not strict in any sense, but she believed sex was for marriage. My father ... didn't."

"Oh," Iris breathed. "Oh, no."

"He didn't rape her, if that's what you think. He might as well have, though. When she refused to be his mistress, he killed her with whispers. He destroyed her reputation. He paid his goons to threaten her friends. He got word back to her family in Afghanistan, telling them that she was selling herself for money. He might as well have raped her, Iris. The damage was almost the same. Complete isolation. She lost her job. She couldn't go home or ask her family for help, because by that point they considered her dead. She had to work odd jobs as a waitress, saving up money to study for a bar exam in another state, and when she could, she packed me up and moved. Finally got work as a lawyer again." Blue's forehead wrinkled; his scent was anxious, sad. "She named me after him, Iris. I never understood why. I wasn't even certain why she told me what happened, who he was. I think it would have been kinder never knowing."

"I agree." Iris could not imagine what it would do to her if she learned something similar about her own father.

Blue sighed. "She's a survivor. She used to tell me that pride never put food on the table. That dignity and pride were two separate things, and that as long as a person had dignity, it wouldn't matter what they had to do, what hardship or sacrifice they had to endure. Dignity was backbone. Dignity was bending but not breaking."

"Reminds me of *my* mother," Iris said.

"Another tough lady," Blue replied. "Do you know anything about her childhood?"

"Not really. Just ... basic history. My mother told me that our ancestors were from East Africa, but that they left almost six hundred years ago to roam up into the Middle East and Europe, eventually settling in France. My mother was born in the Pyrenees. I don't know why she left, but she went to Scotland first, Argentina after that, and then finally America."

"Where she had you."

"She was in her late twenties. She had already worked as a performer for several years, but she quit after I was born. Every now and then she would agree to some shows—and I'd go along—but she was careful to keep me out of everyone's way. I had a bad habit of ... shifting when I got emotional. I didn't truly perfect my control until I was twelve, which meant a lot of isolation."

"How did you go to school?"

"I didn't. My mom taught me at home and every now and then I'd go in for some state-required test. I thought about college, but I didn't see much use for it. Life and books are better teachers, and you don't have to pay money for those."

Iris propped herself up and studied his face. She reached out and tugged on his beard. "You still haven't told me how you know her. My mother."

"Iris—"

"I think we're past the point where you have to shield my delicate ears, Blue."

He sighed, squeezing shut his eyes. "I think this is worse. She ... tried to kill me. Or save me. I'm still not sure which."

"She did *what?*"

"See, this is why I didn't want to say anything."

"Shit." Iris covered her face. "Did she tell you why?"

"Apparently, Santoso told her to. I was getting too close to him, and your mother had to follow orders or else risk her cover."

"Oh, my God." Iris rolled onto her back, hands still over her face. "Did she use a gun?"

Blue hesitated. Iris peered at him through her fingers. "Tell me."

"I don't see the point."

"There doesn't have to be a point. My mother tried to kill you. I want to know how."

He squirmed. "She used a bomb. A tiny one."

Iris groaned. "Jesus. I don't know whether to laugh or cry."

"Let's settle for not talking about this anymore. I don't want to turn you against her or anything."

"She used a bomb on you, Blue."

"And I forgive her. The end."

Iris stared at him, and something else tickled her brain: a memory, a scent.

Oh, Lord.

"Blue," she said slowly. "You were covered in a particular scent after my performance at the Miracle. A perfume. I don't suppose you remember it, do you?"

Blue's jaw tightened. "Maybe. Why?"

"It smelled exactly the same as what my mother was wearing when she found me in the casino."

"Really." He looked at his hands. "That's … some coincidence."

"I thought so, too. Maybe you would care to explain?"

"No," Blue said. "I really wouldn't."

And Iris was fine with that.

CHAPTER SEVENTEEN

Almost twenty-one hours later, after a brief stop in Hong Kong to refuel and change pilots, Iris found herself on the other side of the world.

Jakarta, Indonesia.

Iris did not have a passport, a fact she had alerted the men to before leaving Las Vegas. Frankly, she had expected some of them—especially Blue—to pat their chests with an, "Oops, forgot mine," but apparently in their line of work having the appropriate documentation for a last-minute jet around the world was just as essential as credit cards and a loaded gun. The only thing they all shared in common was the need for a visa, something Fred assured them would be taken care of. Much like Iris's passport.

Sure enough, the moment the jet landed at Soekarno-Hatta International Airport, a very tiny man rushed on board bearing a bulging brown envelope. There were no handshakes, not much talking, just a swift demand for all passports, which he slapped down on the coffee table with a grunt. The next five minutes were spent stamping and gluing, accompanied by a constant litany of soft mutters that sounded about as stressed out as the man looked and smelled. Sweat beaded on his forehead; his white dress shirt clung to his back.

Blue stood behind Iris, and she was more aware than ever of just how tall and strong he was. Looking at him, being near him, made her remember all those hours in his arms, and even though her body ached, it was good—a well-worn feeling that was all the warmer because the person responsible for it was at her side, and she trusted him to stay there. Trusted him to love her as much as she loved him.

Of course, it scared her, too. Her bad experiences lingered. But that was fine. She could live with a little fear.

The man finished affixing the visas with a flourish that consisted of a wide, bright smile that was shockingly cheerful. He returned the passports, including a gleaming new beauty for Iris. The picture on the inside looked like a close-up from one of the Miracle's posters, with her face transposed onto a white background.

The man left, and customs arrived at the jet—the two conveniently missing each other—and the process of entering Indonesia was completed with yet more stamps, no conversation, and a fat wad of bills that one of the agents slipped inside his uniform.

"I love money," Fred said after the officials left. "And I love working for people who possess vast, unending quantities of it."

Dean grunted. "I bet you sing 'Material Girl' when you're in the shower."

Fred smiled, sticking an unlit cigarette in his mouth. "Better than 'Mandy,' Mr. Campbell."

Dean narrowed his eyes. Artur patted him on the shoulder.

A sleek Mercedes van waited for them outside, and tinted windows made it impossible to see in. A short, svelte woman in a tight black uniform stepped out of the driver's seat. A scarf covered her hair, but her brown eyes were covered in green eye shadow, and her lipstick was an unnatural shade of red.

"Mr. Fred," she said, smiling. "How was your trip?"

"Lovely, Arti. Any messages?"

"Only that the man you inquired about arrived several hours ago, and with company: the young man in the picture you faxed, as well as an older woman."

Iris forced herself to breathe. Fred smiled. "Arti, meet our guests. Everyone, meet Arti. She's nice *and* good with a gun."

Arti blushed, giggling with what Iris could only define as extreme passion. She sounded like a hyena. Blue nudged Iris with his elbow, but she refused to look at him. Laughter would be highly inappropriate, even if it was partially due to the news about her mother and Danny.

The drive from the airport went very slowly. Iris, after each passing moment inside the city center, found her opinion of Jakarta sinking lower and lower, until she could—at last, without guilt—admit to herself that she had entered the unequivocal definition of a hellhole.

It was no doubt a pleasant, perhaps even beautiful place to live for those familiar with it, but Iris was not familiar, and though she knew it was incredibly small and shallow of her, she did not *want* to be familiar with this sweltering, steaming city where the air slapped her across the face with its grinding pollution and scents of burning garbage and open sewers; where the appalling poverty, the filth, was relentless, much like the high cries of the gaunt street children who pressed against the van with such desperate, hungry despair she wanted to gather them all up for a meal and a bath and as much money as she could cram into their skinny little hands.

The traffic did not help, either. Despite Arti's best efforts, the van became lodged on a side street like a kidney stone in a urethral tunnel of smoking vehicles. No place to run, no place to hide, no way to help; Iris watched the world pass in muted color, movement: green and blue pushcarts laden with soft drinks trundling down the muddy sidewalks; a sea of corrugated iron rooftops, narrow muddy streets, and, in the distance, the spires of modern steel and glass, which seemed like an affront to the extreme poverty all around her. People on scooters and bicycles slipped past; they wore surgical masks over their faces. Pedestrians were everywhere, walking faster than the cars parked in the road.

Iris looked at Fred and found him chewing on the end of his unlit cigarette. She remembered him as he had been, the odd, bumbling FBI agent, and part of her missed that man. She wondered, too, how he had managed to live the act—all of this, an act—and how a man who read minds was supposed to exist without hating everyone around him.

"You do it very carefully," Fred said, turning to meet her gaze. "You keep yourself shut off or shut away, and in places like this or Las Vegas, where the people just don't stop, you make sure you don't listen. You tune it out, pretend all those little voices are static. Because if you don't … well. You go crazy."

"So, do any of us have happy endings with the gifts we've been born with? Is there one person who has never suffered for them?"

"None that I can think of," Blue said, and Iris pushed deeper against him. "Of course, everyone has something."

Fred pinched the end of his cigarette between his fingers. "So, would you give it up? When you weigh the good you've done with your abilities, would you really just throw up your hands and say, 'To hell with it'?"

Blue said nothing. Iris watched his gaze travel to Artur, almost as if he thought the Russian might have the answer. His friend simply stared out the window at the rain clouds haunting the sky. The soft gray light made his face look exceptionally pale.

"I have no regrets," the Russian suddenly said, turning away from the clouds to look at them. He took off his glove. "No regrets at all." And he touched the seat. His forehead creased. "You are very deceitful, Fred. This is a new vehicle. Never driven until now."

"Of course," Fred replied, still playing with that unlit cigarette. "There was nothing I could do about the plane, but after what you did to me at the hotel, I called ahead and made special arrangements."

"You know that will not stop me from learning more about your organization."

"And I know that anything you find will just be a distraction. All you really want is Santoso. Or maybe just a good fight with a higher-than-average chance of receiving a bullet in your brain." Fred spit out his cigarette. "Wuss."

"Wuss, my ass," Dean said. "We're armed and dangerous back here, man. Watch your fucking mouth."

"Enough." Blue gave them all a hard look. "Fred, where are you taking us?"

"We have a house in Menteng. It's an old neighborhood near the business district. Lots of embassies and important political types live there. The security is good. We'll get some intel from the folks observing Santoso's Jakarta facility and then come up with a plan for getting Serena and Daniel out of there." Fred glanced at Artur. "You want to read someone's soul, be useful and go find something of Santoso's to touch."

Iris thought of the facility, Santoso in that small room watching her shift, begging for a bite. "How long does a person need to be in contact with a thing before you can get a reading from it?"

Artur sighed. "Not long. Moments, even, will produce something."

"And does it fade? Does whatever you can do get weaker depending on how long it's been since that contact?"

"It depends." Artur gave her a curious look; all of them were staring at her. "Why?"

She hesitated. "Because *I* am something Santoso touched. He hit me. Here." She traced a circle in the air above her cheek. "And I bit him."

Blue reached out and caught her hand. His scent tasted sour with anger. Iris said, "Don't. It could have been worse."

Artur's eyes darkened. He raised his hand, but stopped just before touching her face. "If I do this, I will see everything. Not just Santoso."

"I figured."

Blue twined their fingers. "You don't have to do this, Iris."

"I know," she said, then looked at Artur. "Come on. Do your thing."

"Of course," he murmured, and very slowly placed his palm against her cheek.

Given Fred's reaction back in Las Vegas, Iris expected a charge, a rush, some kind of physical or mental response to Artur's touch. And there *was* something—a skipped heartbeat, maybe—that made her chest feel odd.

Artur closed his eyes. His hand fell down to his lap, curled like a claw against his thigh. Iris heard the thick rumble of motorcycles. A lot of them. Traffic moving again, maybe.

"Well?" Fred asked.

"Santoso is there," Artur said slowly. "But this mind—" His breath caught, and he looked at Blue with such consternation Iris felt a stab of fear run from the crown of her head to the base of her spine.

"Aw, shit," Dean muttered. "This isn't going to be good."

Iris agreed. But before Artur could explain, the roars of the motorcycles got loud enough to be more than an annoyance, and the frown on Fred's face twisted into shock.

"Incoming!" he shouted. Blue pushed Iris forward, covering her with his body as the back windows shattered. Hands reached into the car; Iris glimpsed men wearing black helmets and white T-shirts. The motorcycles' engines were deafening.

Fists smacked flesh; Dean and Artur kicked open their doors, pushing back their attackers as they reached beneath their shirts for their guns.

"Get down!" Fred shouted at them, but too late. The air cracked, blood blossoming on Artur's shoulder. He staggered, falling back into the van. Iris barely noticed; she was too busy staring at the bullet hovering at the base of Dean's neck. He reached around and grabbed it, pressed his lips to the gleaming surface, a truly dark smile curving his mouth as he stared at their attackers. The men blanched, but did not retreat.

Blue left Iris—one moment there, the next rolling from the

van, crouching by the open door while Dean dropped the bullet and began firing back shots at a red rooftop. One shot, one body, again and again, his aim unerring. Blue protected his back, fighting with his fists as men seemed to pour out of nowhere, all of them swarming the van. Most of them did not have weapons; the plan, it seemed, was to overwhelm. Arti hit the accelerator, but all she got was bumper. The car in front of them could not be budged. The windshield shattered; the small woman slammed up hard against the seat and then fell forward, her head hitting the horn. She did not move again. The air wailed.

Iris's nails lengthened, turning black, and though she refrained from committing to a full shift, she poured power into her muscles and leaped from the car, fists swinging. Blue called her name, but she ignored him, falling into the dance, fighting to protect. Perhaps more of the cat showed through than she intended; the men, some of whom looked as though they had been recruited directly from local homes, off couches and in front of televisions, fell back when they looked at her face.

"*Sepang,*" they whispered, eyes filled with horror.

"Get back in the van!" Blue shouted, sliding up beside her.

"You first!" she snapped.

"They're here for both of you!" Fred snarled. Tears ran down his face; he held Arti's bloody face between his hands.

"Shit," Blue muttered. "Santoso."

"No," Fred said brokenly. "Your father."

Blue stared. Dean swore, pushing him back toward the van, dragging Iris with them. The mob followed, still cautious; on the outskirts she saw the original attackers, still wearing their motorcycle helmets, none the worse for wear. Letting the poor hired masses do the dirty work. Iris gave them the finger.

Artur got out of the van. His gun hand dripped blood, but he kept the weapon trained on the men behind them. Just as they reached the vehicle, something sharp pricked Iris's back. She knew what it was the moment she felt the pain—the memory was too fresh—but she could not believe her god-damn terrible luck as she reached back and yanked the dart out of her shoulder.

"Iris," Blue said, but even as her vision wavered she saw something small protrude from his chest like magic, a thunder-bolt, and she reached for him, reached and reached, and she was *not* going to lose herself this time—no, no, *no* ...

Iris heard shouting, Artur or Dean, and imagined Blue crawling to her, calling her name. She dreamed about fight-ing, men falling down, men grabbing her body and carrying her. She dreamed she was stolen away.

Again.

Blue could have blamed the dart for taking him down, which it would have despite his best efforts to the contrary, but the real truth was that as soon as he saw Iris dragged away—his friends distracted, overwhelmed by sheer numbers—he gave up the fight and practically waved his assailants over.

"Take me with her," he mumbled, and that was it. Darkness.

The next time he opened his eyes it was in a poorly lit room with sweating concrete walls, a wet concrete floor, and bars over a narrow slit of a window. The air was hot and smelled like piss. His body hurt. He could taste electricity all over the building, but nothing in this room, or inside the locks of the door.

He was also not alone.

His brother, Daniel, sat on a threadbare mattress, back against the wall. Bruises covered his face, his right eye was swollen shut, and blood caked his shirt.

"Hey," Blue croaked. "You look like hell."

"Back at you," Daniel mumbled, as though it hurt to open his mouth.

Blue rolled his eyes around, looking for the door. "Is there a reason you haven't broken out of this place yet? Seems like you could just knock down some walls or something."

"Serena," Daniel said. "Santoso, well-informed man that

he is, said that he would kill her if I tried to leave. Of course, he also said he would kill Iris and you and all my friends at the circus. I decided not to take the risk."

"You missed a good opportunity."

"Thanks so much for making me feel better."

"Sure." Blue frowned, trying to sit up. "So this is one of Santoso's facilities?"

"This is where I've seen the man, so yeah, that's my guess."

"That doesn't make sense. Iris and I were taken down by men working for our father. Why would he have us brought us here?"

"Our father?" Daniel closed his eyes. "I'm not sure I want to know the answer to that question."

Neither did Blue. "We need to get out of here and find Iris and her mother."

"They made me watch," Daniel said, his voice deepening into a hoarse rumble. "The surgery, I mean. Santoso ordered it as soon as we landed in this country. Dragged Serena into that operating room and went right for her skull. Took out her eye and Santoso watched, laid there like it was candy for him. And then they did the same to him, except he got something new in return for the pain."

Blue felt nauseous. "Was that before or after he beat the crap out of you?"

"Both. Man said I had it coming. Makes sense, if he knows our father."

"Our father who is supposed to be dead." Blue attempted to stand. His head pounded, vision spinning, but he kept his balance and leaned hard against the wall. The humidity made it difficult to breathe.

"No time to be cautious," he said to Daniel, trying to focus his concentration on the area beyond the door. He found two heartbeats a short distance away; guards, probably. "Can you undo those locks with your mind?"

"In my sleep," Daniel said.

"And can you run?"

"Because I look like road kill?" He smiled, grim. "I deflected the worst of the blows Santoso's men gave me. Not all, though. I didn't want anyone to get suspicious. But yes, I can run the hell out of here. And God help the idiot who tries to stop me."

Which meant that Blue still had to take care of the guards. So he did.

No chains this time around. No naked women lounging on pillows. Iris woke up on an operating table instead. Leather restraints crisscrossed her body from head to toe; there was a ball gag in her mouth. She smelled blood, bleach, sweat, the lingering miasma of anger and pain. A sliver of fear. Her mother. She smelled her mother.

My mother was here, and they hurt her.

From the look of things, Iris was next. She hoped that Blue was still free, but she had a bad feeling about that, too.

She could not move her head or her body—wiggling seemed to be her limit—and shape-shifting into full leopard seemed out of the question. Her hands, however, were another matter entirely, and she shifted her nails into claws. A leather strap pressed just beneath her hand; she began picking at it with her fingers, sawing and raking. She cut her own skin by accident, but the pain was nothing compared to the idea of getting the hell out of there.

She heard footsteps outside the room and shifted her hands back to human. The door opened. Broker stepped through. Coiffed, relaxed, pressed, and ready to plunder. Iris wondered if any of his relatives were Nazis.

He stood, just watching her. Iris stared back, and after a moment he sighed. Walked to the table and let his eyes travel up and down her naked body.

"I foresaw this," he said quietly. "And I thank you for doing your part in bringing together all the players. I do, however, feel some regret for the way you have been treated. Santoso is a very jealous man. An intelligent man, with a good eye for business, but nevertheless quite shallow, incapable of seeing the larger picture of things. He wants respect he will never have, and no matter how many exotic body parts he attaches to himself, he will never attain the class he desires. Unlike you and me, on the other hand. Unlike others of our kind." Broker touched her forehead, tracing a circle between her eyes. His skin was cool.

"I had a sister," he whispered. "She and I worked toward the same goal, but she took a slightly different path and was shot in the back for it. I will not make the same mistake."

Broker stepped away. His expression was grave—disturbingly so, because his scent showed no emotion, no fear or anger or lust. Just cool nothingness, perfect control. "Santoso wishes his technicians to harvest your ova, Ms. McGillis. Your mother was too old for the procedure, but you are prime. He will grow your babies in a test tube, with himself as the primary sperm donor. A terrible thought, I know. But do not worry...." His voice dropped to a whisper. "I will find more suitable fathers."

Iris wrenched herself against the bindings, but they held firm. She screamed at Broker, too, but the ball gag cut her words until all she could do was make inarticulate noises that sounded more animal than human. Which made sense, because she suddenly realized her body had shifted; fur leaked over her skin, her muscles thickened, her face altered shape.

"Lovely," Broker said.

It got easier after a while. The killing. Blue had fought using his mind as a weapon for his entire life, and now—now, with the line crossed—the sick feeling in his gut was fading. He did not know if that was good or bad.

He and Daniel both had guns taken from the guards whose hearts he'd stopped. There had not yet been a need to use the weapons—in this, stealth seemed like the better option—but Blue had a bad feeling their luck might be running out. "They must know by now that we're gone," Daniel said.

"Yeah," Blue replied, glad he had shorted out the connection that powered the facility's alarm system. Something that would not be noticed until an actual emergency.

The two brothers raced down a narrow, cramped corridor made of peeling linoleum and poured concrete. The few windows they passed were covered in bars, the glass so aged and clouded it was impossible to see outside—the polar opposite of the facility in the Nevada desert. The air was hot and sticky and smelled like a toilet had overflowed somewhere nearby.

Bioelectricity fluttered ahead of them; two individual heartbeats. Blue thought of Iris—he thought of her every time he felt a heart.

But these hearts had voices. Not native Indonesian speakers, either. Blue heard a woman with a crisp American accent and a man who sounded as though he had just gotten off the plane from France.

"He's already here. He's insisting that he see them now."

"Impossible. I was told the men are *disparus*. Missing."

"Then we will have to think of something, yes?"

"Oui. L'homme est dangereux."

Blue and Daniel shared a long look, and in his brother's eyes he saw a mirror of his emotions. Was it possible their father had come for them? Had Santoso truly ransomed them out—the old man coming out of hiding to personally make the exchange? For any other father those actions might make sense, but Felix Perrineau Senior was not a man of self-sacrifice—or even sentimentality. At least, not to Blue.

Footfalls—the man and woman, coming around the bend in the corridor. Blue looked at his brother, found complete agreement, and the two pressed flat against the wall, waiting until their targets were so close Blue could hear the whistle of their breath, the buzz of their hearts inside his head. He reached around the bend in the hall, grabbed the first thing he found—a slender shoulder—and yanked hard. The woman fell into his arms. Blue covered her mouth and pressed his stolen gun against her cheek.

Daniel was right behind him, but he did not have to use his hands. Blue heard a choking sound; on the other side of the bend the man stood frozen, eyes bulging so far out of his small baldhead that Blue half expected them pop right out.

The woman Blue held was equally short, with her brown hair slicked back tight in a bun. Gaunt face, tiny glasses, almost no lips. Blue said, "You scream, I'll kill you. Nod if you understand."

She nodded.

"Good. Where are Iris McGillis and her mother being held?"

Hesitation. Blue shook her so hard her teeth chattered, but he stopped when he heard distant voices. The woman sucked in her breath. Blue jammed the gun into her mouth.

"Move," he whispered, and he and Daniel led their prisoners to a small locked room that opened easily with only one telekinetic push. They filed in, relocked the door, and Blue pushed the woman against a table. "Tell me," he said.

She swallowed hard. "Top floor is where all priority projects go. The two women would likely be there."

"And if they're not?"

"This facility covers a city block, and there are many rooms, many labs, and many surgical bays. I am afraid you will simply have to look the good old-fashioned way."

"Right," Blue said. "And Felix Perrineau? Where might he be?"

Her mouth clamped shut, and any doubt Blue had that his father was here disappeared. He and Daniel traded glances, and his brother wrapped a large hand around the back of his man's neck. He leaned close.

"You're right, you know. My father is a dangerous man. But if you don't cooperate now, we'll fix you and your friend so good you'll be thinking he's a fucking saint. *Vous comprenez?*"

The Frenchman understood. Even Blue understood. They got what they needed, though it was a good thing Daniel happened to be fluent in *la langue d'amour,* because the little man rattled off a stream of words Blue would have been helpess to understand. He watched his brother pale beneath his bruises.

"What?" Blue asked sharply.

"It doesn't make sense," Daniel muttered.

Blue's hand curled into a fist. "Tell me."

"It's true, our father is here. Santoso requested a ransom—originally for me, and now for both of us. But he's not asking for money."

"Then what?"

Daniel shook his head, closing his eyes. "The price is Iris. *And* our father."

Chapter Eighteen

So. Being a sex slave organ donor was not enough; Santoso wanted Iris to be the mother of his children, too. A little army of über-shifters.

God. Kill me now.

Or better yet, get me the hell out of here. Iris was not about to give up her little ovum for a test run attempt in some tube. Even if Broker was offering his "help."

I will find more suitable fathers, my ass. There's only going to be one father, and I already found him, thank you very much.

Though frankly, the idea disturbed her on a level far deeper than personal preservation. Santoso and Broker clearly had different interests, but if both of them wanted to begin a breeding program with captive shape-shifters . . .

Or maybe Broker's people have already begun it, and you're just new stock. That might be the reason he's willing to betray Santoso. The babies you could make are worth more than keeping that creep around.

Bad, bad, bad. Even just nasty.

The question, then, was whom Broker really worked for. There was no way he could hope to do this on his own. So was it the Consortium Blue and the others had talked about?

The group supposedly responsible for putting Santoso in power? Psychic criminals? Mafia with telepathic abilities? Corporations run by men and women with ESP?

More like folks with a superiority complex. Broker practically implied that he and I were members of a master race.

And hadn't the Nazis run their own breeding camps? Forced women to bear perfect little Aryan babies to seed the German nation? Was that what this was all about: building wealth to push an agenda that involved an advanced eugenics program?

But why? Just because they can? What would be the point?

She understood Santoso's motivation. He was obsessed with the supernatural. And sex. And her.

She almost preferred that to Broker.

Her mouth was dry. She needed water badly, though the current lack of it did not concern her all that much. They obviously wanted to keep her alive—if not horribly comfortable. As for people watching her ...

No security cameras—none that she could see, anyway—but even if someone was ogling her body via monitor, Iris was past the point of caring. She needed to do *something,* because there was no guarantee of a rescue. Not here and not now.

She tried to be subtle, though she worked at her leather restraints until her claws felt like they were going to peel off, and still she sawed and picked and worried, until after a while she could feel the beginnings of a tear, some give. *Almost there ...*

Voices in the hall. Men. Iris's claws receded.

The door opened. Santoso entered. White gauze covered his left eye. Behind him an old man followed, leaning on a cane. His hair was bushy and white, his shoulders broad. He had a handsome face, a strong jaw, and piercing blue eyes that Iris would have recognized even if she had not already seen them on CNN.

Felix Perrineau. His sons looked just like him. They smelled like him, too, though he had an edge of sickness about him. Something wrong and dying, like rotten meat. She was shocked to see him.

Broker entered behind the old man. He shut the door.

"So this is the prize that is worth my sons' lives." Perrineau's voice was clipped and cold as ice, his eyes just as unforgiving. "With so many women to choose from, I am surprised that this is the one you break my back with."

"She is unique in all the world," Santoso said, trailing his bandaged hand up her leg. She endured his touch in silence, imagining her teeth clamped down on his neck, draining his blood.

"Unique and trussed up like a pig." Perrineau snorted. "And you say she was with my boy? Has he had first taste, you think? Or is she a whore like any other?"

Iris glared at him. Perrineau smiled. "No, maybe not a whore. Maybe a lady. Just maybe."

He reached for the gag and unbuckled it. Santoso watched, a trace of pride in his eyes, as if he were showing off his prize mare to a jealous colleague.

Broker remained as impassive as ever, though Iris knew different now. He did care about something: getting her.

Perrineau removed the gag. Her tongue felt huge, the roof of her mouth cracking as she tried to work up enough saliva to speak. Perrineau clicked his fingers at Broker, and the man silently fetched a cup of water from a nearby basin.

"There, my dear." Perrineau helped her drink. "Is that better?"

"Yes," Iris whispered.

"Good," he said, and leaned so close she could see herself mirrored in his eyes. Hard, cold, calculating eyes. "Tell me, Iris McGillis. Are you fucking my boy? My boy Blue?"

Iris gritted her teeth so hard she tasted blood. Perrineau narrowed his eyes. "Santoso. What do you have planned for this one?"

"It is none of your business," he said stiffly.

Perrineau swung around. "This *is* my business, you little fuck. And until I am dead it will remain so. You work for me.

You answer to *me*. Do not be cocky simply because of our deal."

This is my business. You work for me. Oh, my God.

Santoso's jaw flexed, his eyes darkening into something ugly. This was not a good time to be Felix Perrineau.

"You wanted to see her, sir, and so you have," Broker said quietly. "What else would you like?"

Perrineau gazed down at Iris. He touched her hair. "I want to know why this one is special."

"I'm not human," Iris told him, but instead of showing shock or disbelief, all he did was nod. Santoso lurched forward, but stopped just short of Perrineau. The old man paid no attention to him.

"I will tell you a secret," he whispered. "I am not so human, either."

"That's no secret," Iris replied, just as softly. "I know your sons."

Perrineau smiled. It was not a pleasant expression. "A word of advice, Santoso. If you keep this one from the Consortium, they will punish you. I think they might even do worse than what you have planned for me."

"She is mine," Santoso said. "And I will kill anyone who says different."

"Ah," said the old man, glancing at Broker. "Then I suppose the future is written, is it not?"

The hint of a smile touched Broker's mouth, and though it was already disturbing enough knowing that Blue's father was, in essence, a criminal mastermind, she found the idea of Perrineau and Broker working together even more horrifying. Santoso truly did feel small-time compared to them.

She thought Blue might feel the same. If she ever saw him again.

You'll see him. A man like him doesn't give up.

But if she kept thinking about Blue she was going to cry. Which would be the worst thing she could possibly do. No weakness allowed.

Perrineau straightened; the scent of sickness grew stronger for a moment. Iris wanted to rub it out of her nose.

"My sons," said the old man, still looking at her. "I want to see them now."

"Broker will take you to them," Santoso said. "I have other matters to attend."

"Really." Perrineau arched his brow. "Matters like this girl? You cannot control your dick even long enough to kill me?"

Iris held her breath. Santoso looked at Broker. "Take him down to his sons. I will be there soon."

Stupid man, Iris thought, listening to the contempt in Santoso's voice. She could smell the predator in Felix Perrineau, could see it in his eyes, and she felt a burst of pure aching relief that Blue had not been raised under his control. How Daniel had made it without turning into his father was also testament to his strength. Or his mother's.

Perrineau arched his brow. "I'll await your presence downstairs, then. Try not to wear yourself out on the merchandise." And without another look at Iris, the old man left the room. Broker followed, closing the door behind them.

Leaving Santoso. He smiled, gazing down at her body as if it were some kind of prize. Iris tilted her chin, goading him with her eyes, making him look at her face even as her hands and arms transformed, her entire body swelling with lean, long muscle. She saw the light reflect golden in his one eye, and she thought of her mother, the scent of her still strong in this room. The leather bindings creaked, the weak one held together by only a shred.

Santoso stared at her body. "You look ready for me, Iris. I think I'll like you this way. So strong beneath me."

Iris strained against her bonds. She felt the snap, the immediate easing of pressure around her body, and it made her smile.

"Okay," she said. "Show me what you've got."

Our father is here, and he's going to sacrifice himself for us.

Right. Somewhere, Hell was freezing over. And Blue wanted to be there to watch.

"I'm having a moral dilemma," Daniel said, as they raced up a flight of stairs, pursuing not their father, but the possibility that Iris and her mother might be nearby, trapped on one of those upper floors. "I'm trying to decide whether or not we should let our father know we've escaped—thus voiding his deal with Santoso."

"You mean, you want to rescue him."

"Um, maybe?"

Blue grabbed the railing, pulling himself along. "We are two sorry sons of bitches, Daniel. We don't even know if we like our father enough to save his life."

"It's not high on my list of priorities," he admitted. "But I sort of feel obligated."

Blue grunted. "Good karma?"

"More like ... doing for him what he's doing for us."

There was not much Blue could say to that. Especially when he felt the same. Which was ... more than disturbing. He had spent years hating his father, though it was an emotion his mother had tried to dissuade on more than one occasion. A surprise—he had always thought she would advocate revenge, especially as her legal practice specialized in protecting abused women.

But in the case of the old man, his mother had always kept a remarkably even head. No hard passionate fury or indignation. Unforgiving, yes—but stoic. Which, in turn, had created an odd split inside Blue's own heart. He hated the man, but he occasionally found himself wondering what it would be like to have him as a father. A real father. A good father.

The facility—wherever they were—had a surprising number of floors, and its decrepitude continued to astound Blue. There were security cameras, but they were mounted mostly in the battered halls, with none in the stairwell accessible only by punching in a code—something Blue bypassed with his mind.

On the sixth-floor landing, with four more flights to go before they reached the top, Blue heard an elevator ding. He found himself slowing, and a moment later heard a voice that stopped him dead. Daniel staggered, eyes wide.

"Dad," he whispered. Blue held up a hand, silencing him. The voice outside the stairwell was deep, commanding, and utterly unmistakable.

"What do you mean, they've escaped? Dammit. Why am I surprised? Santoso is a fool, the worst kind."

"You could have removed him," said a man, his voice smooth, cultured. "Your word is law here."

"And train another? No, Broker. Santoso might be waste of breath, but at least he keeps the wheels turning. And right now that is all that matters."

Whatever Perrineau said next was lost. Blue braced himself against the wall, forcing himself to breathe. Daniel leaned in close.

"Did I just hear that correctly? Did our father imply that he runs an organization that kidnaps, rapes, and murders?"

"Yes." Blue's throat hurt; his heart hurt. Everything hurt. "You're surprised?"

"No," Daniel said. "But why did it have to be this?"

Blue did not know whether to laugh or cry. His father was a monster. Not only that, if this was his business, then that meant he also worked for the Consortium. Which explained why he knew so much about Dirk & Steele.

He played me. He never intended to turn in the agency. He just wanted me to find Daniel for him, no questions asked.

And that was exactly what Blue had done.

Daniel walked to the stairwell door; Blue ran to catch up with him. "What are you doing?"

"Ending this," he said. "No more running from him, Blue. No more attempts to coexist and stay out of his way. No more. He's hurt too many people."

Blue thought of Iris, how she needed him more than he needed to confront his father, but Daniel walked through that door, and Blue found himself following as if there were a string attached to his gut, yanking hard. Their father was nowhere in sight, but they heard his voice and tracked him to a room filled with long tables and men hunched over ledgers and computer keyboards. Calculators clicked. Accountants. Blue imagined them poring over profits—the cost of a child or a woman's dignity; the beating of a heart, the removal of a kidney. Slash, dash, cold hard cash—all to be slurped up by his father. Mr. Good Samaritan. The king of philanthropy, with a multibillion-dollar foundation devoted just to helping others. The hypocrisy was disgusting.

Felix Perrineau leaned on a cane. He blinked when Blue and Daniel entered the room, his only expression one of surprise. His mouth tightened.

Daniel grabbed the old man's jacket and shoved him against the table. Papers flew up and away—and not from the impact. Blue felt a telekinetic wind brewing—a storm.

The man with Perrineau did nothing to stop Daniel. *Broker*, Blue thought, remembering some of what Iris had said about the man. His eyes were cold.

"You son of a bitch." Daniel muttered. Accountants scattered, gasping. Perrineau showed no surprise at his son's presence—or violence.

"Ah," he whispered. "The sons coming home to roost. How remarkable, seeing the two of you together."

"As if you care," Blue said. "We're just a game to you."

"Don't presume to tell me what I feel, boy. Not ever."

"You're in no position to give us orders," Daniel spat. "Not after what I've seen. Jesus Christ, dad, I knew it was bad—you're more mafia than the Godfather—but this, *this*, goes beyond criminal. Why would you live your life like this? Whatever gave you the right?"

"There are no such things as rights," Perrineau said, staring into his son's eyes. "Only power. And I took what I could, as much as I could. The world loathes weakness, boy. It is an affront."

Blue, keenly aware of Broker watching them, placed his hand on Daniel's shoulder. "Let him go."

His brother's jaw flexed, his eyes bright. His fingers jerked loose. Perrineau sighed, smoothing down the front of his suit.

"Your face, son. Who did that to you?"

"Your pets," Daniel said. "Santoso and his men."

Something flickered through Perrineau's eyes; Blue almost imagined it was anger, but it was so fleeting he could not be certain it was even real.

"Why are you here?" Blue asked, fighting desperately to keep his voice calm, to tamp down his emotions. It was hard. He was too angry, too confused—and, even though he was the one standing here, too afraid for Iris.

"Why did you let yourself get caught?" Perrineau retorted, but waved his hand in Blue's face before Blue could answer. "Never mind. I sent my men after you and the girl. She was one of the conditions of your release. Taking you, on the other hand, was extra. For my benefit only."

"Santoso set a price and you jumped? I thought you were the boss."

Perrineau's lips thinned. "A man keeps his power only so long as he lives without weakness. You, boys, are my weakness."

"Bullshit," Blue said. "The only way we would be a weakness to you is if you cared about us."

"And who's to say I don't?" asked the old man softly. "You? You care to lecture me on love? You, standing here with your thumb up your butt while the woman you're fucking is upstairs, strapped naked to a table, alone with a psychopath? Where's the love there, boy? What kind of man are *you*?"

Blue's breath caught. "Where is she?"

Perrineau snorted. "Find her yourself if she means that much. Prove you're worthy of something that fine."

Blue backed away toward the door. "Daniel."

"Wait," said his brother, and he turned back to his father. "You came here to die. You know that, don't you? Santoso plans on killing you in exchange for our release. *If* he can be trusted."

"I have safeguards in place to make sure he follows his word. Though with the two of you free, I suppose I might be able to change my plans. Just a bit."

"Just a bit," Daniel echoed. "Why did you do it, Dad? All of it. Not just this, but everything else. Pretending you're dead, searching for me, blackmailing Blue. *Why?* The only thing I was ever good for was being your verbal punching bag."

"And what a fine bag you were. So easy, so soft." The corner of Perrineau's mouth curved into a smile. "I went to the trouble because my sons believe I am a monster. Callous, uncaring, amoral. And it is true, every bit of it, though I have no regrets, not a single one. Unfortunately, however, my time is running out. I am dying, and that is something I cannot change, though for a time I thought I could. I believed that I had the strength to make the sacrifice required, but I did not. *I did not.*" Perrineau closed his eyes. "I was offered a chance, an opportunity to participate in an … experiment. A shout against mortality. The only requirement was blood. Your blood or Blue's. My sons. And I could not do it. I tried, and I could not." He smiled, grim. "Moments of weakness, boys. Those are what kill even the mightiest of men."

Blue unclenched his jaw. "So, when did you decide you weren't going to hurt us?"

Perrineau passed a hand over his face; he suddenly looked his years, and more. "Months ago. Daniel had already disappeared. I thought he would come home, but my … disease … spread, and there was still no word. So I turned to you. I thought it would make an interesting opportunity."

"You could have just explained, instead of using blackmail."

"You wouldn't have believed me. Blackmail, on the other hand, kept you to your word. You found your brother."

"Santoso found him first," Blue said. "He wanted to use him against you, didn't he?"

"The little fuck has illusions of grandeur."

Blue glanced at Broker, who managed to look bored. "And the Consortium? How do they play into this?"

Perrineau shook his head. "Go to your woman. Kill Santoso if you must. If you and Daniel are free, my job here is done. I can go home to die."

"Sir," Broker said quietly. "I am afraid that is not entirely accurate."

"Oh, really?" snapped the old man. "Care to explain why?"

Broker pulled a gun from his jacket. "Actually, I would."

Blue's reaction was too slow; Broker pulled the trigger. The blast took the old man off his feet, slamming him into the table. Daniel cried out.

Broker slammed into the wall with enough force to make a dent. The gun slipped from his fingers and Blue scooped it up. Daniel's face was terrible to look upon; Blue thought if their father had ever chosen to express any true rage, this was what it would look like: white face, white lips, the tendons of his neck standing out like the thick roots at the base of a tree.

The brothers ran to Perrineau; the old man's breathing was shallow, his lips blue. He had enough strength to grab their hands, though, and to pull them to his wounded chest, coating them in blood.

"You're in danger," whispered the old man, his eyes burning, feverish. "Both of you. All of you. Your people, Blue. The Consortium—"

His voice broke, breath rattling in his throat. Blue looked up and found Daniel staring at the old man, his face stricken. Behind him, Broker still hung against the wall.

"Why?" Blue asked, feeling a scream rise high in throat, drowning in a terrible inexplicable grief. Laughter had seemed so appropriate only days ago, and now … now he wanted to cry.

Broker's mouth twisted. "He left his fortune to the both of you. Equal partners in all his endeavors, legal or not. But if you're dead, the money goes to the Consortium. And all those billions will help us quite nicely." He gazed down at Perrineau, whose eyes were closed, his heart stuttering to a broken stop inside Blue's mind. "We did not need him anymore. And we do not have time to break the both of you like we broke him."

"So why didn't you just kill him in his sleep?" Daniel whispered. "Do the same to us? Why the show?"

"Why not?" Broker asked softly. "I was bored."

I am going to kill you, Blue thought, and maybe he would have—but an odd thing happened: The building began to shake. First the floor, then the walls, until everything was swaying and jerking, bucking the world on the back of a slow bronco. Some of the accountants were still in the room, huddled in the corner. They closed their eyes, covered their faces.

Daniel staggered. "What is this? A bomb?"

Blue grabbed their father. There was room for only one person under the wooden table, and Blue shoved the old man beneath. He grabbed Daniel's leg and yanked him down, forcing them together in a tight huddle. Broker shouted, but still he hung spread-eagled, with the first hint of real emotion— anger, fear—appearing on his face.

"Earthquake," Blue said, remembering too late that quite a few of those had been striking this area.

"Jesus," Daniel muttered. "I hope the ceiling doesn't come down."

But it did.

CHAPTER NINETEEN

Iris was still smiling when Santoso took off his pants. He wore no underwear, and he was quite aroused.

"I hope you realize I'm a hard woman to satisfy," she said. "I don't know if you're really up for the job."

Santoso touched himself, which was stomach-churning enough without the additional sight of him running his tongue over his lips like a porn star wannabe. Some of the circus women had foisted those movies on her; Iris knew what she was talking about. And he sure as hell wasn't any Rocky Piledriver.

Or Blue Perrineau, for that matter.

Santoso took off his shirt. His chest glistened, tattoos rolling against his lean muscles. He walked to the counter and opened a drawer. He took out a gun.

"I am going to undo your restraints," Santoso said. "If you hurt me, I will kill you. I have your mother now. I do not need you alive unless you are willing to pleasure me."

Liar, Iris thought, remembering what Broker had told her. Santoso had not harvested her ova yet. Until then, she was safe. Mostly.

"What happened to Songbird?" she found herself asking. "Did you tell her the same thing?"

Santoso bared his teeth; smile or grimace, she could not tell. "Songbird was all used up when you met her. All those women, ready for fresh replacements. But the facility ..."

Oh, yes. Definitely a grimace. Even, she thought, rage.

"Why did you blow it up?" she asked, willing him to watch her face as her hands slowly loosened the leather.

"I did not blow it up," Santoso said through gritted teeth. "That was Perrineau's doing. He was jealous of the idea. Could not stand the improvements I made to the business. So he destroyed them when he had the chance. Broker told me so."

"Really," Iris said, questioning how much of what Broker said was the truth; wondering, too, how many people were going to die before this was all over. "So when you discovered you had Perrineau's son in your possession ..."

"It was the perfect opportunity. Like now." He moved close, his gun wavering with each step. He was too excited to hold it steady. Iris wondered if he would come if she breathed on him. Not that she wanted to try.

"You have someone waiting for you," she reminded him, feeling everything inside her go still and small, focused like a needle point on the man in front of her. Just one chance—one chance to do this.

"Perrineau is already a dead man," Santoso said. "He can wait."

He reached out to touch her. Iris moved. She wrenched herself sideways, rolling off the surgical table, still tangled in the thin leather restraints, but not enough to completely handicap her. Santoso shouted, running around the table, but Iris rolled sideways again, this time getting free. Her body melted into the leopard, though she kept her voice, her humanoid face. Let him fight a Sphinx. She would kill him as a riddle.

The two of them circled each other, and just as Iris had anticipated, he did not shoot her. Instead he ripped off the bandage covering his eye. The flesh around the socket was red, swollen, but there—there in the heart, cushioned—was a flash of gold. A familiar eye in a terrible face.

"It is remarkable," he whispered. "The properties of your kind. Your flesh truly is more than human."

"I'm going to kill you," Iris said, looking for her mother in that gaze. "I'm going to burn your bones."

Santoso smiled, swaying on his feet. "You will have to touch me first, Iris. You will have to lay your hands on my body. Maybe you will change your mind about killing me then."

Iris did not feel like responding to that. In fact, she did not feel at all like talking—or, for a moment, fighting. The world felt wrong, as if it were tilting, tilting, and it was not until it began to shake, to rumble, that she realized her luck. Santoso, distracted, took his eyes off her for just one moment.

It was all the time in the world. Iris went for his throat. The gun exploded; her side felt warm, but his blood was warmer, and it was rushing down her throat so sweet, so sweet, and that was all she needed—more than freedom, more than her life—and she held on tight as ceiling tiles hit the floor, as furniture toppled, as glass shattered.

She thought of Blue, of his voice and hands, of his—*you will never be alone, because I love you, I love you, Iris*—

Then the world went dark.

Blue was not quite man enough to admit aloud how close he came to pissing himself when the ceiling stopped less than an inch from his head, but he figured that was okay, because everyone was screaming like it was *Apocalypse Now*, and frankly, he doubted he was the only one suffering from a weak bladder.

He tried to speak, but his mouth was so dry it felt like sandpaper. He worked up enough spit to swallow—and *dear God* he was going to die, *holy crap, holy shit* that ceiling was close to his face—and blindly stuck his hand out, searching for his brother. "Daniel, you there?"

He could barely hear his own voice over the cries around

him—those accountants, still in their corner—so he tried again, coughing at the end of his brother's name. Daniel did not respond—there was no hint of his voice or his body—but a moment later the ceiling groaned and shuddered, dust and shards of debris falling against Blue's face, choking him, and just when he thought again that he was going to die, he sensed movement, felt the air churn, and beneath his lashes caught a hint of dull gray light.

Freedom.

"Blue." One word, croaked from a throat that sounded cut by razors. It was as close as he thought it should be, only he had not reached out far enough. His brother had rolled when the ceiling came down.

"Blue," Daniel said again, his voice almost lost beneath the chaos of weeping and shouting—not just in this room, but from others nearby. "Blue, you have to get those people out. I can't hold—I can't do this much longer."

I can't do this much longer.

"Shit," breathed Blue, staring up at the crumbling, buckling ceiling with new understanding. Because *of course* it had stopped, and not just because something had gotten in the way.

Blue tried to scoot across the floor toward the break in the ceiling. There were people in his path, some with the same goal in mind, and Blue not-so-gently kicked them out of his way as he fought to reach the hole. Iris filled his vision, his last glimpse of her collapsed in the street, and he gritted his teeth, pushing harder. If a ceiling had fallen on *her* . . .

He made it to the break. Some of the accountants were already struggling through. Body hurting like hell, Blue stifled a groan and reached. Hands unexpectedly grabbed his wrist and pulled him up: strangers, one floor above, trying to save his life. Blue had to climb—the ceiling itself was hovering only to his waist, but the wreckage and debris piled on either side of the hole created an impressive obstacle that had him stifling groans as his knee ached.

There were people topside encouraging him to climb out

the entire way, but once he got a good hand- and foothold, Blue reached back down to help pull out the few remaining survivors. He called Daniel's name only once, but got no response. Called for his father, too, but received the same silence.

Blue tried to remember how many people had been in the room with them at the start of the earthquake, but his brain refused to process that much information. When the trickle slowed to nothing, though, Blue scrabbled back down into the hole, getting down on his knees. He crouched in the darkness, trying to see, searching for heartbeats with his mind. He found one very close—reached out—and made contact with a slender ankle. He pulled hard, twisting around so that he could haul backward with all his strength. After a breathless struggle he pulled an unconscious woman into the light. He pushed her toward the waiting hands, then shimmied back into the darkness beyond the edge of the hole.

"Daniel!" he shouted, looking for another beating heart. He found one—and only one.

"Fuck," his brother muttered brokenly, lost beyond Blue's ability to see. "Get the hell out of here. Now."

"Absolutely," Blue said, trying not to think about the crushing weight floating so tenuously above his body as he scooted toward his brother, led only by the pulse of his heart.

"I'm serious," Daniel said, and this time his voice was worse, raw, on the edge of a sob. "Jesus, Blue. I can't move. You won't move me."

A chill broke through him. "Tell me."

"No time," Daniel whispered, and Blue found himself shooting backward, feet first toward the hole and its shaft of light. He shouted, trying to slow himself, but all he got were cut fingers and a mouthful of dust as the ceiling directly in front of him collapsed with a thunderous, deafening thud. The air shook with the impact—Blue shook—and he let himself be dragged to safety just as the portion of the ceiling beneath him dropped more than a foot, sending everyone down in a rough tumble that hurt like hammer blows to Blue's limbs and aching head.

Daniel.

Blue did not move. He did not dig for his brother. He stretched beyond his shields, searching, and found no trace of a heartbeat beneath the rubble. No pulse. Nothing.

Hands tugged on his shoulders. Blue shrugged them off, pushing himself to his knees and then to his feet. He swayed, dizzy. All he could do was stare at the portion of the ceiling below him, imagining his brother, Daniel …

No time.

Blue closed his eyes, Daniel's face swimming in his mind. His brother. His brother, gone. And his father.

Deal with it later. Later, when you're still alive and out of this hell. When you have Iris.

Blue began looking for a way out.

The air smelled like blood and feces. Blue decided that if a scream could have a scent, this would be it. Hard, bitter, dirty. He also wanted to scream, but had no time—not yet—and he pushed through the chaos of the dying and injured, moving from one floor to another, searching with his heart and mind until he felt crazy bite him on the edges, until his throat felt so full of fear he choked on it, leaning over his knees and gagging so long and hard he thought his stomach would fall up through his esophagus.

"You," said a familiar voice, sharp. "You, Perrineau. Where is my daughter?"

Blue looked. Serena stood beside him, swaying, dressed in a simple white hospital gown. She held a small naked child in her arms. Blood trickled from a soaked bandage over her missing eye. Seeing her was like seeing a ghost; he thought he was hallucinating. He had forgotten she even existed.

"You're alive," he said, surprised but unable to muster much emotion. "Where were you? How did you get free?"

"Don't ask stupid questions. My daughter. I want her."

"I don't know where she is. I'm looking."

"She is alive," Serena growled. Her good eye flashed, a golden light in the dusty haze. "She is alive. I know it. I am her mother and I know it."

"Alive," Blue echoed. "Yes. I know it, too."

Serena's jaw tightened—hard words were coming—but the child in her arms began to stir, and she glanced down at him; quick, almost startled. Breathless.

"I did not mean to take him," she murmured, tearing her gaze from the child to look again at Blue. Her eye was no longer hard, but instead haunted, filled with the ghost of so much pain that Blue felt it echo in his heart. "He was in the operating room beside me. For a harvest. Kidneys. He is a burden I do not need, Perrineau. I do not know why I took him. My daughter needs me more. I must find her."

"I will find her. Your daughter has me."

"You are *nothing*," Serena said, but Blue touched her face—gentle—and she shut her mouth with a snap.

"I am the man who loves your daughter," he told her softly, feeling the rest of the world fall away as he looked into her golden eye. "And I am the man who will find her. So go, Serena. Just go. Save the boy. Trust me to do this."

"No," she whispered, but Blue had already begun to back away, and he broke into a run before she could follow.

He traversed what remained of the hall, cutting through swaths of daylight as he passed immense cracks in the building; hot, humid air soaked through, turning the ruins into a sauna as he struggled on instinct, searching desperately for a pulse that might be familiar. He had never been able to tell a person from their heart, but for Iris—for her, lost in this mess, alone with Santoso—

Alone and buried. Like Daniel.

Blue heard a groaning sound: the building, his world, slanting sideways. The ceiling sagged; bodies and furniture sprawled through open doors. Window glass crunched beneath his shoes. No electricity ran through the wires in the walls; power was dead and gone.

"Iris," he murmured, leaning against the wall, trying to

shut out the distant wails of voices and sirens, the trickle of water, the smell of screams smeared on his body.

If you lose her . . .

No Iris, nothing would be left. This was do or die. Blue sucked in his breath and tore down his shields, scrapping them to nothing but dust. Unprotected, raw; the onslaught, previously controlled, ripped into him like a hacksaw against his brain. No protection; his heightened sensitivity cut his mind. This area might not have power, but the rest of the city certainly did, and holy God, it hurt.

Blue shuddered, holding his head, trying to swallow the discomfort as he searched for heartbeats, bioelectricity, anything that whispered *Iris*. Anything that made his own heart say, *Yes*.

You can't identify a person based on the beating of a heart, whispered a little voice. *No matter how connected you feel. No matter how much you love her.*

Nothing to lose, though. Nothing but his life. Blue kept moving, one hand against the jagged slumping wall as he tripped and hobbled, the world fluttering inside his head, his vision sparking with light and spots of darkness. Daniel flashed through his thoughts, their father, but Blue pushed them both away, throwing his mind over the sparks of human electricity flickering sporadically through the building around him.

He smelled bleach, acrid and stinging. His eyes watered. Ahead, life; a body glided free of dust and shadows. Another impossible ghost.

"Hello," said Broker. Blood covered the side of his face, his clothing. Blue could not imagine how he had managed to survive—or escape so quickly. He did not have a weapon. In fact, his left arm hung at a strange angle. Dislocated, broken, or crushed, it was impossible to tell.

"Where's Iris?" asked Blue.

"Close." Broker maintained his distance, his features almost lost in the haze of the settling building. The earth rolled gently; an aftershock. Broker kept perfect balance, barely swaying. Blue did not quite manage the same; he staggered, forced to lean against the shuddering wall until the world stopped moving. Broker's heart pulsed inside his head.

"Tell me," Blue said.

"Tell you?" Broker's smile was strained. "What if I told you instead that your brother is not dead? What if I made you choose?"

"I'd choose Iris." *And so would Daniel, if our positions were reversed.*

"Always the woman," Broker said softly. "You could find another. There are easier ways to love."

Blue pushed away from the wall. "If you won't talk, you're of no use to me."

"So you will kill me. Easy for you now, correct?" Broker leaned deeper into shadow. "You should know, Mr. Perrineau, that one day you will kill me, and in a most permanent fashion. I have foreseen it. That is part of the reason I wanted you dead. It was not all about the money."

Blue almost expected a gun to materialize in the bastard's hands, but Broker continued to do nothing but stand, watching him.

"Iris," he said again.

Broker closed his eyes. "The end of the hall."

Blue did not move. "Hey."

"Yes?"

He smiled. "Why don't we make it today?"

Broker's eyes widened, but all it took was a thought. A quick finish, with no last curtain call. The man hit the ground hard. Blue searched himself for guilt and found nothing at all.

He ran, leaping over debris and hands outstretched for help. He searched for heartbeats in that last room and found only one—faint, growing weaker by the moment. And then it stopped completely.

Blue had to kick down the door, but it had already come off one of its hinges, and the wood slammed into the floor. It was dark inside, but part of the ceiling had collapsed, and Blue fell to his knees, clawing through steel and plaster, cutting his hands as he dug through the mess, fighting to reach Iris. There was so much to pull aside, though—too much, a suffocating weight—and the thought of her being buried alive ...

His hand touched her leg, and then more. Wrapping his arms around her waist, he braced himself and leaned back hard, hauling her out with a shout. He rolled them both until she lay flat on the floor. Naked, partially human, covered in patches of spotted fur. Not breathing. Her heart silent.

Blue tilted up her head and breathed air into her blood-smeared mouth, pumping her chest with his fists. *One, two, three—breath—one, two, three—breath.* But she did not respond, and the world suddenly turned upside down inside his head. At first he thought it was grief, but the spinning and shaking did not stop, and the air roared so loudly that the only place he could hear was in his chest, which rattled and ached. He felt heat, and a part of him recognized fire, an explosion—probably some gas line in the building going boom. Black smoke filled the room.

Blue did not move. *No Iris, nothing left,* he thought again, and he lay his hands upon her chest, reaching down into her heart, begging with everything he had for that tiny muscle to spark, to pulse, to *live*—to become again, Iris. Iris, golden—Iris, shining—Iris, smiling and warm and laughing beneath his body.

And as he filled himself with her, it seemed to him that there was power inside his body, electricity pulling and pulling from the city into his skin. Blue felt as though his hair was floating, and next would be the flesh, muscle, bone. Full of power, a conduit, he pushed his hands harder against Iris's chest, shoving outward with his gift to surround her heart, to massage the muscle with electricity. To strike it with baby thunderbolts.

He got a beat, and then another. Strong, even, steady. Iris's eyelids fluttered. She murmured his name, and he dragged her close, pushing them both into the corner. Iris coughed. Blue coughed, too. The smoke pouring into the room was bitter, painful, but there were no windows and Blue could see the edge of a terrible fire raging just outside in the hall. No exits, not above or below. Blue finally noticed Santoso sprawled on the ground. He was missing his throat.

"Are you okay?" Iris whispered, hoarse. Blue choked, rocking her as the air and heat murdered them. His eyes burned, and not just from the smoke.

"Got you here," he rasped. "I'm good."

"Me, too," she said, staring out at the rolling smoke, the fire. And that was it for him: the end. He tightened his grip around her body, turning them so that his back was to the flame. Iris said his name.

And then, quite suddenly, he felt a waft of cool air against his neck and the bone-crushing grip of two hands grabbed his shoulders. One moment, fire—and in the next, Blue found himself sitting in a small stone courtyard littered with debris. His lungs hurt, but not enough to dampen his enjoyment. Coughing, he hugged Iris close, pressing his lips into her hair.

Dean crouched beside them and Blue grabbed his arm, dragging his friend in for a hug. Dean was covered in oil stains, filth, dried blood. He patted Blue on the back. "Too many close calls, man. I would have come sooner, but those guys who attacked us in the street shot our asses full of drugs and dumped our bodies in a ditch. Don't know why they didn't just kill us. They probably thought the locals would do it."

"I don't give a damn," Blue rasped. "Thank you for saving our lives."

"Whatever," Dean said, gentle. "You're lucky we woke when we did. We're *all* lucky. The earthquake hit just as we were getting our acts together. A whole neighborhood came down around us. But after the dust settled, all I had to do after that was find your trail."

"My mother?" Iris asked.

"I saw her in there," Blue said quickly. "She was alive, rescuing a child." Iris closed her eyes. "And Daniel?"

"Right here."

Blue turned, staring. Daniel sat directly behind them, dressed in plaid boxer shorts. His face was still a mess, as was the rest of him, but he was alive. Impossibly, wonderfully, alive. He stood and walked to them, crouching for a bear hug that only days ago would have seemed as ridiculous as surviving the weight of that damned ceiling.

"I can't believe it." Blue wondered if this was it and his mind had finally left him. "You were dead. I couldn't hear your heart."

Daniel ran a hand over his face; his entire arm trembled. "I sure as hell didn't see any white lights down there, so I'm pretty sure I was alive the entire time."

"Then how did you survive?"

"Same way I lived through my fire act. I built telekinetic shields directly upon my body. Almost like bulletproof skin, with a special air pocket over my face." His grin seemed to verge on the edge of hysterical. "I was able to hang on until your friend found me."

"I stumbled onto his trail and saw that he was still breathing," said Dean. "The rest is history."

"And all that talk about being pinned?"

"Didn't mean I was paralyzed," Daniel said. "I just couldn't move, and I didn't have enough strength to get out from under that debris and hold up the ceiling at the same time. I made my choice." He hesitated, shadows gathering around his eyes. "Our father is still down there."

"Yeah," Blue said. *One thing at a time. Too much has happened for anything else. Just take your moments.*

Like this one, with Iris alive in his arms. With his brother here. With his friends.

That was all he needed. Everything else was a luxury.

The air was hot and wet. He could hear sirens and screams and honking horns beyond the confines of the small courtyard. A banyan tree, with its fig roots crossed and fused into a lattice, gave them shade, and after a time, a slender Indonesian woman emerged from the house beside them with bottles of water. The earth occasionally rolled.

Artur and Fred returned. They'd been out scouting, taking the measure of damage at the facility. Blue thought a psychometrist and a telepath made a good team, covered all the bases.

"Santoso?" Artur asked, his skin black with ash and dust.

"I killed him," Iris said, touching the blood flecks at the corner of her mouth. The Russian nodded, and did not say another word. Not that night, and not the next when they boarded Fred's plane and left behind the wreckage of Jakarta.

But when he asked Fred to divert the plane to San Francisco, they did as he asked. When he left to go to the hospital, all of them followed.

And waited.

It was an odd thing, Iris thought, being part of a family. Not just circus family, not just blood family—which had always consisted of only herself and her mother—but something bigger, which was just as tight, just as dependable, and which seemed so much at odds with the life she had built for herself. The only life she had known until mere days ago. The only life she had thought she would *ever* know, because she was too afraid to have anything more.

Permission to love, she thought. *Thanks, Daniel.*

Iris sat in a soft chair beside Blue, just outside Elena Loginov's private room at the UCSF Medical Center. They had been there for an hour, taking over for Dean and his wife, Miri, and before that others: men and women who seemed normal enough, but who looked into Iris's golden eyes with knowing smiles, as though her secret—so carefully guarded—was written in a halo above her head. She wondered what her mother would say about it—if Iris ever saw her again.

Iris did not like the smell of hospitals, though in all honesty, this was the first time she had ever been in one. It reminded her of Santoso's lab. Bleach, fear, death and blood; she felt immensely sorry for anyone forced to linger; worse, for the individual compelled to die in such a terrible place.

The door to Elena's room stood partially open. Artur had gone in two days ago, and never come out. His friends brought food, took away the trash, tried not to comment on the occasional odor. Artur said nothing to any of them. He simply stared at the pale delicate woman lying on the bed, her body covered with tubes.

Blue kept fidgeting. Iris placed her hand on his knee, and he grimaced. "Sorry. I feel like I shouldn't be here."

"You didn't mean to hurt her."

"That's only part of the reason. It's the electrical equipment, Iris. I can't relax. All of this, everything that's happened, has been hard on my mind. I need to . . . get away."

"You're not just talking about the hospital, are you?"

"No." He took her hand, tucking it against his elbow. "Maybe you'd like to come with me. We could bring the cats. I think they'd like Colorado. It's . . . quiet there."

He sounded tentative, as though he was not entirely certain of her response. Iris bit back a smile. "You think I'd say no?"

"I think you've had a rough couple of days. You might have second thoughts."

"And if I did?"

He shot her a dark look. "You're the only woman I'll ever want, Iris. You think I'll let you walk away without a fight?"

"They why did you ask?"

"Because I love you," he said, his voice low, gruff. Iris did not try and hide her smile. She had little time for anything else, though; a moment later a chill rushed over her body, the scent of spring, something wild and rich. It made her head swim, as did the unfamiliar male voice that suddenly emerged from the room. Iris and Blue looked at each other. There was not any way someone could have walked past them, and there was no other entrance to the room.

"Rictor," they heard Artur say, in a voice so close to dead it was a wonder he still breathed. "I did not expect you to come. Not now."

"I had reasons for taking my time," said that low rumbling voice. "I wanted to see what you would do. How far you would go for her."

"I suppose I failed, then."

"No, you did not. Which for my purposes is a shame. If you had succeeded in your quest to acquire a new heart, Elena would have recovered—but she would have hated you for it, would never have forgiven you for saving her life by taking another."

"And so she will die for that? Morals?"

"Don't be an ass. You know better than to question her character. Besides, it's a moot point. I can heal her."

Iris heard a chair scrape back. "Then why have you waited? All this time she has been wasting away—"

"You don't understand, Artur. You never will. Just ... shut up and let me work."

Blue squeezed Iris's hand. She did not know Elena; she barely knew Artur, and she sure as hell did not know what was going on, but she waited with the same breathless anticipation because it mattered to Blue—and, she realized, to herself. This was his family, and now it was hers. Maybe. She was willing to give it a go, anyway.

Moments passed, and Artur cried out, hoarse. "Rictor. I can feel her inside my mind again."

"Her heart is good as new. She'll wake up soon."

Hesitation, a breathless silence. "Would you like to stay and ... greet her?"

"And say what? That I played a game with her life, only to see if I could make her hate you? No," Rictor said softly. "I lied to her, Artur. Out in those woods when we escaped from the Consortium. I lied when I said I didn't love her."

"I know," Artur said. "A man does not look at a woman the way you look at Elena and not love her."

"Caught."

"Again."

Iris heard a deep long sigh. "You are lucky to have a mortal life, Artur Loginov. So blessed it makes me sick."

And that was all Iris and Blue heard, until minutes later Elena croaked her husband's name, an event followed by several low, choking sobs. Blue looked like he might have a nervous breakdown himself.

Iris very carefully closed the door. She and Blue walked away.

Chapter Twenty

The official resting place of Felix Perrineau Senior was in Paris, France. But his body, three days after his real and final death, found its last home in a humble wooden coffin lowered by his sons into a dirt grave surrounded by old growth cedar, ferns, and moss. The funeral was small. Only five people attended. They all held umbrellas, but not one of them was in use. No one seemed to mind the rain. The ranch house was only a short walk away, and quiet; Perrineau's old security force had been dismissed. Neither Blue nor Daniel saw much use for them—if their enemies truly wanted their deaths, those men with guns would be as helpful as dolls playing dress-up.

"He died too soon," Daniel said, taking off his glasses when the lenses became too wet to see through. "I never thought I would say that."

Blue agreed, but he was not his brother; he could not bring himself to say the words. All he could do was look at the box in the hole, inhale the rich loam of a forest lost in rain, and think, *This is what it comes down to. This is the culmination, the end, and all that matters is what you lived for, because afterwards, you're just a memory, good or bad. An image in the eye of heaven.*

Of course, not even his father could claim that much. No black and white for the old man. Blue did not know what to make of him. Not anymore. A monster, yes. A facilitator of terrible things. Never any doubt of that. But as a *father* ... a father who had given up his life for his sons ...

Iris squeezed his hand. She stood beside him, tall and slender, her red hair gleaming like roses in sunlight. Blue's mother stood on his other side, Brandon just behind her. Brandon did not look particularly sad. Merely ... contemplative.

"I think now would be a good time for the truth," Blue said to his mother, looking past her at the man who was the spitting image of his dead father. "Who are you?"

Brandon tore his gaze from the coffin, and studied Blue's face for one long moment. "I am your family. I was not his family, but I am yours. If you want me."

Blue hung his head. "A simple answer would have sufficed."

"Between Felix and I, life was never simple."

Blue glanced at Daniel. His brother shrugged. Mahasti, finally stirring from her own deep contemplation of the coffin, said, "Brandon was once a very dear friend to me. Until recently, however, I thought he was dead. Your father's doing." She shot Blue a hard look. "He and I are engaged. Brandon will be your family regardless of your wishes. I suggest you accommodate him."

Iris coughed; a quick glance revealed her biting her bottom lip. Blue could not muster quite the same level of amusement. Daniel looked startled as well.

The rain began to come down harder. Iris leaned into him and Blue slid his arm around her waist. He kicked dirt into the grave, where it thudded on top of the simple pine surface of his father's coffin.

"Rest in peace," he said. "Burn in Hell."

There was paperwork to sign, business matters to attend to, all manner of staff to coordinate and take care of—the various sundries of inheriting a multi-billion dollar business, legal and criminal—but the day after they planted the old man in the ground, Blue, Iris, and Daniel fled south to Las Vegas. By mutual agreement, Mahasti and Brandon were left behind, in charge. Blue thought it very brave of Daniel, trusting strangers.

"Not really," Daniel confessed, when Blue said as much. "I'm just desperate to get out of there. And, to be honest, I don't really want his money."

Blue understood. Their father's wealth was tied up in blood, much of which he had firsthand knowledge, and his only answer to all that suffering was a tenuous plan to give away his share, every last penny. Use all that power, all those ties bought by cold hard cash, to reverse as much of his father's dark legacy as he could. The Good Samaritan born again. The irony was not lost on him.

Reilly's Circus camp was as busy as Blue remembered, but this time there was a part of him that almost welcomed the place as home. Certainly, a great shout went up as soon as Daniel and Iris were spotted. Samuel came running, grabbing both of them off their feet in giant hugs that sent them swinging. He did the same to Blue with only a little less enthusiasm.

"This is a good day," Samuel said to Iris. "We were worried."

"Very," said Pete, walking up behind them. Dark circles surrounded his eyes. He hesitated for a moment, then held out his arms. Iris fell into his embrace with a sigh.

The entire camp seemed to descend upon them; Iris gave Blue a helpless wave of her hands before being sucked deeper into the crowd. Blue, amused, watched her. He knew all she wanted to do was find Petro and the others, but this was just as important.

"She's happier now," Daniel said, sidling close. Blue wondered how he had escaped the mob. "Look at her, Blue. She's hugging them."

Not big hugs, or long hugs, but the effort was there. Light pats on backs, an arm briefly curled around a neck—highly demonstrative for a woman who had avoided all human contact only days previously. Blue could tell by the look on her face that it still made her uncomfortable. He understood. He was not the highly demonstrative type, either. Except with her.

"What about us?" Blue asked him. "You happy, Daniel?"

His brother was silent for a long time. "I don't know. Maybe. I still have a lot of ... issues I never worked out. I wish I had been able to."

"Yeah. I was pissed off when our father was alive, and now I'm pissed off he died. I just can't be pleased." Blue glanced at him. "But if you have any problems with me ... "

"I do. Not because I think you deserve them, but because ..." Daniel hesitated. "Did Iris tell you about the pictures? I wasn't joking, Blue. I don't know where he got them, but they were always around. In the beginning, when I was little, he called you his first son, his real Felix. Not born with a silver spoon in his mouth, but someone who would make his own fortune, because he was tough, strong, smart. Not like me. Not like the little boy who knew his daddy, who *wanted* things from him. Even if all I wanted was a little respect. I swear to God, he made me feel guilty for being alive. And he did all he could to isolate me. To mold me into what he wanted."

Blue had trouble answering him; he was still trying to absorb the fact that his father had actually bragged about him, albeit for a monstrous purpose. "It didn't take. You fought him off. I'd like to know how. You mentioned your mother."

"She was stronger than he ever gave her credit for being. And his employees liked me more than they liked him." Daniel shook his head, sighing. "I don't know, Blue. I guess I was as stubborn as he was. The more he pushed, the more I pushed back, until all I wanted was to be nothing like him." He smiled bitterly. "Did you know he killed my dog?"

"Shit."

"Yeah. A little stray I named ..." Daniel sucked in his breath. "Sorry. I'm not going to talk about it. Now's not the time."

"Whenever you want," Blue said, and then, quieter, "Did he know about your ... other abilities? Your telekinesis?"

"You say it so matter-of-factly." Daniel snorted. "No. Maybe, yes. I'm not sure, Blue. A lot of things got broken inside the house, though, when I was growing up. We replaced a lot of windows."

"And you're not scared anyone else will find out?"

Daniel sighed. "The one thing I learned from our father is that if you fear something, or someone, that object or person will have power over you. So I stopped being afraid. Or at least, I learned how to control it. I get up on that stage every night because I really don't give a shit. After everything else that's happened in my life? All I want is to be happy. To forget all of that. To forget *me*. And this does it for me."

The two men stood for a while longer before Daniel excused himself, slipping away into the crowd to mingle with his friends. Blue did not join him. He felt a bit like an outsider, but that was fine. He had no intention of going away; he would grow on these people eventually.

He finally ambled off, hefting the duffel with both his and Iris's things. As he walked to her RV, his cell phone rang. It was Fred.

"I wanted to say thanks," the agent said. "You helped."

"I suppose we did," Blue replied, a bit underwhelmed by this lackluster expression of gratitude.

Fred sighed. "Okay, you saved our asses. That better?"

"I can live with it. I could live with it even better if you had some deep dark secrets to spill about the people you work for."

"Sorry. I will tell you this, though. Unlike Santoso and Perrineau, and all the other casualties at the facility who were recovered and sent home in body bags, there's still one person missing from the compiled list, and he can't be found *anywhere*. You want to guess who?"

"Broker," Blue said, a good dose of dread coursing through him.

"Yup. And I don't know about you, but in this line of work,

I don't trust people to stay dead unless I have their corpse right in front me."

Unfortunately, Blue felt the same. "What about the Consortium? Any more information on who their leader is?"

"No, and if your father knew, he took it with him to his grave."

Blue thought about the old man, replayed his death in his head. "Did you know he was working for the Consortium?"

"I wish. If we had, we would have taken a different tack."

"There's always Artur. We could ask him in to take some readings of his belongings."

Fred did not say anything for very a long time. "Are you proposing a collaboration? That we ... work together?"

"I think you'd have to take that up with Roland."

Fred grunted. "How's Daniel?"

"Confused. Just like me."

"Right," Fred said. "Confused and filthy stinking rich. Billions await you and your brother, most of it tied up in various criminal organizations. You be careful, Blue Perrineau. And give my best to Iris. Tell her ... it was fun."

"Yeah. A real barrel of laughs."

"Better than crying," Fred said, and hung up the phone.

Late that night, Iris lay in bed with her lions. Petro and Lila needed therapy, and she was happy to oblige. Blue was just outside the RV, sitting on the steps with his brother. Daniel had stopped by to say goodnight, a tiny gesture that had become a two-hour conversation.

Iris eavesdropped shamelessly, feeling inside herself a rare contentment as she listened to the two men discuss their childhoods, and their father. The more she heard about the old man, the more intensely she disliked him—except, every now and then she remembered his face as he stared down upon her in Santoso's lab, and in her memories she always thought she saw compassion. Brief, but undeniable.

The mind could play such tricks.

She heard Daniel say goodnight. He had an early morning

meeting with the hotel executives. According to Pete, his fire act had gotten good press; the suits wanted him to have his own show. With Iris. An ironic pairing, to say the least. She was not sure how she felt about working for the Miracle, given what little she knew about its owners. It felt ... wrong, somehow.

The stairs creaked; Iris got ready to move Petro and Lila out. Before Blue opened the door, though, she heard another sound, and felt inside her heart a sharp tug, like ropes around glass; close to shattering.

"Serena," Blue said.

"Mr. Perrineau. Or perhaps, just Blue."

"Just Blue is fine," he said, and then, in a softer voice: "The eye patch suits you."

"If you say so. I am still ... adjusting."

"Better you than Iris."

"Yes. I could not agree more."

"Iris is just inside. I'll go wake her up. Unless ... you *are* going to talk to her, aren't you?" Blue sounded alarmed. "She has questions, Serena. Where—you can't *do* this to her."

"I have no answers, Blue. I betrayed my daughter."

"I think a simple apology might go a long way."

"You are naïve."

"Maybe, but I still think I'm right."

"Because you know her so well? Because you think loving her makes you an authority?"

"Because I know she loves *you,* and that won't change, no matter what you tell her."

Silence; Iris held on, breathless. "I think you forgive me."

"Maybe. Or perhaps I'm just patient."

"No," she said slowly. "You are a good man."

Iris could almost hear Blue smile. "You sound shocked, Serena. Good men don't exist where you're from?"

"They do not. Or in such rare quantities as to be likened to dreams."

Iris shook herself and rolled off the bed, running to the door. She pulled it open, and there stood her mother. Blond hair, sharp chin, a black eye patch covering half her face. She looked like a pirate, and there were hard lines around her mouth that Iris did not remember. A different woman, maybe. A secret life.

"Iris," she breathed. Golden light coursed through her eye, splashing her skin, trailing fire down her throat. She took a step toward her daughter, and stopped, staring. Iris stared back. They stood like that for a long time, saying nothing, just looking at each other. Drinking everything in.

"You must hate me," Serena said softly, with such quiet pain that Iris flinched. Blue drifted backward, into the shadows.

Iris fought for words. Her heart hurt like hell. "I don't understand you. But that's not the same thing as hate. Far from it."

Serena nodded, wetting her lips. Slow, tentative, she held out her arms. Iris did not hesitate. She jumped down the steps, hugging her mother hard, savoring the sensation of being held in return, enveloped by touch and scent, which was wild as bramble, green with wood and sap and some cool breeze off the moon.

"I'm sorry," Serena murmured. Lila and Petro pushed through the door of the RV, and the two women sank to the ground, letting the lions crawl over them. Con and Boudicca were suddenly there as well. Iris glimpsed Blue by the holding pen.

No one spoke for a long time, until finally, Iris said, "Why?"

Serena looked away from her; Iris stared at her eye patch, and remembered Santoso. "Because I had obligations that could not be ignored, promises I had made before you were born. It was for your benefit, Iris, though I knew at the time you would not thank me for it." Serena finally met her gaze, and her face was stark, haunted. "I tried to protect you. Part of my agreement for going undercover with Santoso was that you would be cared for."

"And I assume being stalked by Santoso was not part of the plan."

"No," she said grimly. "In fact, it was orchestrated."

Blue finally emerged from the shadows. "What?"

Serena flinched. "When Santoso arrived in this city, he found Iris by accident. He took a liking to her—an appreciation that quickly turned into obsession. My employers were intrigued by this, and decided, against my wishes, that you be allowed to ... hang. To see what would come of Santoso's interest, and whether it would distract him enough for other things to come to fruition." Serena swallowed hard; her scent turned sour, bitter. "They would not listen to me. I begged them, Iris. I did everything I could think to persuade them, and they would not budge."

"You couldn't just quit?" Iris asked, horrified.

"You do not quit these women," Serena said. "No one does. But there are ways around them, and perhaps because of that I did some ... foolish things. I had Fred install a camera inside your RV so that someone could keep you under constant surveillance. And I orchestrated Kevin Cray's attack on the cats. I hoped that if they were taken from you—or if you were threatened enough—you would stop your performances at the hotel. Leave of your own free will."

"My God," Blue said. "You fired that shot at her. *You* were the sniper."

"No," Serena said, looking him in the eye. "Fred was. It was a favor to me."

Iris sat back, leaning against Con's broad side. A tremor ran through her body, her head, her heart; her entire world was shaking. "I can't believe this. I just ... can't. How could you?"

"I had no choice."

"Bullshit."

Serena's gaze hardened. "I will make no excuses for my actions, Iris. I did what I had to. Count your blessings that you have had an easier life."

"Not so easy," Blue interrupted. "You've been in contact with Pete, too, haven't you? You asked him to fire me."

"Oh, not Pete," Iris said, but Serena nodded. Iris rolled back her head, staring at the sky. She could barely see the stars past the city lights, and for a moment she hated it all. Hated her mother, her life.

"I thought I was acting in my daughter's best interests when I asked him to get rid of you," Serena said to Blue. "I did not trust your motives."

"Who *do* you trust, mom?" Iris asked, wanting to scream. "You sure as hell don't trust me."

"That is *not* true. I was protecting you. This life, what I do ... it is not for you, Iris. You are better than that. You are ... sweeter."

"Sweeter," Iris echoed. "Not so sweet anymore."

"I know," Serena said sadly. "I know."

"So," Blue said, much later. "Are you ready to cry yet?"

Iris bit back a hard laugh. She lay on her back in the dry grass of the holding pen, nestled against him. Two lions, a tiger, and a jaguar pressed warm around their bodies, the world drowning in the sounds of heavy breathing, the occasional groan and purr. A nest made of fur—and one very good man. Iris ran her hand up Blue's arm. She was still trying to see the stars.

"I'm too confused to cry," Iris said. "She's crazy."

"She's perfectly sane. Just like my father. At least your mother had your best interests at heart. Mine ..." He stopped, sighing. "I don't understand him, either. Why he had me go after Daniel. Why he couldn't just bring us together. He said it was because we never would have listened, but I keep thinking it was just another one of his games. Always games, down to the bitter end."

"And you'll never know if he loved you," Iris said.

"You have to make your own love." Blue's arms tightened. "Find your own family."

"But it still hurts."

"Yes," he said softly. "It does."

Iris kissed his cheek, his throat, sliding her hand beneath his shirt to touch his skin. He shifted, rolling so that he could hook his leg over her hip and slide her near. His body was heavy and warm, his arms strong. She listened to his heartbeat.

"We're taking a risk here," Blue whispered. "If I ever lose control—"

"If *I* ever lose control—"

"You wouldn't. Not like that. I trust you, Iris."

"And I trust you, Blue." She peered up into his eyes. "I love you."

His jaw tightened. He brushed back her hair, his thumb sliding down her cheek to the corner of her mouth, making her breathless with the heat and hunger rising slow.

"I love your eyes," he murmured. "I've loved them since the beginning."

And I've loved yours, she thought, heart aching, thinking about her life as it had been, and what it could be.

"Shape-shifters mate for life," she told him. "You think you can handle that?"

His mouth curved. "I'm looking forward to it."

"Ah," she whispered. "Then I say we pack up the cats in my RV and we roll ourselves to your cabin in Colorado. Go sit on a mountain and commune with nature."

"What about the Miracle?"

"My mother owes me one. She'll pull strings."

Blue smiled. "And what will we do on that mountaintop? Be at one with the world?"

"I was thinking more along the lines of being one with each other."

"And if we happen to make a pit stop at some little pink chapel? Maybe rope ourselves a preacher who looks like Elvis?"

"I'll be dazzling in fur."

He laughed, but only for a moment. He caressed her left hand, pressing his lips to it and lingering. "I'll buy the rings tomorrow."

Her breath caught, heart thudding itself into a lovely ache. "I think I'd like that, Blue."

They stared at the stars. The city drowned out the night, the dark expanse.

"Blue," she said. "Turn out the lights. Just for a minute."

So he did.

MARJORIE M. LIU

THE RED HEART OF JADE

The grisly murders are just the beginning. Dean Campbell, ex-cop and clairvoyant, is sent to investigate. He is with the Dirk & Steele Detective Agency, that global association of shapeshifters, psychics and other paranormals devoted to protecting life. But there are those who live to destroy.

In Taipei, he finds the remains of burned-alive men and women that reveal a pattern far more deadly than any he has foreseen. Someone knows of a power that can change the world, and of a woman who can complete him: Mirabelle Lee, the childhood sweetheart he'd once thought dead. Now, all that remains is blinding light and searing pain. And beneath it all is…

The Red Heart of Jade
